RIDDLE OF THE SOURCE

Also by G. Russell Gaynor:

Mind of the Man-Child
NightWalkeR
Zodiac: Book of Aries

© 2008 Quicksylver Publications, All Rights Reserved

RIDDLE OF THE SOURCE

Lost Children of Earth Series
Book II

By G. Russell Gaynor

To Punkin – I may not always be quick,
but you will forever be my sylver.
Thanks for my first.

Prologue

The Voguran Leeches moved slowly, but there was no need for precipitation. The Saljah had reached its mark in my brain. I was debilitated, left with barely the power to maintain my own consciousness. I could hardly perceive my own body, let alone access *Vision*.

"Oh, Jamoreh," I reflected, "... *thou hast no idea!*" For with his one action, his provident arrangement of lures and traps, he had struck two blows against the Light-Children. While I was sure they could quickly recover from the loss of Elkazzar, the loss of Vyzoron could hardly be taken in the same stride.

When I had first attained my Vision, Zargo told me what it would mean to all of the Prodigian and it was on that day I gave him my oath: Vyzoron would be neither Light-Child nor Man-Lord. With this time I had been given by the Black Priest, I could not help but think I had failed that resolve. Though it was indeed Vyzoron who once saved most of the members of the Crimson Court, too many times I had acted on the basis of what Elkazzar believed. I can still recollect the day when a group of Absularians, calling themselves the Fourth Tribe, attacked after hurling bombs of Saljah Dust into the courthouse. Vyzoron's talent had enkindled the dust, and he then contended with ten powerful warriors, thrashing them soundly with his Staffling. It was not yet a week later when I touched upon my Vision to deal with three Man-Lords who had a strong disagreement with the Royal Guard as they carried out their orders to arrest a rather popular figure in Man-Lord society. One who had abused the principles of the Great Bridge and had abducted several Tyros, bringing them to The Territories. Zargo would have preferred Vyzoron to stay clear of such arguments. Preservation of life was not something exclusive to either tribe, but the perspectives of what should and should not be allowed was a much more involved dispute. After that, it became all too easy to abuse the power and authority of Vyzoron and it was not long after that the Man-Lords developed the Power Stones that managed to weaken even the *Vision* after a while. It was a convenient enough excuse for me then to not even patrol their lands. *Forgive me, teacher, I have failed!* But Zargo would give no response to me, none that I could hear. In time soon enough I knew I would be joining those of his present tongue.

I could not move my eyes but I knew they were there; the second stage of the Circle had commenced. The leeches' glow slowly rose to the point where I could see it as my eyes were locked on the night sky. The chosen pair would emerge from this engagement of posturing, showing what little note of speed they possessed; that of crawling to their victim. But that was only one result of the circle; I shuddered to contemplate the effect of the second. Each of the leeches established contact with my brain. Any chance of using my motor functions was negated. But the connection would soon seep into the range of the metaphysical... into my mind! Then I would know nothing, see nothing... feel nothing. I would be left in a world of pitch and shadow with the only sensation registering through that blockage would be when they had finally made physical contact. But the trap for me was not an argument of perspective, it was a fact. I thought it a better application of what time and opportunity I had left to reconsider... *William!*

ONE

Blackness... mixed sporadically with pellucid streams of silvery light that fanned wide, appearing like scarves caught on the very same wind which drove him. It was through the scarves he fell, and they burst like mixtures of smoke and water around his body. For each one he penetrated, traces of it clung to him until he was clad in silver robes. Though the descent was without control, there was no integrant of fear.

[*THOU ART UNAFRAID?*] a voice called out to his mind and he recognized it immediately. It was the voice from his dreams.

"Falling," William whispered, his eyes strained to see where he was falling to, "...is hardly cause for alarm. It's the sudden stops that get you!"

[*STAGGERING!*] the voice replied. [*THEN WE HAVE HAD ENOUGH OF THIS. IT WAS MEANT TO MEASURE THY FEAR BUT THERE IS NO FEAR WITHIN THEE.*]

"I would not say that." His feet stood on firm ground. There was no wind, no falling. The blackness was displaced by the sun that hung high in the sky. William looked first to the ground upon which he stood. The sky would have to wait. The surface was hard, made so by the passing of many strides. Though the brown dirt and white sand were in contrast to the normal red clay of his home, William's attention was drawn to his sandaled feet.

"This is... unexpected." He looked up to the sound of footfalls but the source of the sound was not what his eyes focused on. He stood beside a building made of bricks composed of straw and mud. It was made to look like a temple and William's mind quickly collected what he knew of the construct. "Most unexpected!"

"Surprise," a different voice spoke to him. William could already feel the differences between the one in the blackness and the one he heard now. "Something with which you should be familiar, yes?" William turned to see a man wearing clothes much like the sort he now wore; a type of sheepskin skirt with the skin turned to the inside; the wool had been combed and tied off though their patterns did not match. William's chest was bare but he wore leather bracers on his wrists and forearms. The man who approached kept his arms inside his cloak which also kept his face from view. Still William noticed the outline of the man's broad shoulders. He was slightly taller than the confused young man and it was obvious not all of his pursuits were of the intellectual sort.

"I am finding that it helps to be a quick study," William answered as he let his eyes drift from the approaching man. He scanned over the architecture of the buildings, the style of dress, the look of the people that were now just coming into view. Now he could hear birds and see them flying overhead. It was not that these things did not exist until then, but his mind simply had not registered them and he felt it was not an action of *his* mind that made it so. The color of their skin matched the environment. It was hot and very bright given the time of the day.

"Mesopotamia?!" he asked, turning his back to the man who slowly allowed his left hand to come from underneath his cloak.

"Very good!" the man replied. He held a Staffling and as his other hand took hold, his stance widened. "Though that is not a name used here." His movement was smooth, methodical and though William looked at his surroundings, he never took his attention off the shadow the man cast against the ground.

"I'd go for a thrust, if I were you," William said softly, already feeling his body ready to react with even more speed than he had against the nameless woman or the white-haired assassin. The man turned his head and realized William's tool of resolve. He chuckled and returned his hand to the underside of his cloak. The Staffling did not even make a bulge. "Neat trick," William added. "Does it fold?"

"Name me something that doesn't."

"Things that break," William answered quickly.

"Nay!" the man answered as he walked toward the main street, merging in with the foot traffic. "They fold too. They are simply changed by the experience."

"Good point," William said as he followed the man. He had been given no instruction to move but after that particular comment, he quickly realized he had not been told to stay either. "Then how about-"

"All things fold!" the man insisted as he pushed his way through the crowd. William kept up with him but exerted much more effort to dart in between the gaps that presented themselves. "The will of men, the love of women, all things!"

"Sounds like someone could use some Dr. Phil time," William quipped. The man who had become his guide of sorts stopped and spun on his heels. William could not see his eyes but he did not need to see them to realize his sense of humor was not appreciated. "And the sooner, the better."

"You are late!" the man said as he returned to his trek. "And as I was sent to collect you, *I* am late. Come!"

"I suppose the word *please* is outside of his vocabulary," William muttered. It was not a defiant remark, to be sure. It was a test. He looked for a reaction and when the man paused briefly, only to walk faster, William knew the man's hearing was not normal… it was augmented; and as he put his gaze upon the mysterious figure, he recalled the incidents when he looked at his mother. Though only days ago, it was the memory of a lifetime long since expired. He had concluded the instincts he had felt were not the result of his mind going insane, but rather his untrained ability surging to apply itself. This time it was summoned and as he stumbled down to his hands and knees, he knew his uninvited entry had been harshly returned.

[*MOVE*!] He heard the command again but had already learned not to question it. He rolled to his left and the man's staff just missed his head.

"The power of the Staffling," the man said, spinning with his missed effort to keep range with William. He brought the weapon down to hammer it against William's head but it was caught by William's hand.

"Flows from the wrist!" William replied, spinning on his hip to foot sweep the man while taking hold of the weapon with his other hand and prying it out of the falling man's hands. He could hear and feel his opponent fall as he spun away. The weapon, the *Staffling*, had a feel in his hands. A feeling of comfort and empowerment that was new and strange to him. "Whoa!" William awed as he finished his rising spinning maneuver. He was no longer in the middle of a busy street, but in the middle of a small arena. A Staffling cruelly found the fold of his right knee, his left kidney and the right side of his neck. He fell to the ground, unable to move.

"So, you understand power," the man said, rolling William over onto his back. He stepped back from the floored youth and allowed the weapon to spin in his hands. It was obvious he was more comfortable with the weapon than William even wanted to be. "Perhaps now you can discern when and how to apply it."

"*Perhaps?*" William thought as heat flushed through his body, re-engaging his senses and the ability to move. It was nothing short of anger as William pressed against the ground with one hand and he threw his feet up. He had seen athletes and practitioners of martial arts kick up in the same fashion though they had always used both hands. William still felt the Staffling in one hand and was not about to drop it just to stand again. He was in mid air when he noticed the man lunge forward.

"Predictable!" the man said in disgust as he moved to sweep William's feet and return the favor.

"Sez you!" William said as the end of his Staffling jabbed the mysterious man in the face. His approach was retarded and he was stunned. William landed and his eyes squinted as he folded his body and rolled along the ground. He could see ripples of air pass from in front of the man and rip through the ground where William would have been standing had he not moved.

"I'd say that was a good *when*, wouldn't you?"

"This is no game!" the man yelled as he turned and threw his rage into a clumsy swing of his weapon. William blocked the weapon but was surprised when his feet slid nearly two feet from the force behind the attack.

"Aahhh, you're just mad cuz you're losing," William ribbed, believing that if he angered the man enough, he would lose all balance and therefore be vulnerable. The scream the man uttered told William his efforts were moving in the direction he wanted them to go. The next ripple, however, caught William before he could dodge and he was lifted up and thrown back nearly thirty meters before he touched ground again. He hit the ground softly though, his body already rolling before his shoulders touched earth. But the momentum was tremendous and he soon lost his form. He rolled to a stop just in front of another pair of sandaled feet.

"Might want to add a study into *why* while we're at it," William moaned in pain and did not try to move too quickly. Somehow he knew the other man was not pressing; that he had time to get clear his mind and deal with the pain. He looked up at the man standing over him but the sun was directly behind his head and all he could see was the outline of his face as he bent over to look William in the face. There was an undeniable calm to him and just seeing him relieved William of his pain and stiffness.

"Yes, I *would* say you have a good point there." The man's voice was like a thousand soothing hands to William's soul, massaging his fears and doubts. It brought him to the belief that life without them was empty. "Son?"

Two

23:35 hours and the door closed behind him. He stood there, waiting for the feelings to subside. He put his hands on his hips and took in a very deep breath before blowing out slowly, holding his breath before the next inhale. He closed his eyes and reflected on what was just said. He removed his emotion and just looked at each person for what they were: persons of authority and incredible control. He heard their words for what they were: panic and fear. There was nothing they could say or do to have any authority or control over the report. They could not even deem the report faulty or unsubstantiated, not with the footage he had taken. One day in the very distant future he would have to come to terms with what he did and the trusts he had failed... he knew that. Right now he sufficed himself on the belief that he was following orders... that had always been the code! If there are superiors involved, do what you are told. He learned that on the waves, the hard way and damn near died for his insolence. The lesson was really hammered home while he was in the Marines; the three experiences that immediately came to mind made it all too easy to maintain *standard operating procedure* when he wore a badge and a gun.

"Whatever gets you through the day," he whispered as he finally breathed in, brushing back his sun bleached-blonde hair.

"Talking to yourself again, Webster?" a voice sniped at him.

"Boy, you sure know how to take advantage of the fact that I'm not armed," Peter answered as he turned to face the approaching Special Agent Allan Turner. Per usual, he was not alone, but seldom did the Federal Brat parade around with so much meat on his block. Webster took a look at the two agents, one on either side of Turner, and his eyebrows registered his amazement. *"Turns out they do make 'em bigger than Moreland,"* he thought.

"I'm right here, Webster," Turner chided as he walked right up on him; barely a meter separated the two men. Webster wore his normal smirk as he looked at the two large men. They had been briefed. The dark-haired mammoth on Webster's left was just itching to make a move. The redhead on the right, however, could see the Thousand Yard Stare on Webster's face and was already rethinking his perspective. Webster looked back at Turner and they locked eyes. Peter shuddered toward Allan but did not touch him.

"Belay that move, Perkins!" the redhead shouted but it was too late, the other man was already committed. Webster waited for the first hand to touch his person before he exploded into action. The first objective: make sure Tiny did not get a second hand hold of him; he was able to deflect the second with relative ease. What was easier was the way he grabbed the first hand and twisted it to a point where the large man was forced to release

Webster. A spin, a vicious chop and a kick later and the dark haired man could neither stand nor breathe normally. Webster laid the man down like he was spare parts to a trimmed steak, his eyes already on Allan or what he could see of him. Redhead was not advancing, but he had moved Turner to where he stood behind him.

"I don't want to get into this with you, sir," the large man said, holding up his hand showing his open and empty palms. It was also not a bad defensive posture and Webster recognized it.

"I'm not a sir, I work for a living!" Webster whispered as his eyes squinted, measuring his chances on getting by Tiny with a sweet enough move.

"I hear you, Sergeant," the man replied taking a step back and pushing Turner back with the retreat. Turner looked as if he was trying to get around the man but the one-handed grip was enough to keep Turner safely out of Webster's grasp. "Semper Fi!"

"Do or die," Webster replied as he took a step back. He could hear someone approaching the door he had come out of. *"Looks like the deliberation is over."*

"Think you're funny, don't you?" Turner barked as he jumped up and down to get a good look at Webster. "I'll have your badge for this!"

"Perkins touched him first, sir," the redheaded man said receiving a slap across his back.

"You shut up!"

"*All I need is a .22*," Peter thought, hoping against hope that some sort of firearm would just materialize in his hand. When the door opened and he got a whiff of the cologned man, he realized that a gun was not going to be the only wish he was going to be refused.

"Webster!" a voice snapped at him. Peter cast his brown eyes on one of the assistants of the 'Powers That Be' in the Federal Bureau of Investigation, a skirtless secretary, as he called them. "Austin wants a word!"

Allan stopped in mid-rant and swallowed hard. "Deputy Director Howard is in there?"

"Yes, Allan, I am in here!" Howard shouted from inside the room and there was no mistaking his disgust. Peter smiled as Allan frowned. "And I would appreciate it if you would let Special Agent Webster return to the room."

"Special Agent?" Allan echoed and Peter could not hold it in anymore.

"I'm not armed because my guns are part of the evidence chain, you prickless wonder! I'm still in the Bureau."

"You got a name?" Webster asked of the large man that was still serving as Turner's shield.

"Special Agent Robert McNally," the large man answered, almost clicking his heels together.

"You just out?"

"Three months now, Sergeant."

"Webster," Peter corrected. "I took off the stripes when I picked up the badge. Yourself?"

"Lance Corporal, Recon," McNally replied.

"They let you into Recon?"

"They did at that!"

"I just bet they did," Webster nodded as he turned toward the open door. The skirtless secretary was still waiting. "Obedient little cusses, aren't they?" he said, receiving a snort of laughter from McNally.

"You must think you're pretty funny," Habersham sneered as Webster came back into the room. The sniper's brow wrinkled in confusion.

"Not so's I want to quit my day job, sir," he replied. His eyes drifted to Howard who also looked confused, but it would appear he had a different enigma to solve. "Does anyone want to tell me what's going on?"

"We were hoping you could tell us," Habersham answered. "We lost it. We lost every fucking frame!"

"How the hell did that happen?" Webster snapped. "I brought it in just like I was instructed and everything was reading clean and green when I took that scope off my rifle!"

"We're not blaming you, Webster," Howard declared, still in deep thought. "We just wanted to know who else handled your w-"

"Don't even let your mind go there," Webster interrupted as he walked to the table. There she was, Unreliable, in all her glory. To think they had made him hand in his rifle to use this piece of crap. 'Cutting edge technology,' they told him... what a crock! "Everyone on the team knows how I operate and nobody, but nobody touches my gear! I'd know it if they did." He looked at the disassembled heap of garbage that was his sniper's rifle and he shook his head at all the wiring and computer components.

"*Is it a weapon or high powered blue-tooth?*" he thought as he looked at one piece in particular. He had never before seen the working parts of this gizmo and one piece above all registered as odd to him.

"What the hell is this?

"It's pretty technical," Dawson replied, getting up out of her chair. "Suffice to say that it works something like a GPS tracker."

"A multi-wave satellite burst transmitter?" Peter asked.

"Y-yes," Dawson answered.

"With an independent lithium-lined power source," Webster continued, looking at it. He stopped when he found exactly what he was looking for, a manufacturer's seal. "Activated when the main power feed is cut? Good for thirty hours."

"Exactly," Dawson said, taking off her thick black rimmed glassed, her brown eyes flared brightly with curiosity. "Excuse me, Agent Webster, b-"

"Special Agent Webster," Peter quickly corrected, looking at the good doctor. Truly a transformation with the glasses off. Her soft brown eyes were the color of the falling leaves at the peak of Autumn in the Oregon woods.

"Sorry," she said, taking a moment, "Special Agent. But how do you know about this? This piece of equipment is definitely outside your pay grade."

"Maybe, but up 'til a few hours ago, I had a Simmons."

"What's that supposed to mean?" Howard asked. "Simmons is not an electronics expert."

"He is if he reads a magazine article on the subject. But that's not where I'm going with this. Seven months ago, when we had a stopover in Silicone Valley, Simmons ran into an India 'Electra' Alphonse." Webster tossed the transmitter to Howard and motioned for him to turn it over.

"You have got to be kidding me!" Howard exclaimed as he stepped back and leaned against the wall.

"What is it?" Habersham asked.

"The transmitter comes to us by way of Electra Electronics," Dawson answered, rubbing the bridge of her nose. "Five will get you ten, if we run a diagnostic, we will find a download of everything Webster recorded sometime after his immediate recall.

"I told you that was going to send up warning flags," Dawson glared over to Habersham. "King has been covering her tracks for a long time. Howard taught her how, for Christ's sake!"

"We're not going to get anywhere turning on each other," Howard concluded. He came away from the wall and straightened his tie. He shook his head and smiled. His best student was beginning to teach him a few things now. "All we have to go on is Webster's report."

"You've got to be-"

"And everything he has told us is supported by the evidence!" Howard snapped. "Now enough of the name-calling and finger-pointing! The serial killer is dead but we're dealing with a wholly different situation now." The door to the room opened quickly and a man in a black suit walked in and directly to Howard. He gave him a red file folder, turned quickly on his heels and left the room without making eye contact with anyone else there.

"*Now that was spooky,*" Webster thought as he looked over at Howard who was reading the papers inside the file.

"Will you sign an affidavit to the report you have given, Webster?" Howard asked without looking up.

"Yes, sir," Peter quickly answered.

"Then you are hereby terminated for breach of protocol," Howard replied, closing the file. "Agent Dawson, please escort Mr. Webster out of the building." Peter's mouth opened several times but he never made a sound and he walked out of the building into the cool Virginia air. He looked several times at Dawson, but her eyes never looked the same to him as they had in the room.

"Not even if you were drunk, right?"

"Inebriated, over indulged on the top three narcotics on the streets today and in the middle of my seven year itch, Mr. Webster."

"A simple 'no' would have been enough," Peter said softly. He could hear the cars coming to take him to the limits of the grounds.

"You're in a red file, Mr. Webster. You're lucky you're being escorted off the grounds and not into Leavenworth!" She turned to go back inside the building and Peter grabbed her wrist. Her arm gave too soon, she was expecting something physical and she over-reacted. Her swing was wide and he was already in the inside of her attack. If anything she basically wrapped an arm around his shoulders as he pressed his lips down on hers. He timed his move so that she was opening her mouth to scream. A quick and simple twist and Annabelle Dawson had an arm behind her back and was being pulled into the forced kissed. Since he did not have to block her wild punch, Peter dropped his other arm between them in time to prevent her knee lift from being debilitating. She pulled his hair with her free hand but he only kissed her harder. Her knee tried twice to find his groin but she kept hitting his hand and on the second attempt, he massaged the inside of her thigh. Annabelle moaned her argument as her tongue touched his and her lips pressed back against his. Her arm was released and she quickly put that hand to the back of his head, pulling him into her mouth. Peter wrapped both arms around her and kissed her passionately. Her hands then slapped down on his ears and he was struck deaf. He did not feel her body move away from his, but he did feel his head being hammered into the doorway of the building. The last thing he saw was Annabelle on the tail end of a spinning attack. If his life had depended on it, he could not have named what she hit him with... but she hit hard enough to usher him into unconsciousness!

His eyes opened and it was easy to see Peter's surroundings were not what he was expecting. There were no bars, no guards, no uncomfortable beds. Instead, his body rested on satin sheets on top of a king-sized bed. Perfume lingered in the air, a very expensive brand from the bouquet it brought to his nose. It reminded him of leave in Paris.

"Was it worth it?" a woman asked.

"Not one of my better kisses, but definitely one worth remembering."

"I see, so you *are* an animal!"

"Anyone telling you differently is trying to get under your skirt," Peter said as he rolled over to look at his hostess. "And from where I'm sitting, there are lesser pursuits."

She smiled. There were more similarities the two of them shared than she expected. He was not afraid; he had face death many times and it had been a long time ago. That was very good. Terminating him would not prove to be too problematic. She brushed back her long, dark brown hair and put a cigarette in her mouth.

"You don't want to smoke that," Webster said, sitting up. There was no sign of doubt or confusion in his eyes. "And if you had anything to do with that red file, I'm already turned on!" Her dark brown eyes shimmered in the afternoon sun.

She stared at Peter for a moment and slowly took out her cell phone. She hit one button on it and waited for a moment. There was a soft beep' she never took her eyes off of Peter.

"Rook? Have you already seen to that small matter regarding the stolen fighter? No? Good. Cancel the order. I have someone that Bomani might actually be able to work with." She turned off the phone and placed it back into her pocket. She took out her lighter and lit the cigarette, taking a long drag.

"Okay, now I'm even more turned on," Webster admitted.

"Good. Perhaps we will remain friends long enough to satisfy a number of fantasies. You have seen much and it might take some time t-"

"Please tell me you got me fired from the Bureau to go after those freaks!" Peter shot back, standing up. She slowly blew out smoke as she looked Peter Webster up and down.

"You will have to clean house first which means a lot of wet work," she said, curious as to what his reaction would be to taking out the garbage.

"Do I get to zero the freaks or not?" Peter pressed. She smiled. The look was familiar to her, though it had been some time since she had seen it. The glare in his eyes comforted her and she nodded.

"Freaks indeed!" she smiled. "Welcome to Cairo, Peter Webster. Welcome to the Descriers."

Three

He sprang up from the battle-hardened ground and quickly turned to face the man. His father! William's real father?! He had been able to conclude from the overheard conversation between his mother and Elkee that his father was dead. But there was weirdness about the Prodigian, proof positive he was one of them, but his regard for them was low and cold. His belief of what was impossible had been shattered in so many ways he had lost count. But with the impossible in need of a serious renovation, hope was born. Hope that somewhere, somehow, his father was still alive and able to embrace his son. It was hope that glistened across his eyes as he turned, hope that fueled his tremendous speed and the same hope that blinded him from the realization that moving from his back to his feet and turning one hundred eighty degrees took less than one-half a second.

"Dad?" he said as the glare of the overhead sun was no longer an inhibition of sight. Hope joined the definition of what was impossible as he drew focus on the same white-haired man who had tried so hard to kill him.

"Please!" the man shouted, falling to his knees and holding his hands up in surrender. "Stay thy hand! I swear I mean thee no harm! I swear, my lord!" William stood there stunned and unable to speak. It certainly was not his father and there were no words that could accurately describe the intensity of his disappointment. It was as if he was falling in the blackness again, only this time it was no test.

But he would not be allowed to just deal with discouragement. That would have been too simple! Life had never served him such a simple hand and it would appear that although he was changing, his life had not. No, he also had to contend with his would-be assassin begging him for mercy and calling William...

"My lord?"

"He is weak!" his sparring partner chimed in and his words served as all the shaking William would need to rejoin the moment. He blinked his brown eyes several times and even shook his head briefly but vigorously. "You should kill him and be done with it!"

"Oh go suck on a Staffling!" William shouted, half looking over his shoulder. He had taken one step toward the prostrated Cov when he took his weapon in both hands and held it over his head, blocking the attack from the rear. He quickly back-kicked, scoring the chest, but William knew that barely distracted his opponent. He quickly pressed with a thrust to the same area of the chest and then a second, followed by a third. Now his opponent was dazed, William had time. He stepped forward and flourished the weapon, building its momentum as his mind focused on spinning around and sweeping the man's feet again. William did spin and smiled as he saw his opponent jump up.

"*So much for dodging!*" William thought as his real target, the jaw, was bashed by the Staffling. The man spun three times as his body continued to gain height as well as distance away. He met with the ground on his chest and fell flat, unconscious.

"Oh just call me Hammerin' Hank!" he exclaimed. He looked at the body of his opponent. The spin and the fall had displaced the cloak somewhat and at least now he could see the man's arms. The skin tone was very much like his, but the musculature on the man was more defined.

"Man, I gotta work out before he and I do a rematch," he whispered turning back to face Cov who had maintained his posturing but was quite amazed to see William's combat prowess.

"Is he..."

"Dead?" William asked as he gave the notion some thought. "Somehow I doubt it.

"But I really don't see what that has to do with you," William said in a tone that grew colder and more distant. "Seeing as how I think one of the reasons why I am here is *because* of you!"

"Thou doth posses a sure and steady mind, my lord," Cov answered as he began to think over the most recent events, growing more confused with each memory. "I tried to kill you?"

"At that level of effort, we remove the word try!" William snapped as he noticed that Cov was confused by his response. He sought another means of explanation. "Certain events yielded a cause and effect out of alignment with your objectives, but it was in no way at the fault of ineptitude or lack of dedication. In short, you messed me up pretty good!" Cov now knew what William was referring to and nodded in agreement. "Hadn't been for a couple of mystery ghosts passing through, I *would* be dead..." William's anger quickly waned as the need for explanation took full rein. "*... just like you!*

"Okay, somebody go get Vanna White cuz I so need to buy a clue." William said, backing away and dropping his weapon to the ground. Cov looked around and suddenly it became clear to him. He reached for a small stone on the ground near him. He looked at William and an evil grin formed on his face.

"Thy Staffling!" Cov shouted, throwing the small rock with intent to put William's eye out. William spun around with Staffling in hand and easily deflected the stone.

"Now this is the asshole I remember," William said.

"We are inside thy mind!" Cov said in discovery, still looking around, amazed at the level of detail and how fixed everything was. Nothing shimmered in and out of thought, as it did during his own internal reflections. But the ground was hard and everywhere Cov touched it was just as hard. The city outside the arena was immaculate in detail. The wind that brought the scent of the flower merchant felt natural and as random as nature itself.

"It is no wonder I failed to kill thee, Kador. Thou art a master before thy time and I was a fool to think otherwise. Thou art greater even than thy father and he was the bane of peace among the Light-Children. Though he never gave them reason to fear him, they did. They always fear that which they fail to control."

"They are so going to hate me then," William replied as he started to look around. The obvious stood out in his mind and he had to give it voice. "There is just one problem, how is it that we are in my mind and I've never been to this place we're seeing? I mean, I've seen pictures of ziggurats and I've read up on this age. But this is like Spielberg in detail and I don't know where we are except that this looks something like an arena for gladiatorial games. If that is the case, then what we're seeing isn't accurate. There were no official games of note in this time period. 'Course, historical accuracy issues don't stop Hollyw-" The sound of moaning drew William out of his review. He turned to see his *friendly* liaison returning to consciousness. "And then there is Mr. Warm and Fuzzy over there. How can anyone I don't know be in my mind?" Cov closed his eyes at the question. A familiar red glow escaped from between his tightly closed lids and William's grip on his weapon tightened.

"We are... in thy mind," Cov said under what was clearly a considerable strain for him. "Of that, I am certain!" Cov's eyes opened as the glow faded and William could see wonder and fear in his gaze. "But this place is not of thy make!"

William turned to see his opponent get up and heal himself. "*I gotta get a handle on that trick!*" he thought as he turned to face the man.

"We are done with the Staffling," the man concluded as his weapon faded, quickly replaced by Blade and Guard. William's weapon was likewise replaced.

"Shouldn't I be in control of shit in my own mind?" William asked aloud as he took good hold of the sword and shield he had been given.

"I know not the power that holds us, my lord!" Cov answered. "But it dwarfs my own even as it permits me..." Cov looked at his hand and clawed at the back of it. He bled for a moment and then healed the wound. "...to live! I remember my life and my attempt to take thy life in Old Sumeria, though I cannot speak as to why I was so motivated."

"Great!" William whispered as the man started his approach. "I'm about to get my ass handed to me and he's going through miraculous self discoveries!

"Thanks for the assist, man!"

The man walked toward William at an even enough pace, but the last step left a blur as his body streaked into William's. Guard met Guard and William was thrown back through the air, stopped cold by the wall of the arena. He dropped to the ground and fell to his knees. The man was quick to press and he lunged forward. His second stride, however, came down in the middle of William's thrown Guard. The metal gave no traction and the man slid toward William unable to stop. Already on his hands and knees, William lunged forward in a very much practiced tackling maneuver. His shoulder met with the man's ribs and though the Guard continued to slide, the man's body was stopped cold. He dropped both of his weapons as his back met with the ground. William looked down on the combatant with defiance, trying his best not to show how much pain his shoulder was in from that hit. The man screamed and William could feel the instantaneous rise in temperature. He could feel the fire approaching but had no idea how to contend with it. He covered his face with his arms and dropped to his knees. He heard the explosion of flames and he screamed as he shuddered. But as he breathed deeply, he recognized he was not burning. He opened his eyes to see fire burning all around him but not touching. There was a red barrier preventing the fire from reaching him. Suddenly, the fire died and William looked up to see the man falling unconscious again. This time there was a slight red glow that escaped from under his hood. Quickly turning, William saw Cov smothering the flames as he kept his eyes locked on the man.

"Perhaps, my lord, we should make ourselves scarce," he suggested as the glow faded from his eyes. William smiled as he stood up and ran over to Cov. As their hands locked, Cov propelled both of their bodies up into the air and the speed of the action brought a cry of celebration out of William. He looked down on the arena and his opponent, who was once again getting up. But he did not give chase. His Blade and Guard became a Staffling again and he turned to walk out of the arena. William looked around at the building tops, both the worn parts of the metropolis and those newly erected.

"Talk about the friendly skies!" he screamed as the acceleration came to an abrupt halt. William looked up and saw Cov, wearing the same clothes he had when he made his presence known at his parents' house, his glowing red eyes glaring back at him. He would not be calling him 'my lord' now. This was the assassin that had nearly killed him, and now he had been given yet another opportunity. But before William or Cov could act, William could see the man begin to fade. For a brief moment, he could see through the man and the anger burning in his eyes was extinguished, transformed into utter desperation. The man did not want to die a second time.

"*Put it together, Bill!*" William thought as he looked back down at the... "*What's going on?*" William gasped as he looked down. The city, like

Cov, was beginning to fade. From the outer boundaries to the center of the city, his beginning point, which was not a temple so much as a huge construction site, the city was falling off into floating fragments. Falling off... into the blackness! William was not afraid of it, but that did not mean he wanted to go back to it!

"[**No**!]" he said softly, but his voice was the only utterance that held that capacity. He reached back to the remaining sections of the city with his hand and his fingertips seemed to be the focus of his will. He shuddered as he felt something pass through him, from inside him to the city. A sudden flash of light brought an end to his flight and blinded William for a moment. When he could see again, William was back at the side of the building, Cov was still in hand, wearing sheepskins, looking much more solid, but quite out of breath. He quickly pulled away and crawled to the limits of the wall, looking at William strangely, as if he was looking at something alien to his very existence.

"What are you?!" he hissed as he pressed against the wall.

"Right now," William answered as he stood up. "...I'd say pretty much unappreciated. You're welcome." William looked around and saw the hooded man approaching once again.

"No way," William whispered as he tilted his head. He then looked up at the sky and there it was; the sun, the sky, the birds... and as William looked back down, the people.

"This is... unexpected," he said once more, receiving the very same response.

"Cov, do me a favor and just watch this time. Whatever happens, don't interfere!"

"I give thee my word!" Cov quickly answered as he stood up. "But give unto me one answer: twice you have acted to save me and I have quested to kill thee at least as many times."

"Why?" William said, guessing the question that weighed so heavily on Cov.

"Please," Cov pleaded for an answer.

"Why not?" William smiled. "I don't even know you and right now you're not trying to kill me. What reason do I have to kill you?"

"Self-preservation, Master!"

"First, I'm nobody's master!" William said quickly and with more vigor than he probably intended. He had studied his history, or at least the history he thought was his, and slavery was one of the less savory lessons to learn. "And second, you saved my skin back there when my guide tried to turn me into a charcoal briquette. Consider it me saying thanks. Now if you will excuse me."

17

Cov looked at himself and placed his hands on his body. He glowed red for a moment and dismissed the power as he ran after William. "Let me go with you, Master!"

"I told you, I am no one's Master!"

"All the more argument that thou hast risen to a station whereupon thou hast attained mastery over every man," Cov answered and he could see the disgust growing inside William. "But if it is a point of contention with thee, I shall remain with the response of my lord, my lord." Cov flashed a genuine smile and bowed as he spoke.

"And if I don't like that either?"

"Master still remains a viable option," Cov stated pointedly.

William sighed in disgust. There were more important matters to concentrate on at the moment. His assassin was an unexpected addition and so long as he kept to William's directive, he changed little. A few strides through the crowd and William was once again in the arena, holding a Staffling. But he was no longer wearing skins. He wore cloth, much like a Roman Centurion with similar armor.

"Uh oh," he whispered as the man turned to face him, still clad in the cloak and hood but he too wore armor. "I don't think this is a replay so much as the next level." The subsequent Staffling works and the hard falls to the ground proved his theory to be all too accurate.

It was a relentless pace as he was taken through the most basic techniques of the Staffling, Blade, Edge, Bow, Crosser, Blade-Stave, Whip, Slingstone and Bolo. Surprising himself, William was not as inept as he thought he should have been. His trainer was good, seeming to always be some fraction stronger, faster and more skilled than William. Things remained that way so long as William said nothing. If there were any quips offered, the man seemed to lose his center and that was when William could find flaws in the man's technique.

He sat on a bench when his opponent and trainer finally stopped wailing, bashing, cutting and stabbing into him. "We are done for now," he said sternly. "You are too fatigued to learn anything else."

"And when I was too weak to lift my Blade, what was I learning then?" William barked.

"How to lose," the man answered as he turned to leave.

"These lessons are all well and good," William huffed, "... but what about lessons on unarmed combat?"

"*That* you seem to be practicing all on your own," the man replied as he faded from sight.

"Yeah, like I got a choice," William sighed, wiping the sweat from his head and neck. He looked up at Cov who stood at the very top of the seating area and was constantly looking in other directions and pondering.

"Sorry if my bleeding got a little boring," William shouted.

"God of Light be praised," Cov gasped as a bright smile flashed across his face. "I know where we are!" Cov quickly turned and ran down the steps, thinking that mode of transit better than gliding. He had not liked the experience the last time his feet left the ground. "Mas- My lord, I know where we are!"

"I cannot tell you how much I am jumping up and down on the inside!" William snipped, closing his eyes and taking a moment to rest.

"Nay, my lord, we must not tarry!" Cov eyes flared red and invigorated William instantly.

"You know," William said getting up. He was wearing the skirt of sheepskin with bracers again. "The makers of Gatorade ever get wind of you, you're a dead man!

"Okay," William continued when Cov gave no sign of being amused. "Guess it helps to be an Earthling."

"We are here, my lord, at the very beginning!"

"What? Talk to me like you would any other non-Prodigian."

"The beginning!" Cov cried, grabbing William by the shoulders. "The Source!"

Four

"What exactly is your damage?" Antal asked. He had grown tired of what seemed to be an endless supply of aggravated sighs. "Why don't you just pace if you need to do something with the extra air you're sucking up and blowing out!" Their eyes met for a moment and Cole looked at his watch. Antal looked away without anything further to add. A few moments passed and Cole sighed yet again. Antal laughed and it was not long before he had company.

"Oh, I'm sorry," Cole chuckled. "I just hate waiting around."

"What are we waiting for then?"

"Believe it or not, a meeting I arranged and now wish I hadn't." Cole looked at his watch again but there was no use in it. Even if he had the abilities of those he recorded, it would not change the time. Though it would do wonders for the freezing wind coming off the delta.

It had been a quiet night for most people, nearly everyone in the New Orleans area, and in many ways he was not an exception to the rule. But that was the problem... it had been too quiet. All reports had the Man-Lord assassin coming to New Orleans. Even at her most expedited tempo, that should have given Bill Cole enough time to get into position and eliminate her. How did a near-rogue FBI team get from Dallas, Texas to New Orleans, Louisiana without tripping any of the their watch points? Of course, he could only ponder that once he abandoned the chase of resolving how they went from one city to the other so fast. Cole had landed in New Orleans with two hours left on Brooks' timetable. The young operative only used half of the remaining time. To make sure he had some big guns, Cole had sent up a flare. The woman known as Milana was dead. She had done very well in flushing out the Light-Child Guardsman and had even brought him within range of Fellman's rifle. But Fellman had lacked the nerve to pull the trigger and by the time he worked up the nerve to take the shot, Cov was airborne. The only good that came from the entire exchange was that The Descriers were short another wannabe operative. Of course, that meant the noose around Bill's own neck was just a little tighter. The Man-Lord assassin and the Guardsman were reported dead over an hour ago, but there was no way Cole could leave without taking the meeting he had requested. These people were already short on patience and Cole had had enough of playing with matches. Now that they had been soaked in gasoline, the prospect of having fun with them was even less likely.

"Good evening," the man called out and Brooks jumped. There was no panic in his movements but Brooks was used feeling when people moved up on him. But this man gave no such feeling, no scent and no sound.

"Somebody pinch me," Brooks whispered. It was a tall and slender man who approached. He moved from what seemed to be a perfect stance to a casual stride just as the column of water he was standing on reached the docks.

"Don't worry," Cole assured, "...water is the only form he's quiet with. Though his control of air comes in a close second."

"Good evening," Cole said, walking to meet the man. He wore his full length black leather coat around his shoulders and a very expensive tailored suit.

"Did we interrupt the party?" Brooks muttered, receiving the man's cutting glare. Brooks spat in defiance. The man's hazel eyes quickly cut to the ground where the spittle was supposed to land but it stopped inches shy of the wood. It slowly lifted to eye level and the man stared at it before looking at Cole.

"The blood must be running thin these days, Bill."

"He's new, Niles," Bill spoke in a manner that was usually charming. But as the spittle quickly evaporated, he knew that Niles was already in a mood his charm could not reach. He decided not to try and shake hands. "This is Antal Brooks. Brooks, allow me to introduce you to Niles Taaveti."

"Antal," Niles repeated. "The Hungarian spin on the Roman Antonius." He looked down in thought. "Something to do with the estimation of value."

"Invaluable," Brooks answered. "My name means invaluable. Niles' eyebrows lifted in surprise. There were so few *Mites* who knew anything of history let alone language.

"So it does," Niles replied, walking past Cole and directly up to Antal. "Why do you suppose your parents were so presumptuous?"

"Oh no, it wasn't presumption," Brooks answered. His eyes had yet to blink and he certainly was not about to give ground. "It w-" Brooks' hand went to his own neck as he began to choke. There was nothing pressing on his neck or chest. There simply was no air to breathe!

"Niles, pl-"

"Keep your dogs on a tighter leash, Cole!" Niles snapped as he spun around to face Cole. "And I was not aware that we were on a first name basis."

"We aren't, Mr. Taaveti," Cole said, looking down. "But I wanted to be the one to tell you that Milana is dead."

Antal fell to his knees, gasping for air that suddenly had been allowed to flow into his lungs.

"What?" he said, showing a surprising amount of surprise and emotion. The moment passed quickly as his brow folded down over his eyes. "How?"

"The Guardsman got the better of her, I'm afraid," Bill answered. "He displayed nothing but a surprising amount of power and control since he arrived. Our sources told us he was a reject of the Council at one time. We did not expect him to get so close to achieving his objective."

"WHAT was his objective?!" Niles whispered as he lunged twenty feet in one stride and took hold of Bill's chest, lifting him from the ground. Bill did his best not to scream. The last thing they needed to do was kill a half-dozen dock workers who were in the wrong place at the wrong time.

"He was sent to do what the Head Master failed to do!" Bill winced, controlling how loud the pain made him speak. "There was a report that Elkazzar would appeal to the Council and report on his progress, but that has not yet been confirmed." Bill's cell phone started ringing and Niles' eyes drew into a tight squint as he gleaned a surprising conclusion.

"You have an informant among the Prodigian?" Niles asked, lowering Bill back to the ground, releasing the finger-splayed, flat palm grip by which he had held Bill's chest. Taking a few breaths to rub his chest, Bill reached for his phone as Niles spun around and lifted his arm. The switchblade had been drawn, opened and thrown in one smooth motion and Antal was running in behind the attack. The blade went through the fabric of the suit sleeve but sounded as it had struck stone and ricocheted in several directions all at once. Niles extended his other hand for Antal's neck but his palm wrapped around a peculiar black rod the newcomer had placed just in front of him. Brooks smiled as he hit the switch and volts of electricity flowed into Niles' arm. He too did not scream, but not because he had held that strong of a monitor on himself, he was in too much pain.

"How's that blood looking now, asshole?!" Brooks said as he pulled the rod out of Niles' grasp.

"Brooks!" Bill whispered sharply as he looked at the source of the call. He had to answer it, there was no other option.

"See to your call, Cole," Brooks said, thrusting the device into Nile's side, sending more electricity into his pain-locked body. "I'm just working on our Foreign Policy!" Brooks cut the device off long enough to drive his fist into Niles' face. Cole jumped at the power with which the punch was delivered. He too had underestimated Antal Brooks and he knew that without the ability the concentrate, neither the Prodigian nor these Elementals were any different than the common man. A second thunderous punch landed and Bill was sure that Niles felt less than common.

"Cole here," he said into the phone.

"Is there a problem, Bill?" she asked. She had done this too many times for him to be surprised by the call. If anything he was wondering why she had not called last week when he forgot to lift the lid on the urinal. Then again, it had been the Men's Room.

"Mr. Brooks and Mr. Taaveti are getting acquainted," Cole said calmly as he watched Antal stand Niles up and shock him again.

"You see," Antal whispered, "...you and I need to come to an understanding." Niles tried to mount an offensive; a quick heel punch for the face. All he needed was a moment to focus his talent. As the heel punch missed, Brooks could feel the wind starting to pick up. It died when the rod delivered its sting to Taaveti's genitalia. Niles' eyes stretched wide open and Antal's headbunt forced them to close. "You are just visiting our little piece of the pie!" Brooks continued. "You're just like so many damn Americans who do not know their place when they travel to somebody else's country! Walking around like you own the place!"

"Now, I know you have gobs of power coming out of your pores and to that I will concede that maybe the whole party quip was a bit out of line." A jumping side kick snapped Niles' knee. but he was shocked before he could scream. He was lame and because of the timing of the charge, Niles had bitten off his tongue. But Antal was not done. Lifting Niles up by his hair, Antal shoved the rod into the arm pit of his opponent.

"So why don't we do this," Antal offered. "I am going to apologize for my earlier comments. Even though anyone coming in on a pedestal of water, looking like the latest boy toy outta San Francisco *ought* to know somebody's going to say something!

"Anyway, I will say I'm sorry, then I will let you go and you are going to do your Mr. Wizard thing and heal up. Hell, I'll even throw in a few ooohs and ahhs if you like. But we squash this here and now, wipe the slate clean, and approach each other as men, because that's what we are. You read me?" Niles managed a nod. Antal released Niles and stepped back but held his weapon at the ready. The comfortable thing about dealing with Elementals is that they can't read minds and therefore Niles did not know that Antal had set his device to deliver an arc charge.

"Excuse me, sir," Antal said in a strong and genuine tone. He jumped as a wave of water came up and took a literal hold of Niles' body. The water went inside the suit and Antal's view of Niles was lost. When the water passed through, the only thing left was Niles' empty clothing ensemble.

"Mr. Taaveti?" Antal said as a hand gently rested on his shoulder.

"*You* may call me Niles! Forgive me, but I have gotten rather used to Cole's limits of capability."

"We all serve a purpose," Antal Brooks replied.

"To be sure!" Niles agreed. "But you are breath of fresh air among the De-"

"Dead Stones?" Brooks offered. "Don't sweat it. I understand where that perspective comes from. If I could do half of the things your people could do, I'd think less of my kind too."

"It would seem you already do," Niles said.

"Let's just say I'm ready to start improving the bloodline."

"Fine!" Niles whispered, holding out his free hand. A good handful of earth came up out of the water and into Niles's grasp.

Taking his other hand away from Antal's shoulder, Niles formed the earth as his hands went from a flesh tone to a bright orange and red. Brooks leaned away from the man as the heat was incredible, but it was not long before the slender man had fashioned a dagger that he cooled and offered to Antal.

"I hope you will accept this as a replacement to your switchblade." Brooks took the weapon and was surprised to find it cool to the touch. It was perfectly balanced and appeared to be sharp enough to cut just about anything. "When you plunge the blade into the ground, I will feel it and take it as a summons of great importance and react accordingly."

"Whoa! Not sure I'm ready for that much authority."

"What authority?" Niles asked and as he and Brooks locked eyes, an accord was offered and accepted.

"Well, if Mr. Brooks should survive," she said calmly.

"Uh, it's not Mr. Brooks' health I'm concerned about," Cole replied. "I am just hoping I do not have to kill him to keep Taaveti alive!"

"I doubt it will come to that, though I am surprised to hear Brooks is faring so well."

"Have you received the report from Atlanta?"

"Yes, I have," Cole answered. "I was trying to report to Mr. Taaveti the status of his operative."

"And that is when the two *gentlemen* decided to get acquainted?" she asked, already knowing the answer.

"Indeed."

"Well, as soon as the boys are done playing, get to Atlanta as soon as you can. Make contact with Redding an-"

"Redding?!" Cole was shocked for two reasons: he was still alive to receive another assignment and that he was the assignment!

"You know how much I hate to be interrupted, don't you?" she said in a very calm yet cold tone and Cole quickly quelled his feelings on the matter and cleared his throat. "Much better. Make contact with him and resume observation of the target. Maintain a low profile, but recognize that as of this moment, you are hereby upgraded to Sentinel status!"

Bill closed his eyes and barely answered his acknowledgement before closing the cell phone, ending the call.

"You look like you just saw a ghost," Brooks said as he was putting his new dagger away.

"We've just been moved to Sentinel status," Cole answered.

"And I must report what has happened to Milana," Niles said as he started back toward the water. He stopped and looked back at Brooks. "Tell me, is this any better?" Niles dove off the dock but did not make a splash when he hit water, not even a ripple.

"Much!" Brooks said as he looked out over the waters but did not see Niles anywhere. He looked back at Cole and smirked.

"Hey, how long can he hold his breath?"

"You mean before or after he generates air around his mouth?" Cole asked walking toward the car. "We have got to catch a flight... to Atlanta."

"Kinda figured," Brooks muttered. "Not much to Sentinel in Seattle!"

Five

"'The Source'?" William asked, lost as to what the word meant for Cov, though it was unmistakable that held great significance. He ran to keep up with the man as they left the arena and tore through the streets, going back to the very spot where William's visit had begun.

"When there was but one tribe of man!" Cov shouted. "One tribe, one language, one God!"

"People are making that claim now," William returned, ducking a ladder carried by two men and then jumping a cart.

"Nay, my lord, thou must listen!" Cov was too excited to be reasoned with, though he had enough of a mind to pay heed to his direction and speed. William opted to just listen and let the man get it out. "This be no argument of opinion I speak of. This be the truth!"

Cov turned and started to run even faster and William had to work to keep up with him. Through marketplaces and by homes, the duo streaked, and William was able to roughly calculate how fast they were running. He elected not to share his findings. "I must be missing a decimal point somewhere," he half-concluded, though a sensation in his deepest instinct told him he was in denial and not even the cheetah was graced with such swiftness of flight. Still they ran, winding their way back to the beginning.

"Damn, that fl-" another flash of light blinded William and the next sensation he felt was a wall that stopped him cold. He fell back into the street, taking several people with him. "...flashing light must've covered some serious distance," he muttered.

"Get up, my lord," Cov directed, pulling William from the masses that were calling him everything from an idiot, to clumsy, to some maladjusted accident of the loins of his parents.

"Hey!" William shouted to one particular man. "I got your loins right here!"

"My lord, greater concerns press us onward!" Cov insisted as William's brow registered a point of contention.

"Hold on!"

"My lord!"

"I said hold on!" William shouted and Cov immediately prostrated himself. William would pick up on that in a moment, his mind was engaged in something else.

"Hey, you!" William shouted at the man had who insulted his parents. "Come here for a second."

"Go eat a goat!" the man replied as he continued to collect items from his spill with William. "A dead and rotten goat!"

"Your Momma's a dead and rotten goat!" William fired back. His voice sounded as it should to sustain an argument, but his face exemplified that he was in the midst of an experiment. The man looked up and drew a short blade from his hip. The way he held it, William knew he was not trained in the combative arts, but the weapon still looked able to cut. If nothing else the man had to be given respect just for being armed. He drew back the blade but William saw something in the man's eyes... they shifted!

"*He's not going to swing,*" William ascertained. "*Just trying to scare me. Interesting!*"

"My friend," William said, bowing to the man, "my words were wrong and I apologize for my haste. It was most inconsiderate of me." As he held up both of his hands, William looked at them, confused by his own actions. He took a pose as if he was offering to embrace the man.

"*To say this is getting weird is both late and redundant,*" William thought as he smiled at the man warmly. Immediately, the man's face of anger broke and he put away his weapon, embracing William in earnest.

"We are both men and we both spoke with words from mouths drowning in anger. We both know better and you have apologized. I accept your apology if you will but accept mine."

"*Just go with it, Billy,*" William thought as he closed his eyes.

"Already done, my brother!" he replied slapping the man on the back as the embrace was sustained.

"Cov," William said, his arm still around the shoulders of his newfound friend "...see to it that the man's items are returned to his cart and the broken things are mended, if you please."

"I cannot, my lord," Cov replied, looking down. The man laughed heartily as he slapped William in the chest.

"And how would your servant go about doing that?" It did not take William long to see the fear in Cov's eyes and thought it better to dismount from this situation as soon as he could.

"I don't know how he does half the things I've witnessed," William answered. "I think he has been moved too much by your goat comment. He lost his brother to a stampede of them."

"Goats?"

"Yes!" William continued. "You see they were both very young and the herd had been scared by a fierce animal. The boy fell hit his head and I'm afraid the mere mentioning of goats does this to him."

"Oh, my brother, I am so sorry!"

"Nonsense," William said kindly. "How could you have known? How could have anyone have known?

"But I will see him inside and then come back to help you."

"You are going to help build?" the man asked as he stepped close to William, taking a firm hold of his shoulder.

Dropped the volume and increased his grip. "Might as well play the drifter card."

"Is this not good work?" William asked. "Forgive me, I have not been long in the city and-"

The man pulled William toward the side of the building. "That much is very clear!" the man said. "Now listen, my friend, you are young and idealistic, so you are the very sort they are looking for.

"I will not speak ill of the King," the man whispered, "but this is insanity! A tower unto heaven?! Impossible!"

William Anthony Ferrous staggered back away from the man as the words Cov spoke played over and over in his head. The era of the architecture and clothing. The temperament of the people... impossible was indeed the right word for the moment.

"Nimrod is doing this?" he barely managed to asked.

"Yes," the man said with some confusion. "Is there a different king in your homeland?"

"Yeah, and she works for the FBI," William thought.

"No, my friend," William answered. "It is only that I had heard rumor the tower would be built next season and not in this city."

"Then you were told wrong, my friend."

William returned to the street and helped the man with his things and sent him on his way to market, promising to visit him there with some coin. He returned to his starting point and sat on the ground. Cov joined him and placed his hand on the young man's shoulder.

"The Source," William whispered. "The beginning!"

[*We were all one people once, my lord,*] Cov projected. [*The history, as it has been told to me is this*:]

As William heard Cov's words echo through his mind, he found himself in the middle of a time-lapse film effect as more and more builders flooded the area and labored on the tower to make it as high as they knew how to make it. There were feats of sabotage and even cases of material fatigue. But it was obvious the king would not be discouraged by any circumstance. The brief glimpses William was able to make out of him was that he was something of a tyrant, but very much driven.

[*When we first discovered our abilities, we tried to share it with our fellow man.*]

"And they were labeled sacrilegious?" William guessed.

[*And were quickly executed,*] Cov answered. [*They took their ability into the shadows but many were still lost, ousted by their friends and families. But still our numbers grew and our talents increased. That was* when the Elders were first formed and they conceived The Source; to use their abilities and perform something along of a telepathic surgery on every single mind which opposed them.]

"So first they got to Nimrod and made him think up the whole Tower of Babel idea," William continued as the construct neared completion right before his eyes. "And while the Tower was being built, they prepared the languages that would be... *downloaded* into every mind."

"Man that took some chutzpah!" William concluded, his mind not able to embrace all of the details. "How many Elders were there in the beginning?"

"According to our history, there were nine," Cov answered as he looked upon the construction with a pride he could not explain or control and his hand steadily went to his eyes to wipe away tears. William patted him on the shoulder as he stood up.

"I was afraid you were going to say some low number like that," William said as he looked up into the sky. The call of the trumpet brought his gaze back down to the ground as the time-lapse effect slowed to normal speed and Nimrod's approach was announced. The crisp blast of the horns struck a chord with young Kador as he looked around.

"That's it!"

"What is it, my lord?" Cov asked, standing up.

"You said we are in my mind, but this is not my memory which means it is someone else's. Someone else who also was not here when the events we're watching really happened."

"How dost thy know of this, my lord?"

"Too many mistakes," William answered. "The design of the city isn't accurate." It was close, how the buildings appeared here and how they should have actually appeared. Also, the addition of the arena was way out of line, but obviously intentional.

"I would not know, my lord,' Cov admitted. "Thy mother art more given with historical fact. Her achievements as a scholar art well documented!"

"Leave it to Dad to fall for a brain," William answered, still walking and spinning, taking everything in.

"*This place was built for me*," William thought as he smiled.

"Cov, I need you to stay here. Whatever this place is, it is sustaining you so you can't follow me."

"But where are you going?" Cov asked.

William looked up and took in a deep breath. "Exactly where I tell you to send me. Straight up, if you please, and preferably at the same time the arrow is launched into *heaven*."

Cov stammered as William looked at him. He was about to speak when Cov nodded and took them both to the top of the tower.

"What dost thou seek?" Cov asked him as he made sure the two of them were unseen by normal eyes.

"Right now, man, I'm going on pure instinct. I've got a hunch but I'll need a bird's eye view to figure it out. Just make sure you stay out of trouble while I'm gone. Here and the arena seem to be you best bets for privacy and safety.

"Fear not for me, my lord," Cov assured. "Once the shaft is loosed, they shall not be looking for me or my kind."

"Good point."

Nimrod took his time ascending the tower and there was plenty of ceremony to make him feel important. But William was in no great rush. This was the first time he had such a powerful fear of the unknown. But it was not the details that he was afraid to find, he simply knew that no matter what he found out, it could not bode well for him. And without so much as a warning or a check for his status of readiness, Cov hurled William's body straight up into the air where his ascension was equal to the speed of Nimrod's Arrow. Looking down and extending his perception, William could see the massive amounts of energy being released from eight different points in the city.

"I thought there were nine- Oh my God!" William looked down on the city and the surrounding valley and river. For the most part, the energy spread as far as he could see... for the most part. What drew his attention were the places where the energy did not flow through so much as it flowed around. He could feel minds in those areas but they were not touched. Worse still were those places where the energy flowed to minds that were unaffected. In comparison, these numbers were drastically lower than those that were not touched, but William felt an uneasy twisting in his stomach for both groups. Exactly what would have been *his* response to someone trying to reprogram his mind, only to fail?

Six

"What a night," King said as she finally took a moment to sit in the back of the ambulance. She adjusted the makeshift sling and massaged her arm. Though it did not happen often, Lydia was not surprised to see Alfred Simmons come to her and wrap a blanket around her shoulders.

"You seem to keep losing these," Simmons said, taking a seat beside the team lead, handing her a cup of coffee.

"Who the hell had time to go and get coffee?" she asked and Alfred smirked as he gestured. Lydia followed his hand and looked up to see Jack toting several bags and a large tray of warm beverages. The cup he was handing to Marianne no doubt had some sort of herbal tea. Lydia could not remember which kind she insisted on drinking when she was rattled, something else that did not happen often. But Jack's mental rolodex probably had it cataloged down to differentiating the source of the disturbance.

"And Tara calls *me* Momma," she whispered taking a sip of her coffee... black with one and a half sugars. "When did he find the time?"

"I guess he figured it the best use of his time since he had to drive Peter to the airport." Alfred was quick to take a sip of his tea. Knowing Lydia as he did, it might be some time before he would not be talking.

"Who the hell called Webster back to LA?" Lydia snapped as she stood up.

"Howard," Alfred answered, motioning for Lydia to return to her seated position. He still smelled of smoke and burned flesh but he was physically unmarked. "But I don't think the plane is bound for LA so much as Virginia. He's probably already halfway there by now. Jack didn't take him to a public airport. They had a Leer waiting."

Lydia sat down and sighed. She looked around the crime scene, the one without a body but it still had all kinds of wreckage. With the exception of Simmons and herself, no one on her team was sitting too close to another team member. Cooper would have been sitting close to Chalk but he was not fit for company at the moment. Jack had seen to the senior police officer on site as well as the top ranking fireman. He was laying groundwork for any possible angles he might have to work in the very near future. Everyone was still and quiet, trying to find that all too elusive handle on the moment.

"Except for Mifflen," Lydia chuckled, taking another sip of coffee.

"Tara?" Simmons asked.

"Do you know how many times we've all looked at her and wondered how long it would be before she came completely undone? Well, look at her now, over there pacing, plotting and scheming her next move.

Looking every bit the professional we should all be exemplifying. We look like we just got out of World War II and our entire platoon ran out of ammo.

"And don't you look to be the very picture of mental stability, considering you were on fire a couple of hours ago," Lydia added.

"What can I say," Alfred said with a surprising smile. "It looks like this skinny white boy can take the heat!"

Lydia winced in pain and put her hand on her forehead. "Oh, Simmons, that was very bad!" she chuckled.

"Indeed," he agreed. "But there is a smile on your face. Mission accomplished."

"So I'm supposed to be smiling at all of this?!" Lydia asked, probably louder than she expected.

"Wouldn't kill you, Momma," Tara answered. "In our line of work, if you're at the end of the day and you're still wearing your badge... then smile, because you've done well!" She smiled as she turned and approached the ambulance. "So is it the end of the day?"

"Well," Lydia answered, looking down and gathering her thoughts. "We don't know too much more than we did when the day started, but the reason for the season has been handled and my team is still alive." Lydia tried to smile up at Mifflen but now that the redheaded woman had drawn closer, she could see so much more detail in her face. But it was not the sort of 'greater detail' that brought any comfort to the senior agent. It was more like knowing when you cannot get out of the way of a punch meant for your head. You pray you have time to brace yourself and pray harder that you can take the punishment. "Yeah, Tara, I'd say the day is done."

"Then I've done well," she said softly as she held out her badge and gun to Lydia. "Too bad there won't be anymore days, not for this Sooner."

Lydia put down her cup of coffee and took what she was being offered. Tara had always been something of a wild card to her, but she was beginning to understand her and if nothing else, felt a great amount of pity for the woman. King had been tracking weirdness for a long time but Tara had been living it and it appeared she would continue to live it. Whatever was riding her was not going to give her a choice not to.

"You're no Sooner in my book, Mifflen," Lydia whispered, wrapping her good arm around Tara and pulling her close. "I might have been dumb enough to call you a mutt before, but you've always been pedigree, baby."

"Thanks," Tara said, fighting back the tears of the moment.

"If it means anything," Lydia continued, "go with my blessing." Tara shuddered and tears broke through.

"It means so much, Momma!"

Lydia pulled back and wiped Tara's eyes. She forced a smile, killing her own urge to cry. Damn, Tara had become the daughter she always wanted! "Then I won't waste time telling you to be safe and not get too close to this kid."

"Way to sneak it in anyway," Tara cried. They embrace again and Lydia winced as she used her other arm to hug Mifflen. Tara felt her pain… and her love… and cried even harder. She stammered something but it was not intelligible.

"I know," Lydia whispered. "Me too."

Tara stepped back and smiled at her boss, her mentor, her friend, her sister and, for a few moments when both of their lives were on the line, the most protective maternal figure Tara Mifflen had ever known.

"Help me, Jon," she thought. *"Help me keep this moment. She won't cry… not because she doesn't want to, but because she knows it would break my heart."*

"She definitely knows that," Jonathan replied, giving her as much comfort as he could. Her eyes dried up and she took in a deep breath, adjusting her vision to look upon Alfred Simmons who made the gesture for Tara to call him.

"Stay low, Tara," he said.

"As low as they'll let me, Simmons." Tara turned and walked over to Jack Moreland who handed a fireman the tray and bag he was holding. He lifted Tara off her feet with his embrace.

"Jack, thanks for being Dr. Feelgood, man," Tara whispered. "You're the best!

"And if you let her get away-"

"It'll be because she wants to get away," Jack interrupted, rubbing her shoulders.

"Good point," Tara agreed as she nodded and walked over to Chalk who stood up to say his goodbyes.

"Any chance I can convince you to run like hell?" he asked, hugging her.

"Oh I plan to, Doc. Just not in the direction you'd prefer."

"Then take care of yourself, Mifflen, and…" Chalk reached inside her jacket pocket and took her pack of cigarettes. "…you won't be needing these."

"Would you believe that was one thing that bitch burned out of me?" Tara replied. "I can't even get my head around sucking on one of those things without getting sick!"

"Good for her then," Chalk said as he stepped back and sat down. He could not get his attention off his leg for too long. The second crossbow shot nearly removed it just below the knee and he had never felt that kind of pain. But as soon as the bolt was removed Harold had repaired the damage, leaving only a minor bruise. Dr. Caleb Chalk was not long for the world of civil servants.

"Keep an eye on him," Tara whispered to Marianne but went rigid as Cooper pressed her lips to Tara's. Her eyes flashed wide with surprise as the kiss was more than brief, and surprise turned to mind-numbing shock as Tara found herself kissing back. Their lips finally parted and silence was too weak a word to describe the sound.

"That was more for me than you," Marianne said with a devilish grin. "I hate not getting the last word."

"Last word?" Tara stammered.

"Do you know how many times in the past week you've freaked me out?" Marianne asked with a bright smile. She could have been just as thrown by the experience as Caleb had been. But at the moment of her death, she had heard Harold tell her everything was going to be alright and she rather liked the fact that he was right. "That kiss in no way brings us even, but maybe it'll let you know what sort of seeds you plant.

"That, and I get to tell Peter that you kissed me and told me to deliver the sentiment."

"Jesus, Cooper!" Tara exclaimed. "It was one moment where you two had to hold a cover. Get over it!"

"Get over it, my ass!" she argued. "That man has got a serious set of lips on his mouth. I'll use any excuse that comes up to get another taste of that.

"'Sides, you weren't too bad either," she chuckled. "You're not getting more confused, are you, Mifflen?" Tara grabbed Cooper by the back of the head and pressed her mouth down hard on the young Korean woman's.

"Ouch!" Lydia whispered.

"Fire when fired upon," Jack added.

Marianne's hand pressed against Tara's shoulders but the protest waned quickly and when the pressing hand took hold of her sleeves, Tara broke the kiss. "No Coop, everything's clear as a bell. Call me."

"Well," Caleb added as Cooper stood there stunned. "At least she didn't *say* anything to freak you out this time."

"Momma," Tara said as she walked back.

Lydia held up her hand in protest. "Whoa there sport! We already had our goodbye."

"Yeah, but I don't freak you out anymore," Tara said softly.

"No, baby, you don't. I'll handle the paperwork."

"Good luck with that. They're gonna want you out, ya know. I could sure use one serious bitch on wheels!"

"Ain't that the truth," King agreed. "But we all have our demons to face. Yours happen to be real demons; mine are just assholes! But I still have to face them." Tara could feel Jack's head lower to his chest.

"*Dammit King!*" she thought. "*Jack's a good catch, the hell with the Bureau!*"

"*The reason why the Bureau is what it is,*" Jon replied, again soothing her. "*... is because of people like her, Sweets.*"

"And what about me?" Tara asked, forgetting she did not need to speak out loud for Jon to hear her.

"You are one seriously intent demon smasher," Lydia responded. "That kid doesn't know he's about to get a big boost.

"And if you send up a flare-"

"I know," Tara nodded. "You'll bring the Marines!"

"Bump that!" Lydia argued. "I'll get my hands on a couple of comic books and bring to life a few mutates."

Tara laughed and nodded. "Yeah, that should do it."

"See you two around," Lydia said.

"Us two?"

"I think that is my signal," Harold said as he slowly approached. "And Lydia is right. I came here running from my people and their problems. Now one of those problems has spilled over into your lives. This needs to be set straight. It is what both Eric and Palshaya would have wanted.

"And what about what you want?" Jack asked in a tone that was unmistakable. Lydia looked at him but his eyes were on Harold Smith.

"I can no longer have what I want, Jack," Harold answered. "They have both been killed and the debate as to what really killed them, I may never solve. But I will do what I can to make sure no one else faces such contemplations. I have been talking to Simmons and through our mutual talents, I know William's address. And despite the veils of Adrianna, I can tell you there has been another attack that the young man has survived."

"WHAT?!" Tara and Lydia snapped and looked at each other.

"Please be calm," Harold requested. "The one who struck down Webster before he could shoot Yudara again was one of my people and he raced to William's house to set another trap for him. William has survived and the man is dead!"

"Damn!" Jack said, putting his hands on his hips. "That boy is tough enough!"

"Indeed," Harold agreed as he stepped back, holding out his hand for Tara to join him. "And while things are quiet, perhaps this is the best time for the two of us to make ourselves known."

"Good idea," Tara replied as she walked over to Harold.

"Think fast, Mifflen," Lydia snapped as she tossed her back her pistol. Tara's one-handed grab made her look back at King in surprise.

"Looks like she did more than kicked your smoking habit," Lydia smiled tossing Tara four more clips.

"Reload much?" Tara joked.

"Not nearly enough!"

"I hear you," Tara said as she took Harold's hand.

"Take care of our girl, Harold," Jack said as he waved.

"And don't forget you're popping out in front of a crowd," Alfred added, motioning toward the policemen and firemen.

Harold's face was flushed with color and slight embarrassment. He nodded as his blue eyes flashed blue and anyone who was not part of Lydia's team also flashed blue light from their eyes as Tara and Arvius, Blood of Salpanor faded from sight.

"Man," Marianne said in a loud sigh, "I sure hope Tara can keep him alive!"

Lydia chuckled and rubbed the bridge of her nose. "I think I can say that Peter would be proud of you for saying that, Cooper."

"Speaking of Peter," King said as she stood up and faced Simmons.

Alfred was adjusting his glasses when he looked up at King and flashed that simple and yet reassuring smile. "My sister wiped his rifle and his belt just after he got the call."

"Did she wipe her copy too?" Lydia asked walking over to Jack who looked like he did not recognize the woman all of a sudden. It might have had something to do with the look she wore on her face.

"I don't think-"

"Right," Lydia interrupted, "don't think. Verify and make it so! No copies, Simmons. This is too big!"

"I concur," Alfred said, taking out his hand held computer.

"Think he can out hack his sister?" Jack asked, gazing into Lydia's eyes. Vulnerability! A stroke of paint he thought he would never see so flush in this painting called Lydia King. "She's as smart as he is."

"That's what is says on paper," Lydia whispered, taking hold of Jack's arm without breaking stride. She led him toward one of the squad cars. "He taught her everything she knows and I taught him how to fool the system."

"Damn, Lydia!" Jack exclaimed. "You are-" her lips intercepted his words and Jack was all too ready to respond with equal passion as he took her up carefully in his arms. They broke from their kiss and Lydia ushered him to the car.

"Sarge, I need your cruiser," she said.

"Yes, ma'am," was all that the officer said and Jack opened the passenger side of the door.

"What about that report Howard wanted file the moment we knew anything?"

"Jack, I don't know anything right now. And I'm not going to know anything until the sun comes up and not for a few hours after that.

"So Jack, don't say a word, not a single, solitary sound unless you are telling me how wonderful I am or how much you want me. I'm calling time-out on the world and I need you." Lydia got into the car and neither of them spoke during the drive to the closest suitable hotel.

Midnight saw the two of them in passionate embrace and Jack knew that for a few moments, when passion blinded him from reason, that he was hurting her arm. And she would register the pain, she even cried, but she never stopped loving him and he would not stop loving her. As the black veil of the night sky was broken by the rising sun, they were still clenched together, both of them wondering where they had found the strength; the next kiss teaching them what should have been painfully obvious. From fired passions to moment of spent bodies huddled together, they touched each other deeply. When Jack started to subside, Lydia took the lead and the exchanges of control were smooth and simple. In the very beginning, Lydia cried alone, but not out of pain for her broken arm. Upon their last kiss, she felt Jack's tear fall on her shoulder and she kissed him harder, held him closer and loved him more deeply.

"When did she get up?" Jack thought as he rolled over to see her typing into a laptop computer. *"To say nothing of when she called Simmons to get equipment."* He looked over to the side of the bed and saw breakfast. Orange juice, no doubt with pulp which was exactly how he liked it, and one very sloppy bacon, sausage, egg and cheese explosion over a syrup drenched biscuit.

"So this is how it feels," he said softly with a smile on his face.

"Every time," Lydia answered, still typing her report.

"You about done?"

"And then some," Lydia answered, choking back tears. "It's not a report so much as a summary."

"Which means they'll be flying you in for a debriefing."

"That's the plan."

"Is it, Lydia? Is that the plan?"

"It's my plan, babe."

"Well, it was what it was," Jack thought, his fears confirmed. She wanted him, probably more than he wanted her – if such a thing were conceivable. But Lydia King had a way of doing things and until she was

done with Bureau, it would not be done with her. But Jack had seen and done enough. There were bigger fish to fry and there was no way he was going to let Tara and some half-baked alien go at it with a bunch of strangers. There were other leads and Jack knew that Harold and Mary Smith were not unique. Dallas had proven that. But he would work faster alone and someone obviously had to stay with the kid, as he was the focal point of the trouble.

Then Jack Moreland chuckled, discovering he was as hell bent as Lydia. He did not know how what she was doing was going to ever get back to this case but he was used to her being smarter than him. She had lost her team. Tara was just the first to say it. She would work her way through the FBI and make another one. The possibility of such a creation actually made his nostrils flare with anticipation.

"*But she doesn't need me in her head,*" Moreland concluded. "*Just like I don't need her in mine. These bitches play for keeps and they are so much better than us. We have to work the best way we can and pray there is enough of each other left at the end.*"

"Okay, so read it to me," Jack said, sipping his orange juice.

"Well," Lydia said with a sigh, "you know the lead up to all of it, case number LA6-97889... blah, blah, blah... I don't really have a beginning yet."

"Then say that," Jack offered. Lydia looked over at him and quickly put away the urge to start over what had been greater than great just hours ago.

"Hmmm, that's not a bad idea," she said, typing slowly with the one good arm she had. "It is difficult to even begin a report on a case such as this. For over fifteen years, the FBI has had an open and running file on mysterious killings and assaults by person and/or persons unknown."

"Sound good," Jack said, eating his breakfast. "You're not really writing a report so go with what feels right." Lydia nodded but said nothing else as she went back to her writing and silently, Jack started a dialog of conflict and contradiction. The words he thought before now felt like foolish bravado and she was worth having in his head... she was worth fighting for.

"*Maybe,*" he thought and let her finish the report.

"*You can feel the tension, can't you,* Momma?" Lydia thought. "*Oh Jack, in a different world, time and place... but not here and not now. You've got to cook a little sweetheart and where I'm going, I'll be damned if I take someone I love along with me.*

"*What happened to our world? When we began all of this, we were looking for one sick son of a bitch. We found a daughter instead but she wasn't a serial killer at all... she was a pawn and if the pawns bring that kind of power, what the hell will the knights and bishops do?*" Lydia wrote her very empty report and Jack was right about her intentions. She wanted a debriefing… she needed a debriefing. With Howard in Virginia, that is exactly where they would send her and now King knew she could not trust her mentor as much as she thought. That meant Peter was more than suspect. He could have just been following orders or he could have been making it up as he went along. Either way, the evidence chain had been broken which meant she had time, but not much.

"I'm such a little fish in a big ocean," she concluded. *"And I am making awfully big waves! Talk about suicidal!"*

Seven

Another morning. Again the sun rose and brought light into his room. It was a convivial light, innocent and pure. It did not carry visitors from another world that I was conscious of. But it seemed to be searching for something as the morning drew on. Eventually it found William's face and seemed to settle there. I am sure the light continued to move with the sun which was its source but the light that touched William's face found reason to shine in silent celebration. The boy glowed as if he was a smaller sun before all of us, there to light the way and keep us from the darkness of our ignorance. It was the psychic residue left from the young man's power feed that signified to all of us that William was indeed on the mend. But something else happened which none of us could have prevised. As he lay there, the light of his own power mixed with that of Cov's, which had lost its tumultuous capacities, and shone all around him. I looked at my own form to see that slowly and ever so surely, a bond was forming. But it was not only with me that the bridge of raw psychic energy was forming. I could see one forming around Adrianna and another about her mate, Gordon. Adrianna was quick to urge us all to allow what was happening and as I was so sedulously invested, I was quick to agree.

In all of my time, I have witnessed this phenomenon thrice: twice with Zargo and now once with his son. Comparatively speaking, Kador received and wielded his additional power with more perception and efficiency. Zargo had been left in a coma for nearly five lunar cycles after the series of events which created his first experience and was laid quite ill for half that time upon his first conscious attempt. His son, however, rested in a deep, peaceful slumber. There would be no nightmares on this day. No visions of horror to plague the young boy's mind.

To put the matter in its most simple form, William's thought had grown, matured and had achieved a level of sentience. It had manifested its own will. While his conscious mind slept, the recently joined unconscious mind tapped into William's newfound power and was beginning to project itself out into the world. The bonds we saw and felt forming were actually fingers on the hands of the newborn babe, just coming to terms with its own existence. All together, William was simply too busy to experience dreams.

Adrianna was good enough to advise me of that which I already knew: the seemingly endless nightmares. As she spoke, I applied my talent to peer inside his mind and again I was refused. There were too many images through his conscious mind, each of them violent and powerful. How the boy rested at all was a mystery to me.

"His father was known for violent dreams," I remarked.

"Another foolish myth," Adrianna quickly argued. "That man could sleep through bomb testing!" Forgetting to whom I was talking, I nearly asked her to name her source of information but as I looked into her eyes, I managed to prevent myself from posing such a foolish question, though I suspected from her smile that the realization registering on my face relayed to her what I tried to conceal. The sky was still black and dark when Adrianna ushered us from her son's room and down into the kitchen where she was good enough to prepare for us a very fine meal. I was amused at her insistence to use the mechanisms necessary for the common Tyro to prepare food.

"Did you like the meal?" she asked as she gathered the plates and utensils.

"Yes, very much so," I quickly replied.

"Then don't look a gift horse in the mouth," she said. Gordon smiled but said nothing as I was left with nothing to say. She quickly returned to the table with a tray of coffee and assorted baked sweetbreads. I fear I found my weakness of the realm and its name was Bear Claw. We engaged ourselves in what Tyros call small talk but it more resembled an opportunity for parents to brag about their son. I was happy to oblige them the time.

The afternoon brought a bird to William's open window. The young man's eyes opened to behold a sparrow sitting on the window sill. As the bird chirped, a soft smile formed on William's face and his eyes focused on the creature, cosseting it with his vision, absorbing every detail. Slowly closing his eyes, William engaged his mind's eye. He smiled at this new world he found himself within. Yes, he had doubts and fears but would his condition be any different had he no powers of the mind? William's answer to that inquiry was a resounding 'no'! There was not one child that he could think of that walked free without concern. He knew of several who told themselves there was nothing to worry about, but denial was never anything that could be practically argued.

So with fears in hand and in tow, Kador decided to initiate an experiment to get a feel for his new surroundings. Nothing had really changed, but now he knew how to see more. He was about to see if he could probe the mind of the gentle sparrow.

"He's up now," Adrianna said pouring yet another serving of coffee. She sat down and placed her hand on Gordon's shoulder. "Would you mind making him some breakfast?"

"Breakfast?" Gordon said looking at his watch. "It's almost three o'clock! For once that boy has a decent excuse for staying in bed so late, but I don't see why we should start pampering him." Truly I was more than prepared to remain silent in the presence of this man. Despite the relations we shared, our perspectives have never meshed. But I was too struck by his reaction to remain silent.

"Pamper?!" I repeated. "Gordon, he hath embarked, on a long and troublesome journey. Already he nears the completion of the first leg in so very short a time. His mind knows a level of pain your word *migraine* cannot begin to conceive."

"Fly along now, friend," William whispered as his head came up from the pillows and he turned to put his feet on the floor. The sparrow gave a soft song before turning and flying off. William smiled as he watched his afternoon acquaintance fly away. It was then that he questioned why the small bird had not already flown south for the coming winter.

"Late bloomer," he told himself as he let out a yawn that announced he was awake to anyone in the house who was not sensitive to his mind and its emanations.

"My training was not painful," Gordon shot back as he walked over to the refrigerator. I did not appreciate the jealousy I heard in his voice, but I refused to speak to his inadequacy to offer commentary inasmuch as he was an Outworlder.

"Thou didst receive nine years of training," I answered. "And thy studies dealt with defenses of thine own psyche."

"And?"

"And such lessons are elementary!" I answered. "Significant of course," I was quick to add. "But of a lesser degree of complexity than the lessons Kador hath received in mere hours. I would not be surprised if his mood this morning ran somewhat afoul. Best we be prepared for this and allow it to pass without commentary."

"My son, a grouch?" Adrianna said, handing me the means by which Tyros shared what they considered to be vast amounts of information regarding their many and varied realms. It was called a newspaper. "Elkazzar, you still have a lot to learn about the best thing to come out of the combined efforts of myself, Zargo and this so-called Outworld. The three of us, along with the immeasurable contribution of Gordon Ferrous, have conspired to create a most, how should I say it, *unique* individual.

"In fact, that is probably one of the most fascinating aspects of this world. Aside from my husband, of course."

"*Of course*," I thought.

"There is so much diversity, distraction and conflict about. But when they are most challenged, they never fail to act together. Truly a remarkable people!" She smiled as she took a sip of coffee and I marveled once again at a beauty the Prodigian had yet to rival let alone best.

"Perhaps thou art more correct than you may know, dear Adri," I said taking her hand. "I freely and openly admit to thee I feel as though I am his student when we converse."

"And if you're going to hang around here," Gordon said. "You will need to change that particular word choice bank you're working from. You're a Head Master for Christ's sake, so I know you were trained in the speaking arts."

"Indeed I was, Gordon, thank you for reminding me," I replied as I lifted my cup for another sip. "And there is someone at the door." The doorbell rang and I could feel Adrianna's body shudder as her body was prepared to engage in combat. "I believe it is a messenger of sorts," I added, keeping my gaze upon the woman.

"More like a delivery girl," Gordon said, looking at a monitor that showed who was at the front door. If nothing else, Tyros were resourceful. Gordon left his station at the stove and walked down the corridor to the front of the house.

My attention returned to Adrianna who had relaxed only at hearing her husband's words. She was deciding what to do with the electricity she had brought out of her wall when I have her hand a sharp squeeze.

"Not everyone is your enemy, Adri. To this day there are still a number of Man-Lords who maintain Zargo's passions and philosophies. Try to relax." There were few words to describe how she cut her eyes toward me. I had crossed a sacred boundary but there was no way to erase the misstep.

"You're a fine instructor, Elkazzar," she said softly, taking her hand out of mine. "...I will always graciously give you that. But do not ever again try to tell a mother NOT to worry about her child. I am as relaxed as I can be right now. As much as circumstances will allow!

"And where the hell were all these brethren of Kador's father when I was banished from New Sumeria? It's not like any doors opened in Utopia for me either." There was nothing I could say and I let my eyes drop to the floor, considering how I would feel if it were Vada-Ri and not William. Would I even be able to accept my mentor's guidance?

"He's going to die, isn't he?" Adrianna cried. "Just like his father!"

[*Enough!*] I projected into her mind, forcing my will over hers. Unprepared for my attack, and out of touch with many of her combative talents, I forced her to look into my eyes, holding the rest of her body still. [*Indeed he doth possess his father's passion and his mother's skill, but thy son is like no other before him! I know thy pain, Adrianna. I too have lost my heart! But what sits in this space before me is not the Blood of Abinadab!*

Whereto hath the Counselor I knew gone? Where hath gone the woman whose words put to an end incidents which could only have ended in war?! Where is the woman who was strong enough to breathe life into the Unlawful Son? Where is, my old friend, Kadorgyan's only true hope?]

Her eyes softened and became the orbs of wonder I had not had the blessing to immerse my mind into for over thirty years.

In a moment's grace my mind carried our conscious minds back to the first time we met. So many summers ago; hot, dry... how slowly the time passed in that session of the Council. The sunlight poured through the holes in our dome-like roof. I do not know what Tyros would call such holes. I was running through the Northern Courtyard, late for a gathering of the Council of Order. And there she was, most suddenly, directly in my path. Too engrossed, I was, in arguments that I knew were waiting for me that I did not see her and we collided.

"Pardon me, my lady," I said, helping her up.

"No, my lord and Councilman," she answered. "...'tis my fault. My mind was not on where I was as much as where I wished to be." I was caught by her verse, but had not the time for investigation and I merely excused myself to resume my jaunt to chambers.

The Council was meeting to discuss the matter of punishment for a crime committed. After some eight cases of shameless pleading to the board, I had grown tired of the rather tedious duty. Then they brought her forward...the very same young woman! No question remained in my mind as to why she had been preoccupied earlier.

"What art thou accused of?" the Caller spoke aloud.

"Ambition," she answered in a voice I would not have been able to guess she possessed. It was so clear and so very strong. "A desire to set right what is wrong in my community." Her eyes were set on the High Voice and I quickly noticed the look of recognition in his eyes. He knew her somehow, but I had never seen her before, much to my own deprivation.

"Listen not to the ramblings of this woman, my brothers," Achar, High Voice of the Council barked. "She is but another testament to the pressing need to rid ourselves of the Deviants, cursed traitors to the traditions of the Prodigian!"

"I beseech thee, my lords," I found myself saying, though I had no reason for my words. "Hold thy judgment till I may speak on these matters." The faces of my colleagues were not too different from my own. I was flabbergasted by my initiative which, up to this point, had been non-existent. But I had spoken, and in that time no retractions allowed. Worse yet, I had spoken in defense of that which was already condemned by Achar. Not a maneuver exercised by those who wanted a healthy future in the Council.

"Mine ears have yet to hear the full charge or the circumstances. As we are gathered to preserve order, might we then take in this incident and give a ruling based on the truth and all of the facts... or are we simply men who cast fate to whim and a singular perspective?" The High Elder nodded in agreement and the Caller stood to speak again.

"This woman, Adrianna, Blood of Abinadab, has made it her... ambition to hold a seat on this Council."

"More specifically, my lords, to become a counselor," Adrianna spoke again, her voice holding her strength, her glare possessing even greater conviction.

The mumbling rose from the benches as the thought of allowing a woman to hold such power graced minds and shook hearts. The mumbling grew to conversation and conversation broke into chaos. Chaos which took the guise of debate between myself and Achar. Chaos which took eight days before a judgment was made. The Council felt that a woman could not respectfully serve her community in such a position and they therefore decided to test her by giving her the rank and responsibility of a counselor.

At first it was a victory for Achar. The poor child was trembling when the verdict was being read and she was also shaking over time as she tripped over every trap Achar and his stooges put in her path. She was about to resign her ambitious claim and accept whatever punishment the Council saw fit to appoint when a newly appointed Master took her by the shoulders, in a very similar fashion to which he held her now, and shouted to her to plant her feet and stand. To find and yoke the strength she demonstrated in the Great Chamber. That young woman had taken those words to heart and won her position, the first woman appointed to the post. But that would only be the first signpost of greatness for Adrianna. The first of many. It was no doubt that Zargo saw such things in her. Though he was far from the first man to see them. Far from it!

I released her and moved to attempt a reading of the newspaper but I was interrupted as her hand found my arm.

"Thank you, Vyzoron," she whispered, reminding me that she did know of my secret. How could she not, when it was her husband who had shown me the way to the power and when it had been she on several occasions who took the guise of Vyzoron to dismiss any thoughts that he and I were one in the same. Though for Adrianna attaining *Vision* was a deadly practice, she was never one to hesitate from assuming the mantle if it meant helping me. "You have always been there for me. A true friend then and a true friend now. Thank you, again!" I smiled and nodded, even patted her hand. But I could not look into her eyes again. Not at that moment. It would have served no one.

Gordon walked back into the kitchen toting a rather large gathering of blooming foliage. Several exotic varieties kept in a finely hand-crafted porcelain vase.

"Wow!" Adrianna said as her eyes lit up. "You didn't."

"You're right," Gordon said. "I didn't. Believe it or not, these are for William." Adri took the flowers and placed them at the center of the table.

"The card says from a *Queen*?" Gordon advised. "Looks like the boy is back in the social game too!"

"I didn't know our son was familiar with royalty," Adrianna replied as she and Gordon laughed. I was about to join them when I felt him. Though for all practical purposes, my detection of him had come late.

[*Good morning, Elkee,*] William projected and I felt a sense of elation from him that he had managed to surprise me.

"We're not getting rusty, are we, old friend?" he teased as he put his hand on my shoulder and I jumped again. My perceptions had put him at some twenty meters away. "As you say to all of your students, 'we warriors are charged to maintain a steady and sturdy guard'.

"Good advice, would you not agree?" he asked, taking a seat at the table. I realized his parents still did not know he was in the room. "Come now, Elkee," he ribbed, "twenty meters is out of the house. Are you saying I got up, got dressed and left the house without you feeling anything?"

"Well played," I admitted. "I shall have to heed my own teachings, Kador."

"You do that," he said as he got up and walked up to Gordon and Adrianna as though he were just entering the room. They traded hugs and Gordon placed an empty glass in William's hand as Adrianna pulled out a chair for her son... the one I had not seen him slide back under the table.

My eyes drew tight and I focused my actual vision as well as my talent. My eyes saw a young man who appeared to be refreshed and ready for whatever the world would send his way. All of my probes were sent back, giving me only one image: me, as I was in the chair I now sat in, but with a sign over my head that read: "Keep-a-knockin' but you can't come in!"

"*And the game is afoot!*" I thought.

[*No, it isn't,*] Kador projected. [*That's old news, Elkee. It's been afoot, for over 5,000 years now. Since the Source!*]

Eight

"He's still moving south," the young soldier reported, sounding far too fearful for his position. "But his speed has increased to forty knots! Christ!"

"Jesus, kid," he whispered, adjusting the throttle to maintain his intercept point. "You act like you've never seen a man do forty knots in open water... without the benefit of mechanical means of propulsion. Hell, I've seen 'em do sixty-five when it suited them." He checked his altimeter which read forty feet, well below radar, but any fisherman out in the Gulf of Mexico would have a story to tell their kids if they spotted him. But at Mach 1.75 they would not be spotting him long.

"Just stick to the facts, son," an older voice responded with something of a Texas twang to his voice. "Just think of this like a sci-fi movie without the popcorn."

"Ho-kay...a wise old cowboy," he remarked, finally getting a signal on the tracker. He hit a sequence of buttons on his console to bring up a map of the region. As the image tightened, his vehicle's coordinates, speed and direction were confirmed. Moments later the same information appeared for his target. "And the facts just told me that I am getting close. This could be it."

"Dugout, this is Alpha Scout," the operative spoke into his radio. "I have confirmation of transmitter. Repeat: I have confirmation of transmitter. Will intercept target in... fifteen seconds."

"Received, Alpha Scout," a soft female voice replied. How many times had he heard those tones and wondered what sort of frame could emit something that felt like satin over a radio! "Beta Scout also has a lock but you're first up. Expect Beta twenty seconds after you engage, Delta Scout in thirty."

"What say you let the wine breathe, darlin'," he mused. "This won't take long."

"That's the problem, if you ask me. It never does!"

"Ouch!" he replied as his vehicle started to shake. "Ho-kay, we've got turbulence."

"At thirty-seven feet?!" she snapped. He could hear her stand up from her desk. "The hell that's turbulence. He's on to you, Alpha. Abort!"

"Roger that," he said, quickly moving the stick to the left, pushing down the left pedal and his vehicle banked hard and fast. "Alpha has gone to port!"

"Received, Alpha," she replied in a somewhat calmer tone. "We have you eastbound. Take a peek at your six."

He reached up to his console and entered in a different sequence of buttons. His map was replaced with a view of the camera.

"Alpha's going to starboard," he yelled, pulling on the stick harder than his first turn. He was breathing hard as his vest expanded to deal with the increase of pressure. "I got a bogey!"

It had been given the name The Dugout because anyone working in it was an MVP, and that was actually the title given to the operatives just to punctuate the point. They functioned something like an army, though they did not report to any particular government. They did, however, hold the reins of a few; some large, some small. Size of the government did not rate as high as their Expediency Index Curve, whereby they had some mathematical genius rank countries based on geographical location and population as well as the various types and sizes of their businesses.

The controlling members of the Dugout were scholars, researchers, investigators and, when circumstances demanded it, enforcers. The higher-ups had reported a problem, a pest-control problem actually. Seems that there were a few uninvited guests having fun at the family picnic and so they rang the phone at the Dugout. Step One: figure out what these guests are and where these guests came from. Step Two: once Step One is achieved, make contact with the guests and tell them that unless they change their rather destructive ways, they basically needed to bugger off. The biggest problem with the plan: Step One was initiated on July 30th, 1979... approximately sixteen months after the higher-ups got together and found out that they were not so high up. They had picked up their toys and gone home. Since then, they put every nickel they could squeeze out of every development or project into Research and Development. That, combined with a few gifts of fate and some government manipulations, and the higher-ups were so elevated they needed oxygen masks. The Dugout was just one of the results of their efforts.

Thirty years later the higher ups decided to resume Step One. Three teams had been dispatched and not a single operative had lived to share the experience. So the phone rang again and Step One was changed: Converse, Capture or Kill. Needless to say, when things were pushed to the third option of Step One, there really was no Step Two.

Sabrina Bey had been recruited like all the other operatives, but her time in the field had been relatively brief. Her IQ, her love of computers and electronics, her ability to multi-task and her dedication to maintaining an incredibly healthy body separated her even amongst the MVPs, and it did not take them long to promote her to Coordinator. Now she was the eyes, ears and strategy of the Dugout and a liaison between the facility and the higher ups, which were now called the Owners. As Coordinator, Sabrina was often the sole contact for a number of the lower-ranked operatives. Despite the incredible things Tyler Banning could do, he was still low-level.

"Did he just say he's got a bogey?" Bat Boy asked.

"He sure did," Sabrina answered as she keyed in the camera controls for Alpha Scout. She lifted her glasses into her red hair and lowered her face to the special screen. You had to be directly in front of it and you had to be close in order to see it, so there would be no need to kill Bat Boy if he became as curious as his late predecessors. "Dear God in heaven!" she whispered as she looked at a man riding on water fast enough to keep up with a Multi-Frame. But she had a problem with the man looking just like the target her MVPs were trying to chase down. "Looks like we're dealing with some fair-minded individuals." Sabrina quickly went back to her communications console and tuned in a different channel.

"Delta Scout, Delta Scout, this is Dugout, do you copy?"

"I gotcha doll!" Delta replied. "How could I say no to that voice?"

"Do these guys ever get a clue?" Bat Boy asked.

"B. B., that's why they use a *stick* instead of *controls*."

"Delta Scout do you have a reading on the tracker yet?"

"I sure do, Dugout. It is approximately three miles away from my rendezvous coordinates and opening. What the hell?"

"Something like that Delta," Sabrina replied. "I need for you to stay on the tracker and go ballistic the moment you are engaged."

"Now you're talkin', Dugout. Orders received and confirmed. I am breakin' off."

"But that cuts the support for Alpha Scout, doesn't it?" her young aide asked.

"Bats, there may not *be* an Alpha Scout for too much longer," she answered, looking back at the special screen. Alpha was making him work for it. The moves were small but at their speed, small moves were enough. "Come on, Alpha," she cheered softly. "Shake and bake him!"

"We've got an inbound message from Gamma Rho," Bat Boy cried out. The timing could not have been better!

"Pipe it into me," Sabrina said, giving the console a push, her chair rolling down to her computer console. She hit her code and activated the system. "G., you gotta have something good for me!"

"I hope its good," Gamma said with an unusual ring of hope to his voice. "It was good for me to watch. I'll send you the data file for details, but from what I saw, these bastards have a weakness after all. Electricity!" Sabrina's eyes lit up as she pushed herself back to her communications console. She did not bother telling Alpha Scout. With the speed at which she typed, it was quicker to send an override command.

"You like a good barbeque, don't you, Bat Boy?" she said with an evil smile. The Dugout had been taking their lumps and Sabrina was no exception. She had run into one of them who called herself Milana. There had been seven members to her team including her and their lead, a man she thought was Achilles reborn. The woman Milana had proved to be too much of a Paris and somehow worked her way out of a six point attack scenario. A feat Sabrina had gone in thinking was impossible. But when the woman grabbed the front of the semi-truck, Achilles had gone flying out of the windshield and the trailer jack-knifed. It was to be expected with the cab going from forty-five miles an hour to a dead stop. Achilles had been bound for a concrete column. It turned to sand just before he reached it, and he walked away from that landing. But she had only been toying with him... with all of them. She had pushed the truck with such strength that Sabrina had to jump over the side of the railing. One hundred and thirty feet later, she hit water and lost consciousness. Apparently Milana had thought Sabrina was dead. No one else on the team received that error in judgment. Sabrina would have no remorse about what she was about to do. "Tell me, how do you like your ribs?"

"Can't shake him!" he whispered as the number of warning lights doubled on his console. "What the hell is going-" half of the power to the engine was lost and the constrictive cockpit went dim. The Multi-Frame cued it was going through a format change and the engine cut altogether as he heard a man screaming. Checking his rear view, it did not escape his notice that the small orange light at the bottom of the monitor was on. Dugout was watching and she had done something. The craft smacked down on the water hard, but he was able to able to keep the nose straight. He did notice a body skip along the surface of the water like the flat stones he and just about every other kid had tried to make jump across the pond. But a human body was no flat stone.

"Right," he thought. *"Like we're moving at speeds like I used to throw rocks."*

The man skipped several more times before rolling over to a kneeling pose with one hand on the water, along with one foot and one knee. He slid to a stop, but he did not sink!

"Alpha Scout, this is Dugout! Listen up, cowboy. We found out that the people do not like to shit sparks."

"Who does?" he asked himself before opening his channel. "Roger that, Dugout. I am already configured for aquatic mode and the stinger is charging."

"Persistent and resourceful," Niles thought as he looked at the strange vehicle that moments ago was flying better than the speed of sound

but now rested on the water as if it were made to do so. He looked at his clothes. As to their condition, he could do nothing. But the burn wounds were easily remedied. Attacking anyone of his people, with the appropriate talent, upon the waters was asinine. It was too easy to utilize the element to heal their bodies. In truth all six of the elements could be applied for healing purposes, but water was the simplest and most effective to use.

"Obviously someone is watching the Watchers," he whispered. He had already suspected as much. Unlike the Prodigians he found himself pitted against, Niles and his people had a very strong respect for powerless humans. No matter how many he and his cohorts killed, more of them soon followed and took their place. "A proverbial Hydra," he smiled as he pondered his next move. "Ahhh, of course! Let us play serpent games with the mythical serpent." Niles took a deep breath as he stood up straight and released his hold upon the water. He knew the visual effect would be stirring.

"Oh no you don't!" he said as he punched in a sequence of buttons, pushing the throttle lever forward. The Multi-Frame once again changed in its configuration and started to sink under the surface.

"Dugout, this is Alpha Scout, I am going sub-aquatic. Advise Beta Scout of my coordinates."

"Good hunting, Lazlo," Sabrina said softly in response. It was as close as she could come to giving him a kiss goodbye.

"Okay, freak!" Lazlo said as he piloted his craft under the water.

"*Oh my!*" Niles thought. "*This year's model offers a few more options, I see. No matter.*" Niles dived with such force and speed that the wake turned Alpha Scout off his course of following. Still he managed to right his craft and continue his pursuit.

Niles did not care to toy with the human and his weapon. He had already felt its shock and it would be too perfect a world to believe that it was not capable of producing another jolt, and in open waters the effect could have been more than debilitating. Getting his bearings, Niles turned toward the shore, increasing his speed even more. He could no longer see the incredible submersible when he reached the coast, diving into it as if it were so much water.

Lazlo was close to the surface of the water. The wake the man created made it difficult to draw him into focus. In a way, he was glad the man escaped. The engines were about to give and the batteries were down to less than ten percent of their charge. He surfaced long enough to get his bearings and was surprised to see the panhandle of Florida in front of his eyes.

"From New Orleans to Pensacola Beach," he whispered, entering in another sequence of commands. But there were too many lights flashing, too many things failing on the Multi-Frame for it to reconfigure.

"*Oh well, it looks like its going to be a long ride home,*" Lazlo thought as he piloted his craft to dive again and begin the long trek back to the pick-up zone.

He paced for just a few strides. Wasting energy was one of his pet peeves. But as he looked at his watch, he remembered that wasting time ran a very close second. He stopped pacing and started imagining the punishments he would create in order to convey to Niles his level of disappointment.

"*Perhaps if the corrective measures were put to his wife and child instead,*" he thought. "*He might have a much more profound reaction.*" He looked at his watch again and sighed in disgust. The daughter, he would start with the daughter first. He turned to walk away when he felt a familiar sensation that drew close as fast as it could. He stopped and took in a deep breath. Partly to calm himself and partly because he had been cheated the exploration of an interesting tangent.

"You're late," he said.

"Forgive me, my Master," Niles said as descended from the sky and landed in a kneeling position. "They have become something of a pain, these Tyros."

"Damn the Tyros!" he man snapped, his fists clenched tight at his side. There were few things that Niles, born to the name Lavisdion, actually feared. The tall, dark figure that he called Master and Dominus was certainly one of them. He had seen the man wield awesome amounts of power with a simplicity which only served to make him that much more fearsome. Niles did not entertain any notions of fighting the man. Such dreams led to a quick demise. So he made sure not to make eye contact and gave a quick silent prayer. "What of Milana? Is it as I felt?"

"Your senses are only too accurate," Niles answered with remorse. "She was killed by the one she was assigned to turn. I am sure she plagues him even in death."

"Does that image give you comfort, Lavisdion?" Dominus asked, his anger had subsided, somewhat. "Because I'm afraid it does nothing for me. The damn Watchers hold more influence in the Territories than we do!

"Descriers!" he said in disgust, turning away from Niles, allowing the man to breathe easier.

"Yes, my Master. I met with them and it was as you predicted. They introduced a new operative."

"The one you passed the marked dagger to," he added.

"Yes, Master," Niles said with a large smile on his face. "I told him that if he ever needed our help, he should plunge the dagger into the earth and I would feel it and come to his aid." The man nodded and Niles Taaveti, born Lavisdion, could see genuine appreciation across his Master's face. He had indeed done well.

"Good. Very good. But be sure to have the damned thing monitored," he commanded. "We may have to orchestrate an incidence of great need, if only to build a greater trust between you and…"

"Antal, Master," Niles answered. "Antal Brooks."

"Antal, hmmm. Well, with the Prodigian Guardsman dead, we are left with no available candidates save the boy. He is our last hope. But do not fear, that I shall tend to personally! We wouldn't want one of your accidents to bring his life to an end, now would we, Lavisdion?" Niles had no answer and his Master simply continued. "We will need another operative. Milana was gifted but ultimately short-sighted and I do not place her inability upon you. Choose another and have them make contact with the Light-Child."

"Light-Child, Master?"

"One thing I have come to take comfort in," he said as he turned and walked away. "… is that if nothing else, the Prodigian are predictable. The boy is alive, they'll send another. Your operative must intercept them. With that said, send two. Make sure they are not of equal rank.

"And make ready your first guard. We may have need of their services." This meeting was done but he would not take the breath to dismiss him. Niles, however, did not move until he was absolutely sure his Master was out of sight. Now was not the time to be baited into breaking a protocol.

"No, if my Master wants me dead," he thought, "…he will have to look harder for his reason!" It was nearly ten minutes before he lifted his head. He breathed much easier and then set off to put into action the orders of his master.

NINE

"Fathers give unto me thy strength," he prayed silently. Congregating in the place he was slowly approaching was taxing enough. The circumstances for this calling, however, weighed upon him even moreso. It was a dark, damp place, spotted with small streams of droplets along the jagged rock walls. Dreary, the chambers seemed to him, like what the bowels of Hell must be. For the most part, it could be said the room was circular, but it was not hand formed, presenting more of an elliptical shaping. It was capped by a natural crystal dome which was the inspiration behind the naming of the assemblage. He walked to the center of the room, to the large chiseled stone that had been fashioned to serve as a podium. The foolish masses would be behind him as he faced the northern wall, an arc of seating cut into the rock with seating for five. This was called the Bench. On the ground level, to the extreme left and right, there were two seats. Moving inward and upward there were two more seats of the same size and sophistication. Above those two, in the center of the Bench but high above all was the largest seat of the room. The four lower seats were reserved for the High Priests of the Elements and the largest belonged to the Grand Lord, Master of the Crimson Court. One day, that seat would be his and on that day, coming to this place might bring him pleasure. For the moment, his seat was well behind him, along the curved bench behind the podium. His particular place was just out of the light which was the only thing that suited him about the Court. He sat with the other Priests in front of the Congregation, the servants of the Court. The Crimson Court was a place of power, law and order of the Man-Lord sect though the last attribute was highly in question by those outside of the tribe. Still, it confused him! Why in all the realms of the tribes would matters of such import be settled here? It was not fit to house prisoners that you did not wish to perish! Yet this was the Great Hall of Utopia, the only place the Crimson Court would convene. As he took his place and waited for the young and old, the bright and the blind to find their seats, he sighed in disgust. Jamoreh could think of many endeavors which would be better recipients of his time and attention than speaking his attendance, but he did and quickly turned to walk to his seat.

In this calling to council, he had to attend. He could not trust this matter to proxy. Jamoreh did not care much for things of the Territories or the Outworlds. But he did care for himself and anything he could brand as his own. He would attend the Court to protect his own!

The horns sounded as the Elders walked in and took their stony seats. Most already knew the topic in argument and it gave too many an air of pleasure. It had been some time since the Blood of Beriah had known trouble from the Court.

Jamoreh sat there, wrapped in his large cloak, running his fingers through the hide of the Black Fang which covered his shoulder. It had been a simpler time when he took the beast, one of the most feared in the Territories. But he feared nothing, save perhaps for the power of this room. He would one day have to control it in order to achieve his destiny. His nostrils flared as others spoke their attendance and then began to clutter in various groups to converse quietly amongst themselves. A few were bold enough to steal a glance at the Black Priest, but none were foolish enough to attempt to hold a stare. He focused on his breathing, something Yudara had taught him to do when he could feel the fire of his anger building.

"This be beyond ridiculous, Daleifner," he muttered in disgust. "The Court has outlived its purpose."

"Quite true, Master," the young servant replied, always kept in his master's shadow. He brushed back his long dirty-blonde locks and looked about the chamber. "But a word of caution. Hold thy rage, sire. To destroy it now wouldst work against thee."

"Aye, little one. Aye."

Ten times altogether, the horns sounded as they had so many times in the past. This was the call to order. Ten times more he pondered his fate and that of the woman who had been brought before the Court. Were it not for the man who stood as his father, Jamoreh would have ionized the lot of them ages ago.

"The Crimson Court is now called to order!" Indomar, the Chief Congregate, called out as the three High Priests of the Elements entered. The largest, Petra, stopped in the center of the room, just in front of the podium, between it and the Congregation. He lifted his hands and employed his tremendous talent to raise the Court's Power Stone that was held under the floor just in front of the Bench. The moment it cleared its housing, the infant-sized stone fed on energies that still confused the greatest minds of the Territories. It gave life to the barriers surrounding the Court. Neither thoughts nor bodies of any sort could pass through the barrier.

"All is in order," Petra announced, wrapping his bear hides around his broad shoulders. "Let us proceed." The large warrior took long strides, two if not three times the length of an average frame's gait. He sat to the far left as the Priests of Water sat opposite him and the Priest of Fire sat just above and inside of Water. They took their time getting to their seats, always a painful exercise for Jamoreh. At least the Grand Lord did not walk with increased airs. He knew his power and stations and neither needed any further display.

"Enough! I say to thee all, ENOUGH!" the young Priest shouted as the last horn sounded. "This is an outrage and what is more, blasphemous to the memory of those who created this Court, to say nothing of the reason why they struck this ground for this gathering." He rose and walked across the floor as he was given to do on most occasions when he attended. Given his rank in the proceedings, he was allowed. Being the man they all knew, this much was expected. But it was still early in the Calling of the Court.

"Calm thyself," Petra spoke in his normal boastful tone. In his time of service, no one had ever given the young Black Priest an order. They merely employed their station over his in an attempt to make him see his lack of power within, at least, this body.

"I must ask thee to accommodate noble Petra, my young friend." The white-haired Colhozeh always spoke in a soft tone, always gentle and orchestrated words already weighed so that his speech would command the desired effect. Little wonder then, that he held the rather violent body of the Man-Lords in check as the Grand Lord of the Court. Even their typically impetuous nature was quelled by his reason. But he noticed that speaking in the voice he had chosen had yoked no change in Jamoreh. That was not a first, but the matter at hand was complicated enough. "Take thy seat, young Black Priest. Thou shalt be heard by this body, but all must be known first." As Colhozeh laid his wrap of fox hide and leather over the bench, the Black Priest bowed to his station. A glare from Jamoreh locked upon Petra's unwavering eyes as the young Priest returned to his seat. "And I wot not the circumstance of this manner. Indomar, continue please."

"By thy leave, Grand Lord," Indomar answered as he bowed. He approached the podium and cleared his throat. He did not look at Jamoreh, but he did wait for the Black Priest to at least reach his seat and sit down.

"I call forward a healer. Dolas, Blood of Vandigry." All heads save one turned to see a familiar face enter the Court. His smile was popular and his manner most welcomed.

"Greetings, great lords," the venerable man said upon entering. He received general answers from the audience, the three High Priests and a standing bow from the Grand Lord. "How am I brought unto this calling of the Court?" The aged doctor asked.

"Thou doth stand as witness to the condition of the woman of the name Yudara, Blood of Beriah, tasked to extirpate the Unlawful Son, named Kador, Blood of Xargagyan. Wilt thou render the truth on this matter?" Indomar asked, walking to his seat. He knew the physician would answer affirmatively, everyone did. But the Court was strict to the way of ceremony.

"I shall give the truth as mine eyes hath seen it, my lords," Dolas replied, looking at the silent Priest whose face held more rage than his aged eyes had seen in the worst storms. He began to feel through the pockets of his vest and robes. "You see, the woman is in a state of-"

"Dolas," Colhozeh interrupted, still speaking softly, "... thy testimony shall be summoned anon."

"Oh!" Dolas said in genuine surprise, drawing a low chuckle from the Congregation and small from the High Priests. "My apologies, Grand Lord. I confuse such with every attendance."

"Always, old friend," Colhozeh smiled before returning to the business at hand. "Art there any other this body shouldst recognize as witness to the matter before us?" The Grand Lord waited a few moments and then stood up. "It is therefore put to the Priests and Congregation to name who shall speak against."

"The voice of Hattil shall speak against the woman Yudara; under penalty of execution shouldst she be found in guilt." Hattil was one of the ten Priests of the Court. There were five of Color and five of Voice. The fair-haired Hattil held the highest seat among the five of Voice. It was his voice, however, that had tripped across the Black Priest's line and the trap was released.

A scream of fury echoed throughout the room and shook all that were present, save the small contingent of guards who were waiting, again, for such an action. Five of them responded before Jamoreh had taken a second step; a very quick reaction, but reckless nonetheless. The first guard arrived too soon and his attempts to restrain were deflected. His body was grasped and lifted with the ease one might have lifting a small stone and as such, he was thrown into the four guards approaching. Everyone in the room knew of the power of the man now enraged. It was the stuff of legend. Only his age and lack of maturity kept him from the seats of the High Priests or the Grand Lord. The three remaining guards failed to keep the Black Priest from taking his fourth stride.

Hattil quickly formed a shield of pure force, but it gave like a spider's web trying to forestall a war hammer. With Hattil in hand, Jamoreh ascended, still screaming his outrage. Hattil's body was stopped by the far wall as Jamoreh pressed on his chest. In the grasp of backlash, Hattil was easy prey, but Jamoreh could not claim him here. Not like this.

"Raise one hand to my sister," he whispered, feeding bursts of energy to Hattil's pain receptors. "... and I promise thee 'pon the next instant, it shall be found at her feet, still twitching weakly and in desperation for its pitiful master!" The Black Priest's left hand held Hattil's wrist and only blood was escaping the iron grip. His right hand held claim to the neck, the nails of his hand had been extended to penetrate the skin and tickle the jugular vein.

"Jamoreh!" Indomar yelled. "There hath been no challenge made or accepted. Shouldst thou kill Hattil, it shall be regarded as a crime."

"Aye, a crime!" Jamoreh shouted his reply, his eyes never leaving Hattil's.

"Thou doth understand my aim here, yes?" he whispered.

"There must be one to speak against her," Hattil pleaded. "Wouldst thou prefer in my stead the Gray Priest Shuppim to me?" Hattil was no fool. Sometimes, the only way to beat a raging beast was to give it the appeal of different quarry.

"Release him!" barked Petra who had righted the guards and was the first member of the Court to arrive at the wall where Jamoreh had his captive pinned. "This be not the way to save thy sister. Thy removal from this hearing shall be the only result of such actions shouldst they continue."

The two bodies slowly descended as the young Priest released his grip of death. He turned a second cold gaze upon the largest and most outspoken of the Four High Priests of the Elements. But to Jamoreh, Petra, High Priest of Earth was a weak fool. There could be no place for him... no place at all save deep in the very Earth he presided over.

"Thou dost not speak in a tongue I care to comprehend," Jamoreh said, walking past with no bow or any motion acknowledging the older man's position.

Petra whirled around in a rage uncommon to his demeanor and flung his head to move his unkempt reddish-brown hair out of his eyes. He had grown very tired of this whelp who called himself a man. The boy may have had power, but Petra possessed great skill. Skill with which he had faced Elkazaar of the Fairies twice and had found glory on both occasions. He had nothing to fear from this young, arrogant shell of a true Priest. He moved to both speak and strike but the hand of the High Priest, who was again late to the Court, took a firm hold of Petra's mighty arm.

The High Priest of Earth turned and put his deep brown eyes on the one who would dare such a bold and fatal mistake. Drawing focus on the culprit, his body relaxed and he let out a calmed sigh. It was Bilshan, the High Priest of Air, the oldest and most respected member of the Court if not the most respected Man-Lord. The old man was bent in his stance, as was usual, allowing his *Owl Cloak* to drag the floor at its corners. The white feathers had turned gray in their time, but seemed to look more distinguished as they were now of a more silvery hue, matching the elderly master's long hair and beard. He supported himself by his grip upon Petra and his cane, something he had possessed since his youth nearly 1,000 years ago. His hands and face withered and wrinkled with time, Bilshan's sky-blue eyes had no rival. His stare was as cold as the surest steel and in the moment of a heartbeat, it could be as warm as the heart of the sun. His strides were small and feeble in appearance, yet somewhere within his frame was the aura that commanded respect. He possessed two powers: one which all the Prodigian possessed, but the second came from the fact that no one knew how much power he wielded. Bilshan was always the one called upon when there were to be any talks with the Light-Children and had served as Grand Lord several times but never wished to hold on to the position. He would always retake the seat of High Priest of Air, the most powerful of the High Priests. The Court fell silent as he moved through the room. Even the Black Priest would be quiet until Bilshan had taken his place. There was something eerie about the old one. He had lived much longer than the norm for Prodigian and though bent, he did not appear to be seeking a grave anytime soon.

"I entered the courtyard just before the barriers lifted," he said softly to Petra, who was all too happy to escort his good friend, guardian and mentor to his place on the Bench. "Either the path to this place has grown longer or my steps shorter."

"High Priest of Air, Lord Bilshan!" Indomar shouted. He was the only member of the Court to be announced and as always, Bilshan returned a warm smile and deep head nod. Colhozeh rose from his chair and bowed deeply as all the other members stood and dropped to one knee in unison. Even Jamoreh bestowed to the ancient one this respect. His reply was always the same; a slight "Oh!" and then a soft chuckle.

"Late again?" he asked Petra who struggled not to laugh.

"You are late, as usual, my old master," Petra said with a bright smile. "But thou hast never been too late."

"I am old, give me time." Opting to take the stairs up to his seat, Bilshan looked over the Court. It was much easier to do so from this height.

"*Aye*," he thought, "*...it doth rest well in the heart to see such things. How can one wotteth if he hath done well by his kind, if indeed he doth care about such things? Is he to wait until life's fire is but a cold and black ash, incapable of bringing either light or warmth? Nay! A man shouldst know such things whilst there remains time to change all which must needs be changed and grow to the light which shall keep him eternally!*" Bilshan smiled as he looked upon his compatriots.

"There shall come a time, strong Petra, where if you are noting, I shall arrive upon a later and later hour until such time I shall not arrive at all," he smiled, muttering incomprehensible words as was his nature.

"No, my friend," Petra argued, "...I implore thee not to speak of such a dark time of our kind."

"Well, large one, perhaps in the time I have left to me, I may instill enough light that all might survive such a darkness, if my passing wouldst herald such a thing." The old one spoke in a kind tone, something almost lost in the past. In the beginning, the Man-Lords had been a sect who simply did not agree with the laws the Council of the Light-Children had created and put into action without so much as a voice for and of the people. But with the passing of time, the image the Light-Children had created, the image of the *Deviants* had become an all too cold and cruel reality.

"What hath transpired here?" Bilshan asked and the answer was projected to his mind by Indomar as it was his task and Colhozeh called for the Court to resume.

"Hattil, as he is still able, will speak against," Indomar barked.

"Then who shall speak for?" Colhozeh called.

"The voice of Jamoreh, son of Beriah and brother to Yudara, shall speak for the woman in question."

"The speakers are chosen, the Court shall engage in the substance. Hattil, take to the podium and give thy word so that it may pass into record and for judgment," Colhozeh directed, keeping an eye on Jamoreh.

"By thy leave, my lord," Hattil answered, waving for Dolas to join him. The two rose and walked to the platform.

"Dolas, what is the status of Yudara?"

"She is kept now in cellular stasis."

"And her life force?" Hattil asked, failing in his attempt not to look at Jamoreh, whose fists clenched tight at his sides.

"She lies but a whisper's breath from fading forever," Dolas answered. "The injury was to her heart and without applied talents the wound would have been fatal." A slight murmur rose from the members of the Congregation. It was silenced as Jamoreh's head snapped around to see who was speaking.

"And thou hast taken the memory from her mind so we may all see her failure in removing the one called Kador of the Blood of Xargagyan?"

"Aye, my lord, I have," Dolas answered, looking up at Colhozeh. Doth the Grand Lord admit the viewing of this memory crystal?"

"Let all be known, fair healer," Colhozeh replied.

The healer removed a black gem from his purse. With little concentration, light sparked from its center. As the light grew stronger, it turned to the hue of a memory crystal in use, a soft bronze-yellow. Dolas lowered his hand but the gem remained and light was emitted for the top of the stone, creating a three-dimensional image, as if each viewer were there, within the memory. The first image was of Kadorgyan and there was much in the way of verbal response. Most of it was born of confusion. The Unlawful Son was reported to be many things, none of them good. But Kador was obviously of strong health and sharp mind. The image expanded in time to see a young Tyro female kissing Kador and the emotion of the touch flushed through the chamber. Most closed their eyes from the sensation. Those that were strong enough to keep their eyes open realized that Yudara had closed hers. Jamoreh's face was still stern, but his anger had been displaced with wonder.

The next image viewed Yudara driving behind Kador. Only his thoughts were heard and when he countered her attack, commentary from the Congregation became louder and they were too involved in the unfolding story to be silenced by Jamoreh's glare.

"That was indeed a brilliant counter," one man said.

"The lad doth possess the spirit of a Man-Lord, as did his father!"

As the recounting continued, more praise for Kadorgyan could be heard. Jamoreh was at the point to where he was considering the entire Court when he saw his sister send the Outworlder whelp across a field.

"Ah-hah!" he cried standing up. "You see, a true Man-Lord at work. Her skills art more than-"

"Jamoreh, please be silent so we may see *all* of the tale," Bilshan said as Kador landed one of his kicks, the viewers shuddering as they felt his power.

"*This fight is far from over,*" Bilshan thought.

"The boy doth weather punishment, that much may be said for him," another voice called out.

"Methinks there is more of Zargo than we dared hope for in this one," Petra said softly. Kador's dodges and counters brought cheers from the crowd.

"To think, he is yet untrained," another viewer remarked. "The boy art a warrior to be reckoned with."

"And these Tyros fight hard for him. A born leader, like his Blood!"

"Silence!" Jamoreh screamed. "The High Priest hath asked for silence and I hath been given no reason to deny his request."

All was silent for a while. It was when Yudara claimed the end of the battle that Jamoreh once again came up from his seat.

"She has won!" he cried. "Why, in the name of the Zeldron Star hath we been called here to decide her fate?"

"All hath not been told, my Black Priest," Dolas answered. "She hath forgotten her weapon...or she hath been made to forget it."

Jamoreh's eyes widened as he watched Yudara stagger back to the scene of the battle. So much fire and smoke, Tyros scattered about in pain and fear of an impending death, and the passing of the minds of Fairies already dead or dying. But he could feel her weakening. Pressed she should have been with the power she had applied. But tired?! She should not have been so unsteady as to not be able to walk.

"Nay!" Jamoreh whispered when Kador's voice called out through the Court. It startled nearly everyone else just as strongly. Bilshan sat unchanged. He had seen this all before and for him, it had not been that long ago!

Not long ago when he trained a young man recently removed from the Light-Child order. His name was Xarga, Blood of Gamshygar. But the name of his blood had been marked and was removed as he joined Man-Lord society. He was an intuitive and very capable man, earning himself a place of respect and a new name for his blood… the name of Xargagyan. Xarga was elevated to the High Priest of Fire and took the mantle of Air when Bilshan was called to serve as Grand Lord. Whenever the old one left that status, Xarga would rejoin the Congregation and work his way back up to High Priest, save for the time when the then-current High Priest of Fire, Addar, Blood of Keentolk abdicated his place for Xarga. Xarga's first born was Zargo and both Bilshan and Xarga poured all of their knowledge into that lad only to find their combined efforts could not fill him. Kador somehow moved like Zargo. The comment claiming that the boy was untrained was incorrect by many lessons. But Bilshan's stone visage was broken when Kador took canisters of helium out of the trunk of his car.

"Aye, that is Zargo's boy!" he whispered. Petra gave sign that he had heard his old master. Colhozeh thought it best not to and his black eyes remained on the viewing.

But Bilshan's sharp mind perceived something that was not part of young Kador's explanation. Kador's clothes were lined with tubing and he had placed small canisters of compressed hydrogen about his body. A risky move, had Yudara's flame ever reached them. But whenever he felt the effects of the helium, he would release some of the hydrogen. Though the effects were not cancelled out, he was not affected as much by his own trap. Yudara had no such defense and was therefore completely vulnerable. Bilshan had always been one who believed that thought and skill would always win out over power, strength and aggression. He was enjoying this testament to his philosophy, but he knew the time for enjoyment would be fleeting. The image was drawing to its close and Yudara was powerless and wounded. Still, she was close to her Crosser, though that did not seem to press Kador.

"*And the wound to her heart?*" he thought as he caught glimpse of Kador's conveyance.

"*Where is the bolt that was lodged in his* Sugar?" he thought before his brow lifted. "*Ah, wound to the heart indeed!*"

Ten

Normally he was not the sort who enjoyed loud noises. But the clamor coming from the yard touched his heart in a way the finest orchestras failed to reach. So he watched. The moonlight along with the illumination provided by the torch stones was perfect, once again, and it was not too hot, not too cold. He stood above the performance in the cool night air. But then again, he liked it dark. He cradled his cat and stroked its charcoal fur, it purred in splendor to his touch. Beneath him, there was little to be cool. The weapons were heated as steel ground against steel, sparking alight every so often. The bodies wielding the weapons surged with heat as they pressed themselves for more speed, more strength, more power. Then there was another sort of heat altogether from the maidens who tended to the courtyard and a few of the masters there. They watched the combatants as he did, but there were more differentiations than mere angles of perspective. In truth, they cared little for the outcome so long as it did not mean some sort of gruesome injury. He did not let their presence or their passion pull from his enjoyment. So he watched. Sapphire blue eyes descended upon the scene that brought such elation, his view often heightened by flashes of light reflecting off either Blade or Guard. When they met, it was another verse of the flashing and clanging chorus, mixed in with enough misses to give the illusion there was a wind storm building. But there was not change in the weather. Not so much as the change in the scenery. A single man, who had started the contest unarmed, stood against five armed and armored warriors. He took the Blade from the second opponent, the Guard from the fifth. In the watcher's eyes, the young man moved with a perfect grace as he bested each of the five. For each man that was taken and removed from the contest, a fresh man would take his place. So he watched as the second wave was bested leaving the fighter with the last five. He looked upon the one, the young man in the center, the one who was his future, his legacy! He was a wonder to behold. Long golden hair and deep brown eyes were the first things the eye could see. They were so much like his mother's. His physique was too close to perfection to be called anything but, and his body moved like the wind. His balance was impeccable.

"The young prince fights well," Korach said as he approached, draped in lengths of cloth that he wore like robes. He was of no declared bloodline, a convert from the Man-Lords and one in whom the King placed a great amount of trust. Over time he had gained more power than he had been allowed in the Crimson Court.

"He doth know no other way!" Elior said softly in response, acknowledging the efforts of his son. "Becoming quite the Bladesman, my son! I know not of one who hath his potential of skill."

"Save the fifteen fools who dance about him, making him look glorious in battle!" Ezra said under his breath as he stood back from the railing of the overlook.

"Be silent!" Elior snapped at one son without taking his eyes off of the other, the slight frown he was beginning to form quickly returned to a bright and proud smile.

Korach walked up to the King and stood beside him. He was nearly the exact opposite of the King. He was balding where the King's hair was dark, thick and long. Korach was loud and abrupt, the King was soft and quiet and slender compared to Korach's broad frame. His rich, deep voice roared as the Prince defeated the last of the fifteen. The maidens who tended to the court showed their appreciation as well as their availability to the sweating prince's needs.

"Father!" young Abiron cried out, thrusting his sword in the air. "Didst thou bear witness to mine efforts?"

"Aye, indeed I did and 'twas a gracious treasure for my eyes! Thy skill is without equal, my son. Without equal!"

"Well done, brother," Ezra called out. Slender, dark haired and pale-skinned, he was the sort easily overlooked, especially in the shadows of his brother's golden radiance. But with the Prodigians, seldom does what one sees correspond to what one gets. "Surely thou art the sword arm 'pon which the throne may rely."

"And a good thing it is, as well," Korach added. "What with the King's only other son passing the time of day with naught save animals. Take to the vermin whose company thou dost prefer, or to the weeds with which thou hast plagued this castle, but thou shalt be silent. Is it not enough that thou art seen? Must thy voice also be heard?!"

Ezra's gaze did not leave Abiron's. There was no need to question Korach. He was allowed to speak as he wished, even in the presence of the King. The brothers were used to this. Growing up together had prepared them well. Abiron's sword slowly lowered as he bowed to his younger brother conveying a message that need not be said or projected mentally. Ezra bowed and bolted for the far wall, where the overlook and the outside castle wall met. He was slender but not foreign to movement. His strides were smooth, quick and silent. He augmented the power of his legs and jumped over the side of the wall. Elior could hear some of the maidens gasp as he fell out of sight. He reappeared shortly thereafter, riding upon a winged horse. A creation of his, made from a dying gelding he found in the wild and to whom he had given the name Hagar. Her legs were not much for running, but her back was powerful and he had created a way for her to move through those muscles. He could still remember trying to teach her how to fly. It was difficult at first but she had adjusted and was now always somewhere near him.

"Aahhh you see!" Korach declared. "You see, he doth prefer his damned animals!"

"Small wonder that Prince and Counselor do not get along if that is the case," a female voice replied and Elior smiled at the sound of her.

"My Queen!" Elior whispered as he spun around. Quickly his hand went to her face to once again feel her lovely skin and once again she moved her face to her shoulder to keep his hand there for as long as possible. Her long fiery red hair covered half her face but not for long. The King's talents were superb and his telekinesis was more tender than his silken touch. "It has been too long, my Queen!"

"Elior, my husband, thou shouldst know the power of thy passions." Her hands took hold of his arm. She could feel the sinewy strength beneath the fabric of his sleeve. "I have but just recovered."

"Jaffe, thou art beautiful!" Elior declared, ignorant of anyone else around him. "I am thy humble servant."

"The King is the humble servant of his people. It is the Queen who serves the King. Dost thou not agree, Korach?"

"My lady is most wise," Korach said as he bowed, anything to get his eyes off of her form. The fates were cruel nursemaids to make him suffer her existence, to make any man suffer it! How many had he seen the King put to death for having overly anxious gazes? Too many for him to forget and add to their number.

"And though I am anxious for all the passion my lord and master can powerfully bestow, I have been sent on errand to thee."

"Who wouldst dare to send my Queen to be an errand girl?!" Elior said, moving closer to her. She filled his eyes and his heart and the King was not known for his patience or courtly considerations. But Jaffe knew this and thought it best not to speak.

[*Calm thyself,*] Jaffe projected, her soothing tones carried over from her voice to her projections and Elior was her slave. His eyes closed at the weight of her touch. [*But the matter is private; Cov hast been dispatched from this life*] Elior's eyes opened and though he did still have passion for the woman in front of him, his gaze betrayed the fact that his mind was elsewhere. [*It is Mevkrean who hath need of thy audience and counsel.*] Elior quickly relayed the message to Korach and Abiron before turning quickly, setting his cat upon his shoulder. He broke into a run but it was swift and silent. He ran for three powerful strides and jumped from his place on the overlook to the most expedient corridor that would take him to the headquarters of the Elite Royal Guard.

No matter how much he studied it, the section of the wall did not change. The dark gem would not glow again. Cov was dead. He began to question himself, which was always his reaction to failure. There must have been something he should have done. A stratagem he should have initiated or anticipated. But with the information he had been provided, there were no such concerns. The boy was supposedly harmless and Cov had not been dispatched because the Head Master had failed, but because the Light-Child Councilman was not succeeding fast enough. He was reminded of a Tyro saying that warned of what happens when one hastens. Now his own speed to act had cost him a guardsman. Cov had not been the best, but he was ruthless and he had held nearly a Man-Lord capacity for dispensing pain, something that should have served him well among the Tyros. They were not a bright people but pain was an excellent means of conversing with them. But he was dead now and far worse, Mevkrean knew that he had none of the answers for his approaching King.

"Too damn ambitious!" he whispered, his fists on his hips. His dark ebon skin glistened in the torch light. He did not believe in using power stones of any size or capacity. His brown eyes squinted at the undeniable truth.

"Cov was a good man, my Captain," Insra said in quick support of her commander.

"Nay, he was not," Mevkrean argued. "And such was the base of reason for why he was dispatched to Old Sumeria. The Council sought not the best man. They yearned for the foulest. But thou hast mistaken my words, Guard Lieutenant. I stand neither for nor 'gainst Cov. The error I speak of is within me! I have failed the King!"

"Giveth unto me the discernability of who hath and who hast not failed me, Mevkrean," Elior said as he entered the room, his cat jumping to a large map table in the center of the room. Elior's eyes immediately went to the board. Indeed, Cov's stone had turned dark while Elkazzar's and those who traveled with him were still very bright. Elior's fist was lifted to strike the wall but he did not send it. Instead, it opened and laid flat on Cov's stone as Elior's head lowered. Korach stepped forward, his hand tightly on his Blade's sheath. He glared at Mevkrean who was not moved by the visage, and he quickly returned his attentions back to his King.

"How did this come to be?" Korach yelled. There were many who felt that Korach was given far too many freedoms. Mevkrean was counted among that small but growing group. "Why hast thou not yet recalled his form?" Mevkrean made it a point not to answer Korach. He held no official rank and though he was often called the King's Counsel, Elior had advisors for such purposes.

"Captain?" Elior said softly.

"There was nothing to recall, my King," Mevkrean answered, drawing the attention of everyone in the room. "Whatever took Cov, took him entirely! That which normally remains was consumed upon the instance of his death."

"And the site, fool!" Korach's anger had reached the point where he spat as much as he shouted. Not that he needed to shout as he stepped even closer to Mevkrean. A distance reserved normally for those he knew intimately or while needing secrecy. "*Where* did he meet his last fate, Mevkrean?!" But again Mevkrean did not answer. He simply lowered his head and Korach burned with rage as he slowly lifted his hands and let them fall. "Dost thou know who killed Cov?"

"Korach," the Prince started to speak but he received Korach's glare, which was slightly empowered. Still the King was without action and the Prince stepped back.

Mevkrean let his hands fall from his waist. He kept his eyes on the King, but it seemed as though he held less and less presence while Korach assumed more authority. This was not a first, but Mevkrean was not about to have his name added to the list of foolish victims who were not prepared for Korach's allowed rage.

The room no longer felt like a place belonging to soldiers. It felt alien and Mevkrean had too long listened to his instincts to abandon them now. Calming his mind and focusing his thoughts on the report he had to give his King, Mevkrean removed his helmet and ran his other hand over his bald head. He waited for Elior to once again direct him to answer a question spouted from anything other than royal lips and when he did, the large solider took in a deep breath before he would speak.

"From what the Tracker-Warriors were able to gather… the first inclination declares Kadorgyan as the author of this event."

"Ka-" Korach stammered as he staggered backward. He looked around the room for a silent moment and huffed in rage lunging forward, grasping Mevkrean's throat. "Thou shalt pay for thy incompetence!" With ownership of the large man's neck, Korach was quick to draw his Blade, turning to face Insra.

"Remember, thy loyalty is to thy King!" he said firmly.

"Thou art not the King!" Insra shouted as she looked to Elior. "Your majesty? Your majesty!!"

Augmented muscle pitched against augmented muscle and though Korach strained, his progress toward killing Mevkrean was pitifully slow. Their eyes locked, one within the other, trading a test of strength between their minds as well.

"Father!" Abiron pleaded, watching his childhood protector and the instructor of many of his lesson being strangled.

"Abiron, thou art excused," Elior said as he looked away.

"Enough..." Mevkrean choked out as he slowly lifted his hand to Korach's forearm and at the very same speed pushed Korach. "I say to thee, enough!" Mevkrean held the Korach's mental onslaught at bay as his hands squeezed at the forearms even harder.

"Thou art a blind fool, Korach!" he whispered. "Blind to the gifts the King bestows 'pon thee... blind to the folly thou leavest in thy wake, in the King's name! Thy power hath made thee blind to reason." Pain distracted Korach and his mental attack subsided but Mevkrean did not invade his mind. He simply maintained his defenses and continued squeezing. "Just as thou art blind to my strength!

"Assemble!" Mevkrean cried and Insra drew her sword. Three of Mevkrean's men phased through each of the four walls; three came up through the floor and three more through the ceiling. All of them were Elite Royal Guardsmen with weapons at the ready. Korach took a more defensive pose as Abiron turned about the room, seeing the glory of the man who had taught him strategy shine once again. He smiled at the Captain and his elation was noticed as Mevkrean looked over, Korach nearly on his knees in pain. He wanted to speak, but enough had fallen foul and already he could feel those of the guard more loyal to the throne than any officer, much like he was many, many years ago.

"Your majesty!" Mevkrean struggled to say. Elior looked at his Captain for a moment and as his eyes fell from the leader of the Elite Guard, he nodded.

"No act shall be made against thy blood. I swear it!" Mevkrean moved forward, toward his King and was about kneel when Elior held up his hand in denial. "But thou hast offended the throne, Mevkrean. Surrender now and thy death will be swift."

"There are many who might die!" Lorthar roared as he approached the King, his axe set to remove Elior's head. Mevkrean lifted only a finger and the soldier stopped cold, his weapon still ready, his killing urge still hungry, but both kept by a discipline of greater mettle than his axe.

"By thy leave then, your majesty," Mevkrean said with a deep and gracious bow. But there was little time for further words. He reached his hand, his Guard and Blade flew to his grasp.

"Find the wind. Be the smoke!" Mevkrean barked as he jumped back from the King, phasing through the wall. Korach tried to focus his thoughts and force Mevkrean to become solid while he was passing through but the *King's Counsel* was struck with pain as not all of Mevkrean's men left the room at the same time. Only eighteen of the twenty left, the last two were teleported away by one man who had already phased out. A military withdrawal, by the numbers, each man covered at least once, no one left vulnerable to reprisal.

"By the Fires of the Fates!" D'Hano cried at he entered the room. He was another one of Mevkrean's Guard Lieutenants, but it was no secret the two did not get along well. "Assemble the Elite Guard!" D'Hano ordered as he ran to the King..

"Stay thy wrath," Elior whispered as he aided Korach's recovery effort. "Mevkrean is no easy catch and there are more pressing matters. Triple the guard about the Great Bridge and assemble every Blade and Guard of Absularian Blood in our ranks! Search every home, leave no stone undisturbed!" D'Hano turned to make these orders a reality but he was grabbed and spun around to face the King. "And bring me thy best Bladesman along with four others. You have a mission of death in Old Sumeria!" D'Hano left and Abiron offered his body to steady Korach.

"D'Hano's men will need a Tracker-Warrior," Abiron stated. "I am trained in the arts."

"Thou art indeed a Prince of the Throne, but I will not have thee going about chasing after abominations!"

"But Father-"

"No, Abiron," Elior insisted. "Not in Old Sumeria. If thou art so eager, thou shalt apply thy talents to the search for Mevkrean.

"Now go!" he commanded, ushering the young man along. "Fetch they weapons and thy armor and prepare thyself for an enduring search."

"Mevkrean is a Master Tracker-Warrior," Abiron pointed out.

"This much I know. But he also instructed thee. Let us hope thou wert an attentive student."

"Your majesty," Abiron said as he bowed and then ran off to collect his things, leaving Korach and Elior in the room alone. Elior approached the wall and touched the stone representing Elkazzar. It flashed bright white but nothing else. The stone verified that the Head Master was alive but it no longer had the ability to locate the man; an interesting feat given how they were made.

"The Prince spoke true, your Majesty," Korach said. "D'Hano's men will need some sort of guide."

"Then by my blood, they shall have it," Elior said as he pondered his next move. "Summon the Wolf Lord!"

As the men poured out of the building, Mevkrean looked down on them. He smiled at the young prince who ran to complete his tasks quickly but did not possess an earnest face.

Then there was D'Hano to consider. If he was blessed, he would finally have his opportunity to kill the man. But then what? The move beyond the next clamored about in the back of his mind. He and his men numbered a full score and for a time they would be a force to reckon with. But they had no home now, or at least, that is what the King would believe so he would set his chasers out immediately. In his haste, Mevkrean would find the room to enact a plan he had always hoped was just his darker nature composing but would never need to be engaged. Times were more than dark now. The gradual decline of the King concerned more than Mevkrean and there were places he knew he could find help. But he would not implicate the first among them.

"Know this, my men...," Mevkrean said in an even tone. "...the first of thee who wouldst rather remain loyal to the Throne, speak now and upon my blood, no harm shall befall thee. The ground we tread is treacherous and may yet consume us all."

"Then let it choke on my bones!" Lorthar called out and there was some laughter after the comment, much more than the Captain expected. But eight did decide to resign their commissions. Mevkrean kept his word and they all lived as they left, an act that outraged Insra.

"A man's word must count for something," Mevkrean explained.

"But now they will know where we are," Insra argued.

"Dead bodies would tell the same tale," he replied. "And those men will report to the King and he will react accordingly which means we will leave these high perches and move about the streets. Come, my friends, there is something of import I have always wanted to know."

"What is that, my Captain?" Lorthar asked as they all began to run quietly.

"Why doth our King fear this Unlawful Child so?!"

Eleven

"Did you sleep well, son?" Adrianna asked, placing a hand on the back of her son's head.

"Didn't sleep at all, Mom," he answered. "At least not like I normally sleep. My eyes were closed, my body rested..." he looked at his body and smiled. "...and mended. I even snored!"

"Sounds like normal sleep to me," Gordon remarked.

"Except for one thing," Kador said as he looked up into his mother's eyes. It was not that he could not see the fear they held for him, but the fire to explain himself was immediate, nearly desperate. "I was aware of everything around me. I can tell you when the three of you left my room. I even know what you were thinking when you were in there," he said, turning in his chair to look at me. He did not project anything, he did not need to. It was clear he knew my feelings for his mother and we would be discussing those feelings at some later point. "I can even tell you what you had for breakfast, down to the proportions.

"And Mom's right, Dad," he added, "you do need to lay off the salt!" Adrianna chuckled and my eyebrows bespoke my interest in what the boy was telling us. "But it started to fade out about three hours ago," he continued. "Then, I could've told you what the neighbor's dog was thinking about. But now..."

"Your perceptions are kept to your own personal space," I interrupted. "This is how it should be, my son. In time your power and skill will grow to the magnitude you have experienced. You may even go beyond those parameters. But for now, your senses have returned to what is still paranormal to this world, yet quite normal to ours." He smiled as I returned my attention to the newspaper.

"Wow, look who's starting to sound like one of the untouchables!" the young man remarked, smiling at me. Gordon chuckled as Adrianna covered her mouth to prevent laughing out loud. I managed to return to the boy a gentle smile, one that killed his. "Nice try, Elkee, but you don't have to lie to me." He had not changed the tone or volume of his voice but it was evident that something had been added; something which removed the comedy and lightness of his retorts. Adrianna looked at her son as Gordon looked at me. "I know my perception capability is beyond *normal* for both environments. Knowing that doesn't mean I'll become conceited, arrogant, power-hungry or the saint of the world. That's probably the same unfounded assumption the Prodigian made about my father."

"*Probably*?!" Gordon shrieked. "I think you hit the nail on the head!"

"Maybe I did," he agreed. "Can't say for sure though. Nothing can be sure without proof. Condemning the Light-Children or the Man-Lords on a whim would make me like them. It's just like you and Mom taught me, 'two wrongs don't make a right'." Gordon placed a plate in front of Kador and his eyes flared wide.

"Think you can handle that plate, son?" Adrianna asked sitting next to her boy.

"If I can't, it won't be for lack of effort!" he answered as he put a napkin in his lap.

But Gordon was not done. I could feel his animosity toward me and the Prodigian entire, despite the fact he had married one. "But William, you have to remember that regardless of who really killed him, both sects are equally responsible for his death."

"That is not the focus of the matter!" I said in a strong voice. "What truly matters is that his mind is able to conceive of and perhaps perform *all* of our abilities."

"And that has what to do with my point?" Gordon huffed.

"Easy, Dad," Kador said as he quickly got up from his chair.

"Easy nothing! An eye for an eye," Gordon said, spinning to return to the stove. William followed and took hold of Gordon's shoulder.

"Look, I know that you and my father were close. You two must've been really close friends. But I can't just go to the Territories taking names and heads. That wouldn't be right, even if all of them were in on it. I'll find the truth. Anyone and everyone truly responsible will have me to deal with, I promise you. But I have to save that rage until I find the truth. I can't afford to use it one second before I need to. Not one second." Gordon turned to face the lad and their eyes locked before they embraced, the son consoling the surrogate father. The room was silent. My eyes never moved from Gordon, even after he and Kador parted. He walked over to the sink and just looked out of the window. Kador quickly returned his attention to his plate and Adrianna's eyes floated around the room. William broke the silence by holding up his glass and examining it, trying to figure out why it was empty. Adrianna got up and smiled, walking over to the refrigerator as Gordon returned to the stove.

"I thought you said he was going to be grouchy. Looks like he grew a tapeworm instead," she said as she filled his glass with fruit punch.

"Who got flowers?" Kador asked, looking at the arrangement and vase.

"You did, son" Gordon answered, adding food to William's empty plate.

"Okay, so who messed with the card?" I folded my arms. Amazing!

"No one touched the card!" Adrianna was quick to answer. "We read the note on the side but-"

"Excuse me!" he said holding up his finger. "But in given company, the word touch being limited to the implication of using physical form is rather obsolete!"

"Quite true, my boy. I read the card," I admitted. "How did you know it was... *messed* with?"

He lifted his glass to his mouth, taking in a third of its contents. He had also lifted a fork-full of food to his mouth before his eyes rose to meet mine. I could not tell if he was testing me or wanting me to become angered.

"The card was too clean," he finally answered. "I couldn't even get a sign that Linda touched the card or the envelope."

[*Very good, William,*] I projected, nodding my head with pride. "Sometimes no proof is proof positive."

"But what if someone at the flower shop wrote the message, like they do with call-in orders?" Adrianna was pressed to stump her son. My student was now a teacher but she was competing with a dead husband whose genius still exceeded the living.

"Impossible for it to be a call-in order," Kador answered. "The scent on the flowers is Linda's perfume. Plus the residue on the stems tells me not only did she go to a florist, but she chose each one of these by hand. Serves to reason that she would've written her own card." William finished his plate and glass and directed a smile at his mother.

"Well done indeed...William," I said.

"Call me Kador," he replied, smiling at me.

I was beginning to think that this very young man was turning out to be the answer to all of the problems our people had. Not only because of his potential for power, but because he was a living symbol that the Man-Lords and Light-Children could not only live together, they could love each other as well.

"*Oh Fathers, what fate have I been blind to?!*" I thought. "*I am a fool and only a shell of a man!*"

My eyes, locked in their endeavor to take him in, I had been watching him but for the first time I came to see Kadorgyan! Instantly it became clear to me. Suddenly every veil pronounced by a pontificating, posturing Councilman or passionate, exalted member of the Royal Court turned transparent, dissipating from in front of my eyes. Between my fears of again failing my former Master and tripping over the love-sworn ideals for a woman I would never posses, I had fallen short of reason! I had promised to protect my people from all our enemies but in standing true to that word, I had no firm conception of who our enemies were.

"Riddle me this, my friend," Zargo once said to me after one of my more trying exercises. One that was a precursor to *Vision* and had proven incredibly difficult to resolve. The latest attempt had produced less than satisfactory results and my mentor, who was my junior in age, counseled me. "Now that thou hast given thy word as Councilman, who is thy worst critic?"

"Hast my mentor taken a different turn?" I answered with a question. The Fates blessed me that day, for such an error of etiquette usually resulted in disciplining. "Surely I am my own worst critic?"

"And why for is that?" he asked, a familiar grin forming across his face and yet another I had missed; the ability to review my memories enabled me to see it later.

"No one wotteth me better than I, my Master. I know my limitations and if I do not, I shall be the first to learn of them."

"Indeed!" he agreed.

"This is in regards to the exercise!" I declared.

"Is it?" the most favored words to leave his lips.

"I did not commit myself fully to it, Master. I made every effort to give the appearance of the effort rendered was all I had left, but the truth is that I tire of this exercise and the objective for which it was created. I do not want to reach *Vision*!"

"Nay?"

"But I do!" I said, closing my eyes and feeling a hatred for myself so deep and enraged that I would have struck myself had it been one of the forms of combat in which I had been trained. "I do and I am lazy! I hath failed thee for the pleasure of a moment's respite from thy drills. I know the reason already but I looked only to my fatigue, my hope that thou wouldst let me pass this point if the effort appeared strong enough."

"Thus, you opted for deceit?"

"Aye!" I cried, throwing myself at his feet. "Thou art well within thy right to abandon me in lieu of a student who wouldst at least try!"

"I have that now," he replied calmly and I cleared my eyes of tears to look upon him. "But I wouldst hope thou hast found the truth of thyself. Thou art thine own worst enemy for good reason. The deepest of truths of thyself cannot escape thee. Denial is a thumb in a cracked damn with far too many holes already! Elkazzar, thy answer was correct: the worst critic of self is thyself."

"What be the point of this, Master? To see me undone?"

"Lose not the eye of wisdom which has just begun to open, Elkazzar," he instructed. "Look 'pon thy oath and realize, if indeed thou dost lay effort to protect the Prodigian from our enemies, first thou must protect us from thyself. For surely thou art also thine own worst enemy!"

So quick I had been to assume that the Deviants were always the enemy and the only enemies of my clan. But my Master had been a Man-Lord, one of their most powerful. He had ushered me into a higher echelon of perception, taught me how to invoke *Vision*... yet still I was inept of sight. To bring Kador to the Territories, to show all of our clan and the others of the Prodigian, that would be to challenge the unwritten law of the Unlawful Son. He was nothing of what we were told to expect and everything they feared. Once cracked, that foundation would give, only to crack others and soon even the throne itself would have to be held accountable. Results from those in power would be expected and without them, explanations would have to be submitted and reviewed. The people would have to be appeased and perhaps that was an extreme for which they were not prepared. No, not prepared, an eventuality that they would rather have avoided.

"But how could the King have foreseen this?" I deliberated. *"The orders he set before the Council had nothing to do with observation – it was a notice of execution, to terminate with extreme prejudice. And how I have gone about my duty, confounded by my pride and my power. Oh, your majesty, thou hast chosen well thy fool for this errand!"* So much had already been done to complete the task. I could no longer take the Council's vote to have the boy observed as a testament of hope. More likely it was an effort to afford time for those who were truly the architects of this boy's death. Because so much was at stake and with the rising conflicts with the Man-Lords, few mistakes could be afforded.

"*Nay*," I concluded, "*this I cannot do!*" The Prodigian would deal with the fate of their own actions. It would not include the life of this innocent one. For how could he be taken into such a world and still maintain some mien of his original humanity and dignity... his original beauty? I could not hold Kadorgyan to this eventuality, though it could very well deliver the verdict of doom to the Prodigian.

[*Hey you!*] Kador projected to my mind and I shuddered in surprise. [*You know, in some circles, being all drawn off in the company of others is considered rude.*] His tone was soft and musing. Beneath the forming smirk of devilish overtone lay the spark of acuity. [*Hope I didn't take you from anything too important.*]

"Perhaps you did," I sighed. "But I suppose that does not matter here and now."

"Kador, I cannot-"

"Eat another bite," he interrupted, playfully peering under the table. "I know, this Tyro food has got you stuffed beyond the point of reason."

"No, that is-"

"Is not as important as you finally getting around to telling me where you were when I was being raked over the coals last night." I looked up into his eyes and it was as if time had repeated itself. In the instant of a blink, I was no longer a potential mentor. I was a student again, at the feet of my Master who would not accept my definitions of inability.

[*The pieces aren't together yet,*] he projected. [*And until they are, I have to keep going. You wanna come with me, fine. But with or without you, I am going forward with this!*]

"I would rather visit the Territories with a knowledgeable guide," he said softly but not so soft that Gordon and Adrianna could not hear him. "But if that's not in the cards, fine. I'll roll with that punch too. I'll just improvise," he said, maintaining his smirk. I could feel Adrianna shudder as my eyes closed. We had both heard that bravado framed in different words and we both knew the chances of changing his mind were as great as changing his father's had been: minimal! He stood up from the table and took his plate to the sink. The room was silent.

"Now about that explanation," he said.

"You have to know what you are risking!" I pleaded.

"Can't be too much more than I put on the line last night," he shot back with a stare. "Just sitting here I put one thing together: if I leave the Prodigian in the state they are in now, I am no better than the fools that killed my father and banished my mother to what most had to have hoped would be a one-way ticket to hell.

"All in all, everyone in this room has slipped up and tripped up. All of you are weighing in on my future and I get that. Between parent, guardian and friend, I get that. But I am a Prodigian! My ancestral home is the Territories. My culture is not the one that I am living in right now. Yeah, it's a part of me. All of this will always be a part of me just as part of me will always be William Anthony Ferrous. But that name and this place are disguises, shells where I could be kept safe. Now, does somebody in this room have the chops to tell me that this safety is real?" he said looking around the room. His eyes fixed on his mother and his face softened. "That wish has died! It's about time we put the Clark Kent costume away and deal with Krypton."

"**Why**?!" Gordon said at just under a scream. I had not believed his voice could hold so much power but I jumped as did Adrianna. Kador knew it was coming. He may have not known from whom, but he knew the outburst was overdue. He turned to look at Gordon. His face was not as soft, Gordon did not need tenderness, it was not a language he could translate at the moment.

"It is what I choose to do. It is what I was meant to do. It is what I would be doing if my father were alive. Should I change up because he's dead?" He did not wait for an answer as the faces he looked upon took the inquiry as rhetorical. He turned and walked out of the kitchen. We could hear him going up the stairs to his room.

I could not look at either of them, I felt too responsible for this turn of events.

"Easy there, hero!" Adrianna whispered. "I think we've had enough martyrs for now." She stood up and walked over to Gordon who said nothing as he took her in his arms. He closed his eyes as her head lay against his chest and she began to cry. He opened his eyes and tears began to roll down his cheeks.

"Go to him, Elkazzar," he said softly. "Elizabeth could train him, but we all know you're better at it. Train him and make it so that he...he at least stands a chance."

Her crying eyes opened and looked at me as I stood up from my chair. "Please!" she mouthed and I nodded. I nodded and took the path to follow Kador.

"Very well, William," I said, entering his room. He was sitting on his bed, reading a magazine, sucking on a lollipop.

"Kador," he corrected.

"Very well, Kador," I said. "Fine. But if you wish to venture to the Territories, we must see to it that all you have received mentally can be applied by your mind and body. We must sharpen your skills.

"We will start with the most simple, hand-to-hand combat techniques."

"No offense, Elkee," he said, turning the page with his mind, "...but I think I've got that one covered."

"Oh do you now?" I said, finally finding reason to smile. "Well, young man, you are about to find out just how incomplete you are. For just as you never truly read Linda's card, so you are lacking in the finer points of our arts. Mind you that which is the most difficult to instruct, you have demonstrated an acceptable level of adroitness."

"Adroitness?"

"But," I continued, ignoring his judgment of my locution. "...while your instincts are indeed impressive, your skills lack experience and-"

"Nothing takes the place of experience," he said, hopping up from his bed. "Okay, whatever you say, Elkee. But aren't you getting a little old for this type of training?"

"Indeed!" I said glaring at him. The nerve to imply that I might be unable to perform at my peak. Surely I knew this and my body needed more augmentation in combat these days than it had in my younger seasons. But for him to mention it was unacceptable. "It just so happens I have made a few arrangements which also should tell you what I was about when your

77

situation was dire. Though what I was able to arrange serves as an explanation, I have-"

Alright, hold it right there," he said with a gentle smile and a touch upon my shoulder. "No apologies, man. You were doing what you thought you had to... just like what I was doing by even going out last night." He looked down in realization and shook his head. "Dear God, what was I doing? I put Linda's life in this mix. What if that bitch had made her move while we were on the date?"

"She would not have," I answered. "Not initially anyway. The *Deviants* have made a science of understanding their enemy and how to eradicate them."

"Easy on the Roget's, Elkee," he replied, but again I ignored him.

"And while attacking in the company of one you hold dear might serve to distract you, there is a greater chance that any harm befalling them might enhearten you and turn the tide of battle."

"Damn, they study that sort of thing?" he asked.

"It is their way," I answered before taking a pause. "But it is wise to study how power should be applied to avoid wasted effort.

"However, you are expected in the backyard," I said as I started to fade slowly from his sight. Slow teleportation was so much more costly, but incredibly more effective. As hard as it would be to attain a plateau of superiority with Kador, it was necessary if he were going to accept me as a mentor. "I have gathered three specialists to complete your training."

"You mean three Prodigians?" he said in a surprising voice instilled with youthful hope.

"No, I mean three invaders from the Moon," I answered, returning his own smirk. "Downstairs. Backyard. I suggest that you not keep them waiting."

He took a deep breath before putting on his sweat suit. As he tied his shoes, he looked up to a picture of his family that had been taken when he was sixteen. The Ferrous' were the first family of the community to celebrate a sweet sixteen for a boy. Gordon and his mother 'pulled out all the stops'. The entire house had been decorated and the backyard was a field for many games. Now it was a training field for combat and God knows what else.

"The more things stay the same," he said, picking up the picture. On the back of the frame was an inscription: 'To our son on his sixteenth'.

"It was a good time," Adrianna said as she entered the room.

"Not even a year ago," he whispered. "I was so young then."

"We all were younger, baby," she said, placing her hands on his shoulders.

"You okay with the change-up?" he asked, still looking at the boy in the photograph. "You were supposed to be teaching me, remember?"

"I think it's time that Handyman started calling the plays," she replied, fighting back her tears. William nodded and put the picture down.

"Besides, you'll need me to make heads and tails of that place you found in your mind." William started to turn around but she held him where he was. "I'm your mother, baby. I will always be part of you. The blocks I put in your mind are gone, but that doesn't mean I no longer know my way in."

"Why didn't you tell Elkazzar?" Adrianna asked of her son.

"Grace for grace," he answered. "He's holding on to a few secrets of his own."

"Two wrongs making a right?"

"Keeping secrets isn't wrong," he answered, placing a hand over one of hers. "You just have to figure out which ones are better left as secrets." He took in a deep breath, saying farewell to the memory but not goodbye.

"Going through a different kind of puberty now, right?" he said, gently moving her hand away from his shoulder. He would not refuse her love but he could not encourage coddling, despite how much he wanted it.

"That's a good way to look at it," she answered, stepping back, saying goodbye to a dream. "And I'll be here to help you with that place in your mind. Next time I'll even try to come with you. I think I might be one of the few who can accompany you."

"Yeah," he said, walking for the door.

"*So young,*" he thought. "*So young to the ways of the Prodigian. Here I am staring adulthood in the face and I have to go back to learn what most of these people must've learned before they could even walk!*

"*I learn the powers with which I can defend myself and perhaps take a few lives along the way.*" Memories of Cov and the female assassin flashed in his mind. He wondered how long his list would be before his own name was added to one.

"So much pain in the world," he concluded. "I was dumb enough to believe I could be one of the few to take a little out of this world. What is it they say about best laid plans?" His head was low as he walked downstairs. After another flight, he would be in the basement and from there he would enter the backyard... and his weaning.

Twelve

He stepped out on to the back porch with his head hung low, his eyes closed. Kador seemed to me as if he was marching toward his execution and I could find no fault in him for the countenance. From what I had gained from his mother and my scans of the one called Rachel, William was usually uplifted by the act of becoming acquainted with new people. But the reason for this meeting prevented his normal processes and tainted the occasion. He stopped at the edge of the porch, breathed out slowly and opened his eyes. He saw three new forms, each wearing cloaks and hoods, but he was moved by none of them. They stood in the middle of the lawn, with at least a good meter between them. The cloaks kept their faces from him and I was taken aback when I saw his eyes shift, taking in the forms of the bodies underneath the fabric and the dimension that cloaks could not hide from sight.

"*Who taught you this?*" I thought, making sure to keep my mind shielded.

He studied them quickly. The structure of their shoulders gave him an approximation of their strength. He then looked at their feet to judge each stance and gauge their balance and combative depth. But what was he using for a reference? To say nothing of how he had divined the technique! I took a step closer as he prepared to speak. Something told me I would soon want a better view.

"Good afternoon," he said in a voice much stronger than I expected. "Welcome to my home."

"Well at least he has manners," Vada-Ri returned. Her stance and speech were cold and offsetting. A Mistress of the Council, she failed to at least match the offered caliber of courtesy.

"I am William Anthony Ferrous," William continued. "I was born to the name Kador, Blood of Xargagyan. I am honored to have you here at the home of my parents."

"Thy name is Kadorgyan," Vada replied. "The *William* façade must come to an end. It was, after all, but a ruse to give thee opportunity to mature and approach the abilities of thy people, the Light-Children."

William was surprised by her response and he looked at her more closely. My premonition was correct. His eyes drew sharp on Vada's form and I could feel them, his instincts flashing thoughts into his mind. They worked in coordination with his memory as he recalled when he had last heard that voice. His chin lifted less than an inch and her hood blew back, revealing Vada's face. The white hair was all he needed to see. He stepped away from the porch and toward my daughter. I would have been struck nervous except for the look on his face. There was no anger, no justifiable hunger for retribution. He was curious!

"This is no introduction," he said softly as he drew closer to her. I could sense a change in his tone. "Perhaps the word *formal* could be added to make all of this ceremony necessary, but you and I have already met. In combat, if I recall correctly."

"'Twould seem not all the abilities of the mind are yet beyond thee," she answered and her words lashed into him and my hand clenched into a fist.

"Vada-Ri!" I shouted. "We are not here-"

"No!" William said quickly but just as softly. "No, Viz, the woman is entitled to her own opinion."

"Father, why does he call you Viz?" Vada-Ri asked as I tried to keep my shock from registering across my face.

"Why don't you ask *he*?" William cut in. "Or are you intimidated being this close to an *animal* you couldn't put down? Even though you had help and I was alone." William got the exact reaction he was looking for, the heads of the other two turned to look at him and Vada. Their eyes were tightly locked within each other's glare. His brown eyes peered into her green ones and while Vada-Ri was trying to impose her will over William, he was putting all of his effort in making Vada confront herself and the lack of honor in her actions. How she had betrayed the ideal of the Light-Child and had behaved like a Man-Lord. She was not only stronger than him, but she had more experience in this sort of thing. But young Kador's approach negated her advantages and all the effort she threw at him, she was actually throwing at herself. Her denial gave way and her eyes fell from his and she looked down at the ground at her feet. I thought I would faint. William walked by my daughter and on to the next form. Igrileena pushed her own hood back and her brown eyes quickly drew focus on William as he approached.

"This is Igrileena," I said, knowing of her tendency to be laconic. "She is one of the foremost combatants I have ever had the pleasure of working with. She was born a Man-Lord, but found the oppression of her gender too much to bear."

"So she became a Light-Child?!" William asked, already knowing from my memories that the Light-Children had not exactly experienced suffrage.

"It is better to have a slight chance than no chance at all, Outworlder," Igrileena answered quickly. Her tone was not much more receptive than Vada's.

"A pleasure to meet you," William said, offering his hand. Igrileena looked at it questioningly.

"Use it or remove it," she said as her hands lifted to her hips.

"Nice group you got here, Viz," William said glaring back at me.

"That is the second time you have called him this. Why?"

"Whoa, and they can count too!" William said to me with a smile. Igrileena's eyes flared and short of engaging any of my talents, I knew I would be too slow to stop her from attacking. But as her anger tried to trigger her actions, she found Kador was already looking at her, already prepared to move...too prepared for her to feel comfortable in continuing with her initiative. He was faster! She had not used her best speed but he was untrained! How could he move so fast?!

"Funny thing about impulses," he said, glaring into her light brown eyes. "They can make you do the darndest things. Make you act before you've had time to think.

"I call him Viz because he's quite the visionary. All you have to do is get him talking about the Prodigian and the next thing you need is a blanket and something to wipe the drool." The next in line snickered at his comment and William left Igrileena to meet the last of the three.

He was huge, towering well over six feet tall and like Igrileena, he too decided to push his hood back. But he offered his hand to William.

"This is Vastiol," I said, stopping in front of the large Absularian.

"Well met, young Lord Kadorgyan. It is indeed an honor to meet you at last." William was pleasantly surprised.

"The honor is mine, Lord Vastiol." William offered his hand and Vastiol grabbed his forearm.

"Vastiol is an Absularian," I started. "He-"

"And his people are immune to the abilities of the rest of the Prodigian," William finished, smiling at me. "You forget I have a general knowledge of the Prodigian."

"And how did *you* happen across that?" Vada asked, her former attitude had not stayed away too long.

"I bought it on E-bay!" William shot back. I was certain he would keep the exercise of the power feed just as his father had kept it, quite secretive!

"Igrileena," I said, knowing my daughter was not going to take his answer well, "...will be responsible for your combat training while Vada-Ri will instruct you in the finer applications of your mental energies. Combined, these lessons should bring you to the point to where you at least an interesting match for Vastiol here."

"I get it," William answered, smiling at Vastiol. "Absularians are immune to mental powers and most of them are stronger and faster than the norm. Even the Prodigian norm! Yeah, that should be real fun."

"He shall also provide thee with instruction in muscle conditioning," Vada added. "Thou dost look as if such lessons are in need."

"You could use a tuck here and there yourself, bleach-head!" Vada started to move and William was already set to spring. But Vastiol took one step and was between the two as my hand took a firm grip on William's shoulder. He stopped, turned to look at me, sighed and relaxed.

[*That's one!*] he projected, a little physical force came with it.

[*Yes, and I'm sure it won't be the last,*] I replied. I kept my hold of his shoulders and decided to usher him toward the house.

"The important thing for you to remember is that she is here to teach you how to employ your powers.

"Vada-Ri is a Master. One of the most gifted of our kind!"

"More powerful than you, Viz?" he asked quickly and I just as quickly ignored the inquiry. I also felt it most advantageous not to advise him that facing Vastiol was but the first of two tests. I actually expected him to best the Absularian. But he would have to face me and be able to hold his own fairly well before I would allow him to journey to the Territories. At least, that was the dedication I made to myself.

"She will show you the different forms of energy your mind can wield. Yes, you have already seen this in my mind but her view has greater depth, the reaches a mind like yours can appreciate. Your prior contests have all been bedraggled and improvident. It has been the offerings of fate and fortune that your engagements have been short term."

"Right," Williams said, nodding. "All of my fights up to now I've been sloppy and it's just been blind luck that no one's gone the distance with me yet. Got it!" He laughed as we continued to walk.

"I amuse you?"

"Only when you get nervous," he said softly. "Which is looking more and more like all the damn time. You surround yourself with pretty words that are not in the main of speech because you equate that with intellect and believe somehow intellect will save the day."

"You make it sound as though it cannot," I countered.

"Oh, it can. But a dictionary burns just as fast as an atlas." I stopped walking and released his shoulder. The sensation struck my heart, shooting so far beyond my intellectual fortress wall that it affected my physical form. He was teaching me! And even though I had no idea where his thoughts were leading, I knew he was right. He stopped and turned to look at me and I was helpless against the tide of the moment.

"And all of that means?"

"You can say all the pretty words and you can know exactly where you are and how to get to the next place. Neither of them does a damn thing to put out the fire!"

"And the fire comes from?"

"The fire is fear, Viz," he replied. "The reason why you plunge into knowledge in the first place. It doesn't matter if you say 'Gadzooks!' or 'Shit!', anyone paying attention gets the same message. It would be different if you were the sort that had to explain themselves in such a manner. Then you would have an argument of listening to what you're saying versus how you're saying it. But you're at home with the fouls of language and until your throat gets tight, you like using them.

"And as for your kid," he said, rescuing me from looking a complete idiot in my silence (a judgment I now know would have been mine and mine alone), "...I get the fact that she is here to show me style, some precision to balance out the power."

"Indeed!" I said, starting toward the house again.

"That's all well and good, provided I don't use her lessons to re-style her face!" His somewhat comical tone was gone and his supposition was too close to becoming an objective. He had been thrown by her reaction of him. Had it been an issue of color, he was at least exposed to that. But Vada was a woman who had no concept of him outside of rumor and she was refusing to see him. Such a thought process confused him and *Deviant* minds often destroy those things that confuse them. As proud as I was of William, I had to remember he was half Man-Lord and his emotions were a very powerful catalyst.

"Yes, she is a bit abrasive," I said. "I'm afraid her father has taught her to have a general distrust of anything associated with Man-Lords and to dislike anything relating to the Outworld. It seems her mentor has taught her all too well."

"Right," he said, stopping in his stride to turn and look back at her. She was talking with Vastiol and talking at Igrileena. She was smiling. "And here I am, a half-Deviant Outworlder. Two strikes against me before I even get to the plate!" He kept his gaze on her as she took Vastiol's arm and led him away from Igrileena who could not have cared less. He shook his head and I felt ashamed.

"You people have got a lot to learn," he said in a defeated tone. "You don't see the ground bitching about the origin of the person being buried in it. Then again, maybe it does. We just can't hear it!" As he reached the back door, I could understand why his tone sounded so depleted. He was fatigued! A position from which he would quickly recover. But his anger had generated an amount of energy which demanded to be released. Instead of lashing out at Vada-Ri, he put that energy to another application.

[*If you have to hate me, do so for the things that I do!*] His projection was strong, echoing in our minds like a loud drum. Vada was not braced for the projection and she would have collapsed to her knees had it not been for Vastiol's speed. Igrileena lowered herself to one knee. I staggered back a step but I was not so taxed with the force of his projection that I did not notice how he was controlling it, keeping it inside of Adrianna's shields.

[*Do not hate me for the things I cannot control. I did not choose my blood but I am not ashamed of it! It was my hope that those of greater intellect would have more substantiated prejudices. But you have proven to me that ignorance will always be only that, ignorance. It does not become any more enlightened if it is projected through the mind.*] His eyes closed and a single tear escaped each one. His body trembled as he maintained the magnitude of his projection as I could feel a gentle wind begin to swirl around him. I looked for its source but this wind had nothing to do with meteorological characteristics. It was actually coming from William! I looked to see if any of the others could see this but Igrileena was on her hands and knees, Vada-Ri was on the brink of unconsciousness and Vastiol was more focused on their condition than what William was doing. In this case his immunity prevented him from knowing the source of the matter, and William appeared to be in as much pain as the rest of us.

[*You beings of such* great *minds are as pathetic as the rest of us! Perhaps more so. At least we know of our faults and some of us are willing to admit them. Your power has blinded you and made thee so much more the greater fools*!] Blood started to slowly drop from his right nostril. The strain was beginning to tear at his physical frame. He had exceeded his limitations and I moved to stop him. But his eyes, those damn eyes, they flashed open and wide and through the pain and rage he laid his gaze on me and I was petrified. I was meant to hear him and to acknowledge him, nothing more.

"[*I will learn what I can from each of you and anything else that comes across my path. There is something to learn from everyone and thing!*]" he projected and shouted aloud. The back door opened and Gordon came running out. His three strides revealed to me that Kador's control was greater than merely within Adrianna's shields, his outburst had been contained to the backyard only. Gordon stumbled forward before falling to his knees just out of reach of William.

[*No!*] I projected as I brought forth my Staffling and deflected an Edge thrown by Vastiol. He had heard William and deduced the rest. I shouted my protest which kept him from throwing his second. The breeze had been replaced with a stiff wind and I was taken again into my past to the first time I had seen Zargo summon *Vision*. Not much was missing from this instance, not much at all!

"[*Hear me all… for in all strides that I receiveth, so shall I giveth. For this hath yet to be drawn to reckoning; my Blood hath been wronged. A crime hath been laid against mine hearth and I swear to thee all, upon my undying soul, we shall be avenged!*]"

The wind stopped and the loud echoing voice subsided and it took a moment for me to clear my eyes so they could see properly. Vada was unconscious, as was Igrileena, and Vastiol was seeing to them. I readied myself to catch William, surely his body was about to give. But it did not. He was spent, but his body was still sure and steady. He reached down and helped Gordon to his feet.

"Sorry," he whispered and he would not say anymore.

His eyes never looked at anyone save Gordon and myself. But I could read his thoughts and he did not believe they deserved his eyes, any of the three of them. In Vastiol's case I was surprised, but William had seen something in the man's openness, something with which he did not agree.

I looked up and on the raised porch stood Adrianna who looked down on her son with tearful eyes of pride. The kind of which she had not felt since she witnessed Zargo create a pulsar out of quartz rock. I smiled at her. I knew she could not see me, Adrianna was caught between today and yesterday and I would do nothing to cheat her of every deserved moment.

It was Gordon that brought me out my sense of elation. His eyes were sternly focused on me and I almost laughed at his attempt to have his stare match the power of his stepson's. It was like comparing the vision of Medusa to that of a blind man. But it was his resentment that fueled his stare, and I was forced to recollect the relationship he had held with my teacher. There were not many occasions where Zargo had not spoken highly of his Outworlder friend. Such discussion could clear a room more quickly than an agitated skunk. They were close and I knew exactly what thoughts passed through his mind as William walked back into the house. It was an age-old question that had many suggestions but no proven answers: who had killed Zargo, Blood of Xargagyan?

As I stepped into the house, outside of the field of William's influence, another question came to mind: where was William?

Thirteen

"I tried to tell ya, Sweets. There are some things you'll just need to get used to."

"Don't even!" Tara cried, still trying to catch her breath. "No freakin' way you're going to... to... *float* there and tell me I need to get used to dodging 747s!"

"Actually," Arvius stated, looking up. "I think it was a Lear Jet. It was a little small for..." Arvius lowered his view to see Tara giving him a stare as cold as stone. His words choked in his throat and he thought it better not to complete the voicing of his observation.

"You know, Harry," Tara said softly, "the more I get to know you, the more I know Mary was very special. You hear me, Harry? Very, very special!" She shifted her seat to get more comfortable but she heard a crack and the large branch she had been set down upon gave. Arvius missed grabbing her arm by inches but quickly steadied himself in the tree and drew focus on her falling form. As she started to slow down, there was another crack and his perch was forfeit.

Tara started to breathe in a sigh of relief when she felt her body slowing down. She gasped when the force taking hold of her body gave way, dropping her to the ground.

"Graceful to the last, eh, Arvius?" a soft voice called from the trees. Tara scrambled up and drew her pistol and gave herself a pause. She was no longer a Special Agent of the FBI so she would have to take the matter of firing her weapon more seriously.

"Not that I have a shot here anyway," she thought as she looked around. She could see nothing but trees in all direction. *"Oh God, don't let them zero me out like this. Not this soon into it."*

"Interesting prayer," the voice commented and again it sounded as if Tara and Arvius were surrounded.

"Is he sending that into my head?" she whispered.

"No," Arvius answered as he got up. "But Palshaya used to do very much the same thing. I just can't remember how she did it."

"Not the studious sort, eh, *Harold*?!" the voice inquired in a tone indicating it already knew the answer.

"I don't suppose you carry a spare firearm?" Arvius asked as he began to turn in circles.

"The only one on the team who didn't, actually," Tara admitted, gritting her teeth. "Sure wish I was Webster right about now."

"Why art thou here?" the voice asked.

"Uh-oh," Tara said softly. "Harry, you do know you've got one of your Old Testament friends around, right? Right?! Arvius?!" Tara spun around but she could not find anything to indicate Harold had ever been there with her.

"*Jon?*" she called out in her mind but again there was no response. She looked around, from side to side, searching for the slightest movement. Her left hand supported her right, ready to aim and fire at a moment's notice. She pulled from her training of the distant past and the much more recent memories of Palshaya that still passed through her mind.

"Okay," she whispered, quickly steadying herself. "Remember, you used to be an FBI Special Agent. Those things just don't... ewww," she sighed as she looked at the point from which she fell.

"Thou art frightened!" the voice returned. "Scared like a little child!"

Tara started shaking but she could not tell if she was cold or scared. But if it was the former, why had it taken so long for her to realize she was cold?

"To thy left!" the voice shouted and Tara swung a wild hook to her right. Her gun hammered against something that gave under the force of her attack.

Chidon spun away from the woman, surprised by her reaction, but the blow lacked any serious power. As he fell down, he teleported, but his timing made it look as if the ground had swallowed him. Tara gasped and put her hand to her mouth. A heartbeat later, something hard struck her at the heels and swept both of her feet forward. She fell hard to her back and was stunned. Chidon stood over her, his Edge, having already reduced her weapon to fragments, was set to draw blood. Elkazzar's instructions had been quite specific and in the wake of all that happened, completely justified.

"In the name of the Head Master I shall ask thee once more. Why-"

"They're here for me, Chidon," William said as he stepped into the clearing. Chidon's eyes quickly dropped to look at how William was walking. The Silent Stride was not a difficult task to master, but still had to be taught! Noticing his stare, William smiled. "I pick things up pretty quickly," he said.

"Aye, I have nary a doubt. Yet from whence?"

"The assassin was particularly quiet," William said, losing his smile. "It's the same place where I met this young lady." He shifted his eyes to Tara and smiled again. "Special Agent Mifflen, if I recall correctly."

"Well, I'm still Mifflen anyway," Tara replied as she sat up slowly. "Seems every time I see you, I'm getting my clock cleaned!"

William chuckled, "So it would seem. Let me help you up." Tara took his hand and stood up. They smiled at each other, a common reaction of those who survive life-threatening instances together. It was a bond one would rather not make, but once made, it was the sort that never died. Dead leaves and breaking twigs drew the attention of all three.

Arvius was running again. He had seen Chidon and he knew what that meant. Palshaya had told him husband several times of Chidon's skill at the hunt. The man was particularly adept at taking runners from the Territories. In any other place, he knew his chance of escape were slim. But perhaps there were enough trees to provide him ample cover from Chidon's well-noted bow.

"Die, runner!" Chidon whispered, drawing bow and arrow in the same action.

His eyes already had his mark; his only delay was linking his hand to his sight. By the time he heard William scream 'no', the arrow was already away and it shot just hairs over a large branch and a meter under another before it approached Arvius. The runner's left shoulder dropped at the last moment and he fell forward into a roll that was anything but combative. The shaft continued on and tore through a tree before stopping deep in another, nearly seventy meters from its archer.

"His shoulder was my only clear target," Chidon whispered, shocked that he had missed but not distracted enough to not draw another arrow from his quiver. When his hand met the bow string, there was no arrow and he looked over at William who was holding his intended missile.

"Should I have said 'nay' instead of 'no'?" he asked.

"Thou hast proven thy Blood, young Kador," Chidon said, turning his left shoulder to William. "But thou hast no place-"

"You're the one with no place here, Chidon!" William barked in a voice that even made Tara straighten her posture.

"*Wonder if King's got any illegitimates she failed to mention,*" she thought.

"You're on foreign soil, baby," William continued, "and unless you people have done a lot of arranging with the powers that be, which I sincerely doubt, you're the one who has no authority here. Now when we get to where you live, then you can return the favor but if you reach for another weapon, you'll need to kill two targets!

"And I know what you're thinking," William said, stepping back. "You're thinking I'm not faster than your bow. And you're right. But we both know I'm faster than you! Your play." William turned the arrow around in his hand so that he could throw it just as he had thrown the crossbow bolt from the assassin. If anything, the weapon he now held seemed to want to strike true, despite the target.

Tara saw him manipulate the arrow and the scene of how this young 'boy' had killed the assassin flashed in her mind. He was lying. He was faster than that bow!

"Gentlemen, gentlemen," she stepped between the two men because to her perspective, the mysterious bowman was not going to back down and the young mystery man of the week did not need to. "Allow me to interject. You mentioned a title that I'm familiar with. Did you not say in the name of the Head Master?" she asked Chidon who kept his eyes on William. Normally this would have been considered bravado, but Chidon had set bow and arrow against William before and found the boy's agility to be profound. And with the images he had received from the woman, resolving to work out how a Tyro knew how to send such thought at a later point, he agreed with her opinion. The boy was faster than the bowman *and* the bow!

"Because if that's the case then we're basically on the same side. So this has nothing to do with authority and everything to do with not wasting resources." She looked at both of them though for some reason she knew the boy was not going to act first so her primary focus was on the archer.

"Thou shouldst know thou hast a criminal in thine community," Chidon said sharply as he put his bow away.

"At least one," William said as he started toward Arvius who knew better than to move and be the trigger that would release either of them into action. Palshaya had told him of Chidon and the *Deviant* woman that killed his wife had both been bested by the boy. Nothing good would come from a confrontation. "Care to point out any more?"

"*Uh, okay, that sounds personal,*" Tara thought as she crept towards Arvius.

"Implications are the tools of weak men," Chidon said, loosening the strap that held his quiver.

"Says the man that cannot understand them!" William replied as his head came forward slightly and his face lowered. His knees bent and his hands moved away from his sides. He dropped the arrow and began to rub his fingers together. A gentle wind began to blow over the ground, kicking up the topmost leaves. Tara was only two strides from her destination when she stopped. She turned around and looked at William.

Tara wondered if she had missed it before. Maybe back at the side of the road, in that wooded field, she had been too busy dying. But there was nothing pressing now. Harry was alright. A bit shaken and obviously terrified of the bowman, but otherwise Tara had no distractions.

"*What are you?*" she thought and the breeze stopped. She looked down at the ground and then back up to William who was looking at her.

"Lost," he whispered before he turned and walked away. "You touch him, I kill you!" he directed at Chidon. "It is just that simple. You guys are welcome to come into the house. No need for you to be skulking in the cold out here. Welcome to the home of my parents."

"Thanks," Tara said quickly.

"Indeed, thank you," Arvius added.

"Already a step above the imports," William muttered beneath the ears of everyone except Jon who quickly related the words and the meaning behind them to Tara.

"*There's three more of them?*" she thought.

"*I'm not to sure you can say **of them**,*" Jon replied giving more detail than what even William knew or thought about his trainers.

"*See dead people?!*" she thought as she started to follow William. "*Hell, I know shit they never told their mothers!*"

"*It only gets weirder from here, Sweets,*" Jon warned. "*Pretty soon you'll run into Prodigians who can do what you do and do what they do!*"

"*Uh, that would be **too** soon,*" she corrected. "*And by soon do you mean you can see the future too?*" she inquired.

"*I can, but that's not what I was doing. And don't ask me to do it either. The future is always changing. It's so volatile, you wouldn't believe it!*"

"Yeah," Tara whispered. "In the last few days I've come to believe a lot of things."

Fourteen

A shudder moved through the room that had become the pond of silent proposition and gasping substantiation. The depiction of the events that led to Yudara's defeat had been the pebble and the abilities of the son of Zargo rippled through the Crimson Court as the images finally fell dark.

Bilshan sat up straight as his brow drew tight. He looked at the various gaped eyes and mouths that were slowly bringing themselves back to the moment. He knew it was a trip not worth taking. Because to come back to the same moment was to act as if what they had all just seen had not happened and as if the boy did not exist. For those that knew *of* Zargo, they wrestled with the myths often exchanged even in this great hall. For those that knew the man, he was no longer dead, but reborn and improved!

"What speed," one of the Congregation whispered. Bilshan nodded. Not yet a man and Kador had managed to rival his grandfather's speed, though he was not quite as fast as Zargo... not yet!

"*Speed*?!" Colhozeh thought. "*The skill! The accuracy! Phenomenal!*" He was sure to keep a strong guard on his mind.

"This be her last conscious memory, my Priests and Lord," Dolas said as he quickly collected the stone. Indomar stepped forward to move the hearing along but his words were not fast enough.

"Interesting!" Shuppim said in a manner that was very much out of character for him. The Gray Priest stood up receiving Jamoreh's coldest stare. There were few who did not fear the Black Priest's terrible wrath. Shuppim was one of those precious few.

"*Interesting indeed*," Bilshan thought. "*To say nothing of unexpected.*

"Now which maiden speaks to me," the High Priest of Air continued in his contemplations. "*...Chance or Fate? The extended company of either has always been... precarious? Yet one of them tends me now and I must be an agreeable host.*"

"The Court recognizes the Gray Priest," Colhozeh said. "But thou doth realize the floor is granted to those who will speak against?"

"Aye, Grand Lord, that much is certain," Shuppim said bowing, again cutting his eyes over to Jamoreh. Without the application of talent he could feel the rage building, but the Black Priest's troublesome shadow was tending well to its Master and clung now to his arm, silently beckoning Jamoreh to maintain his place. "But in truth, it cannot be recorded that mine words taste true of either argument. Mine is simply an inquiry of the evidence presented."

Colhozeh nodded as he leaned forward, taking a quick look to the seat of the High Priest of Air. "*God of mine fathers!*" he thought as he looked to see that Bilshan did not rest back in his chair, slouched, looking as if at any moment he would fall asleep; his customary mien during meetings of the Crimson Court. Colhozeh kept his smile to himself as he hammered the gavel down.

"It is well within thy right to post thy question, Gray Priest," the Grand Lord replied. "Proceed with thine inquiry."

After bowing, Shuppim threw his long, black braided locks back out of his face and looked to Dolas focusing his soft brown eyes on the healer. "It be thy word choice which calls me to bring forth this question, healer."

"I am thine," Dolas replied as he bowed.

"Thy service and skill hath been a strong blessing to our people and our cause," Shuppim answered, giving a nod of his head. "Yet thou didst say these images were the last of her *conscious* thoughts."

"Aye, I did," Dolas said quickly, swallowing hard afterward.

"But we be of the Prodigian, man!" Shuppim shouted. "I put to thee to restate thy claim, taking into account *all* of the collected thoughts!"

Dolas swallowed hard again before he looked over to Daleifner who was not looking at the healer. Still there were many who followed Dolas' eyes to the Black Priest who was looking down and slightly removed from the hearing at the moment.

"I cannot, my lords," Dolas admitted and the murmuring voices were provoked.

Colhozeh called to his fellow Court member three times before he looked at the High Priests who nodded in agreement to the thoughts they received. Turning the gavel over on its other side, the Grand Lord brought it down to the plate and it made a resounding boom. But it was not the sound that brought silence to the Court. The meeting of the two metals emitted an energy that stimulated the pain receptors of the brain. Unless one was braced for the emission, a headache was the result. While the members of the Court spent time healing themselves, Colhozeh was allowed to speak.

"Members of the Crimson Court *shall* come to order!" he said in the same soft yet powerful voice. He then looked back at Dolas. "Dolas, dost thou mean thou collected thoughts experienced after Yudara collapsed?"

"It makes no difference!" Bilshan said, stamping home his point with his foot. There were a few gasps but most reacted silently and their shock was only facial, as was Jamoreh's. "The Court's time be far too great a thing to spend further 'pon this so-called Man-Lord Warrior.

"Furthermore, as High Priest, I offer unto this Court the suggestion that we proceed to verdict and deny the one who speaks for!"

This would be a day marked for how low mouths could drop in one session of the Crimson Court. Bilshan, supposedly the benefactor of every living entity, was speaking against Yudara.

"Thou dost speak within thy given power," Colhozeh said, somewhat shaken himself. "And the penalty is known to thee?"

"Is it not execution?" Bilshan asked.

"Aye, it is, old friend. It is."

"Then my motion was stated properly," Bilshan huffed, looking as if he had more pressing matters to tend to. "Off with her, incapable wench that she is!" Bilshan looked over at the Black Priest who looked more like the antithesis of life as he glared at Bilshan, but the old one did not waver and Jamoreh's attention was drawn to Petra who shifted in his seat, hoping he would be noticed. He made it clear that had Jamoreh moved, he would not reach the High Priest of Air.

"This is unlawful!" Jamoreh shouted.

"Jamoreh," Colhozeh explained. "If a High Priest or this station doth make motion in the Court, it is within the right of the Court.

"Bring forth the Executioner!" Colhozeh commanded. "Dolas, thou art hereby given leave to restore Yudara to health so she canst receive her punishment." Dolas faded as he bowed, taking himself to the holding chambers beneath the Court.

"But the High Priest has moved for judgment not sentencing," Jamoreh said running over to the Bench.

"And his suggestion hath been accepted," Petra answered. "There be only one sentence for failure against a Light-Child in challenged or tasked combat. That is death!" The High Priest of Earth was taking a taste of pleasure from all of this, though he was still shocked by Bilshan's motion.

Bilshan's eyes never left Jamoreh for an instant and his brow never relaxed. He was waiting for something, that much was evident. But no one cared to lay a hypothesis as to what.

"Hello, my brother," Yudara said returning with Dolas and her voice softened the hardest stone that was his visage. He closed his eyes as if the sound of her speech had touched his body. He turned to face her and walked toward her. "Dost thou fare well?"

"Nay, my heart!" Jamoreh said, letting his eyes show his emotion. "They mean to take thee away from me, my sister." He took her in his arms, embracing the only person he could truly love. He cared not for those who saw his display of love or his tears. In her presence, he was a different man. "But I shall not fail thee!"

"It is I who hath failed thee, my brother," she said softly, returning his embrace. "I am not worthy of thy love. I hath shamed thee, the Blood of Beriah and the Man-Lords. I do not deserve to remain among my kind."

Jamoreh's eyes opened in revelation and he stepped away from Yudara to look in her eyes. She was confused to see a familiar spark in her brother's gaze. So many saw him as an animal, but she knew the scholar, the poet, the warrior and the brother who had been greater than any offering from her father's loins and her mother's womb. This look of hope confused her, but it frightened her as well and she shook her head 'no'. It was a recommendation her brother did not accept.

"The sentence given to my sister doth not apply here. There hath been an error in judgment!" Jamoreh put his fists on his hips, proud of every word he had uttered. Yudara wanted to scream.

"Nay!" she finally managed to speak. "To challenge judgment and be proven false brings my sentence unto thee! I beg thee, Jamoreh, nay. Let me pass!"

"To die with thee exceeds a life without thy touch," Jamoreh said softly to his sister before looking back at the Bench. "I hereby challenge the judgment and as Black Priest, I am within my right to do so."

Shuppim was the first to move. If Jamoreh met with the axe, Shuppim could ascend to Black Priest. "I move for judgment for both lives!" he cried.

"A moment, Shuppim," Colhozeh replied. He did not know how this session might end, but it had long ago exceeded memorable. "We must *hear* the substance of the challenge before it canst be judged.

"Jamoreh, thy voice is all that remains between this life and your next. Offer it unto the Court."

"Most gracious Grand Lord, I thank thee," Jamoreh said as he walked toward Bilshan, a pinnacle in the Crimson Court who had never lost an argument. Jamoreh stood ready to deliver to him his first loss. "The judgment found here is wrong for one fact and one fact only. True enough, my sister was bested in combat by this Kador, Blood of Xargagyan, with the help of Tyros numbering less than ten. That is not in argument.

"Yet the point I bring forth marks the question of what *is* this Kador? For the purposes of this Court he hath been branded a Light-Child. I say to thee all he doth have the blood of a Man-Lord in his veins and that blood cannot be denied."

"A banished Man-Lord!" Shuppim argued.

"I say to thee nay!" Jamoreh quickly replied. "He is the son of the banished Light-Child of the name Adrianna, Blood of Abinadab. The Man-Lord of the name of Zargo, Blood of Xargagyan hath ne'er been brought to this Court in judgment."

"Then that motion is thus given!" Shuppim put to the Bench.

"To submit such a motion now when no name of that Blood canst give defense is unlawful and therefore disallowed by this Court. Is this not true, Air Priest?"

"It is true, Black Priest," the old man answered.

"Then I put to this Court that my sister was bested by one who is half Light-Child and half Man-Lord, and there canst be no such judgment against a Man-Lord losing to their own kind."

"But this Kador be not anointed as a Man-Lord," Bilshan offered.

"In the honor of Zargo whose name art still of power and honor in our history and in mine power as the Black Priest, I anoint as Man-Lord, Kador, Blood of Xargagyan!" Jamoreh's fist slammed down on the bench to punctuate his motion and his argument which was clearly gaining ground.

"A High Priest must accept this offering of the Black Priest," Colhozeh said, reminding Jamoreh that he had not yet won his fight.

"I accept," Bilshan said quickly. "Kador, Blood of Xargagyan, the Unlawful Son, shalt here and forever be one of the tribe of the Man-Lord."

Jamoreh threw up his arms in victory as Colhozeh covered his mouth, and therefore his smile, with his hand. At last he knew what his mentor, the ageless Air Priest, had accomplished.

"Release the woman, Yudara," Bilshan commanded. "And, in accordance to the proclamation of Jamoreh, Black Priest and honorable Blood of Beriah, let all unsanctioned hostilities set against Kadorgyan, brother of the Man-Lords, cease here and now for it is unlawful to proceed against our own kind unless deemed necessary by the Crimson Court, for such is our law! Only withstanding the right of challenge." Colhozeh smacked the gavel down to dismiss the Court and its barriers. He then put the hammer down and quickly excused himself. He had to be out of the range of eyes to release the laughter he had been holding back. He saw Bilshan moving about and decided he was going to see to himself and quickly the rejoin the Court.

Jamoreh was a stride away from embracing his free sister when he heard, understood and felt what had been done. That old worm! He would one day dress a spear with his overly-aged head. The Black Priest turned to see the ancient Man-Lord grinning without the slightest hint of humility.

"NOOOO!" Jamoreh screamed, drawing pure energy from the room. As it collected in his hand, Bilshan directed a weak, thin beam of coherent light. Weak it was, but strong enough to strike its target and trigger a chain reaction of instability throughout the energy form, causing a pre-intentioned explosion, directly in Jamoreh's hand.

"My, the power that boy can generate!" Bilshan said as he stepped down from the Bench.

The Air Priest waved off the approaching guard as he slowly made his approach to Jamoreh, still laid low by the blast. He placed a locking glance upon Yudara and made his way across the floor. Bilshan chuckled as he heard Petra clear his throat, warning Yudara to tread carefully. By the time Bilshan reached the Black Priest, the young man was not yet fully conscious and was dealing with backlash and the power of the explosions. Bilshan extended his cane, which now had a sharp steel point to it, letting it come to rest on Jamoreh's neck.

"To yield now is to live," Bilshan said coldly, as if he was preparing himself for the act that he would not enjoy, but would nevertheless endure. "It is thy choice."

Jamoreh was able to hear and see, but his mind was not ready to defend himself. The tonicity of Bilshan's stare let the Black Priest of the Crimson Court know how close he was to death.

"I yield," Jamoreh answered. He had never been known to speak so softly.

"Good," Bilshan said, the blade retracting as he removed the cane. "Then recall all of thy agents from the Outworld as thou hast no business there. Mayhap they wouldst prefer to be among their own Blood again, yes?

"Now rise, young Priest, and tend to thy affairs." Jamoreh could not speak or was he able to move under his own power, but Daleifner was up to the task. Setting his Master on his feet, Daleifner focused his energies directly into Jamoreh's mind and like any other starved entity, he took to the nourishment quickly, eventually drawing in more than Daleifner had intended. But he stood on his own power again and he possessed a clear mind which immediately received from his heart all the emotions that remained. Even Yudara's touch did not shake him from the gaze of hatred he gave the old one. Using her other hand, Yudara took a stronger hold of her brother and pulled. His head snapped around and Jamoreh had to remind himself that it was his sister touching him. He looked at her face and nodded, walking with her as they took their leave.

Most of the Congregation began to disperse only when it was convinced Jamoreh's departure was genuine, that there would be no more entertainment this session. Now they would carry these events to the general citizenry of the Man-Lords (and perhaps a few Light-Children). A few of the Court remained to talk amongst themselves as there were few private places in the Territories. Still a few more waited and watched as Bilshan, once again bent over and leaning on his cane, slowly walked toward the dining antechambers. Good debate always sparked his appetite. But he did not walk alone.

"Oh, my old friend," Colhozeh smiled, "...thou art as sharp as the blade in thy cane."

"Aye, Bilshan," Petra added. "Thou mayest speak of aging and the foundering of thy ability, yet still I am awed by thy motions and speeches.

"Yet thou hast lost a point of power," the Earth Priest continued.

"Indeed," Bilshan nodded. "I have lost an argument, that I did. But in the effort of bringing the son of Zargo to us unharmed, what price canst be set which is too great? It is as though I hath reached out and touched the son of a son who was my brother and friend. Kador be worth the effort."

"Worth all of this?" Petra argued, motioning toward the Court.

"Ohhh!" Bilshan stopped as he looked sternly upon the large Man-Lord. "Thine eyes shouldst see the worth of mine act first! When we art called to Court, what doth receive thy power and is raised to protect us?"

"The Power Stone!" Petra replied, realizing his friend's point and it was a very strong one. "A device we still do not understand, though we know Zargo made three."

"At least three," Colhozeh was quick to add. He too had come to know Zargo and the man's mind was always heavily engaged in thought and supposition. "The other two perform the same service as ours, for the Light-Child Council and the Mountain Keep for the Absularians."

"True, Zargo oft times worked within his own law and many a time that didst not agree with the Court," Bilshan reflected. "Yet he gave to all, denying none. If he gave to one sect, he gave to all in turn." Bilshan looked back on the Court one more time. One last scan of eye and sense to look for the one the Air Priest had assumed would be in attendance. Still, if it was her wish, she had long ago proved that she could hide even from his mind. The touch of Colhozeh was much like his speech, soft and warm, already pulled and pondered.

"Mine eyes didst not see her, my mentor," he said softly, giving a soft squeeze before letting his hand drop. "She wouldst be most proud of thine actions this day.

"But to the matter of Kador, dost thou believe the son will follow the path of the father and the father before him?"

Bilshan's brow lifted in contemplation as his head moved toward his left shoulder and he gave a single nod before righting himself. "He possesseth the mind for it; such was made very clear. It was simple invention which placed him in greater power than Yudara, who is accomplished even among our community of warriors.

"Yet the boy be engaged within his own puzzle, Colhozeh. He must seeth to it 'fore he canst see to any other, or be less the man when doth try. As for what he shalt do with his ability, thou hast overlooked a tendency of his Blood in the recounting we witnessed."

"Passive was his father," Petra said, deep within his memories of Zargogyan, a few of them painful to recall. "At least to the shell of the man, he was passive, though his soul was always committed to a task. Left to himself, he simply explored and created."

"And when disturbed?" Bilshan asked, smiling at Petra who was already nodding.

"It wouldst depend upon the disturbance," the Earth Priest replied. "When he attended his first debate with the Light-Children, he gave to Adrianna what she had given him, open interest. We all know what camest of that.

"But if the disturbance were harsh… say, the unannounced attack of one who imagined he was in a position to judge him… why then Zargo wouldst sustain. He would always sustain! When a fury was visited upon him, he returned his own and when tested, Zargo's skills found a way to suit the instance."

"Aye," Bilshan agreed, laying a soothing hand on Petra's back. They could recall the battle that had been waged between the Earth Priest and the then Gray Priest. Even those who had not seen it remembered it. After the conflict, Petra had been allowed to keep his place in the Court which was an act that had not ever been repeated. Zargo had merely asked for the seat of the Black Priest and the Blood of Beriah had not had the stomach to deny him.

"Upon whatever he receiveth, he giveth in accordance." Bilshan said as he summoned his power. The walk was taking too long and the debate continued. He teleported himself and his two escorts to the dining chambers where the debate would of course continue… but over food!

Fifteen

"Damn him!" Jamoreh shouted as his energy bolt claimed a sculpture of an assemblage of the Crimson Court. Daleifner quickly employed his talents to reassemble the artwork.

"Well, 'tis clear thou hast recovered from the backlash," Yudara said in an amused tone, hoping to bring her brother out of his rage. "Thou shouldst now-"

"I urge thee to be silent, dear sister, whilst I ruminate on my course of revenge."

"Revenge upon Bilshan?" she asked. "Hast thou taken full leave of thy senses?"

"Nay," Jamoreh barked. "I shall not raise my hand to the ancient one. Though such was my first impulse. Bilshan hath served the Man-Lords in ways which yet best my brightest dreams. Fear not, mine heart, I wouldst prefer to take him in as counsel than ever declare him an enemy.

"It is Kador I seek. Oh, the pain that boy shall find," he said, drawing his sword. It was well known that among wielders of the Blade, the Black Priest bested Masters with ease. With a broad swing of his weapon, Jamoreh teleported Yudara and himself to their home. Daleifner soon followed under his own power and Jamoreh looked at him with regret for having overlooked him.

Yudara knew where they were; this was the room where her brother would prepare himself for battle. In the antechambers adjacent to this circular room were the storage rooms of his armor and weapons. A very thorough collection indeed.

"Oh, thou art indeed mad," Yudara continued. "Heed me, my brother and my pride. I hath faced this Outworlder who now stands as a Man-Lord. He is different; judge him not by the company he doth keep for they are not a working of his. He *is* a true warrior!"

"Bah! He was graced with luck and thou wert cursed with folly and treachery."

"Is that truth? Was it not mine own brother who told me in war there are no rules, no ledgers, no officials to call the point? The victor is the one who doth survive, knowing the opponent faced will not rise again?!" Yudara positioned herself between Jamoreh and his weapons room, allowing Daleifner to walk by her. She did not need to monitor his actions. Her body glowed for a brief moment as she was gently moved out of his way. She tried to resist but her brother had been besting her since they were both very young children. Though he was younger and less trained, his power marked him as the older sibling.

"One side, sister, I have a war to win" Jamoreh said. He entered the room and was handed a fine wooden box. Inside was a pair of Outworlder weapons he had taken the time to master. "These guns may yet come to be useful against this Light-Child trash!"

"I have a better weapon, brother," Yudara said in a weakening tone; Jamoreh was too engaged to notice the difference. The sight of Daleifner, however, was another matter. The look of horror on his face as his eyes peered over Jamoreh's shoulder caused the Black Priest to turn and look behind him.

Yudara, in her unfailing beauty, was down on her knees and crying. She was surrounded by a field of gravitons which always served to be a steadfast shield. It was sturdy and once assembled, it did not require further maintenance. She would need her focus to plunge the Blade, its tip already at her own chest, into her heart.

"By the hand of our Creator, if thou dost not heed me then let mine eyes fall from this world. For if thou dost face him, thou shalt fail and he will kill thee and without my brother, this life holds no merit!" There was no need to employ talents to verify his sister's intentions, Yudara was serious and what was more, committed to the act. Jamoreh knew his sister's disciplines and if this was the antecedent, death would be her only option if he questioned her resolve.

"Speak, dear sister," he said softly, putting his guns back into their box. "What hath brought this between us?"

"Swear thy oath to me," she cried. "Swear to me thou shalt not engage in actions against Kadorgyan!"

Again that name! Her words, so softly spoken, stoked a fire in his being. This... *thing* had brought them to this! The man whose name she spoke would pay dearly for what he had done to his sister... that he was willing to promise but thought it best to keep such things from Yudara at the moment.

"Yudara, I-"

"Swear to me or look upon me no longer!" she screamed, easing the Blade inward. The tip was now gone and blood began to run down her chest. She had chosen the same wound point that Kador had struck and the skin, though healed, was still soft and easily cut.

"Stay thy hand, you have my oath!" Jamoreh shouted.

"Your word?" she asked through tear swept eyes.

"And a thousand more, if thou dost desire," he answered, and her Blade fell to the ground along with her graviton shield. Before the next breath she was in his arms and being healed by his talent. He held her tightly, allowing nothing else to touch her. She was sacred to his life, the home of his passions, emotion and humanity. With her he could be just

Jamoreh the Man-Lord instead of Jamoreh the Black Priest, feared in combat and scourge of Order. All those he relinquished for her, his sister.

"What wouldst force thee to do such a thing and threaten that which serves to give this life meaning?" he asked her, feeling her arms wrap around him as tightly. But she was weak and her hold was not sustained. He eased her into his chair and stroked the hair out of her face.

"I know," she whispered. "I know how he fights." There was a genuine fear in her eyes, something he had not seen there before. Could this Light-Child actually be that good? He doubted it; Yudara landed several telling blows on him. The boy was clever and lucky, nothing more.

"And how doth this boy fight?"

"This *man* doth fight with a passion much as your own." she replied softly, unconsciousness was coming for her and she could not sustain herself much longer. The word he had given her was false and they both knew it. But Yudara also knew how much her brother loved her and in death, the pain she would have burdened him with. There was no simple solution to the puzzle, but if given time, she might resolve it. "If thou dost face him with death in your heart, he shall kill thee. Face him for victory, not destruction. I implore thee, my brother-"

[*Shhh, be still, beautiful one!*] Jamoreh projected, sending a low decibel sound pulse through her temples, rendering her unconscious.

"Take her to her chambers!" he barked, standing up and facing Daleifner. "And do not let thy hands touch her form," he added taking hold of the servant's throat. "For shouldst thou fail in this, the Fates shall greet thee before the pleasure of such a touch reacheth thy mind!"

"I will hold to thy command!" Daleifner choked.

"Who is there?" a rough, old and weak voice called out and Jamoreh closed his eyes in anger and frustration. His fist clenched tight and trembled in front of his face. At least for a brief moment.

"*Damn*," he thought as he finally released his grip, turning to walk to the chamber where the old man rested. "*He is awake, after all.*" Jamoreh lowered his head to his chest, summoning the strength of will to endure an exchange between them.

It was a small room, compared to the rest of the household. But it was very round like all the other chambers, the walls just as clay gray as the others though there were no wall hangings here. Those were left for the more frequented parts of the house. No, the only things stored in this room besides the massive rectangular bed were bookshelves overrun with tomes of knowledge which Jamoreh doubted the man had read with any true comprehension. It was a labor to reach the bed past all of the discarded sheets of parchment, trays of half eaten food and gifts from those who endeavored to keep themselves in his favor. Powerful the Prodigian were, but they were not above superstition and he had done well manipulating it... his lordship, the great Beriah, former Grand Lord of the Crimson Court and the victor over Zargogyan... it was odd to Jamoreh how none of those accolades read: *bedridden old fool*. His bloodshot and sullen eyes were gray at the center, but it was clear he was losing his vision. He had always been a healthy man, but his appetite had not diminished in stride with his activity and he was now rotund. What used to be thick, shiny black hair was now a dull gray and thinning. Only the length of his hair remained long.

"I am here, father," Jamoreh said softly, his head still lowered. "It is thy son, Jamoreh."

"No true son hath ever come from my loins," he spat in a thick, bitter voice. "Thou art but an adopted wretch."

"Aye, sir...'tis thy adopted son, Jamoreh."

"Ah, much better," Beriah coughed. "Where is my true blood? Where is Yudara?"

"She rests now, my sire. She hath returned from her mission and is resting now. Surely she shall visit with thee when she is able."

"And thee," he said, disgusted. "What art thou engaged in?" In Beriah's eyes, Jamoreh had yet to prove himself worthy of the blood name Beriah. Despite the fact that he had attained the rank of Black Priest a good fifty years ahead of the pace that Beriah had set, he considered the young man worthless and embarrassing.

"I dispatch myself to conquer the son of Zargogyan." Jamoreh answered in hopes that this news might at long last begin the trek toward worthiness in the eyes of his adoptive father and finally he would be accepted as a son.

"So, he hath been found. Good! If thou art able, destroy him," the old man commanded. "Just as I killed his traitorous father. Now get thee gone and do not return without victory."

"I shall not fail thee, father. The son of Zargo will fall to the son of Zargo's destroyer!" Jamoreh bowed, turned on his heels and walked out of the room with an internal fire brimming over with heat for one thing: blood! He knew that killing the Light-Child would be the best thing for the Man-Lords. Then they could proceed with their plans to assault the Council and even the King. The Territories would finally be theirs. He returned to his room to prepare himself; Daleifner stood ready to garb his master but Jamoreh stopped short of his pedestal, turning instead to the nearest wall and plunging his fist into it. He could not kill Kador. Bilshan was no fool. He would not trust the proclamation of the Court to hold over the wills of the Prodigian, not even the Man-Lord sect. He would have the boy watched and very closely.

"Master? What ails thee?"

"Bilshan! He hath always stood for the Man-Lords yet there are times I question his reason. He hath put forward, through mine own argument and anointing a means whereby I cannot touch the boy!"

"Such is not true, my Master," Daleifner replied as he approached with a bright and hopeful smile. "There be open challenges against both Elkazzar and Adrianna and even a newly anointed Man-Lord canst not interfere in a challenge laid against either."

Jamoreh stood there and looked at the crack his fist had put into the wall. He lowered his hand and smiled at his natural power. "Do not mend that," he commanded and Daleifner bowed in acknowledgement. Jamoreh approached and took firm hold of both shoulders.

"Old friend, dost thou realize why I warned thee as I did, against touching Yudara?"

The Edger's head sank low but it was not long before Jamoreh brought it back up. "Aye, Master. It is a weakness within me."

"Within us all, Leif. Within us all. Save that thou dost not retard thyself from acting upon that weakness, and in a manner violent even for a Man-Lord." Jamoreh brought his servant into an embrace. "But it affects not thy mind, my friend. In my anger I hath wrought a great wrong upon thee and I ask thy forgiveness."

"I am yours, Master!" Daleifner said quickly. "There be nothing to forgive."

"A point we shall spend eternity arguing, my friend! A debate I shall most assuredly enjoy. Come, my Edger. There be battles to plot and *accidents* to invoke!"

Sixteen

It was one thing to hurdle the baby stroller. It was another thing to do the same over three rather large pedestrians. But the 'rabbit' Peter was chasing managed that feat. Webster instead bounced off of them as he tried to push through.

"Why is it that elephants travel in herds?" Peter whispered as he got up, eyed the elusive man he was chasing, and plotted another route to run. He got to his feet, breaking into a hard, fast run through the mid-day metropolitan crowd. There were some that got out of his way but most he collided with, preventing him from running his fastest. Three steps away from his planned intercept point, his prey ran by at a full gait Peter doubted he could match. As he made the turn to pursue, he saw the hot dog stand and the off color green park bench at the corner of the street. The rendezvous point!

"*Ah, the hell with it*," he thought as he signaled the pick up vehicle. He reached for his sidearm and stopped running. He was not quite fatigued to the point where he could not control his breathing, and it made for an easier shot. But there was no shot to take. His jackrabbit was weaving and dodging in and out of pedestrian traffic making it impossible for Webster to get a clear shot.

"Screw it!" he said softly as he fired. A man, in a navy blue business suit, probably on his lunch break, had the shoulder of his suit ruined as Webster's shot tore through it. He fell to the sidewalk and over half the people stopped moving. "Bingo!" a double tap from the pistol and Webster hit both of his target's legs below the knee in the meat of the calf. The young man fell right at the sidewalk and the pick-up van stopped long enough to grab him and then drive away.

"Well I'll be damned!" Peter said, lowering his weapon. "Mission accomplished!"

"Now just what do you call that?!" a voice cried out. The city faded away and he was once again in the empty warehouse. He took off the safety goggles and looked around.

"Said it before and I'll say it again," he whispered with a smile. "That was rad-funky!"

"I asked you a question," he said, somehow getting louder. Peter did not think that was possible.

"I call it a resolution," Webster said as he tossed the goggles toward the approaching technician. "Thanks for the adjustment; they fit much better that time."

"You're welcome," the young man said in a thick Japanese accent. He was surprised to hear gratitude from anyone.

Peter's eyes went to the stairway. He looked first at her, gliding down the stairs toward him. She looked to be a woman in her late thirties, but she had the endurance of a tri-athlete. Normally when given such a special treat, Webster was hungry for more. In her case, he would appreciate a three-day warning.

But she did not walk alone. Mr. Wonderful was on his way to scream at him... again. It was a shame the gun was just some sort of electronic gizmo. *"They programmed in a pretty good kick though,"* he thought as he tossed it to another technician and thanked him too.

"You shot a civilian!"

"He was a co-conspirator," Peter said quickly, and she put her hand to her mouth. She managed to block her smile, but the snicker came too quickly for her stop.

Fortunately the man knew better than to say 'do you think you're funny' to Webster. How he hated these types of operatives! Webster was no different than so many others that she brought into his facility so they could awe at the technology and display, for the entire world to see, just how barbaric they are. *"There has to be a simpler way,"* Augustus thought. He had grown so weary of his labor being used as if it was some kind of toy. And then there was Thidalia. What man could resist her? How many women could be added to that category? Even her laugh was beautiful! In the time he had taken to look at her, his anger waned and he simply brushed back his brown hair and sighed.

"I suppose you will make the claim that your shot had a high percentage chance for being non-fatal."

"Sounds like you know it too," Webster said. "Look, you gave the parameters for the exercise! You started with saying my cover was blown and the guy I was chasing was the reason. Therefore, I silence him, I stand a chance at reinstating my cover." Augustus nodded as he folded his arms.

"Well," he thought, *"at least we know he was paying attention and he's right, though it is a slim chance, it was one worth taking."*

"I'm not saying I had much of a chance," Peter continued. "Especially after the street chase, but in the long run it comes out to at least try."

"Indeed. Please continue."

"Continue? What do you want from me? The guy changed in mid-chase!"

"What?"

"What are you saying, Peter?" Thidalia asked; there was nothing amusing now.

"The guy changed in mid chase," Peter repeated.

"My word!" Augustus thought.

"He was five foot, five inches and around one hundred and sixty pounds. Not too shabby.

"But when I started gaining on him, his legs gained about another two inches and he lost ten pounds! What kind of programming is that?"

"One point seven six inches and nine point seven, seven pounds to be more precise," Augustus answered, still awed. Webster was the first operative to ever notice. "And, having heard that, Mr. Webster, I am all too happy to accept your explanation about your shooting of the civilian as a non-lethal maneuver."

"And that concludes our testing," Augustus said, looking at his clipboard. "If you would just head back to the sensor pad, we will take one last reading and get the two of you on your way."

"Well, alright then," Peter said, somewhat surprised in the change of attitude. But he was not going to look this gift horse in the mouth, nor leave the door open so it could wander off. His time with King had taught him better than that. "Uh, Dr. Caprice?"

"Please, call me Augustus."

"Okay, call me Peter. Listen, I was wondering if I could get your card or some way I could make contact. This facility is nothing short of genius!"

"I think I would like that very much. I shall see to it that your field PDA has my contact information. The name of the facility is Hideaway."

Peter chuckled. "You guys really like your themes don't you."

"Well, yes, though I agree they can get quite comical. And in keeping with that line, your primary password is peek-a-boo."

"Primary," Peter asked.

"Yes, there are two passwords," Augustus explained. "The secondary password will find you in the field. Now if you would, please; to paraphrase the military, we're burning data. Unless you'd like to run this one again?"

"Hell no! See you, Auggie." Peter turned quickly and ran over to the sensor pad.

"What a good idea for a secondary password!" Augustus said, writing it down on his clipboard.

"Well?" Thidalia asked as the two of them stated back upstairs.

"Good news or bad news?" he asked, removing his glasses. It was only when they were off that Thidalia could appreciate his crystal blue eyes.

"Give me the bad first," Thidalia sighed. She was hoping there would be no bad news with this candidate.

"I have yet to read his entire file, but he was in the FBI until recently, yes?"

"Very recently, Augustus."

"He was not the leader of the team, but at the same time he received numerous commendations for his performance."

"This is starting to sound like good news," she said, somewhat confused.

"No, it's bad," Augustus replied. "He wasn't the leader so he has only observational experience of the position. That makes it very risky for you."

"Agreed," she said, beginning to calculate. "Continue."

"He will have difficulty with a team that cannot perform on his level. And from these scores," he said, holding up the clipboard, "...you are going to be incredibly challenged to find anyone to keep up with him."

"How about Brooks?" she said, running through her list of candidates.

"You'd give up Rook and have him work in the-"

"*Brooks*, good doctor," she corrected. "Brooks."

Augustus had to think about for a moment. There was no way Brooks had the hand-eye coordination that Webster possessed, but it was certain he was more physically aggressive. Properly applied the two would work well together.

"You would need a thir-"

"India," she said, anticipating what Augustus was about to say. But that name brought Augustus to an abrupt halt as he quickly donned his glasses and turned to look at her.

"You told me she was dead!" he whispered and started looking around.

"Of course I did, dear," she said with a smile, touching her hand to his face. "I couldn't very well have you sending anymore of your agents to their demise, now could I? I have come to enjoy our times together, Augustus. I know you and India became close, and she did not take well to some of your career choices."

"Take well?!" Augustus repeated in a soft scream. "She killed all three of my partners! And anyone who was with them at the time she found them!"

"You have to admit, given that one was with an Arabian Prince at the time, she is at the very least resourceful."

"She's a homicidal maniac!"

"That you thought was your reason for living, if I recall correctly." Thidalia smiled. She enjoyed watching some men try to squirm out of their own transgressions. Dr. Augustus Caprice was a supposedly happily married man with two children. But that had been before he met India Brown, an operative Thidalia recruited out of the United States Marines where she had been on her way to becoming one of the few women to survive SEAL

School. She was third in the class when Thidalia made the necessary arrangements. Perhaps one day she would be able to tell *Auggie* that his seduction was a plot of her own design. Peter was right. He was nothing short of genius, and like most geniuses he tried to do too much thinking out of his area of expertise. He needed controls and India had delivered far beyond Thidalia's expectations. The very thought that she was still alive made him more reliable and a fair degree more loyal to her own ends. Now he was manageable, like most men should be!

"I can assure you India knows her limitations, and I am one of them," she said, stroking his chin. "You are completely safe. I give you my word."

Thidalia's word was a commodity not traded often and it was given a value that often defied practical measure. Augustus simply nodded and kissed her hand, the customary act when leaving her presence.

"I'll put some numbers together for you," he said softly as he returned to the steps that led to his office. She watched him all the way up before she began looking for Peter Webster. He was no longer on the sensor pad. Apparently they were done taking all the readings they needed to take. She reached in her purse and took out her phone.

"Rook," she said, "Has everything been arranged? Good. No, Mr. Webster and I have concluded our business. Summon Pawn and please notify the plane that it will need to be prepared for a transatlantic flight. Yes, Rook, we are going to the States."

"Looks like I'm coming home, Momma," Peter whispered as he peered through his ultra-small telescope. "No, no, no. I'm on the phone Simmons gave me. It's got that buzzer thingy when something's up. See what you can dig up on an Augustus Caprice out of Austria."

Peter checked his jacket twice. He had to make sure everything was in working fashion. He did not trust the sparkle in her eyes. Plus she was too damn sexy to get a clear reading on. The longer he looked the more chance he stood of getting distracted. If that was something she did naturally, the more power to her. But if it was something conscious, then that little look she gave could have meant a number of things for him.

"As far as my keeper goes," he continued, "...the only name I've been privy to is Thidalia but she seems to be the one calling the shots for some group of watchers calling themselves the Descriers." Peter jumped as his phone started to buzz. He immediately cut off the phone, knowing Lydia was on her end doing the very same thing. He just hoped, especially after the chase through the false town, running around and into rather real-feeling false people, that his piece of James Bond and Wild West Memorabilia could

109

hold its own. He quickly disassembled the phone and put on his clothes. He did not want to keep *Thidalia* waiting for too long.

When he reached the car, the large pale man already had the door open and closed it after Peter sat down. Bomani was still riding shotgun and he still looked like he was still trying to piece some things together in his mind. She had already poured herself a drink. Brandy from the looks of it. Peter straightened his jacket and looked at her.

"Don't tell me I have to eliminate him," Peter said.

"Well, not today anyway," she answered as she watched Rook walk around the car. "But do not put him in a place where he is beyond reproach. He is a resource and sometimes it is resourceful to have a resource removed."

Rook got into the car and looked back at Thidalia. She nodded and Peter saw Rook shift his eyes to Peter. The silent man then lifted a gun toward Bomani.

"*Head shot!*" Peter thought as he leaned toward Rook, his right arm flung hard forward. An instant later, the gun tucked into the holster on his forearm was in his hand and eady to fire.

Bomani jumped as he looked over at the weapon pointed at his face. He jumped again at the sound of the gunshot. Rook's forearm was red and he dropped the gun, clutching his gunshot wound. Peter then shot back his elbow scoring Thidalia's face. She dropped her glass and the palmed dagger she had in her other hand as the partition window shattered from Peter's second shot. Rook fell forward into the steering wheel. Twisting, Peter saw the dagger and could also see that the blade was wet with something that did not have the consistency of water. He slapped his COP .357 into Thidalia's face and she fell unconscious. Peter opened the back door and fired his last two shots into her chest.

"Stay if you want," Peter said, grabbing her purse and getting out of the car. Bomani needed no further suggestion. He took the gun Rook had meant to use to kill him and got out of the car. He could hear Webster slap the side of car and he pondered if the American was angered because he had to make his move before he wanted to.

Bomani jogged until he caught up with Peter, stuffing his weapon in the back of his pants and looking in all directions as Webster's attention was on the contents of Thidalia's purse.

"What's your next move?" he asked, continuing to check all angles.

"Get back to the states," Peter said, taking Thidalia's phone out of the bag. He opened it and stopped walking.

"What the hell?!" he whispered, showing Bomani the device. "This is a freakin' toy!" Bomani took the device and examined it carefully. It was indeed a toy, but parts of it had been removed. The buttons were genuine gems of particularly fine cuts.

"Most of it is a toy," Bomani offered. "These gems are real and I doubt even Barbie can afford them."

"I'd like that back!" Thidalia shouted as she got out of the car.

"Blessed Mother!" Bomani whispered as he looked back at her.

"We'll see," Peter said as he pressed down on the face of his watch. The car exploded into fire and smoke. Peter did not break stride and he never looked back. He had relieved Thidalia of all of her currency. She was set to be impressive in several countries. He took the so-called phone from Bomani, put it back in the purse and threw the purse toward its owner. "She still coming?"

"No," Bomani answered, realizing what Peter was doing when he slapped the car. "She was wearing a vest?"

"Trust me, Bo," Peter said, taking out his phone. He was about to say goodbye to it too. "These guys don't need to wear vests. And I'm not about to say she's dead now, but I am hoping that it takes her a while to piece herself back together at least.

"I've been made. Headed west," he said into the phone before turning and throwing it into the fire. He then put his mind to reloading his gun and returning it to his sleeve holster. He could hear the door to the warehouse door open and it sounded as if Augustus was screaming.

"*They must have been close*," Peter thought, assured of the fact that Caprice would be too fixated on the fire to look around, and in three more strides they would have the warehouse between them.

"Getting out of here is going to be fun," Peter said softly. He was surprised to see Bomani hand him the pistol.

"You are better with this than I and one of us needs to steal a car."

"You know, this could be the start of a wonderful relationship," Peter smiled, taking the gun.

"Allah provides!"

Several computations were run and they all came up with the same conclusion, a new form of multi-wave burst communication was being used. The concept was novel, but it relied on nearly archaic technological principles. That did not keep the signals from being elusive. She adjusted her opticals and made one more search over the recorded transmissions. No further information could be derived which meant she could either continue her research or file a report with nothing but suggested theory to explain the incidence. She preferred neither option. Still, she had a report to make and the Comptroller was seldom in the position to exercise patience over expedience. She took her data and went immediately to the Comptroller's desk. A few braids were out of place but again, she did not have time to for personal grooming.

"We simply do not have a proper reading of this variation," she reported. "We will need to gather more data."

"Normally I would agree," the Comptroller remarked. "However, the conclusion that you have yet to derive is that somewhere on Earth someone, whom you do not know, is communicating with another mysterious entity and we do not know what was said."

"Probably safe to say it wasn't a recipe for quiche," she jested, but the Comptroller continued, ignoring her attempts at levity.

"Nor can we say, since our sensors are not programmed for this sort of signal, how long the two parties were in contact with each other…or if it was only two parties. This must be forwarded immediately, but that is within my functionality parameter. I would direct you to return to your investigation and see if there is another broadcast."

"Yes, Comptroller," she said, her head lowering toward the floor.

"I detect there is a 98.776% probability you have something to say. Please come forward and share your thoughts."

"I would rather see to my research in the field, Comptroller," she said, knowing the fate of those who have lied to the Comptroller.

"Your request has been noted and will be forwarded through the proper channels. Return to your investigation."

She allowed a slight smile as she turned and walked quickly back to her work. Elation was no excuse for poor time management.

Her eyes opened and her body registered unbelievable amounts of pain. She gasped, her body locking, and even more pain ran through her form. But it eventually passed and she began to breathe regularly. She looked around and noticed she was being carried. The face she saw was without expression but it was a beautiful sight. India's eyes had never been more welcome.

"Pawn," she struggled to speak.

"Rest, Queen," India replied. "Rook summoned me by the most expedient means possible. I arrived just as you were about to be consumed by the flames."

"*Damn blast laid me low,*" she thought before she coughed out a chuckle. "*I underestimated Mr. Webster. That cannot happen again!*" She closed her eyes and placed herself in a state of meditation. The healing would not be so painful that way but with the amount of damage the bomb and the fire had done, it was going to be a few days before she was able to move about on her own. Still, she had her Pawn and therefore she was able to take action. Though revenge called to her, it was just another distraction.

There were greater objectives to consider and at the top of the list were the Prodigian.

Seventeen

"How does he do that?" Bomani asked, looking at Peter Webster as if he were something inhuman. He set the back of his head against the headrest and took in a deep breath, holding it for a moment before slowly blowing it out.

"There you go," Peter said, his eyes still closed. "Pretty soon we'll be given clearance and this bad boy will be headed out of here."

"But we are not landing in the United States," Bomani replied as his head came up and his eyes opened.

"You're losing it, you are losing it," Peter whispered. "And you were doing so well too." Bomani closed his eyes and returned to his relaxing position. "Much better," Peter graded. "No, we are not landing in the States but we will be landing at a place where we can expect some support. I'm just about out of ammo and we had to drop our big gun."

"How is it that you were able to get that on to the plane?"

"Detectors aren't looking for devices made out of composite materials," Peter answered, leaning over to Bomani so that he could afford to speak in a lower tone. It was the first time since they said their goodbyes to Thidalia that he actually felt like he was not being watched by everyone around him. "Mind you, this thing is only good for two maybe three more shots anyway."

Bomani opened his eyes and turned his head to look at Webster. The flight attendant walked by, keeping Bomani silent for a moment. She was a fairly attractive woman going about her business seeing that the overhead compartments were closed. But with her back to him, Bomani could see the curves of her waist and the length of her blonde hair.

"I wonder if she is Dutch," he thought. *"Everyone else around here seems to be. With the exception of the mysterious American who sits so calmly next to me."*

Taking down a few pillows, the attendant offered them to several patrons across the aisle from Bomani. His eyes looked at her legs. She was wearing pantyhose, but it could have been stockings, he could never tell that low on the leg. But her legs were shapely and the heels she wore stirred his passions even further.

"Looking harder won't make that skirt any shorter," Peter said in a volume that Bomani thought was too loud as he jumped. The flight attendant turned around. She understood English?!

"May I help you?" she smiled, and Peter opened his eyes, smiling up at the young lady.

"I'd say you've been a big help just with that smile," he answered. "I'm trying to just calm down before this thing starts moving."

"Oh, you are afraid to fly?" she asked, squatting down. The front of her skirt had a slit that ran up to her mid thigh. Squatting low, the fabric separated enough to reveal her upper thigh region and Bomani could see she was wearing stockings. He loved European women! Her lowered stance also displayed her blouse and scarf combination. She had a particularly long neck, but the top button of her blouse was unfastened and he could see her cleavage. She was a very healthy woman and Bomani slowly came up out of his seat to get a better view of her breasts.

"I'm actually getting better at it," Peter answered her, his face looking anything but convincing. "With my work, I have to travel and until someone builds a freeway from the States to the rest of the world, this is it for me."

"But I don't want to keep you from your duties," he smiled up at her, nodding and breathing deeply. "You go ahead, I'll be fine."

"This happens to be one of my duties," she answered with a bright smile. A smile that was erased when she looked over at Bomani who was clearly out of his seat and gawking at the woman. "As soon as we are in the air, I will come back and check on you, okay?"

"I don't want to be any trouble."

"It is no trouble at all," she replied, standing up and smiling down on Peter. Bomani sat down and looked half dazed as the scent of her perfume reached his nose. It was a soft jasmine bouquet but something made it sweet. "I will see you soon," she said, walking down the aisle to check on the other passengers. Bomani missed the glare she gave him and Peter chuckled.

"I have to thank you for that," Webster said as he sat back in his seat.

"Thank me for what?"

"Well, I was just making sure you got an eyeful of her and now it looks like I might get a chance to revisit the Mile High Club."

"How can you be so sure?" Bomani asked.

"First, she's a woman, so there is no 'so sure'. However, while I appeared vulnerable, something these customer service types really go in for, you looked like you were ready to jump her right there in the aisle. Which means when she comes back to check on me, and circumstances support, she will ask me to sit with her at a different seat. That's when I'll lay the truth on her."

"And then?"

"What are we in, first grade?" Peter barked. "Hasn't it crossed your mind that your appetite for women has put you in fatal harm's way at least two times that I know of? Mind you, with Thidalia, I can understand. But at some point you need to wake up and get a grip. Obsessions at this level of play can get you killed! So if you want to split when we land, I'll understand. Kinda wonderin' why you're on the plane now."

"I am here because I have seen Thidalia's work first hand," Bomani answered, taking hold of Peter's forearm. "And so far, my friend, you are the only one still alive. It is one thing to have faith in Allah, and another thing entirely not to tie up one's camel."

Peter turned it over in his mind, what Bomani had said. There was an innate wisdom to every word of it. But Peter was going to stick to his instincts. That was why he put the bomb on Thidalia's car. It was going too easy for him and that was something that just did not happen anymore. Not since he picked up the trail of the so-called serial killer. That was why he lied to Bomani about how many shots he had left to his gun. It was not made of any sort of composite. Simmons had at one time explained to him how the gun got through metal detectors. It had something to do with what he had put into the small handle. So long as it kept doing it, Peter really did not care how it functioned, save the firing process. That he knew and that was all he needed to know. But there would be more truth to be dealt with after his second or third shot with Bomani around. That much he was sure of.

"Look, we put down in London and at that point you need to figure out what you're going to do and why."

It was not long after Peter closed his eyes that the plane pulled away from the terminal and taxied to the runway. As the plane started increasing speed, Bomani leaned over to Peter.

"Are you a spy?"

"FBI," he answered. "Recently retired. I spent a few months tracking down a serial killer only to find that she was some way out, supernatural, psycho assassin with the ability to make things happen with her mind.

"And by things I mean she could throw people, stop vehicles trying to run her down and cause things to burst into super-hot flames. Our Thidalia is part of an organization that has been watching these people because, as it turns out, the assassin was here to kill one of her own kind. He had powers too.

"Anything else?" Peter asked, knowing there would not be. Bomani was on a very serious *maybe* sticker. Maybe he would get a handle of what he had stumbled into. Maybe he would find out in time to be able to do something constructive with that information. Maybe he would live to see the end of it all.

"No," he answered, his eyes fixed on Peter, looking for the slightest sign that the American was either lying or joking with him. "Nothing else. Not now."

Not long after the plane leveled off, the flight attendant did ask Peter to sit with her on a different row and he was gone most of the flight. When he returned to his seat, minutes before the landing, Bomani could smell the woman's perfume on him but when asked, Peter replied that she had held him and nothing else was said of it. Leaving the plane, the lady smiled especially brightly at Peter and barely managed a cordial exchange for Bomani.

"Mile High Club?" he asked as they walked down the access way and Peter began to smile before he stopped unanticipatedly, his forming smile lost to eyes that ran from left to right and back to the left. "What is i-"

"Shut up!" Peter said softly as he looked over to his left. He quickly stepped to the left wall of the tunnel, nearly knocking down one of the disembarking passengers. He began to swear at Peter in French but he did not even hear him. He put his face in the window.

"He sees me," Peter whispered while quickly looking around into the night and then he pulled his head back. The glass of the window shattered and that gave birth to a number of screams and panicked passengers.

"Mix in and stay to the right!" Peter directed and he moved quickly, ducking down low and adding his screams to the mixture.

Reaching the terminal, Peter quickly turned to the right. He could hear another ricochet.

"How in *the* hell!" he exclaimed, wondering how they got into the airport with high-powered rifles.

"Right!" he said. "They watch people who can do shit with their minds. Might have picked up a few tricks along the way."

"Keep that ass moving, Bomani!" he urged.

"I'm right behind you!" he replied, sounding closer than Webster thought he would be.

"*Man's got moves!*" Peter thought as he opened the door leading outside the terminal. A move that made him an easier target but these *poppers* were not professional and there was a rising chance an innocent was going to get clipped. That was not why Peter joined the armed forces and it certainly was not why he had worn a badge. With both of them behind him, he saw no reason to change. If he got aced today, he was playing the game, it happens. But there was a boatload of people who were just trying to get from A to B and had not asked for the extra entertainment tonight.

He reached the bottom of the stairs and he could see two men running in from his right.

"*We are so screwed!*" he thought as he turned to his left. The sound of automatic gunfire brought the old soldier out of him and he spun around, tackling Bomani to the ground. There were no ricochets around either of them and he looked up to see a godsend.

"We got a plane waiting at the private strip," Moreland called out as he came off the trigger of his AK-47.

"*We is right!*" Peter thought as he saw Chalk and Cooper firing from the rear of a near featureless blue van. He got up quickly and was again surprised when he did not need to pick up Bomani. He was already up and running toward the van. Moreland tossed his weapon to Webster who tossed him his shoulder bag.

"Payback is a bitch!" Webster said as he turned, fell to his knee and fired. Three-round bursts only and after his third, both men were down and they were not getting up. A low loud tone came from the van and vibrated in Webster's ears. It was irritating, but it did not keep him from spotting the sniper, thanks to Cooper's help. She had the eye for the art but not the experience. One cannot make an accurate long distance shot on full automatic. But her shots made the sniper seek cover as well as marked the area for Webster. She gave Webster three seconds, two more than he needed as he took one shot, nipping the edge of the sniper's cover. He fell out from behind the cover holding his knee.

"*Bingo*," Peter Webster thought as he fired a second time. The left temple of the man burst red and the man fell dead.

"The man is unreal," Chalk said, reloading his M-16. "He doesn't even have a scope on that AK."

"He would have taken it off anyway," Cooper said, trimming her firing down to three-round bursts as well. Watching Peter was a good reminder of what he had taught her. "It would have been set to Moreland and taken way too long to readjust."

"I see," Chalk said, looking at Marianne who did not look up from her shooting.

Peter stood up as alarms around the airport sounded off.

"Perfect timing," Moreland said as he turned for the van.

"What gives?" Peter asked, back-pedaling. "That was almost too easy."

"That sound might be a little irritating to you and me," Jack said, getting in behind the wheel. "But to our favorite folks it can be rather debilitating, especially if they're using their powers."

"Far fucking out!" Peter said softly as he got into the vehicle.

"Yeah, that's the good news," Caleb said as he turned off machinery. "The sound has a tendency to blow out a speaker, even the one that Simmons made."

"He said it was probably not a good fit," Marianne said, reloading her weapon. Peter smiled and shook his head at the team nurse. "We've all been kinds of rushed."

"True," Caleb agreed as he looked to the rear of the van. Airport Police were running and driving toward the terminal. Three people were running from them, one of them holding her head as she staggered more than she ran. "And it looks like it did what it was supposed to do."

"They won't be able to hold 'em for long," Jack pointed out as he continued to drive. "But that was not the objective today."

"How are you, Petey?"

"Damn glad to be here, Jack!" Peter smiled and relaxed, truly relaxed, as he took out his telescope.

"Figured," he whispered as he focused on the running woman. She was dressed as a flight attendant but she was not the one who had given him special attention. He had made her when he first got on the plane. She had been too watchful without saying anything. Besides, when he and the blonde had been in a more intimate situation, the young woman had not quite seemed natural. Her movements had seemed awkward and she had no rhythm… like a puppet that did not want to be on the stage. That was why he had only held her; she was an innocent, but had he acted like he was not interested in her, all sorts of alarms would have gone off.

What he would have given to have his rifle. It would be another night shot against a Prodigian. Moving or not, the airport asphalt was smoother than that old Decatur road and Jack was driving… no way he would have missed.

"How did you do it, Jack?"

"Got some contacts with MI-6," he shouted as he turned toward the rear gate. "Called in a few favors."

"You got anymore?" Peter asked as he looked up into the rear view mirror. The team sniper (and therefore guardian angel) and the team den mother made eye contact. "Hey Doc, when you got the download on all of this from Harry, how long did he say the effect lasts?"

"It really depends how engaged they are when the sound hits them," Caleb answered. "But Arvius was good enough to hit me with the principles behind calculating their down time."

"Good ol' Harry," Peter smiled, his eyes still locked on Jack's.

"Caleb," Jack said, taking a moment to see the road ahead of him. "If the Prodigian was engaged in making several gunmen invisible?"

"At least an hour," Caleb answered. "And that's rounding down."

"You as tired of being on the *reactionary* end of this as I am?" Peter asked. Jack said nothing but he did take out his phone. Peter smiled as he sat back. "Everyone, this is Bomani. Bomani, this is one helluva cavalry! They also happen to be my family." Marianne afforded herself a smile as she leaned over and kissed Webster full on the mouth.

"That's from Tara!" she smiled.

"Bullshit!" Peter replied.

"I'll never tell while the lights are on," Marianne playfully replied. Peter's rifle smashed the dome light of the van and he reached out for Marianne who was already meeting him halfway.

"Jesus!" Jack said.

"Will I do?" Caleb replied as he sat down in the chair next to the muscular driver.

"Yeah, I suppose so. What flavor lip gloss are you wearing? I'm pretty much a peach or pear man." Caleb looked at Jack and then opted to ride in the back of the van. Marianne cackled out loud as Bomani took the front chair.

"Tootie-fruity," he smiled and Jack joined Marianne in the loud laughter.

Eighteen

[*Don't have a cow, Viz,*] William projected, again verifying his senses were very accurate when apperceiving my state of mind. I put more effort into my standard thought shielding.

[*That's gotta sting,*] he continued in a pronounced sarcastic tone. [*I can still remember the first time we met and you got off on cutting me off by reading my mind and knowing what I was going to say before I could say it. Put the shoe on the other foot and look at you now.*]

[*You have a point to make?*] I asked, not sure at all what I should have said.

[*You might want to remember this the next time you feel like showing off with your telepathy.*]

"Hey everybody," William called from the front door. He came in with a Tyro and... what used to be a Light-Child. I stood up immediately, fixing my eyes on Chidon. "I brought friends!"

"Uh, honey," Adrianna said as she approached.

"Don't sweat it, Mom, they already know about me. In fact Harry here... where's Harry?"

"I am here," Arvius answered, stepping out from behind the Tyro female. "Perhaps I should wait outside."

"Nonsense, Harry," William said aloud. "I invited you in. He's okay to have in here, right Mom?" But Adrianna had no answer for her son. She turned away from Arvius and looked at her husband who was joining the Tyro in a state of confusion. William just scratched his head and looked down.

"Do I have to scream 'No' again or is someone gonna step up and say something?" William asked.

"What happened the last time you screamed?" Tara asked, curious at the threatening tone in which he spoke.

"Major headache for everyone in the room," William answered matter-of-factly.

"Right," Tara nodded, turning to address the room. "Okay, I'm new here, but that doesn't mean I'm looking for a migraine. Harry's with me and-"

"Calling yourself *Harry* these days, Arvius?" I asked in a cold tone, ready to summon my Blade and be done with him. My eyes locked on William's as a low growl escaped from between his lips.

"You can either bend those knees and sit your high and mighty ass down right now, or I can just take 'em off your hands and we won't have to worry about you raising your head above anyone else...EVER!" Gordon started to speak to his stepson but Adrianna was quick to wave a warning to him to not do so. "Now everybody listen up, and you, Robin Hood, make sure the three assholes in the backyard get this too. In this house, there are two voices of law and authority, and neither one of them are of the Territories or their edicts. This man is welcome in this house until *they* say differently, and if you cannot honor the house of my parents with passing respect, I will respectfully pass you through the most expedient wall or threshold!"

"William," Adrianna started in a very careful and soft tone. It always worked wonders on Zargo but Kador was her son, not her lover, and was not bound by the same kind of love.

"Mom," William interrupted again. "He helped this woman and her friends save my life from the Man-Lord assassin last night."

"I saw Tara in your memories but I saw nothing of the Blood of Salpanor."

"Okay, that name recognition sounded like we're going to get back story some time in the near future," William replied.

"So glad *he* said that," Tara muttered, looking at Arvius and then clearing her throat.

"Actually, Harry here was keeping my fellow agents and me alive. He'd heal us up and we'd throw ourselves right back into the fray... for a second or two." Tara looked down but she did not see the floor. She was back off the side of the road, walking through the burned grass and various automobile wreckage, up to a very confident and deadly Yudara. "Man that Yudara was one tough bitch!" My eyes closed and my head sank to my chest.

"Excuse me," Adrianna turned quickly to face Tara Mifflen and her gentle demeanor was gone. William was too attuned to our reactions to miss it and his curiosity was piqued. "... but did you say Yudara?" Tara nodded. "Yudara, Blood of Beriah?"

"We really didn't have that kind of relationship," Tara replied. "Palshaya did mention the Beriah name while she was giving us the business about the Prodigian."

"Palshaya!" I said, nearly coming out of my seat. But I could feel William's eyes shift to me. I doubted he had the skill to make good on his threat, but the room was tumultuous enough! It did not need any further assistance.

"You know her?" William asked.

"Knew," Tara corrected, moving consoling eyes to Arvius.

"She was a Tracker-Warrior," I answered William, standing up, trading my seat for a cooperative effort. "She specialized in finding runners."

"Runners?" William was confused but once again his mind engaged at unfathomable speeds and he looked down. "Prodigians who don't want to be Prodigians anymore?"

"That's one way to put it, baby," Adrianna answered. "Some of them simply leave," she said as she looked back at Arvius. She was still angry with him, and she had good reason but she did not maintain her asperity for long. Now there were other pressing matters to which she would devote her anger. "Others turn quite treacherous and leave their mark upon the Prodigian as they leave the Territories."

"*Still*, Adrianna?!" Arvius cried, surprising all that knew him. "*Still* you would claim that the Light-Children are the Prodigian? Have you nothing to say of the other two sects, or did your time in the Council blind you to their very existence?!"

"Whoa!" William said quickly and loudly. "This is about to get political and nothing good ever comes from that."

"Do you know who this woman, this assassin, is?" William asked Adrianna.

"Did and was," Tara corrected.

"Do and is!" Adrianna, Arvius, William and I said concurrently.

[*And how do you know her to still be alive?*] I projected to my young student.

[*I don't. It would just be too easy if she were dead,*] he responded.

[*Nay, young Kador, it would not!*]

"Will you two stop being rude," Adrianna directed to her son and me. "To answer your question, son, Beriah is the Man-Lord who claims to have killed your father. Yudara is his daughter."

"Oh this is a special kind of sick," William said, walking over to my chair and sitting down. "My Dad killed your Dad so I have to kill you!" he feigned a childish overtone. The room was silent, each with their own thoughts to ponder and have them dispel any semblance of inner peace. William looked around the room for a few minutes. How many I could not ascertain, for I had my own thoughts to contend with.

"Good God, where is the airport?!" he said as he got up from the chair. "With this much baggage there's got to be a plane leaving soon." Tara was the only one to laugh, being perhaps the best adjusted with the baggage she carried.

"Easy, son," Gordon said softly. "You're getting pretty high-handed there."

"Matter of perspective, Dad," William answered. "You raised me to be colorblind and forgiving, to find the essence behind the Golden Rule and live through it. You set one helluva example for me to reach and I've always wanted to make you and Mom happy so I bought it, I bought into it and everything I've ever done has been framed by those lessons.

"Now I'm knee deep in the worst shit I've ever heard of and you want to change the rules on me," William said as he picked up his flowers and took in their scent. He closed his eyes and allowed himself a smile. "So if I am high-handed, as you put it, recognize where that hand came from and if you don't like it, you have yourselves to blame," he concluded, pointing at Adrianna and Gordon. "Now I'm going to go upstairs and call the lovely young lady who sent me these flowers and try to console myself for firing off on my parents in such a fashion that I am the worst hypocrite in the room. Given the current company, that's saying something. My parents, I apologize and I will get it together. Still not quite adjusted to being..." he looked around the room and I could feel his faculty of hope beginning to fade. I tried through my eyes to tell him he was wrong and for a moment he looked at me, breathed in deeply enough to correct his posture and nodded. "Anyway, sorry." He turned and walked down the corridor to the stairs.

"Wow!" Tara whispered.

"Sweetheart, you have no idea," Adrianna said, ushering her to a chair. "You're starving. Let me get you something to eat." She was halfway to the stove when she looked up at Gordon. He smiled and she gave a slight smile in response. "You're both starving," she said. "And if I recall, Harry, you like fried chicken?"

"I had no idea you had taken on the talent of cooking, Adrianna," Arvius said as he approached the table and pulled out a chair for Tara.

"It's been a constant work in progress," Adrianna answered as she opened the refrigerator door. "Before my blocks to his ability fell, that kid was still a jock and a growing young man. That kind of combination I had to respond to. Didn't want him to take a bite out of me!" A light laugh made its way around the room but I did not participate. I signaled Chidon to follow me and I started toward the corridor.

"Is the teacher unable to follow the example of the student?" Gordon said, blocking my way.

"This Golden Rule he spoke of," I started, trying to keep my mind from going through the memories of what form Arvius' treachery had taken. "This is not something I taught him nor would it be. You knew my mentor well, Gordon, and I recognize the color of your stare whenever you embrace his memory and look upon me. And in the words of your ward, that makes you a hypocrite, for I do not see you 'cleaning the slate', even though you have yet to prove your beliefs. This man is a criminal and people died because of his actions and beliefs. I will not be able to forgive him as quickly as my student nor his mother. And Gordon, you in no way block my progress," I said as I teleported myself and Chidon to the backyard.

Gordon and Zargo had been the best of friends and Adrianna's husband had long suspected me of killing my master. He claimed I was the only being of sufficient of power who could have succeeded in getting close to Zargo while bearing malice in my heart. For the most part, his argument was accurate, but that only added to the mystery. The phenomenal power levels one would have to attain to face Zargogyan were almost beyond comprehension. The idea of discovering one who could hide that much power from any possible witnesses, let alone Zargo, mired my resolve. But power was only one aspect of Zargo's legend. In coming to understand the Light-Children, he had taken part in their fixations for precision. Before embarking upon that obsession he had relied on his incredible reserves of power, but he had adapted himself to be extremely skillful and seldom did he even need to touch upon those reserves.

In all the Territories, there was only one Prodigian who came close to possessing the power, skill and, above all, the motive to slay Zargogyan. That would be the very man who laid claim to the victory, Grand Lord Beriah whose time was inexplicably drawing to an end.

Despite our powers, not even the Prodigian are immortal, but for only having seen three hundred years, Beriah was aging very rapidly and held his title merely out of honor and respect. Yet with all of his power, which he wielded with an arrogance that had been silenced by Zargo on more than one occasion, Gordon Ferrous was more comfortable believing I had killed his friend and my savior. My means of departure gave an avenue through which he now took argument to Adrianna as she served beverages to her two new guests.

"Elizabeth," he said softly but the urgency was still very clear.

"Oh this is serious," she said as she floured the chicken.

"Can we speak more privately?"

"No, sweetheart, I don't think we need to. That color Elkazzar spoke of is not just visible to him. We've had this argument too many times to need privacy. Elkazzar would have cut out his heart before drawing Zargo's blood.

"Fine, then we agree he is heartless," Gordon replied. "And I don't think he has a grasp of what he is doing here. Bill is teaching that old man as much as he is supposed to be teaching our son."

"That would be par for the course with William, honey," she said, smiling up at Gordon. "And there are constants in the universe I observe that not even my son needs to remind me of. I don't get in the way of masters.

"No one questions you about the law. No one questions me about how to run this house. No one questions our son abut being a genius and a super-jock."

"Damn straight on the jock part!" Tara cried out before she realized she was supposed to be keeping her thoughts to herself and went back to drinking her punch. Adrianna chuckled and could see why William had spoken up for the woman and anyone who traveled with her.

"You know, she's a Medium," Adrianna said to Gordon, remembering she was in the middle of making a point. "And to finish it up, no one, but nobody questions Elkazaar about how to train someone. That man could teach a man how to give birth!" Tara spit in her drink and Adrianna floated a napkin over to the woman.

"Thank you," Tara said, taking the napkin to wipe her mouth and shirt.

"The man was born with the magic finger."

"What magic finger?" Gordon asked, still brooding.

"The finger that always finds the right buttons to push. He has always known what to say to get his students to perform beyond what they thought their best could be. You think William is pushing him all over the place and to be sure, he is. But he is also gaining William's trust, finding out how he thinks and why. When he finds an opening, he'll tear into William and break him, if he can be broken at all."

"You say that like it's a good thing!" Gordon argued.

"Sweetheart, can you recall what it was like to be a hormone-driven teenager? Now add in the fact that you just realized that every girl who ever said no you could *make* them say yes and make them mean it when they said it.

"There isn't a test you can't pass," Adrianna continued. "All you have to do is look into the teacher's head. Instant answer key! How the hell do you learn anything when all you have to do to know something is invade someone's mind?"

"He's got too many scruples for that," Gordon contended.

"Stack those scruples against being godlike and see which one wins," she warned. "Yes, I put blocks on William's powers, but it was not solely for his benefit! How could he ever lose a game if he used his powers? And what sort of person does he become if he never has to deal with losing?"

"*Wow!*" Tara thought, finishing her punch. "*I can see where the kid gets it from! Now I just got to get a handle on the sort of man would attract a woman like her! Hell, never mind, I can only look up so high!*"

[*You could break your neck and not see high enough,*] Arvius projected to his friend. [*Zargo was the last best hope for the Prodigian! When he died, many of us thought our last chance for peace died with him.*]

"*So that's it!*" Tara thought, staring at Arvius. "*That's why you're here!*" Arvius looked down and Tara stood up from the table.

"You sorry sack of shit!" she yelled, drawing the attention of Gordon and Elizabeth Ferrous. "It wasn't enough that his father died trying to fix whatever the hell is wrong with you people. Now you want to dig your claws into his kid and make him your go-fer?!

"What the hell did you do, Harry?! I've known this woman less than five minutes and already her sense of integrity makes me homesick for *Momma*. Five minutes ago I was dumb enough to think that kind of integrity comes around once in a lifetime and I've gotten to see it twice!

"Why don't you fight your own damn fights, Arvius?!" Tara yelled, taking hold of the scared man. "You got Palshaya to fight your fights for you and now that she's dead you're *helping* around here so the kid upstairs can take your place in line. Get the hell out of here," she warned reaching to her leg and drawing her second gun; a surprise she had been saving for their woodland stalker, but she needed to see Chidon before she would let the thought of having a second firearm go through her head. "Because I'm liable to shoot you myself. Right now, I'd rather face the wrath of that boy upstairs than tolerate y-" Tara grunted as she lost sight on the moment. Her body floated out of the kitchen into the family room where she was placed on the couch. Arvius looked over at Adrianna as she lowered her hand and released her telekinesis. She blinked twice and smiled over at Arvius.

"Kind of an impasse," she said softly. "I don't know what you said to her and I don't want to know. But if I let her drive you off, I have to deal with my son and he's got enough on his plate. She'll be more even-tempered after she's had a nap." Turning back to the stove, she stopped and looked at Gordon. "See how it easy it is to get bitten by the God Complex?"

Gordon looked up at the ceiling and placed his hands on his hips. "Fine," he acquiesced. "He should train the boy. But do you think he should've brought those three in the backyard? Not exactly the sort of people we want a well-adjusted young man to hang around with."

"Will you please keep your voice down," Elizabeth snapped as she walked over to the window, looking into the backyard.

"Don't you think I can keep them from reading my mind?"

"It's not your mind I'm concerned with," she replied. "Elkazzar said Igrileena was born a Man-Lord. She probably heard you." As Adrianna spoke, Igrileena looked up and smiled at her, shrugging her shoulders.

"Scratch probably," Elizabeth concluded. Igrileena nodded.

"Well maybe I don't care!" Gordon yelled and she looked at him, forming a telekinetic bubble in the kitchen. She was surprised that Tara responded to its formation. There was more to this Medium than she had first seen.

"I was wondering when you'd finally blow up," Adrianna said, going back to her cooking. "I knew that sooner or later it would all catch up to you and sure enough, Zargo's in there somewhere."

"You think this is some sort of game?" Gordon screamed and she smiled, knowing she was right. Gordon's floated into the family room and landed in his favorite chair. His wife was right behind him and sat in his lap as the chicken was put into the hot oil.

She wore her smile proudly and her gaze softened him. She wrapped her arms around his neck. As their eyes met, her smile faded and her countenance shifted, becoming one she had received so many times from Kador's father.

"I would like to think of all the people involved in this, that William and I have the best picture of what is really going on here. It is anything but a game. People are trying to kill my son. It only stands to reason that in the attempt, one of them might get wise and figure that if either you or I were to die, William would be more than a little distracted. I have to admit, it's a good plan... probably the only one that will work.

"So, I suggest that you take a moment and collect yourself, honey." She fixed his collar before kissing him briefly. "I know exactly what is going on. Elkazzar is the best person qualified to teach my son. Hopefully he will teach William everything that Zargo taught him." She looked away for a moment, hit with a wave of realization.

"If he knew he was going to die," she thought, *"could this just another means he could guarantee his way of teaching his son? By teaching one of the few men who would be strong enough to go against the will of the Council and the Throne and walk in the Outworld?*

"Damn you, Zargo," she thought. Years of wedded bliss had given Adrianna the comfort of his love, but it had also carried the benefit of being a first-hand witness to Zargo's stratagems. *"How much of this is going according to one of your plans?"*

"What is it, honey?" Gordon asked.

"Nothing," she answered, not sure as to why she was so quick to lie to her husband. Was it that Gordon did not think he was worthy of her after having loved Zargo? Or perhaps he had crossed a line of honor by loving Adrianna? She did not know but she had already spoken and she followed her response with action as the chicken turned over and more meat came into the house from the freezer in the garage. "I forgot to take out something for dinner and we do have a small army to feed."

"That we do," Gordon lifted his brow in agreement.

"Hey, I know I can be a gracious hostess. Why don't you show these pompous Prodigians what a studly Tyro I married?"

"Studly?"

"Oh baby, I know I don't have to explain that one," she said as she kissed him passionately on the mouth. Gordon could see a veil of black light surround them and with assured privacy, he was allowed to receive her passions and express his own.

Nineteen

Chidon looked around, knowing he was not anywhere near the encampment. From what he could determine, he was still near the backyard where Elkazzar had taken him before taking the entire group to their encampment. He reached for his bow but his entire quiver moved faster and flew from his body. His Edge and Blade were next and they moved off into the darkness. Unarmed, he was left to his empty-hand skills and Chidon shielded his mind while taking his combative stance.

"Over here," a voice called out to him and it echoed from one side of his body to another. The archer extended his senses but his efforts were reflected back at him. It was a harsh denial but just less than what would have been necessary to cause backlash.

"Doesn't feel so good, does it?" the voice asked.

"Show thyself, Kador!" Chidon commanded. The light in the room came up and Kador stood five meters in front of Chidon, holding his Blade that was no longer in its scabbard.

"Now, how would you have known it was me?" William asked, brandishing the Blade with a fair amount of skill. "Is it because I am the only one outside of Elkee that will take the time to teach you a much needed lesson?"

"Have a care, stripling," Chidon warned. "Thou art still too new to these matters and it may be thine own hide in need of instruction!"

"You feel like you can teach me, Chidon?" William asked, tossing the sword aside. "Take your best shot!" For a moment, neither man moved, but it was clear which of the two was more nervous. "Didn't think so," William commented coldly as he reached to his back and he produced an arrow, a Man-Lord arrow and Chidon's face twisted.

"You don't recognize this?" William asked, looking at the archer's face.

"If this be the matter of lesson I am to learn, Kador, mayhap there is something for us both to learn. I fired many shafts at thee that night but none of them were of Man-Lord make. I may respect their craft for weapons forging, but I would never apply that shaft to my father's bow!"

There could be no doubt Chidon was telling the truth. William could even feel that had he requested, Chidon would have let him into his mind to verify the statement. He had eased his mind into Elkazzar's and had him teleport Chidon to the basement instead of the encampment. In the time it would have taken anyone to piece it together, he had gambled that the truth would be his. But he had the truth, it was not Chidon who fired the arrow.

It was a truth which brought no comfort to Chidon either. It meant he had been in the presence of the enemy and had not felt them at all. For all he knew, that person was in the very same room with them at that moment. He looked around and once again extended his senses. He could feel nothing save William, and my return to the household. William quickly opened the door for Chidon and offered his apologies. As soon as Chidon was clear of the house, William closed the door and started the walk to his room. He looked at the arrow again and nodded.

"*I should have picked up more than one, I guess,*" he thought as he went up the stairs quickly. He ran up to his dresser and opened the bottom drawer, which was the largest.

"I hate being right," he whispered, looking into the drawer. From that night of dealing with Vada-Ri and Chidon he knew he was going to need room and thusly the drawer had been cleared to become something of his Bragging Drawer though he would not brag of these things. He kept them so he could hold tight to why he was still alive. He put the arrow away next to the bloodied stone and the caught bolt.

"Going to need more room before too long…and that's too bad, isn't it?" William closed the drawer and grabbed his jacket, his car keys were still in the pocket.

"I need to take a pause from all this doom and gloom," he thought as he walked quickly out of the room.

Twenty

The double doors of the tavern opened and instantly the scent of drink and sweat wafted into his nostrils. It was well into evening and the darkness aided him in his cause.

"*And to think at one time I fought the hard fight to have establishments such as these removed from our society,*" he thought, quickly moving to the left side and out of the main light. Though the three he had with him had his appreciation and his trust, there was a lack of comfort in Mevkrean's strides without Insra and Lorthar in his company. The latter was afraid of nothing save his commander's rage and the former had developed to the point to where she was as much the teacher of strategy as she had ever been the student. Still none of the men with him were new to the ways of the soldier nor were they unaware of how their Captain operated. One stayed with him as the other two moved to the right and equally out of the light. Mevkrean looked hard at those two and watched how they moved. He should have been impressed and under other circumstances he would have been. But these two had broken his rules when they demanded to join his unit.

The twin sisters, Salkathi and Murietta of the Blood of Chiram, had come to him under the required age of consideration but had sworn to Mevkrean they would never fail to impress him. It had come to be an oath by which Mevkrean measured all of his new recruits. The twins that only held a slight resemblance in face only; their bodies could not have been further apart without one of them being a man. But they moved together and it was always a picture of grace and focus. He was glad they did not have orders to kill anyone, for it might have been a few moments after they passed their target that anyone would have noticed the poor fool was dead! Salkathi kept to the main floor and when she reached the table most under the stairs, an occupied table, she decided to become quite sociable and took up a conversation with the two men that were there. She took a hand to her long, softly red hair and moved it back over her right ear. A deft move as the lifted arm parted her cloak revealing the fact she was armed with both Blade and the formations of flesh that was well received by most men. Her smile flashed in her emerald green eyes at the two patrons as she leaned on the table and tossed a small coin purse in the center of the table. Given her looks, she was assured her position.

Her sister, Murietta, took to the stairs and found an empty table that would provide her a view of the main floor, especially the door. She kept her hood up to cover her fiery red hair and thus remain unnoticed. She was more comely than her sister and equally more savage. She carried a Blade, but her weapon of choice was her collection of Edges. She probably had one palmed in case it needed to be thrown at a moment's notice. She took a seat and tugged on her hood, her signal that she was in position.

Mevkrean continued to move forward and Olliento took hold of his Staffling and moved to a quiet table along the far wall. "Strong arm and stronger heart," he whispered as he took his seat. Three points of cover. No one posted by the door but among the Prodigian, such a posting could prove costly if they did not sense an approach. No, this was the best setting available with the number of men he had with him. Insra's and Lorthar's team had their own objectives this night and with any assistance of Fate, he would see them again and begin to make some sense of the chaos he found himself lost within.

The fact he had received an acknowledgement of his wishes so soon made the Captain apprehensive, but the source promised information that he could not resist. The *Hasty Jug* was just as good a meeting place as any other and there were neither too many patrons to where it felt like a trap nor too few to where it was an open area where he could be seen by some passing Guardsman. He went to the table he had been given by the messenger and took the chair that put his back to the front door. He thought little of the positioning. The chairs were sturdy and that would mean his lower back had some protection. He laid his forearms on the thick, ale-soaked wooden table, his left fist inside his right.

"Mead," he said as the tavern servant approached. "Preferably warm."

"By thy wish, Captain," the woman replied as she took the seat across the table from him.

"Interesting vassal," he said softly. "Paying thee well, is he?"

"Forgive me for any perceived impertinence," she said softly with an alluring smile. It was a wasted effort, but she was obviously frightened and needed some control of their hopefully brief engagement. "But that be none of thy concern or affair."

"So said the last Man-Lord who perished 'pon my Blade," Mevkrean answered, impatient and not inclined to partake in childish games. They were the landmarks of the inexperienced; feeding into the stories woven by too may bards and troubadours who also had little true experience. But then again, the truth was seldom worthy of song. "Heed this well, wench. I am wanted, by no less than the Throne itself! Mayhap thou dost believe thy bosom sufficient to replace that as the forefront of mine thoughts. I canst assure thee this is not the case! Now get thee done with thy business and return to thy world of trivial pursuits and random bed-warmers!" The woman sat back and gave a surprising smile and Mevkrean needed no further hint.

[*Trap*!] he projected, standing up and deflecting, the woman's telekinetic push with particular ease. Her mind was too fixed on victory and not her surroundings. He shoved the edge of the table into her ribs. Not a telling blow, but one that took her mind off their confrontation long enough for him to move. He could hear the front door burst open as he rolled over the table.

[*Hold*!] he urged as his feet kicked the woman over. He had grabbed the edge of the table as he rolled over, lifting it up on his back. The table was vertical and in front of him before they released their first volley of arrows.

"*Not any students of mine,*" he judged as not one shaft managed to penetrate the table. He lowered his knee into the woman's jaw as his hand measured the texture of the wood. He touched the center of the table and felt each plank, each of the individual lines each section was cut along and found how best to act next. Applying a very small degree of his telekinesis, he pushed at each line, forcing the wood to shatter like broken glass, only the ten arrows were also part of the debris. His telekinetic storm fired back on the charging archers, peppering them with splinters and arrowheads. The injuries were not serious, they barely broke the skin, but as with the woman their minds were in no place to mount any sort of defense. A simple stimulation of their pain centers and all ten men screamed in dire pain as Mevkrean dropped his fist into the woman's sternum.

Standing up and lifting the woman from the floor, it became clear to Mevkrean that none of these fools were Royal Guardsmen.

"Mercenaries?" he asked aloud and the woman's eyes shot open. She was more than a mercenary, she was a *Deviant*!

[*No coin canst make this act any sweeter!*] she cried and Mevkrean staggered from her emotional outburst. She lifted her feet and pushed against Mevkrean's chest. She was free of him and she flipped back, landing with two Edges drawn.

"Using thy pain to fuel thy feats," Mevkrean observed as he slowly approached. He waved the woman to approach. "Come hither, I hathe more power for thee. After this thou shall be able to face an army!"

"I do not fear you, *Fairie*!" she cried, brandishing her Edges. An impressive display until she noticed she was without one of them.

"Fanfaring hath always been a wasted art upon me," Mevkrean whispered as he tossed the Edge back at the woman. "But feel free to try again."

Her hand reached out to catch the weapon, but it moved through the image The Captain had erected. She screamed in pain as she looked at her other arm. Mevkrean had indeed returned her Edge to her. It was lodged in her shoulder and the arm was useless to her. She tried to use her pain to empower herself but she was not used to controlling so much at once. Mevkrean held out his hands and recalled the Edge as well as the one that was dropped. He twirled them about his hands them before throwing them both over his shoulder. He hit two of the ten archers in their bow arms.

"Leave this place!" he commanded without fully looking at the men. They were so overwhelmed with fear they did not move to aid their wounded, but nothing was wrong with their legs.

"Die!" the woman screamed, her newly formed claws raking for his neck. They shattered against his bracer instead, and the backlash stunned the woman; she started to fall. Mevkrean possessed her face with his hand and her mind was vulnerable. His search was not slow nor was it meant to be painless. When he released the woman she fell to the floor, spent and unconscious. Straightening his cloak, Mevkrean gave the sign for his men to follow and he projected to them where he was teleporting. They all found themselves on the roof of the tavern inn and Mevkrean pointed northward. They all turned to see one cloaked figure that was already running away.

"Catch that and meet me at the most southern point," Mevkrean said as he looked southward. As he expected, he saw them.

The roof he stood on was well lit and much brighter than it should have been. Torch stones, no doubt set to burn brighter upon his arrival. His eyes met Abiron's and there was little joy in the reunion. With him stood Akiba and a full score of Royal Guardsmen. Mevkrean's eyes squinted as his three broke off after their prey, though he could feel Olliento's reticence to speak against any order given by his Captain. One against a score was a fool's errand, even for one as accomplished as Mevkrean. But the Captain of the Elite Royal Guard had no intention of standing and fighting.

"Akiba!" he shouted as he summoned his Staffling. A simple hand gesture and most of them ran toward him. They floated on the wind, bounding easily from rooftop to rooftop, half of them falling from sight. "Thy master hath set thee against the jaws of hell. This day may yet be thy last!"

"Too bold, old one!" Akiba thought as he drew his Blade and waved for his remaining men to follow him. He had already dispatched fifteen and the other five remained with him and the Prince.

"This be not wise," Abiron remarked as he ran with the others. "The ferret does not follow the serpent into its lair!"

"This is New Sumeria, boy!" Akiba argued. "Thou doth afford too much praise to Mevkrean. Or mayhap thy loins are not of the mettle face thine idol." Akiba's men laughed as they drew Blades. Abiron looked to his lessons and decided to match his target and his Staffling appeared in his hands.

"*Aye, my Prince, thou wert trained well,*" Mevkrean thought as he checked the fastening pin of his cloak. "*And whilst thou wert my student, thy attention was never diverted.*" Mevkrean took a step back and he was in the center of the roof of the building. He took a simple defensive stance with his weapon. He closed his eyes and applied his talents.

"He is summoning!" Abiron warned, his pace slowing.

"What canst he hope to achieve against a score of trained minds?!" Akiba questioned. "He doth merely strengthen his mental Guard to ward against our thoughts. Fine, we shall pummel him down until he canst no longer stand! Charge, men!" Many Prodigian ears felt the war cry of Akiba's group as they moved in on Mevkrean. They looked up and there were a few who knew enough not to like what they saw and acted accordingly, removing themselves from this place.

He was quickly surrounded by Akiba's men and they were anxious to claim their piece of legend. "I was in the group which brought down Mevkrean, Blood of Thalls and prostrated him before the King!" He knew that somewhere, the troubadours were already busying themselves with embellishment of the truth.

"Then again, they may not need to," he whispered, his grip on his weapon tightening.

"Surrender, Mevkrean!" Akiba commanded as he finally landed on the roof.

"Such a stern command," Mevkrean replied, his eyes still closed. "And forthright whilst thou doth hide behind your men!"

"The King wouldst rather have thee able to speak and answer his inquiry," Akiba whirled his Blade about in a vertical circle.

"This King hath many a healer under his command!" Mevkrean shouted back. "Methinks thou shall be within their service 'fore too long."

"How dost thou hope to stand against so many?" Akiba was agitated and Mevkrean smiled. He had expected this much success. "Some of these men even thy hand took part in training."

"Aye, I recognize those I discarded unto thee," Mevkrean jabbed back. "One doth not assign fresh fruit to swine, Akiba! Thy skill would not know how to wield a proper regiment of soldiers. But these are most fitting."

"Let the healers save what they can!" one man screamed as he broke into his attack run. He swung his Blade for Mevkrean's back but the large man actually ducked low enough for the weapon to miss, his Staffling tripping the attacking man who fell hard and slid on his chest passed Mevkrean.

"Ah yes!" Mevkrean sighed. "Impetuous thou hast been and thou art still. Mayhap thou now dost see the reason for my words of caution." Mevkrean stepped to his side as another man came out of teleportation right next to him and in mid-swing. The tip of the Blade just missed Mevkrean's temple. The Staffling, ever so much longer than the Blade, met hard with the bridge of the nose, breaking it and the man fell to his knees. A thrust to the sternum and the man flew into in the next three who were also charging.

"Fight within thy given form!" Akiba screamed to his men but they could not hear him over their own cries of rage and pain, the former being in the majority but slowly shifting to the latter. Akiba's five remained with him and Abiron stepped forward, straining his eyes to look upon his former mentor. His eyes were still closed.

"What sort of trickery is this?" he asked as he was suddenly taken aloft and he screamed in pain. He looked up to see his left shoulder was the property of a large black falcon. The jeweled collar betrayed the creature's identity.

"White Feather?" Abiron winced.

"Forgive his talons, brother," Ezra called out to his brother as he rode atop the great beast. "But I feared my grip would not have been strong enough to hold thee aloft."

"Why dost thou interfere?" Abiron cried. "Canst thou not see this task is burden enough for me?"

"Stay they wrath and thy inquiries!" Ezra pleaded as he looked back. "And look upon thy mentor."

Abiron put his eyes upon Mevkrean who was still engaged with Akiba's men. Not one of them had scored a wound on the man but he had at least given ground when Akiba and his last five entered into the battle. It was then and being at his height that he noticed the sky. What a plan! The darkness of night had masked it well and all the time he spent with his eyes closed, Mevkrean applied his talents to bring forth a storm cloud.

"That is why he chose the Staffling!" Abiron whispered as Mevkrean jumped up and was infused with the clouds natural power. When he landed on the roof again, he allowed that power to flow freely. There was no need to be accurate to the point of aiming, all of his foes were wielding metal weapons and the lighting arced to each and every one of them, laying them all low. When the smoke cleared, only Mevkrean stood and he looked up at the departing Princes and smiled before taking after his men and the one his men seemed to be chasing.

"He risked much, taking to the roofs," Ezra said.

"Aye, but he had to," Abiron answered.

"How dost thou come to this knowledge?"

"Because he took the act upon himself. Mevkrean does not move upon whim." Returning his Staffling to his weapon's locke, Abiron took hold of White Feather's leg and swung himself up to the great beast's back.

"We must return and take those we can to the healers. My thanks, my brother!"

"A brother of mine need not thank me," Ezra replied, a bright smile stretched across his face. "But thou art more than welcome!"

Twenty-One

If nothing else, their prey was fleet of foot and motivated. But these were not novices that gave chase. They had served too long with Mevkrean to make simple mistakes. And given that their Captain was willing to draw the entire party of Royal Guardsmen upon himself, they were not going to be put off easily. From rooftop to rooftop they moved silently, without word or projection, and yet they moved as one with only one initial objective which was not to gain on their target, but not to allow its lead to get any greater. Several rooftops after leaving their leader, their approach was failing for they were gaining ground quite steadily. Murietta did not hold seniority but she was clearly the lead in the chase with her sister, Salkathi on her right side, Olliento (with Staffling still in hand) on her left. That was not how the chase began but with the sharp turns their prey was making, the point man position had shifted with a fluidity that would have made water envious. None of them jumped at the same time and they did not always run straight at their target. The short range teleportations of their target told those in pursuit that this figure was no master of the known talents, which was comforting to them for none of them were either. Without a Great Door to aid it, twenty meters was the best result it had achieved so far which was directly on par with Salkathi and slightly less than what Murietta could reach. Olliento was clearly not pressed, having succeeded in crossing half a league with a single effort. Teleportation was not a common ability and those who had it were often limited to very short distances.

Another augmented jump and the fox stumbled; the hounds closed to within twenty meters. He redoubled his efforts but all three hounds heard him whimper in fear and waning wind. This chase was quickly coming to an end. He looked back, a second sign of an approaching close to this segment of their evening. They maintained their pace, waiting for the fox to fall or give the third and final signal. He cut sharply to his left, gliding on the wind and diving through a window.

"Follow my mark," Murietta whispered as she was the one furthest to the left. She once again became point of the chase as Olliento, former point after the fox's last teleport, descended to give direct chase though he did not glide so much as he streaked through the portal. Murietta focused only her natural senses. A common mistake was to extend mental awareness toward a target one could not actually see. Often such an extension took time, and a shielded mind could not perform the task quickly. Thus, many would drop their shields and pay terrible prices for the effort. But Murietta's hearing and sense of touch were enough to keep on the heels of their quarry. She could hear his feet as they lost their rhythm and his breathing increased in labor and frequency. His whimper had gained volume and desperation.

He ran down a slender corridor that must have been of sturdy make from the echo it carried to her and she could feel the vibrations of his running through her feet as she ran along the roof.

What she did not expect was her sense of smell to pick up anything! He was inside a building and two flights beneath them. Still, there was no time to question what she felt.

"Guard!" she cried as she jumped up.

"Loose!" another voice called out and four men stood up to the far right of the two women, firing their bows. Murietta was their target as she had no ground from which to enable a decent dodge. But that is what someone was meant to think. Salkathi grunted as she made a V-shaped wind vortex in between her sister and the archers. It was enough to take on the arrows and blow them wide right and left, up and down.

"Strike!" Murietta screamed as she threw four Edges. None of the bowmen even thought to move as they could still feel the vortex between them and the female soldier. The only problem with their deduction was that the vortex was a complete system and from Murietta's side, it increased the speed of whatever she chose to throw into it. The four Edges struck true and all four bowmen fell dead or dying, each completely penetrated by the well-thrown weapons. "Return!" Murietta yelled as she jumped off the side of the building, her four weapons following closely behind her. By the time she caught the third and fourth Edges, having returned the first two to their scabbards, she was landing on the ledge of the building and setting herself to attack. The window shattered and the fox came diving out.

"Defend!" she could hear Olliento command and before the word had passed through her ears, her downward stabbing grips were reversed. The fox was surrounded by metal debris; they must have passed through the dwelling of an artisan, one who worked with silver from the look of it, but it mattered little. What mattered were the missiles that were formed and sent at Murietta who kept her place on the ledge as she deflected seven of the thirty-two projectiles consigned to her destruction. Two she avoided by kneeling on the ledge, and the others were the stuff of the anxious warrior who could not tell what would have missed had they just held their ground. But she could see that the fox had only employed half of the total potential missiles. Sure enough, Olliento came diving through the window, his Staffling held close to the chest, running down the length of his body with the other end between his feet. The second half of the quickly forged projectiles flew back at Olliento who broke his diving form to spin his Staffling, and his body carried through the air. Murietta knew the man could hold his own but that did not make his applications with his favored weapon any less entertaining. He deflected each projectile, and the fox had obviously put more effort into killing Olliento as only ten schards were sure misses. In the end, it meant nothing as Olliento was unharmed. His balance and awareness were incredible! The last projectile he did not deflect so much as he redirected and it lodged into the quarry's left calf. There was a scream of pain and instead of landing on the next building, the fox collided with its ledge. But their quarry did not fall, not so much as it screamed, a hard-thrown Edge pinning the left arm to the ledge. Olliento winced as he landed in the alley between the buildings, bounding up to the roof of the next, and landing just after Murietta.

"And thy sister?"

"I am here, Master Warrior," she called out, carrying the man who had commanded the archers. He was bleeding and unconscious. "Extra weight slowed my progress."

"Thy reason is accepted, Salkathi," Olliento replied, looking around. Murietta had gathered up the fox and smiled at her sister as Olliento's grip on his weapon tightened. The chase was over and he had yet to receive a scratch. This was too easy!

[*Well done, Fairies*!] a voice projected to their minds. It was meant to be a painful message to receive, but they were too defensive to be caught unawares. Still all three grabbed their heads and fell to their knees.

"Attack!" a male voice cried out as five *Deviants* lifted their curtain of invisibility. There were five, a Man-Lord Death Fist deployment.

"Thou hast grown too bold, *Deviants*!" Olliento warned as he thrust his staff into the roof. The next moment, the entire roof caved in and each body that stood upon it plummeted. Olliento reached the next floor first and landed in a kneeling stance, thrusting his Staffling even harder, causing the next two floors to give.

"Salkathi, take these two and follow thy orders," he directed as he threw his Staffling down at an angle. His other hand reached out and Murietta was quick to take it. The Death Fist stopped their fall before they had fallen one floor and floated.

"Ah, now they are easy targets!" Olliento said as he grabbed the end of his Staffling, now wedged into the wall, and swung Murietta and himself up toward the Man-Lords. She still had two Edges drawn, cutting one across the small of the back and another across the face as her legs locked around the neck of a third. As she swung around, choking her victim, she threw her two Edges which each hit home in the chest. Olliento was still ascending when something hit him hard and fast! His back met with the second floor and went through to the ground floor which did not give, and it was all Olliento could do not to lose consciousness.

"So glad not to disappoint thee," the man who now stood on top of him said as he jumped up, drew two Blades and came plunging down.

Still falling quickly, Murietta knew the risks but she knew in reversed situations, Olliento would not have waited this long. She closed her eyes and braced for impact. She teleported, changing her location but not her velocity or momentum. Her shoulder met with one of Olliento's and he was pushed out of the way of the two swords meant for his face and chest. The wielder of the Blades hissed. Murietta rolled to a stop and quickly put her hand to her shoulder.

"If thou seekest an easy kill, proceed toward me!" she said low and coldly.

"The only thing to entice me more than one dead *Fairie* is two brought to their demise!"

"How goes the shoulder? All healed?" he asked.

"Healed enough, *Deviant*!" she growled as she stood up.

"Then let us begin this gambol of anguish!" he called back, stepping into the light he had generated. Murietta could not see the color of his eyes, but she could see steel in his glare. Steel and ambition, a very dangerous combination. He was slender but she could still see a well-defined musculature holding on to the Blade/Edge combination he seemed to favor. He walked as if he was a master, but aside from a blindsiding attack, he had displayed no prowess she could not thwart.

"Thou art not man enough to lead me in any dance. Yet let us embrace all the same," Murietta said as she charged. He responded in kind and they ran down the corridor of the shambled building toward each other. Murietta knew she had one pass, maybe two if she was fast enough. After that, the Man-Lords she had marked would have fully recovered from Olliento's genius opening move.

"*Take a different path*," she remembered the lessons of her Captain. "*One which is thine own!*"

"Haa!" she screamed as she jumped up to the wall and ran along it, her body completely horizontal. The sudden change in perspective did not have the full effect she was hoping for. She wanted to surprise her opponent, and that she had achieved. But instead of trying to figure out how to fight someone coming at him the way Murietta was, he decided to destroy the wall instead. She was caught in the energy blast and the portions of stone and mortar that made up the debris. She fell to the floor, stunned. Jumping again, the slender man sheathed his weapons and landed next to Murietta. He did not know that *Fairies* could be so comely. She was breath-taking; as he slowly moved his hand toward her face, a Staffling hammered down on his hand. He screamed in pain and nearly choked when the Staffling was thrust into his open mouth and the back of his head thrust into a wall. Before he hit the floor, Olliento had collected Murietta and was running down the street, his chest and back aching. Now *this* had been a deployment! Should he be able to shake the *Deviants* from keeping in his trail, he could return to his Captain with a light and sated heart. The chase had been reversed and now he was the fox, but *Deviants* were not trained hounds, simply dogs of the worst sort and after one leap and a short range teleportation (called a *slide*), he had enough time to stop, take good hold of Murietta and teleport to his maximum distance (called a *jump*). At that point he was able to generate enough power to replenish his reserves and restore Murietta and himself. When she awoke, she had no questions, Olliento offered no answers.

"'Twould be most unwise to keep the Captain waiting," he said as he started back for the inner city. Murietta looked up into the sky and saw only the clear night of stars. She breathed easier after that; Salkathi was alive and no doubt had delivered the collected parcels of the chase to Mevkrean. They walked a few strides before they accelerated to a jog. An equal count strides jogging and the two broke into a sprint. Two slides and they were again on the rooftops, jumping and riding the wind.

Twenty-Two

Sugar rounded the curve without her tires making a sound and he smiled. It was good to get out and just be again. Deep down he knew opportunities like this would be few and far between so his foot became heavier. The next turn was not as quiet and the one after that inspired a screaming competition between William and the tires on his car. The tires were louder, but as the road eventually straightened, William's cry was longer and definitely more exuberant. He wondered how many lawns he would have to rake clean to earn enough money for another set of tires. There was no way Gordon was going to pay for another set so soon after getting the last set. It would be expensive, but with the drive not yet over, he already felt like it was worth the price.

"*And the lights are on,*" he thought as he pulled into the short driveway. "*So long as there are no arrow-firing landscapers, I should be okay.*" He picked up the smaller of the two bunches of flowers and headed toward the front door which was already opening.

"I can't see you today, William!" she yelled. "Please, don't come any closer." William stopped and looked at the woman and in that moment of wanting to know, his senses opened up.

Cigar smoke, peculiar cigarette smoke and muffled footfalls. As he looked at her, he saw a shadow behind her that was much too large to be one of the neighborhood's stray cats that she took in from time to time.

Too late! It was too late to say anything. Too much had happened. Too much they had both changed. That was what he was meant to believe.

"Please, no closer," she repeated.

"No closer so I can't see your eyes or no closer so you can't see mine?" he replied, quickly holding up his hand and waving at her. "Wow, did that come out of my mouth? I'm sorry, Rachel. The environment's changing on me and it has its gives and gets. I'm poppin' off attitude to my elders like nobody's business and I don't like some of the changes happening inside my head.

"So I can see why you're not trusting of me," he continued. "I'm not too crazy about William Ferrous either.

"But I would like to think that even at my worst, both of us know I would never harm you," he said warmly and when he saw her eyes close, he approached her. "I won't come around anymore, I promise. But allow me this goodbye, please."

"William!" she whispered and he ran to her, wrapping his arms around her shoulders. Hers went around his ribs and she cried on his shoulder. "I'm so sorry, William!"

"Me too, Rach. Me too!" He kissed her head and slowly pulled back from her. Her grip did not lessen and he fully understood. He gripped the flowers harder and Rachel's hand fell over his. His muscles relaxed but his anger was still growing. Their eyes met and the gentle William was gone! "And you tell-" he looked at her and something held his voice in check. Beneath the tears her eyes were pleading with him.

"*More thought. Less emotion,*" he thought as he handed her the flowers.

"Tell your niece what could have been."

"You bastard!" she cried, slapping him hard across the face and William smiled, rubbing where she struck him.

"Like aunt, like niece!" Rachel turned on her heels and went back in her house, slamming the door behind her. He could hear her crying as he stared at the house with hatred spread thick across his face.

"What did he mean by that?" a man said. He was heavy set and nervous, very nervous.

"My niece and he… were acquainted for a time," Rachel cried.

"Ended on a slap, did it?"

"Obviously not hard enough," Rachel replied.

"*He's armed,*" William guessed. "*And he thinks the gun will solve his problem, if there is one. Yeah, better off leaving,*" he surmised, walking back to the car. "*Of course, I wonder what they'd do with a handful of Prodigians raiding that house and making their worst nightmares look like a day at Six Flags!*"

"*But I don't have a crew like that,*" he reminded himself as he got into the car and started the engine. "*Not yet, anyway,*" he allowed himself a devilish smile as he pulled forward and then turned the wheel to pull out on to the street, going through Rachel's flower garden. There was no sense in lessening the ruse.

"Whoa! Somebody is pissed!" Brooks said as he blew out the smoke from his clove cigarette. "Right through the flowers."

"What?!" Rachel said as she charged the window. She parted the drapes and screamed. She pounded on the window and Antal grabbed the woman to keep her from hurting herself. "That black, sorry son-of-a-freak! I'll kill him. Call the police!"

"Now that we can't do," Cole said, getting up from his chair. He set eyes on Redding and tried not to display his apathy. He was one of those classic survival types but he had justification for all of the weapons he carried.

Redding had been in the Army when he met his first Prodigian. A Man-Lord seeking refuge from the Territories. A rare case inasmuch as

Man-Lords typically respond to their problems with violence. But this young lady had been a convert and the rest of her family was still Light-Child. Amos Redding and his platoon came to know first hand what the unchecked wrath of a *Deviant* can do. Amos and his lieutenant had been the only survivors and Redding had killed the man to earn entry into the Descriers. He had piled up more time in the hospital than all the linemen of any three college teams. His inventory was always being depleted and though he had only two kills (one of them being his Lieutenant), he had a very interesting capacity for survival. But Cole was just beginning to find his balance with Brooks when the call came in, delivered by the gray-eyed Redding, as they were driving to the Pryor household. The latest recruit had already gone rogue and every agent was given clearance for a kill.

"But what I can do is-"

"You can tell me what I can do to help you!" Rachel barked, still being held by Brooks. "He's an alien, isn't he?"

"The first thing you can do is calm down, Dr. Pryor," Cole answered, waving off Brooks. "Or we can simply leave and let you handle this matter the best way you see fit."

Rachel was confused as she looked at each of the men. The one who spoke was not bluffing. "What sort of cop are you?

"One who never took an oath to protect and serve!" Redding answered, running his hand over his buzz cut brown hair. He moved closer to Rachel in an effort to intimidate the woman with his stature.

"*I know a young man who would eat your lunch if I but asked him too,*" Rachel thought as she looked down and Cole waved Redding off as he approached and took a very gentle hold of Rachel, massaging her shoulders.

"I understand you're upset," Cole said with a warm smile. "You trusted him and he lied to you. He's been lying to you all this time... that's what they do, Dr. Pryor."

"What can I do?" Rachel said in a calmer voice. "I really want to help."

"You can start by telling us everything you know about William Anthony Ferrous," Cole said, looking over at Brooks who already had out his recorder.

Rachel walked over to her chair and sat down. She thought for a moment. "*My but aren't we up for the Oscar?*" she pondered. "*That's the flower garden he planted and I haven't been able to grow a rose in that thing for years.*"

"*Like aunt, like niece indeed!*" she thought and had to fight the urge to smile. "*But he gave me an avenue, one I can add a couple of lies to and make it look awfully honest and true. Well done, William. I know you had a* great deal to tell me, bringing me flowers! Your mind was not on your destination and that means you had a lot on your mind.

"Well, now we both do!" she thought, looking at her three so-called friends. She cleared her throat and started her story with the science fair. Somewhere in between that and what she would describe as a near psychotic breakdown, she would recommend they use her house a base of operations.

"As if nearly being wiped out twice in one night wasn't enough!" William yelled as soon as he felt far enough from Rachel's house. Again he was driving fast, but not for enjoyment, now it was a means to contend with his impulse to drive back, shatter the door and kill the three people who had Rachel under thumb.

"And then there's the obvious question," he said aloud. "The one that comes after 'who the hell are these people' and that is 'what in the world do they want'?" It was that last point that brought his foot up from the accelerator and down on the brake.

"Yeah, what do they want? They let me drive away." He looked in his rear view mirror and then turned around in the seat. "And it doesn't look like they're following me."

"You looking for a kingdom in this neighborhood?" a voice called out to William, but the sound did not reach his mind.

"*Of course, it is a major assumption that this has anything to do with me,*" William thought as he got out of the car. He walked toward the rear of the car and leaned against the trunk door, one hand on his chin, the other supporting the former. "*No, she was trying to protect me from whatever was in the house. It has something to do with me, alright. And I can lean towards concluding it wasn't any of the Prodigian,*" he added. "*They tend to judge and shoot first, before they actually get around to dialog.*"

"William?" the voice called to him again.

"So something new," he whispered. "Something new has been added to the game. Another damn angle. Great! Haven't even figured out the ones that have been trying to kill me so far!"

"Hey you!" Linda yelled and William jumped. He turned to see Linda's limousine just setting there beside his Sugar, and he never noticed her drive up.

"Linda!" William said with a smile. "I was just on my way to see you!"

"Yeah, sure you were," she said getting out of the car. "Hughes, I think I can count on Mr. Ferrous to give me a ride home," she said, looking at William. "Right?"

"Definitely!" William answered, nodding.

"Very well, Miss Rasner," Hughes said as he drove off.

The two stood there, taking turns looking at each other, saying nothing but meaning everything. For Linda, the dream had been only a few moments ago and was still ongoing. William was nothing like she thought, and beyond what she thought she wanted. She had sent him flowers to show her gratitude for a wonderful evening, even though her mother told her it was too much; and here he was, leaning against his car just a few blocks away from her house. What was he coming to say to her? Why wouldn't he say it now?

"*Look at her,*" he thought. "*Okay, now I get it,*" he discovered. "*Now I know why the hero keeps secrets like this from his... was I about to say girlfriend?*"

"*But how can I throw her into this? Those people aren't hinged the same way the rest of us are. They can justify the most barbaric crap in the name of council and king. Fanatic spelled any differently is still someone without a means to make their beliefs make sense. And I'm surrounded by a lot of them! If anything, the number seems to be growing. Now I have to ask myself what sort of fanatic has a hold of Rachel?*"

"The old woman is another matter, Kador," a voice responded, and again William jumped, though this time he had company. She stood just in front of the tree line, wrapped in an old brown cloak that seemed to blend with the trees behind her; the wind did not move it. Her black hair was cut short and combed to where it stayed frizzy, with a natural spiking curl. Her skin was just a shade darker than Linda's and her eyes were nearly black, but seemed to be turning lighter to a soft hazel-brown.

"Curse thee for a fool if thou art not like thy father. Stride for stride!" she said as she stepped away from the trees, her cloak shifting from a dark brown to a black.

"Uh, William," Linda said.

"Get behind me, Linda!" William said, taking a step forward, lifting his fists and preparing to move defensively. He could not afford to duck with Linda behind him. He kept his eyes on the woman but looked for other possible attackers.

"Ah, look 'pon this!" the woman shouted with a hearty laugh. "Thy answer comes to thee!"

"William, is this supposed to be funny?"

The woman put her hand to her mouth and it seems as if she coughed. She then massaged the front of her neck.

"Linda, I swear this is not a joke," William answered, realizing the woman was alone, like Yudara, like Cov!

"Maybe this will be easier for your ears, sweetheart," the woman said, sounding as if she just stepped out of a television family show. "As many times as I have visited, I do forget to make certain adjustments, I do ask for your forgiveness," she said softly while bowing. William did not relax but he did lower his hands. The woman smiled at the lowering fists and nodded slightly.

"Yes, you are so much like your Father. You do his dreams a great deal of justice, William."

"Oh, so not even Kador anymore?" William asked.

"I was simply trying to make everyone comfortable," she replied. "I meant no offense. But if I may say, neither of you are making this easy. You're ready to drive those potent little hands into my face and that one back there is ready to hit me with a mace."

William blinked and almost smiled, realizing what the woman meant. "She's not packing a metal club in her purse. Mace is the name of a spray that burns the face, stings the eyes, smells horrible, makes for a seriously unpleasant experience."

"Like Dire Dust then?" the woman asked.

"Yes, something like that," William answered, recollecting the mixture. "Just no glass."

"William, what the hell is this about?" Linda was losing patience.

"This is about me being very, very rude, Miss. You see, William was weighing his options in regards to you and I believe he was about to make a very bad move."

"And where do you get off?!" William barked and the woman's eyes flared at him.

"Right about here, Kadorgyan!" William tried to move forward but fell unconscious. Linda started to scream but her body locked.

"No, no. no. Please, no screaming," she pleaded, her eyes again flaring. She approached Linda and removed her glove, touching her flesh to the young woman's. In an instant she knew Linda and let Linda know her. Like his father, Kador was attracted to the fair skin as well as the dark. It had been her experience that the darker skinned Tyros possessed ever so much more passion and were therefore ideal candidates for training in the use of psionics. But this one was strong, like Kador's mother and the woman had already been proven wrong when she assumed Adrianna's limitations. Her eyes relaxed and Linda's body was released.

"Forgive the invasion of thought, but my means of information exchange is so much more expedient."

"That's not all it is," Linda answered, rubbing her temples.

"My apologies, I often forget my own strength," the woman answered, walking over to William.

"So you're something of an aunt to William?"

"When I can afford to be," she answered, kneeling down. She reached out to touch William's face but her hand was trembling. Already it was trembling! "Dammit!"

"You have to leave soon, don't you?"

"Do not play the silly girl with me, child!" she warned. "I am not drawn in by your favors."

"I'm sorry," Linda replied, looking down. She jumped when William got up and walked toward the car, his eyes still closed.

"No, you're scared and you damn well ought to be! But that doesn't change what you know. It is now a matter of what you will do with it."

"This is a lot to take in," Linda said.

"No argument there," she agreed as William got in the car and started the engine.

"Wait!" Linda yelled.

"My time is short," the woman replied.

"I know." Linda ran to the car and opened the door. She touched William's face and kissed him on the mouth. "To think we were joking about you being a king. Oh my God, William!" Linda closed the door and stepped away from the car.

Another flaring of the older woman's eyes and William's eyes opened. He put the car in gear and drove off. Linda and the woman watched the car drive out of sight.

"I will take you home," the woman offered.

"No," Linda denied, holding up her hand. "I'm going to need the walk."

"So he's just going to think that-"

"That he came out to see you and you two talked, enjoyed each other's company and he drove home, forgetting to give you the flowers."

"He brought me flowers?" The woman sighed and turned to the wood. "You did all of this but you don't believe in Tyros any more than any of your people do."

"That boy's father believed in your kind and I more than believe in him!" the woman scolded. "Mark where you place your assertions, child!" She turned again and took a step forward but her left leg was beginning to fail and she tried to steady herself on a tree but the effort was a quickly failing one.

"C'Silla!" Linda yelled, rushing to aid the woman. She managed to crouch low enough to get her shoulder under the woman's arm. "I've got you!" Two more unsteady steps and Linda closed her eyes and stood up, bringing the woman up with her.

"I should say you do have me... woman!"

"Now don't going playing old soft dying woman on me," Linda urged.

"It is no game I play."

"Now see, that's where you're wrong, and you of all people should know it."

"Then you've made your decision?" C'Silla asked.

"Can't say that I have," Linda answered. "Right now I am not sure if that was a kiss goodbye I gave him or not. I just don't know."

"Not knowing is always a good place to start," C'Silla said, taking out a red-glowing gem and looking up. "Bring me back, brothers." C'Silla started to fade quickly as she looked again on Linda.

[*For your information,*] she projected, [*the wrong decision he was about to make... was that he should make your decision for you. I have not helped you, Linda, Blood of Rasner; I have wounded you and turned your perspective so that you will do on the morrow what you did last night.*]

"And just what was that?" Linda yelled as C'Silla faded from sight. "What exactly did I do?!"

[*You made him, child! You made him... complete!*]

Twenty-Three

The doors opened as Sabrina approached. She looked up at the archway and shook her head, adjusting her glasses. Apparently the Research and Development wing had a new name. 'R and D' was no longer adequate and they came up with a new name. Something the geeks thought would be more in line with the theme of the organization.

"Summer Camp?" she whispered. "Jesus Christ!"

"Careful, you don't know if that was on the list," Hubris added under a muffled chuckle.

"How'd you like to fly a console for twelve hours?" Sabrina threatened and Hubris choked before he stopped altogether. She quickly walked through the wing to where she could hear the machinery. She said a silent prayer as she stuffed her hands into the pockets of her lab coat. She approached another set of doors that did not open automatically.

"Sabrina Bey," she said but the doors did not budge and she huffed out a sharp breath.

"I swear I hate hackers!" she said before she leaned over to the wall microphone. "The Slugger's Wife!" The doors opened quickly and Sabrina walked in, noting what she would do with the salaries of all the idiots who were undoubtedly gawking at her on the other side of the tracking cameras.

"Where is Alpha Scout?" she shouted to one of the technicians who did not hesitate to point to one bay in particular.

"They're working on him in Bay Four," he said in a clear voice and Sabrina's brown eyes focused on his name plate, one she could have missed as it was so small in comparison to the chest it rested on.

"*Thor?*" she thought. "*Interesting, albeit hauntingly accurate. Oh well, it takes all kinds.*"

"Are you sure you want to do this?" Hubris asked, walking a little quicker to be directly at her side. He did not say anything else. Her face translated her silence into an emphatic 'no' with a warning that pressing the issue might lead to an unwanted level of physical punishment.

"Dear God," she gasped as the last door opened. She could not only hear the machinery, she could see it too. There was nothing in what she saw that looked anything like a Multi-Frame. The metal was torn and twisted, fused together in places where it should not have been.

She had reviewed the logs five times. Alpha had done everything by the book and in a couple of cases a little faster than the book said he would be able to perform with his Multi-Frame in the shape it was in. It was one thing to dog that freak for as long as he had, but to be attacked again before he could get back to the rendezvous point and by the bogey he was trailing was something totally unexpected. He had had no forewarning; his sensors were out of power. Had he been able to do a cross-wiring job through his failing battery, he would have discovered the sensor relays and apparatus had already been destroyed. But to take the Multi-Frame so deep, knowing there was a human life aboard…that was beyond inhuman!

"Do we have any life signs?" Sabrina asked the doctor.

"Believe it or not," the physician answered, "we are getting a heartbeat. A pretty strong one!"

"*Lazlo*," Sabrina thought as she stepped closer. She wanted to get a better look but she was not going to interfere with the specialists. They were getting him out and she did not want to impede their progress. All the drills and cutters were working and she knew the men and women behind those tools. She smiled, wondering in how many corporations one could find the boss doing this sort of grunt work. But there he was, Michael Canyon, going at Alpha Scout's Multi-Frame as if it was his life on the line.

"Clear!" the Native American man yelled as a large section of the Multi-Frame came free of the fuselage and fell to the floor. A section large enough for everyone to see Alpha Scout and Sabrina averted her eyes, expecting the worst.

"Fuck me!" Hubris said in a tone that did not convey horror so much as disbelief. Sabrina looked at him and saw a bright smile forming on his face. She mouthed his name as she looked at the crushed vehicle. The paramedics were helping him into a wheelchair, but he looked relatively untouched. There was some bruising, a slight cut here and there, but nothing he could not have walked away from.

"Hey darlin'," he said with a smile. He nodded at Hubris who was approaching. "Bats, how's it hangin', man?"

"A lot better now, man! Damn, how did you pull this one off?"

"Let the man have his way," Lazlo replied, hoping he never had to see one of those people ever again in life. "When I told him how tight it was in the cockpit, he smiled. Knew I was in trouble then."

"So you flipped yourself inside the cockpit?!" Hubris asked, amazed at what he was hearing.

"Sure did," Lazlo answered. "But it didn't hurt none to do some begging and screaming."

"Still putting on the convincing act, I see," Sabrina said as she approached, hands back in pockets.

"Hey boss!" Lazlo replied. "Sorry about the Multi-Frame."

"Sorry doesn't get it done down here, soldier," she replied with a smile. "We're taking this out of your pay!"

"In that case, when you do get around to saying yes to me taking you out, would you mind picking up the tab?"

"No, we're not going out," she replied adjusting her glasses. "And yes, I would very much mind picking up the tab. Now if you will excuse me, I have a report to file and a new Multi-Frame to get built."

"Sabe!" Lazlo said, holding up his hands. "What gives?"

"You want charity," declare yourself as a non-profit," Sabrina answered and turned on her heels and walked away. Her desk was waiting.

She knew what they were all muttering under their breaths. Something about her low body temperature or about her being a nursing dog. She could take that. She was also about to get her ass handed to her on a platinum platter, and she could take that too. But to have Lazlo die on her watch, during a *tag and see* mission, that was something she did not want to live with yet. She got out of Bay Four and allowed herself a moment. She lifted her glasses up to her hair and closed her eyes.

"It was a close one." She placed the voice immediately. Sylvestra Lovonki, Beta Scout. "He is lucky, sure. But don't forget that he's good and sometimes luck only comes to the skilled."

"Thanks, I needed that," Sabrina said as she was grabbed from behind and spun around. Before she knew what was happening, a pair of lips pressed down on hers. She was off balance and was about to fall when Delta Scout, Conway Patterson, wrapped his other arm around her waist. Trained for combat, Sabrina panicked and just pressed against his chest which did not budge him as the tip of his tongue touched her lips. Suddenly she stopped pushing and let out a moan that sounded like she was dizzy between being angry and passionately moved. Her mouth opened and received his tongue, touching it with the tip of hers. When hers retreated, his dashed forward. It was nearly cut off as Sabrina bit down hard. A muffled scream came first and Conway tried to push Sabrina away, only now she was holding on to him and would not be moved. He drew his hand back, made a fist and sent it forward. His wrist was caught by Sylvestra who tapped Sabrina hard on the shoulder as she twisted Conway's arm.

"Let go, he's had enough!" she sternly commanded and surprisingly Sabrina did as she was told. Sylvestra released her grip only after twisting his arm a bit more to spin him away from Sabrina as she stood between the two. "I know you can hear me," she said and Conway lunged at her, firing three straight punches and a hook. Her left hand smacked away all three straight punches and she spun to avoid the hook. She stood, her left shoulder facing him, her flight helmet still tucked under her right arm. Her form was solid but her face registered pain as she shook her head 'no'.

"You sum of a bwithch!" Conway yelled at Sabrina, his mouth bleeding. He stepped back from Sylvestra and started pacing back and forth, glaring at Sabrina.

"What the hell did I just do?" Sabrina thought as she made sure to keep Sylvestra between her and a man who could kill her in three moves... if that many! The exchange between them was just a series of blurs to her eyes. She knew they were fast, but she had never witnessed their speed. She started to consider what those reflexes were like in the Multi-Frames, but this moment had not yet passed. There was still a chance he would kill her.

"You crossed the line, she crossed you back," Sylvestra tried to reason with him. Stopping the straight punches was like trying to bend a steel rod jabbing at her. "Now that looks pretty bad. Maybe you should get that checked out."

Conway glared at Sabrina and Sylvestra kept breaking his line of vision. He knew the technique, using her body to affect his mind. The longer he was allowed to focus on her, the more he would translate his pain into focused rage. The more he could strike with the precision but without hesitation or mercy. But that time was disrupted by Sylvestra's face and all he had was pain and he the knowledge he would have to go through a wingman to get to Sabrina.

"Get to Sabrina," he thought.

"You crossed the line," Sylvestra repeated herself. "Acknowledge!" Conway continued to walk and bleed from his mouth; what was left of his tongue was throbbing. "Acknowledge, Delta Scout!" she repeated, this time pulling rank and his eyes locked on hers.

"Wait a moment," he thought. She had her right side hidden from him. She wore her sidearm on the right side. All of the MVPs were ambidextrous. Their flight suits had the guns on the right side due to the cockpit design. *"Plus she's holding on to her helmet. Alpha's already shown Lambda how effective those things can be... and I did cross."* Conway dropped his eyes and nodded as he turned and walked toward the medical wing. They were going to poke and prod him for an hour at least, but maybe he needed that time to cool off anyway.

She watched him walk away and when he was out of sight, with the sound of his footsteps getting steadily further away, Sylvestra turned to Sabrina and smiled.

"Not the brightest thing you've done in a while, is it?"

"By far it was the most-"

"Spirited," Sylvestra interrupted. "He crossed the line!" She started off toward debriefing.

"I had no idea you were the protective sort," Sabrina said and Beta Scout stopped. When she turned around, her smile was gone. *"Or am I just suicidal and don't even know it,"* she thought.

"Let's get one thing straight. When I'm supersonic and trying to avoid five missiles that all have a lock on my ass, I hear your voice calmly telling me what to do-"

"I'm only calm because I'm not in your pla-"

"And it works... and it works... and it works!" Sylvestra said calmly as she approached Sabrina. She wanted the Dugout administrator to see things the way one of the Multi-Frame pilots saw things. "I wasn't trying to protect you, I was protecting me. Having you around makes the machine work." She turned and started walking again.

"Besides, I let you answer the issue on your own, then I stepped in. You got to let a lady speak up for herself."

Sabrina found herself smiling as Beta Scout walked away. How many missions had she followed them through? How many airborne attacks? How many strikes on high security targets? Never did she think that any one of them would have to come to her rescue, let alone from another one of them.

"*Jesus, Sabe, what* were *you thinking of?*" she asked herself. The answer would have to wait as the communication device on her hip sounded off. It was not a colorful sobriquet, calling it the Hot Line, but when it went off, that was exactly what everyone had come to expect, for the temperature to go up rapidly.

"Bey here!"

"The report has been reviewed," the distant voice repeated. She often wondered if the one on the other end of the line had to consume drugs to sound so disassociated from everything.

"Say again," Sabrina requested. "The report has not yet been submitted."

"The report received from Lambda Scout has been reviewed and you have been given clearance. Your notes on the report are expected within the hour. Acknowledge!"

"*Lambda Scout,*" she thought. "*That's the Minor Leagues. They do only surveillance and low level target eliminations.*"

"This is Bey," she said clearly. "Directive received and understood. I will comply within 60 minutes. Bey out!"

Sabrina put the Hot Line Receiver away and quickly made her way to her office.

"Audio/Visual review," she said aloud and the room began to reconfigure. As she made her way to her chair, her bookshelves spun around and made a very large digital screen.

"Designate file or files?" she could hear her own recorded voice call out to her. More than anything, she wished they could change that voice for her. Throw it through a synthesizer, anything, just not make her hear herself!

"Most recent Lambda Scout submitted report, please," she replied, taking a seat in her chair. Her hands were scanned, along with her eyes, her voice, and eventually a hair sample. Eventually she was given clearance and the playback opened up on Lambda Scout and his backup Rho Beta Scout, a virtual rookie in the ranks, as they were getting on their motorcycles.

"*Poor Lambda,*" she thought, looking at the quite regular mode of transportation. But it was not as if he had never been warned. But when people such as these were created, a certain amount of will comes with every successful mission. Lambda had bought into the God Complex so all of Sabrina's warnings were ignored. Gifted she may have been but she was still mortal. Lambda failed to listen to her and eventually the warnings were no longer off record. He had been counseled but again by only mere mortals. He never listened, and so a price had to be paid. She had seen other MVPs taken down and then literally taken apart for doing far less. But Lambda Scout was a favorite to the Owners. Sabrina was sure he would be back in the Majors before too long.

As Lambda turned his head, she could see that they were at the airport and had made contact with their surveillance target. Lambda zoomed in and took a picture of the woman.

"*Okay, now I know why the clearance on this got bumped up,*" Sabrina concluded as she saw Lambda received the picture and run a check for identification. A check that came back: Unknown Entity. "This cannot end well!" she muttered, wishing she at least had some popcorn for this one.

A flashing red arrow pointing to the right appeared in the bottom right hand corner signifying that the report had already been viewed and this section was deemed as something that could be passed over. Sabrina seldom subscribed to report editors. They were in positions of such little power that they tended to flex their muscles too much whenever given the chance. When the red arrow flashed, Sabrina scrambled to find the remote control so that she could slow down the picture. In doing do, she found her gigantic tin of flavored popcorn, the buttered variety already depleted. She smiled at her remaining choices: caramel and cheddar cheese.

"Leave it to me to get rid of the boring stuff first," she said, picking up the tin and finding the remote control. With her shoes off and feet up on the edge of her chair, Sabrina held the remote control and a handful of cheddar popcorn. She slowed the playback and started to eat.

"*Hmmm,*" she chewed, "*Heading northwest from Rotterdam.*" Sabrina looked at the ceiling and blinked twice. "*Monster,*" she concluded, finding the word somewhat amusing.

After a long ride made longer by Sabrina's remote, Lambda finally came to a stop in the small township of Monster. He kept straight when the car he was tailing made a left. It was a smart move. At that point, going too far after a left turn put you into the North Sea. And this was an MVP after all. He looked to see if there were any potential witnesses. Sabrina gave him the go ahead before his helmet did. He signaled his partner to take hold of his bike and Lambda Scout took a dive off a motorcycle doing about forty miles per hour. He rolled when he hit the ground and on the second roll he bound up and over a parked car, landing on the sidewalk. Running at full stride he jumped again and put two good steps up the side of a wall, his hands catching the edge of the roof nearly three stories up. From the roof, Lambda quickly drew focus on the car pulling into a large church. He took a look at the church and ran another search. The church was immediately put under a yellow veil. It was reported that the church had been demolished, but that report was over four years old. The building looked to be much older than four years but its denomination was listed as Roman-Catholic.

"This is getting sticky," Lambda whispered.

"No kidding," Sabrina agreed, knowing that particular section of the city followed the Muslim faith. But it did not get any stickier for either of them. The flashing red arrows appeared again and Sabrina slowed the playback again and again she did not gain any information. The editors were not always wrong but it was not worth risking significant data.

And then it all happened. It happened so fast, Sabrina thought she was watching one of the Minor League Rookies trying to make a name for themselves. The mystery woman came out and this time Lambda was able to get a good look at the man with her.

"You have got to be shitting me!" Lambda whispered, getting the report that Peter Webster, a recently retired Special Agent of the Federal Bureau of Investigations, was in the Netherlands less than twenty-four hours after being retired.

"Yeah, Lamb, somebody's shittin' ya!" Sabrina said swallowing a mouthful of popcorn and pausing the playback. "Bio-file," she said aloud and the file for Peter, no middle name, Webster came up.

"Interesting, an inside Federal Snitch assigned to a Lydia Diane King as she was investigating..." Sabrina dropped the remote and her popcorn.

"Verify status of FBI Case File LA6-97889," Sabrina ordered as she approached the screen.

"The status shown has been verified," her voice replied.

"Status and location of Lambda?"

"Status, operational. Location, London, England. Be advised, Lambda Scout has another report to file."

"Yeah, I just bet he does," Sabrina said as she moved back to her chair. "Reconfigure office to daily format and get me a secure line to the Owners," Sabrina commanded. "I'm going to need clearance to recall

Lambda to the Major League without taking him off his current assignment. I will also need an ETA for Delta Scout's recovery ASAP!"

"Please state reason for function outside normal procedure," her voice had never been so irritating.

"What are you, fucking blind? There is an FBI file we don't have access to! Just how many of those do you know of?"

"Counting this one, four, but two of those files originated with the Dugout."

"Exactly, you idiot, and the fourth one was never filed electronically. If we can't hack those files, we'll need to send a recon team to snatch that info straight out of Quantico!"

"Reason received, understood and my programming agrees with your need for the requested action."

"Well, now that I have your permission," Sabrina said, leaving the office. She was going to the medical wing to get some drugs. She was not going to be sleeping for some time and the Ballpark was calling her name.

Twenty-Four

"Are you sure you want to do this, baby?" Adrianna said as she walked into the room, her most comfortable chair floating in behind her. William looked at her telekinetically carrying the chair and smiled. "What?"

"You are just enjoying the hell out of yourself, aren't you?" William chuckled.

Adrianna quickly adopted the *'I don't know what you mean'* look, but she looked back at the floating chair and let a smile escape as she turned back to her son. "Yeah, I kinda am!"

"Sorry I curbed your style, Mom," William said softly as he layd back on his bed.

"There's no way you can convince a parent that their child curbed their style," she answered him, cutting off all of the electrical lights and setting fire to twenty candles places all about the room. The windowsill, the bookshelf, the dressers, the headboard and his desk were all aglow with the softest of light.

"Alright, I withdraw the apology."

"Thank you," she smiled, touching her hand to his face and then using her fingers to guide his eyes closed.

"We're just going to jump into it, huh?" William asked, taking deep breaths.

"There are some things you are going to need to reconsider, son." Adrianna sat in her chair and looked at her incense burner that was between two candles on the headboard of William's bed. It did not take it long for it to start producing smoke and with another application of talent the smoke was ushered about the room. "One of those is the preclusion that you must always get ready for something.

"There are some feats of skill and power that do require extra effort, but some things, like relaxing, should be kept simple. You don't go through deep breaths just to run a pass route, do you?"

"Really all depends on what down it is," William answered. He smiled when he heard his mother chuckle.

"Okay, fair enough, but I think you get my point."

"Don't make it any bigger than it is," William said softly.

"Exactly," Adrianna said, sitting back in her chair. "Okay, shields are up, Gordon and Joshua are on guard downstairs."

"You brought that kid over?" William was surprised.

"Actually, he came over to check on me and asked if he could be of any help."

"Kid's sloppy," William remarked.

"You're no Grand Master yourself, *kid*!"

"Oh, nice try Ma! You know my moves are- OWW!" William's body jumped as Adrianna made her connection.

"What's wrong, Grand Master?" Adrianna chided. "Am I coming on too strong for you?"

"Then again," William said in a softer tone. "The kid's got marvelous potential!"

"Better!"

"*Much better than you know, my son,*" she thought, doing her best to insure their connection was one way. "*Oww? That was one of my better shots and all he had to say was oww?*"

[*You're pretty heavily guarded,*] William projected. [*Something I should know?*]

[*We don't really know what we're getting into here,*] Adrianna answered. [*I want to come as close as I can to masking my presence just in case this place you spoke of has its own defenses.*]

[*Just in case?*] William asked. [*You know that these days I know when you're lying or coming out with a convenient truth.*] A darkness swept over both of them and Adrianna gripped the arms of her chair.

[*William?*] She reached out for him but could not feel him. She could not feel anything! [*William!*] But there was no response from her son and Adrianna was lost in the darkness, screaming out against the nothingness as she felt herself falling.

[THOU ART AFRAID!] a voice called out in her mind and she recognized it immediately. It was the voice from her best and most sacred memories.

"Zargo?" she cried out, releasing her fear and taking in the essence that surrounded her. She closed her eyes as the blackness under her eyelids was more tender and defined than the one she plummeted through. "No, my late husband. I have never known fear whenever you were around."

[ADRIANNA! MY WIFE! THOU ART PERMITTED ENTRY HERE BUT I CAUTION THEE... FOR IN MY LABOR I DID FORGE FATE HARD TO PROTECT OUR SACRED PROMISE.]

"Our promise to each other was that life would spring from us," Adrianna remembered as the falling sensation slowly passed and she could feel solid ground beneath from her feet.

[INDEED! NOW OPEN THINE EYES AND SEE HOW THE PROMISE HATH BEEN KEPT!]

She looked upon a vast and clear sky that matched the color of her eyes. A breeze blew across her face and she closed her eyes, taking in the scent of the flowers. She giggled and shook her head.

"Lilies," she whispered as she turned to her left and opened her eyes. A man stood by his cart selling herbs and vegetables. Among many of his offerings were several varieties of lilies. Adrianna gasped at the detail of it all. The clothes everyone wore, including herself, felt so real she nearly forgot she was inside of her son's mind.

"Zargo, what have you done?"

"There you are!" William called out. Mother turned to look at her son and her face was lit with happiness and wonder. William was at a steady jog, looking magnificent and innocent. But as William drew closer, he found that his mother's smile had faded and her eyes glowed with quickly generated psionic energy.

"Kador, get down!" Adrianna yelled as she concentrated on her target. Not knowing what was the matter, William went down quickly, dragging Cov down after him. An act she was not expecting and the confusion stayed her energy crackling-hand. "Get away from my son!" she commanded, her voice echoed as the power she had assembled drew thought of is own and mimicked her voice and her words.

Very quick on the uptake, William got to his feet quickly and held up his hands for his mother to stop. "Wait! Mom, wait! Cov is with me, with us."

"What?!" the glow in her eyes decreased, but did not fade altogether. Cov was a little slower to stand and his attention was on neither his friend nor his mother.

"Perhaps this be not th-"

"Dude," William interrupted Cov, "...yours is so not the voice she needs to hear right now!"

[*Thine ears hath yet to speak to thine eyes!*] Cov projected to William's and Adrianna's minds and mother and son immediately looked around to see the people, who had been passing by without notice, suddenly gathered in great numbers, each citizen bearing a stone and draconian intentions.

"Whatever you do," Adrianna said, turning her back to her son, "...going too far up will take you away from this place so watch your elevation."

"Been there, done that," William answered, mirroring his mother's move. He grabbed Cov and pulled him back to stand behind him. The late Guardsman was at the very least surprised.

"And we don't want to kill anyone," Adrianna added. "Because while I have been to phantasms before, this one has a level of detail I've never experienced."

"Indeed!" Cov added.

"And we don't know what killing one of these people might set off."

"Well," William said, stretching his neck, "if we aren't going to stand and fight, we need to move. You two think you can keep up?"

[*Have a care, master*,] Cov projected. [*Thou are still untrained!*]

"Just try your best, Cov," Adrianna replied as she turned in the same direction as her son. "I've got your block, you run the route!"

"Hike!" William yelled, exploding into a run of such power and speed that Cov was surprised. Still he managed to engage his legs to follow and he could hear Adrianna on his heels.

[*I shall shield us!*] he projected, lifting a shield of telekinetic energy around the three.

"Shield yourself!" William yelled as he plunged into the crowd. The barrier just in front of him served as a wonderful battering ram and moved the crowd to the left, right and back. He had a forward lean to his gait and his stance was lowered. "It's getting in my way!"

"But-"

"Do it!" Adrianna ordered. "I think I know what he's doing.

"Sneaky little bastard!" she whispered under hear breath.

Cov removed the dome shield and turned his talents to augment his body to keep up with William who was beginning to pull away. He also applied power to his senses so he could become more aware of any stones hurled at William.

Adrianna smiled as her suspicions slowly became fact as the crowd could not begin throwing stones for fear of hitting an innocent. Her eyes flared wide when the crowd began to part more quickly and William turned to the closer of the two walls.

"Get them!" he yelled, pointing down the street. "Infidels! Blasphemers!" First one, then another actually looked to where William was pointing. And there, in the middle of the street and a good fifty meters away, stood a young man who was buying bread. He turned to see the commotion and William pointed at him and screamed in a righteous rage.

[*Time for you to feel afraid!*] William projected and the young man dropped his parcels, breaking into a run that would rival an Olympic athlete. Instead of being chased, the three of them became mixed in with the crowd.

The mob was mindless and would have chased a feather had it trembled enough. They began to throw their stones with all the strength they could muster.

[*Now*,] William projected to Cov, [*if you want to protect someone, those stones need to miss!*]

[*I hear and I obey!*] Cov answered, dropping his shield and adding enough of a push or pull to make the few close-falling stone miss greatly. [*Thou art a genius!*]

[*We'll see*,] William replied as he guided the three into an alley.

"Okay, Mom, anybody who knows that kid needs to forget this moment."

Adrianna smiled as she closed her eyes. "That I can do."

"Cov, when he gets to the end of this street, he needs to be invisible. Then suggest to him to make a good left turn into a safe alley."

"It shall be done," Cov replied, also closing his eyes.

Just to be on the safe side, William stepped away from the two as they put their talents to use. He turned to face them, lifted his hands up and lowered his head, taking a pose of prayer. No sooner had he begun to mumble, five men stopped in the mouth of the alley and looked at the three of them. They started to yell when the lead man held out his arm to stop the others and they also took the pose of prayer.

"Guide us, our father," William said aloud, "as we are besieged by infidels who seek to taint us!"

"Father!" one man called out.

"To weaken our faith!"

"Heavenly Father!" another cried.

"To take thy children from thy bosom and feed them poisoned milk."

"Poison!" a man yelled as he started rocking back and forth.

But William did not open his eyes to see any of them. He could not. In the midst of feigning what he believed the others needed to see, something inside of him was triggered. It was not the fruit of any subconscious mode of instruction. Nor was it anything he had gained from his recent plight. He was confused because what he felt did not come from his mind... it came from him! Something had happened that he could not have predicted. He felt them! It was not his mind that detected them, for he was not engaged in anything mental. But still he felt them.

"My God!" he whispered and his exclamation was followed by much of the same as the five grew to twelve and even more were beginning to gather.

[*Whose side are you on?*] Adrianna projected to her son. [*The boy is in the clear. A bit confused, and still very much afraid of everything, but he'll be okay.*]

William opened his eyes and nearly screamed as he looked on his mother. She was on fire but she did not burn, and the fire was not a normal color but more like the color of her eyes. Shifting his eyes over to Cov, his fire was blood red and almost too small to see.

"God protect us as we seek to protect ourselves," he said, turning to face the crowd. Their fires were like Cov's but each one was stronger than the Guardsman's and they cheered William and his words. "Now go to the east and if you see him not, know that he has left this place and be at peace."

"But surely he will return!" a man yelled, gaining some support in the crowd.

"Can the farmer keep his crop from the worm?" William asked, approaching the man. He put his hand on the man's chest.

"*Damn,*" William thought. "*This feels real.*"

"No, he cannot," he continued. "All he can do is keep a vigilant watch over his lands.

"You cannot kill all of the worms. And why would you want to? Are they not also creations of the most divine?" His question went without answer and William nodded as he began to usher everyone out of the alley. "Now go and tarry not. If you find him, deal with him, but if you do not, leave it be." Slowly, with little response of any kind, the people did as they were told. William watched them walk away, waving at the few who looked at him as they passed by. Adrianna and Cov walked up to join William at the mouth of the alley.

"Care to tell me what that was about?" Adrianna asked.

"Haven't the first clue," William answered. "I just went with it and... yeah." William looked down, as if making a promise to himself to remember everything about the moment, especially the feeling, and then he grabbed both Cov and his mother, taking one step forward.

"What in the name of caramel!" Adrianna gasped, falling slightly dizzy from the displacement. She was not ready for the *jump* and she knew it was not a short distance. With her son having carried two people, she was a little confused as to why she was the only one feeling dizzy.

"Wish I could do that in the real world," William said as he looked around. "And there he is." Getting her head together quickly, Adrianna turned to look in the direction William was. She looked at a man holding a Staffling in one hand. A dusty, featureless cloak covered most of his body and all of his face.

"This is the last place I'd expect to find a Man-Lord!" she said, looking the man over.

"How can you tell from here?" William quickly questioned.

"His stance, his style of cloak, even his weapon. Stafflings are meant to be weapons and canes, son. You can look at that weapon and tell that man has no trouble walking and if he does, he's not using the Staffling to assist his stride."

"Really," William answered. The feeling from the alley was still with him and he could see a fire burning around the man. The embers were a mixture of gold, bronze and brown and while William pondered what could produce a brown light, the figure approached. "Oh boy!"

"What is it?" Adrianna asked, her head getting back to where she could actually engage her ability.

"School is in session," William answered as he walked toward the man.

"This thou shalt enjoy, I promise thee!" Cov said, ushering his fellow Light-Child over to a bench. "There be nothing like witnessing two masters engage in combat."

"Masters?"

As the fighting began, she was given her answer. Their passes were wordless eloquence fitting into an orchestral arrangement of power and precision. One could not keep an upper hand over the other for too long in this contest of skill against skill. An hour passed and it was only when William moved in a way completely unorthodox way or said something to anger his opponent that he was able to find a very small opening where he found room to strike clean. His blows were light in comparison to the cloaked man, still the greater number seemed to equal things out.

"Amazing!" she whispered as the two combatants backed away from each other, dropping their Stafflings. Looking to their respective weapons racks, they summoned Blade and Guard, taking perfect stances as they turned to face each other. Only now was sweat beginning to drop from their brows and Adrianna's hand tightened to a fist; the toys were now very dangerous ones. Cov's hand rested gently over hers and when she looked over at the man, he wore the most reassuring smile. She looked for it, probing hard, and the fact that Cov did not resist her at the first sign of her probing convinced her it was not there; the madness that had plagued Cov in life was gone. Adrianna put her hand on top of Cov's to thank him for the comforting gesture.

But that did not change her opinion of the severity of the moment; neither did the general result of the engagement. The quick hits William scored carried more of an effect now, but he was beginning to weaken while his opponent showed no signs of slowing and sought to take advantage of William's fading endurance. His advance was expertly blocked. William had been toying with the man, suckering him in. Still the hammering of the Guard to the head was not enough to defeat the cloaked man. "He has the power and speed of a Deviant and the precision and guile of a Fai-" Adrianna stood up as the cloaked man blocked William's Blade with his sword but kept his movement going and bashed William in the back with his Guard. It was a common move, but there was something familiar with the movement, especially in the pose the man took after the pass was completed.

"Zargo!" Adrianna yelled as she ran out toward her son and the cloaked man. She was in her third stride when she left the ground and fell into the blackness.

[AYE, MY WIFE. THOU HAST SUMMONED ME?]

"Zargo! What have you done?"

[NOTHING SHORT OF WHAT A FATHER SHOULDST DO FOR HIS CHILD.]

"Except maybe live to see your son grow!" Adrianna screamed out in a long-held fury. "You died on him, Zargo! You died on us!"

[*IF THINE ANGER IS ALL THAT THOU HAST TO GIVE, I WILL ACCEPT IT GLADLY.*] Adrianna closed her eyes in shame and cried. When he was alive, Zargo had told her of truths she had never spoken to anyone' that his life might very well be forfeit well before his aims and dreams could find themselves real. [*FOR IT IS OF MY BRIDE, MY BEST!*]

"It is not all I have for you," she admitted as tears flooded her face. The falling stopped, but she was still in the void. "Zargo, I miss you. I miss my husband! I love you, Zargo!"

[*HOW I DO ADORE THEE!*] the voice responded. [*BUT THERE IS STILL MUCH TO DO, ADRI AND THOU HAST FOUND ANOTHER HEART TO CONTENT THEE. NAY, LOOK NOT 'PON THESE WORDS AND FEEL ANGER, FOR THERE BE NONE. THOU HAST FOUND HAPPINESS AMONGST THE TYROS AND THOU HAST COME TO SEE THEIR BEAUTY. THOU HAST E'EN COME TO LOVE ONE OF THEM. ONE OF THEIR BEST, MY BROTHER OF ANOTHER WOMB AND BLOOD. HE HATH GIVEN THEE MORE THAN THY HUSBAND WHO HAS ABANDONED THEE TO FATES MOST FOUL!*]

"You will not speak of my husband in these words!" Adrianna yelled. "Zargo was my light. He is my light still and it was out of the promises I gave him that I even dared to love again."

[*THEN LOOK NOT 'PON GORDON WITH SHAME IN THY HEART,*] the voice replied in her mind.

"*But he is not you.*" She allowed her mind to voice the thought but kept it locked away like so many thoughts about her husband, her grandest adventure, her Zargo!

"I will not," she complied.

[*AND RETURN NOT TO THE PHANTASM,*] the voice commanded. [*FOR KADOR BE NOT THE SAME IN THY PRESENCE. HE SEEKETH THE MEANS BY WHICH TO IMPRESS E'EN YOU, MY WIFE!*]

"Then he will be just like his father," she answered and the darkness was dispelled by a single point of light. It was about the size of one open eye and glowing bright enough to show the way to hundreds. It started to approach her and Adrianna put up her hand.

"I know not how you did this Zargo," she said, stepping back. "But we both know that phantasm is getting its power from somewhere and if it is from you then this will only shorten your time with your son. You two are only too right for each other and with all that he is about to face, he needs you."

[*ABOUT TO FACE?*]

Adrianna smiled in realization and nodded. He knew of Kador only through his dreams and it had been a few nights since the poor boy had actually slept. "Why don't you take a break from your sparring session and ask him," she suggested.

[*BUT, MY WIFE-*]

"Always," she thought as she closed her eyes and severed her link to her son's mind. Moments later, she opened her eyes to find herself in her chair, the candles and the incense still burning.

"I'll be damned," she whispered as she looked over at William's alarm clock. She had forgotten one of the most basic lessons of her childhood: thought moves at the speed of thought. The whole ordeal had taken less than fifteen minutes.

"A training phantasm," she said as she stood up. She had never heard of such a thing, but it made perfect sense. It was the mind that needed training over everything else. Why not train the boy while he slept? She wondered what her mental blocks had cost her son in the way of his development, but she recalled how William had dealt with Cov and soon put her worries away as she looked about the room. Notes pertaining to William's science fair project were strewn about the room and Adrianna allowed herself a laugh.

"Like father, like son."

She walked over to his desk and wrote her son a note. Something he could read and do with it as he saw fit.

> *William,*
> *Well, there were things I was expecting and things I wasn't. Needless to say this all falls under the 'wasn't' column. In the same breath, let me say that it is a wondrous thing and I think we need to keep to your first instinct not to tell Elkazzar. When you are ready, I will tell you about your little world. Basically, it is a construction of thought translated to energy inside your mind. They are called phantasms and generally they are no bigger than a house or maybe an estate. Leave it to you and your father to put together a city. And yes, the city has import to our people, that didn't get by me either. Again, when you are ready. Right now, I would say enjoy it for all that it's worth and move along in your training there as you will move along your training here. Eventually, the two will meet.*
> *BTW – I think you should know, you move like your father, only smoother!*
> *Love,*
> *Mom*

She got up from the desk and with a telekinetic wind, she put out all of the candles and they assembled in a bunch and placed in the seat of the chair as it floated behind her as she made their exit from the room.

"*Sweet dreams* has a whole new meaning, huh kid?" she said as she closed the door and turned out the lights… in that order.

Twenty-Five

Darkness can be a shelter and it was for her, for a time. The water they used was cold, very cold, though it was not due to any conscious manipulation on their part. There were few places in Great Britain that were warm at this time of year and the water going through the pipes could not have been expected to be warm.

The water felt more like daggers of ice that ripped away her night-colored veil and she screamed at the outrageous feelings that shot through her body. Her body moved in as many directions as it could, trying to escape the feeling of every nerve in her body awakening at the same time, each reporting, with undue haste and intendment, to her brain and through her mind!

"Houston, I think we have lift off!" Peter said as he tossed the pail into the corner of the room. Even the clanging of the pail against the cold stone brought her more pain.

"Take it easy," Caleb said from the corner opposite the pail. "She's on the brink of going out again."

"I think I can take care of that," Webster said as he approached. He reached for her face but he was reached first and a very strong arm pulled him back. Peter pulled free of the grasp and turned around, knowing it was Jack Moreland who had grabbed him.

"You want to go out of bounds, do it away from me!" Jack said plainly, without any inflection of bravado. "This is your call, your plan, but it's my team-"

"Then take your team and get the hell out of here!" Peter yelled. "I'm sorry if this is too adult for you!" Marianne stated to walk toward the two, but Caleb Chalk took hold of her wrist. The two pairs of eyes met and where Marianne's wore inquiry, Caleb's wore concern. What transpired was no normal argument, because what was happening to them was no normal situation. They were no longer in the FBI, although what they traveled in and what they wore was of a higher echelon of funding, with that removal came the loss of authority. They were breaking the law and that breakage was having its effect on both men. Where Peter seemed to agree with it, Jack had obviously met his limitations and was not going to go any further. To Caleb, getting them to calm down was secondary basically because even with the tempers lowered, where they were was still, at best, flawed and unsupported. To a man who now had a brain-full of Prodigian biological facts, calling their position dangerous was comical.

"If my team walks, we walk with our prisoner," Jack replied, his voice still low and calm, his eyes never leaving Peter's. The sniper stared at

Moreland for a moment and his brow came up as he blinked. He sighed and started to turn away, coming back with a right hook that pounded Jack's jaw.

"Peter!" Marianne was startled and pulled free of Caleb who was getting up to assist.

"Don't!" Bomani called to them as he came away from the wall he had been leaning against since the woman last gained consciousness. "I do not want to hurt either of you. But I will!"

Peter stepped into Jack, driving his elbow into Jack's sternum and back fisting him across the nose. Jack took one step for every blow he received, putting him against a wall. He was just beginning to draw focus on Webster when foot was lifted into his stomach and he doubled over. He was made to stand straight up with a lifted knee.

"Being Lydia's bitch has made you soft, old man!" Peter said, landing a left hook. His right hook was blocked.

Quickly locking Peter's arm under his left arm pit, Jack turned and slammed Peter into the wall. He brought him back and sent him forward again, opting to release his hold.

"You stroked the wrong wound, sniper!" Jack said, grabbing Peter from behind and slamming him into the wall a third time. He let go and stepped back and Peter slid down the wall.

Bomani saw Peter's declining position in the fight and was marveled at what the man's powerful frame was able to withstand and then put into returning the attack to Webster. He looked at a pile of the materials created when the team had decided to use this place to interrogate their prisoner. Among the items was a short plank of wood with blood on it. It had been used as club before and Bomani, who knew how to fight, thought if he was going against Jack Moreland, he was going to need more of an equalizer than his hands and feet. He took a step toward the pile and his world flashed black. He staggered back and his focus went blurry.

"You took your eyes off of me," Marianne said, landing from her jumping round kick in a perfect position for another attack. She hopped forward and sent her side-kick into Bomani's chest. He hit the wall hard, losing most of his air. He lost consciousness when Marianne took hold of his hair, brought his head forward and then slammed it back.

"Oh no you don't," Caleb said, hitting the switch. The current from the van battery coursed into the captive woman's body and she screamed again. Caleb turned off the device and rushed over to the chair, landing a cross on the woman's chin. She was out again and Caleb stood there, ready to deliver another blow but, when there was no need to do so, he checked her over. He breathed a sigh of relief and looked back at Jack. "She's just out again."

"They teach you that in Medical School, Chalk?" Jack asked, rubbing his chin where the first hook had hit him.

"Among other things," Chalk returned. "You want me to pimp out your sister next?"

"Let me think about that," Jack answered as he grabbed Webster and stood him up. "C'mon Webster, I didn't hit you that ha-" Peter shot back his left elbow, interrupting Jack. His right came back and found Moreland's ribs. He spun around with a wild right hook that Jack caught in his left hand.

"Jesus Christ!" Peter said, awestruck by what Jack was able to take.

"Jack will do," Moreland said calmly. "Now are we going to talk to each other, or do I put you through that wall behind you? 'Cuz I think you lost sight of your target, sniper. And that happens, especially when the shit gets scared out of us!

"It must have put a new load of starch in your slacks, right, Webster?" Jack continued as he slowly let go of Peter's hand. Something in his eyes told Jack the fight was over. Peter was going to take shots at himself before throwing another hand at his friend. "There you were, out of the action but right in the middle of it, like all snipers. You found your perch and you were going to save us all. 'Cuz that's your job, isn't it? To be our guardian angel; to see what we don't and kill it!

"But he got to you, didn't he, Pete?" Jack asked, his voice just above a whisper. Caleb looked down and told himself he was doing so to check the woman. Likewise, Marianne looked away. They both knew what Jack was talking about, all of them had behavioral analysis capability and perhaps this particular *rundown* was overdue. But to go through it meant they would have to go back to that night, and even though they lived through it, they had teased death so much that night that going back might make death mad enough to correct its failing attempts.

"You were in your perch, out of sight and out of sound which is how you like it, because you can hear things sneaking up on you. But you didn't hear him and boy did he get to you. Never felt so much like a child since you *were* a child, right Webster?"

"Jack!" Marianne pleaded.

"Too late to take sides now, Cooper!" Jack barked back, keeping his eyes locked on Peter. Locked on eyes that seemed to be drowning in fear and pain.

"Did you scream, Webster?" Jack asked, knowing he would not get an answer. He didn't need one because the question was not for him. "Did you beg him in your mind to stop?" A single tear ran down Webster's cheek as he looked up at Jack Moreland. "Do you know which one of those assholes I'm talking about now, or does it matter? He was the first man to scare you since your father, and in an instant you remembered what it's like to be powerless, what it's like to be afraid. Dammit man, that is part of what it's like to be alive! The rest is what we do with it *after* we've survived."

"I didn't survive," Peter mumbled. "I was saved... both times!"

"Make that three," Jack said, wrapping his arms around Peter Webster. "I can't let you go down that road, man. I didn't come halfway across the world just to lose you now." The two men embraced and Peter cried. At one time, he beat his fists against Moreland's back but the large man did not move. Cooper quickly put her attention to aiding Chalk but when she turned, she was startled and she screamed. Caleb was unconscious on the floor and the woman was gone. She looked to the doorway of the abandoned apartment home and she saw a tall, pale, slender man leaving the room. He stopped and looked back at Marianne as she was reaching for her gun. She could not move her eyes from him. She recorded his long, straight black hair that ended in inch-long silver tips. His eyes were yellow and cold. She could feel his regard for her and her kind. To him, death seemed appropriate for everyone in the room, but for some reason he did not have the time. She thought she called out, but the command to do so never left her mind. The same for her intention to draw, aim and shoot. None of those things would happen, and Marianne's mind was touched ever so lightly with his ability. She fell to the ground, still conscious but without the ability to move. She did not hear her gun fall to the floor but then again, she did not feel her body fall either.

[*Next time, Tyro,*] he projected into her mind before he stepped out of the room and took up the captured woman, walking away without making a sound. Marianne strained to look back at Peter and Jack, hoping her eyes might alert one of them. She ceased her effort when she saw a projected image of Caleb, still straddling the woman, and herself, standing over her powerless form. That was undoubtedly eye-candy for Jack and Peter. FBI or not, they had another boogeyman to be afraid of now!

Eventually the feeling passed and both Marianne and Caleb were able to move again. Peter and Jack were just coming out of their embrace.

"What happened to you two?" Jack asked, looking around. "And where's the girl?"

"She's gone," Marianne answered, rubbing her temples. She was still sitting on the ground and dealing with a tremendous headache. "Dude, that was one sinister bastard!"

"Tell me about it," Caleb replied, handing Marianne a couple of pills. "Trust me, they taste horrible but they do wonders for Prodigian-induced headaches."

"Just what the doctor ordered," she smiled, taking the pills and quickly putting them in her mouth. She winced as she swallowed and glared at Caleb.

"Just be glad you didn't take 'em with water," he said, walking back to his bag. "For some reason they taste worse that way."

Peter looked around the room, wiping his tears out of his eyes. He did not say anything but it was clear he was getting angry.

"Take it easy," Jack said, putting his hand on Webster's shoulder. He walked over to his own bag and took out a phone that resembled the one Peter had used in Monster.

"If that is the same frequency-"

"Trust me, it isn't," Jack said, looking at his watch. He touched the back of the phone to the crystal of the watch. He looked up at Webster whose brow was drawing tighter by the moment. "It's activated by approximation," he explained.

"Oh, is that how it works?"

"Oh shut up!" Jack chuckled as the watch beeped. He lifted the phone to his face. "Moreland, Jack, verify." A few seconds passed and he made a hand signal to Cooper and Chalk to get everything packed up. "This was expected and, if I would dare to guess at Simmons' strategy, part of the plan."

"Which means?"

"We kinda planted a bug on the girl," Marianne said as she started collecting materials.

"What does she mean *kinda?*" Peter asked, turning to Jack who was also gathering a few items. "I searched that woman top to bottom and that was *after* Caleb gave her something to keep her sedated. So when did we *kinda* plant the bug?"

"Let's just say that between that little sound pulse and Caleb testing the electrodes, she didn't need anything to remain sedated."

"So what was in the needle?"

"A type of bug," Caleb smiled. "But I can't take credit for it."

"Let me guess… Simmons," Peter said, shaking his head. "Damn glad he's on our side!"

"Brother, you don't know the half of it!" Jack agreed and then returned his attention to the phone. "Target is marked and out of pocket." He then put the phone away and went back to packing up.

"Too true," Caleb continued as he went over to one of many black cases. He opened it and a map of the world came up on the digital display. After a few clicks from the machine, a signal was designated.

"Man!" Peter exclaimed. "Is she moving out!"

"He," Caleb and Marianne corrected in unison. A green circle formed around the light and Caleb then closed the case.

"Alfred's got the signal and he's tracking it. It is currently over the Atlantic, heading west and pulling about four hundred and fifty-three miles per hour and climbing!"

"That almost tops what we'll be able to do getting back," Jack said, shouldering his bag. "Let's put a wiggle on it, people!" Caleb and Marianne were already heading for the door with their bags when Peter grabbed Jack.

"You know, that part of my file is supposed to be sealed," he said, looking up at Moreland.

"It still is," Jack answered. "Funny thing about those seals. Sometimes they slip.

"Bottom line, I'm not going to have anyone on this team that Lydia doesn't know about them."

"Fair enough," Peter said.

"Glad you feel that way," Jack said, turning to leave. Peter smiled and followed behind him. It would not be prudent to keep Jack waiting. He did stop at the door and looked back on Bomani. No one had even bothered to say, "what about Peter's friend" or anything of the sort.

"I guess you aren't part of the plan, Bo," Peter sighed, leaning against the wall. "Sorry about that. When you wake up, you'll thank me."

He caught up with the other three and Jack was outside the van looking somewhat agitated.

"You do know what I meant when I said put a wiggle on it, right?"

"Oh yeah, sure," Peter answered, tapping the crystal of his watch. The apartment exploded in flames. "Just had to say my goodbyes.

"Don't you hate it when someone's trying to act like they're out cold but they don't know how to breathe right to sell it?"

"Jesus, Webster!" Marianne said, trying to move away from the man she did not know could be so cold. "He could have had some sort of respiratory problem."

"Not anymore he doesn't," Peter answered, drawing a snicker out of Caleb. Marianne shot him a cold look but the doctor did not lose his smile. He handed her his PDA with the readout of his check up on Bomani. He was the very picture of health.

"But Peter didn't know this!" she protested.

"You wanna bet?" Caleb asked, and Marianne knew better to take it any further. She kept quiet and tried to put her mind on the things to come.

Somewhere, in the remains of a limousine that burned to the ground, there was a toy phone that did not perish in the flames. Inside the phone, a gem, dedicated to Bomani Aten-Avri went dark. The signal was enough for the gem to feel and its reaction was enough for her to feel. The toy was quickly recalled; its other gems still quite intact.

Twenty-Six

He flew low and fast, as he had been told. That did not make his task any more agreeable. As far as he was concerned, he was carrying dead weight better off dumped into the ocean over which he traversed.

"*No,*" he thought, closing his eyes for a moment and trying to clear his mind of the anger. That was the habitual response, not the true response. He was angry at the woman, but he more than understood what she had been trying to do. She had not been fully successful. but what she had achieved was beyond measure and it would earn her yet another damned vote of forgiveness!

[*Leone, did you retrieve her?*] He knew the voice and had been expecting the telepathic communiqué, but he was so very tempted to lie and say she had perished.

[*Retrieve! I suppose that is the exact word for what I did.*]

[*Was anyone injured?*] he asked, and it was then that Leone noticed how soft his voice was.

[*None so great that they will not recover,*] he replied. [*And to answer your next question, she failed to kill the Tyro. However she did touch his mind and your suspicions were true, he was in the midst of joining the Descriers. I should be on my way to the Netherlands!*]

[*I do not agree, nor have we had opportunity to-*]

[*Oh, get out of my head with your need for meetings!*] Leone harshly replied, hypothesizing that the low voice he received was an attempt to mask the telepathy. The one to whom he now conversed was not in a safe place and Leone's retort would threaten to compromise his veil.

[*Simply follow the plan and I will contact you later!*] the voice replied, quickly severing contact. Leone's ploy was successful. He was sure that at some point and some time meetings served their purpose. But they were dying, and their most primary objective was close to being lost. The time demanded action, not debate. Still, he could do little toting an unconscious Light-Child around. He would follow the plan and see her to safety. After that... he would...

"*Dry off,*" Leone thought as it began to rain. The rule was no shields unless attacked. He was in for a very wet and cold journey.

The door to his room opened and he could feel her standing in the doorway. Damn Leone! Of all people to have felt his tirade, it had to be this one. She was already anxious to be gathering information and her sensations were stronger than they should have been. He spent most of his time and talent trying to keep information from her, but with her power growing, it was a task he knew he would eventually fail at accomplishing. But success was not the objective as much as delay. Soon everything would be known. But with any luck, that time would be after their aims had been fulfilled.

"Harry? Everything okay in here?" Tara asked.

"I'm sorry, Tara," Arvius answered. "I was having a… never mind. I hope I did not wake you."

"Thinking about Palshaya?" she asked.

"It won't happen again."

Tara stood at the doorway and looked at his back. Maybe she had been accurate; maybe she had been a little harsh. But the man had saved her life and the lives of her friends. Perhaps this would be a fence she would mend. Hearing nothing from Jon to the contrary, she went into his room, closing the door behind herself.

"I'm not so sure that would be a good thing, Harry. You loved her and she was really in love with you…"

Twenty-Seven

He rode a horse quite dissimilar to the norm. Its intelligence had not been altered in any fashion and it had not been trained in the art of telepathy. The rider had, however, learned the mount's language and was happy with their level of communication. With its natural state of being left untouched, the horse was a stronger and faster runner, and he never had to deal with an attitude or find the harmonious answer to the inquiry of why the beast was being ridden. It was a horse, not a life-companion, and until it tripped upon some miracle of Fate, he would ride it or kill it. But when its hooves thundered against the stones of the city streets, he noticed that people got out of his way.

True, it might have had something to do with the three he had already ridden down, one unable to be healed before the *Wayfarers* took the poor soul. But the Wolf Lord did not grant too much time to supposition. He had been summoned by the King. The Council he was accustomed to hearing from, but the King was something unusual and therefore all the more exciting. Effortlessly he moved from the streets into the courtyard of the castle and then, with the aid of his talent, over the wall into the gardens.

"By the Fates," a voice screamed as his horse landed. He pulled up on the reins and the horse quickly came around. He had been told once or twice that it was impossible to predict what one might see inside the castle walls. She was all but naked and seldom had his dark eyes seen something more striking to the eye. He licked his lips in anticipation and appreciation of what he gazed upon.

Her tanned, silken skin glistened in the night sky. From the energy residue, he could tell she was focusing solar light onto her body. It was a pastime of some of the more gifted energy-wielding Prodigian females. It was an activity she did not need, for even if she had been pale, she would have been no less beckoning. From the last curl of her thick, dark brown locks to the bottom of her feet, she was a wondrous formation and the recipient of many a wayward thought, he imagined.

"Well, this is at best unexpected!" he said as he brought his mount under control and moved his long black hair from in front of his now red eyes. They shifted from their normal brown state as he shifted to a mental state of acquisition but he was distracted by his mount. The horse did so love to jump when he was riding it. The animal was smart enough not to try such things unless its master was on his back, but when he rode, the horse was filled with such gumption, and he never seemed to want to end the run. A second pull of the reins brought the horse out of his passions and more into the rider's control.

"What dost thou want here?" the woman asked, finally grabbing her robe to cover herself. She seemed to be unafraid of his girth or the many dark hides which he wore as his clothing.

"Certainly not that robe!" he answered as he dismounted. "I am Wolf Lord and summoned to the castle I hath been. What be thy business here?"

"I wouldst think that to be of mine own affair, Lord of the Dogs," she snapped. She had as much fire as his horse. Perhaps she too needed a pull of the reins. He took a step closer and she turned her shoulder toward him, a Blade in the hand furthest from him, summoned from a source he did not see. His eyes squinted as a smile formed on his face.

"Now thou hast made a gross error," he said softly, increasing his pace toward the woman. Her dark green eyes flared with power and she prepared for combat.

"How fortunate for me mistakes can be corrected," she said as she took a step forward, thrusting for his chest.

"Arrrgh!" he yelled as he lunged to the side to avoid the blade. She missed, but not by much. He landed on both hands and feet and looked back at the woman. Staying in a low squat, he reached to the small of his back with both hands and came forward with two small axes. Taking a more defensive stance, the woman made a quick fastening knot with her robe and put her eyes to the ground.

"So be it!" he yelled, launcing at the woman, his left hand swinging for her face. An attack she easily blocked, ducking under his right hand's attack. He kept his spin and lifted his foot, a kick she had to back flip to avoid. She sprung up and forward from her landing point. Both axes plunged into the ground where she had been standing and without looking, one of the axes was hurled after her.

She had not yet landed when she felt the weapon's approach. She sent her Blade over her head and managed a last moment block, but there was too much force from the axe for her to counter and as she landed, the deflected weapon made another pass; her Blade was removed from her hand. As it passed again, her fist met with the steel and there were sparks as she punched the axe into the ground. She grunted as his shoulder met with her back and she was forced to the ground, losing her wind. The flat of his axe against the back of her head nearly took her consciousness. He grabbed a handful of her hair and pulled her face up only to slam it forward, his right hand reaching out to his lodged axe and like an obedient pet, it responded to its master's call. It came up from the ground and flew toward him. Her left hand ripped into his leg and he screamed. Her body shrugged him off, caught the axe and swung down for his head, her Blade in his hand preventing her perfect revenge.

"Methinks we have traded weapons," he said as he pushed her back. She was off balance and he swung the Blade for her neck; the metal faded from sight and grasp just before it touched her. Her fist met with his chest and he had seen battering rams hit softer! He flew into his horse and both of them fell over, but he was on top of his mount once again. She threw the axe and he had no choice but to avoid it, sacrificing his horse in the process. His anger seized him but it had company; her talent! Suddenly his rage was translated into so much pain that he howled as he jumped forward, grabbing the woman with both hands about her neck. She fell to the ground with him on top of her and she blasted at his mind with hers; his grip only improved. She could not breathe, she could not think, and in what seemed to be too short a time, she could not see.

[*Wolf Lord*!] Korach screamed into his head and he reeled from the force of the projection. He released the woman and rolled back, his hands once again possessed his axes. [*Thou hast been summoned by the King! Dost thou dare to draw blood upon royal grounds?*] Korach appeared in front of Wolf Lord who stood up and put his axes away.

"Madness is upon thee!" Korach cried. "This be the King's cousin, Kamala, and she be nearly dead."

"Thou didst interrupt," Wolf Lord explained. "A moment more and the life in her would have been dealt with!"

"Bring me a healer!" Korach called out as he stood and faced Wolf Lord. He sighed in disgust and shook his head.

"Thou shouldst be more fastidious with thy life, Korach," Wolf Lord warned. "I beleaguer myself not over the feelings of the King. If thou dost wish to take her place then keep those very eyes upon me." Slowly, but most surely, Korach's countenance did change. "Good boy!" Wolf Lord remarked, looking to his dying horse. He walked over to it and gazed upon the wound. He put his hand to the point and probed. There was no mercy to his action and the horse whinnied in pain.

"Foul fate found thee, I fear," he whispered as he turned to walk inside the castle to his audience with the King. "Now what be this business?"

Four of the healer's sect came running and Korach quickly pointed them toward Kamala and the horse, though he gave no directions for the latter. "Look to the woman," he commanded. "She be the King's cousin and the most favored of them."

"She shall not perish, my lord," the female nurse replied as she knelt down beside Kamala and touched her face. Still unconscious, the woman had obviously been in a fight for her life and nearly lost. She began to apply her talents to resolve the situation while those that came with her saw to the fallen mount.

Elior sat on his throne, but he was obviously troubled as his brow could not relax. There were so many things to consider and it would not be long before he would need to explain himself to the Council. He was indeed King, but the people listened to the Council and he could not afford to alienate them.

D'Hano and four of his best stood off in the corner, fully armed, fully armored, greatly anticipating the task their King would assign to them.

"My King," Korach called out, "...at last, the Wolf Lord has arrived."

"Your Majesty," he boomed as he walked into the room. His eyes went to D'Hano and his assembled men. This was to be a hunt and he would have to be both guide and nursemaid! Wolf Lord stopped and sighed low in tone and volume. "I think my price just tripled," he muttered.

"Do I have the stomach," Elior asked softly, "...to inquire as to why, when summoned by thy King, thou dost drag more than thy feet to respond?"

"It would depend, your Majesty," Wolf Lord answered.

"On what?!"

"What was served thee for dinner?" Wolf Lord jested and D'Hano came away from his spot, reaching for his Blade. Wolf Lord snarled as he fixed and eye on D'Hano, stalling his approach and the drawing of his weapon.

"I see *my* dinner," Wolf Lord replied with a smile. "... but I do not think I was summoned to enjoy Guardsmen and guts!"

"You were not," Elior replied in a tone unchanged and Wolf Lord moved his eyes up to his King and he relaxed. That was one thing that Wolf Lord liked about King Elior, his ability to appear above everything. He looked earnestly at the King and bowed. Elior nodded and stood. He looked down upon Wolf Lord for a moment before descending down the stairs.

"An Elite Royal Guardsman has been killed, Wolf Lord," Elior said, picking up his cat. "Leaving us with questions... many questions. I would like answers and I would like them as soon as they can be found.

"And of further interest to thee, Wolf Lord, mayest be why the Guardsman was dispatched to begin with. The Unlawful Son still lives and he hath been found. By Blade, Bow or Axe, his life must end... and soon!"

Wolf Lord bowed as Elior walked by. "It will be an honor of service to the throne, your Majesty."

"Good, then consider thyself dispatched. D'Hano and his four best Blades shall accompany thee. And that is not a request," Elior added as it looked as if Wolf Lord was about to speak. Elior's cat hissed, punctuating the point.

"By thy will, your Majesty," Wolf Lord replied.

"Get thee gone, thou art already too late to the task and the son of Zargogyan must die!"

"My apologies to thy cousin, sire," Wolf Lord spat before turning to walk out of the throne room.

Elior stopped at the door and turned to look at Wolf Lord. He then looked at Korach who quickly projected to the King that his most favored cousin had engaged with Wolf Lord and apparently she thwarted him one time too many. Elior put his cat down and started to walk after Wolf Lord, but Korach prevented him, enveloping their heads in an airtight shell of telekinetic force to prevent them from being heard.

"With Cov killed and inexplicably so, we may need his barbarisms to right this course we are presently on." Elior glared at Korach and his eyes did not waver. "And with the Unlawful Son dead, D'Hano's Blades may be directed to remove the Wolf Lord's head." Elior nodded his approval as he turned and walked away, leaving Korach to project the directive to D'Hano using the code language of the Royal Guard, as he could not risk Wolf Lord not being able to listen in on the conversation. D'Hano was very happy to get the change in orders and complied with a smile on his face.

"Good news, Captain?" Wolf Lord asked.

"We hath experienced problems with the former Captain of the Royal Guard," D'Hano answered. "He hath been trapped, cornered. His arrest draws close."

"If thou doth speak of Mevkrean, child, mark well just who is the bait and who is trapped!" The hunting six made their way to the Great Bridge.

"Ahh, the Outworld!" Wolf Lord sighed.

"Thou hast been there before?" D'Hano asked.

"Only thrice," he answered, checking his weapons. "Each time for a runner. Each time I brought back no less than three heads of runners. Whilst we are on this trek and a runner is spotted…"

"The bounty and the credit shall be thine!" D'Hano answered, caring not for such things at the moment. The Unlawful Son awaited and with any help of Fate, he would return with the son of Zargo, while Akiba would return with Mevkrean bound and silenced.

"Careful, Captain," Wolf Lord warned. "Thou art too far into thy dreams. What a shame it wouldst be for thee to awaken, find thyself dead and curse the Fates because the moment was missed by thy waking eye!"

183

Twenty-Eight

He did not leave himself time to check the number of bodies he had laid low. That was the work of the troubadours and their amount was never fixed anyway. He made his way to the streets where he eventually mixed in with the citizenry, changing his appearance three times before attempting to take one of the three entrances. As a young man, Mevkrean had been a scout and he had often thought the best place to seek out paths would be New Sumeria, and paths he found. Deep beneath the city, beneath even the sewers and waterways there was an old tunnel system. The tunnels were vast, large enough to march entire armies through. The walls were at least three bricks thick and there was never any dirt or pestilence of any sort. The outermost stones were polished, as if each brick had a glass surface. A very young Mevkrean had worked for hours to remove one brick, revealing the grayish-beige color of the mortar. A great amount of time and effort it took to remove the perfect stone; a stone which proved to be too heavy for a young Mevkrean to lift. So he left it there and upon his very next visit, the brick was gone and a new one was in its place, but it did not have a glass-like surface. That had only convinced an impressionable young man that there was someone else down in the caves who probably did not take well to his visitation.

Over time, he visited the caves five more times and upon his last visit, he explored the northbound tunnel to see how far it traveled. He had never tried to confirm it, but it felt like he was under Utopia, the *Deviant* Seat.

But there were no *Deviants* here, only the best and brightest the Light-Children had to offer. For some reason, they followed him, all meeting at the site of the only non-glass brick.

"Thou art a most welcome sight, Captain," Lorthar said, embracing his Captain and holding him close.

"Lorthar," Mevkrean said softly, "dost thou know the sort of love we share is shaken by this brand of reunion?" The men laughed and the Master Archer pushed his Captain away in great haste.

"A pox upon thy brilliant mind!" he spat at Mevkrean who was still laughing heartily.

"Given the ideas I hath witnessed of late, thy curse is already upon me." The men laughed harder as Mevkrean let his eyes move over them, taking inventory as it were.

Lorthar and his three were here and he breathed easier when he looked upon Salkathi, Murietta and Olliento. Two men were bound at their feet, their minds locked. One he recognized from the roof of the Hasty Jug, the other was in the uniform of the regular army with the insignia of an archer. But there was no sign of Insra and her group.

"Murietta and I are both yet fresh to this place, my Captain," Olliento said in an attempt to ease Mevkrean's troubled mind. "And the one for whom thy concern burns...well, she be no stranger to the worst of the Fates."

"Aye," Mevkrean agreed, nodding. He did breathe somewhat easier.

"And still she hath survived," Salkathi added. "A testament to thy skill and leadership, my Captain."

"Aye," he said again, holding out his hands, "and look where your Captain has brought thee, to the bowels of New Sumeria! E'en the sewers be above us now!"

"At least the sewer bear nary a false witness," Lorthar countered. "I expect dung from the sewer; it was built for such things."

"Lorthar," Mevkrean said softly.

"But there be fouler things perched upon the throne at this moment!"

"Lorthar..."

"A true pox upon him and his blood for what th-"

"Lorthar! Be silent!" Mevkrean shouted, his hands gripped tightly into the archer's leather armor, and he slammed the man back into the solid rock walls, his feet clearly off the ground. "I know not what vexes our King, nor if there be anything to vex him. But keep thy passions away from those boys. They are Princes to the last drop of their blood, and I shall take thy last drop if thy lips curl once more to spat curse upon them. This I command and I care not for your acknowledgements." Mevkrean stepped back, releasing Lorthar. None of the men stepped forward to caution Lorthar on his next action. He was a Master Archer and was known for his vision. Surely he could see his destiny should he continue to anger Captain Mevkrean any further.

"I beg thy indulgence, master," he said with lowered voice and head. "I am thy man!"

Mevkrean blinked as he nodded. Lorthar would sooner die than bring disappointment to his Captain. But tensions were high and his men were being hunted like animals. That he could not have for much longer.

"But know this, my Captain," Lorthar said. "My last drop is thine if it be a choice of their blood or thy life. I wouldst strike them down and come to my death at thy hands without regret."

"Loyal brother," Mevkrean said, placing his hand on Lorthar's shoulder. "If it comes to such, we will strike each other down, for mine eyes couldst not take the measure of those two failing and falling. And I am thine!

"But even this place only holds a short respite for us. Were you and your men successful?"

"Aye, my Captain," Lorthar answered. "We hath a route to the forests which doth cut through all of the Absularian Lands. "And it be a route hard to track, I can assure thee. The path is set for a score, Captain."

"Good!" Mevkrean answered, turning to Olliento. "And what hath thee to report?"

"We caught the one thou didst set us upon," Olliento answered. "This other led archers who laid in wait for our passing. Their arrows failed but it was not entirely due to poor aim."

"A trap set along an escape route. We deal with a clear and clever mind, men. One not too well trained or aware of our ability, but that is an advantage I would rather not count. Especially after tonight!

"I will talk now with the one I was meant to meet this night. Remove his bonds and bring him hither. Olliento-"

"Should he emit thought, Captain, it shall not leave this chamber."

Mevkrean turned himself away from his men and waited. He could hear the restraints being removed and he could feel the mind-lock being lifted. Even with the relief the man felt, Mevkrean could tell it would be some time before the man could execute any talents with any coherence or true power.

"I am confused," he said as he heard the man dragged across the floor to kneel close to him. "We had a pact to meet yet when I didst arrive, I was met by mercenaries, not by thee. I do not recall requesting a trap so much as I requested information. Now, there art ways we can go about this, foolish man. Only one of them will prove to be painless. Rest assured that though our time here is limited, there be more than enough to delve into thy mind and rend the truth from your brain. This, of course, carries the most permanent effect, and I would spare thee the torment if thou wouldst but spare me any continued foolishness. Am I understood?"

"Thou art more than clear, my Captain," the man panted, almost on the verge of tears.

"I be *not* thy Captain!" Mevkrean barked as he turned around. "Not in the least! 'Tis only out of respect of mine men, mine fellow fugitives, that I e'en hear the word! Thou hast ripped us from our world and thrown us all into this chaos! Now, I shall have the reason or I shall possess thy heart in my hand!"

"Then I be dead," the man answered. "Why shouldst the particular path matter?"

Mevkrean made no verbal reply, he did not even scream. He simply held up his hand, his fingers posed as if he were going to grow claws. But he did not. Nor did he generate any visible displays of energy. He simply looked at his hand and focused his considerable concentration. Soon his hand began to tremble and his breathing grew deeper and deeper. At its deepest, his eyes shot open and he thrust his hand forward into the man's chest, each fingertip sinking into the flesh nearly half an inch. The man screamed and grabbed Mevkrean's wrist. There was no augmentation, it was purely mastery of technique and all the strength the man summoned was not enough to remove the hand from his chest.

Closing his eyes, Mevkrean forced his body to generate an electric charge. A charge he let flow through his fingertips directly into the man's body. Again he screamed, but this was beyond the normal limits of pain. The man was discovering things about himself that no man need know. Each small burst was focused through the man's body and into his spinal column. The first burst made the man scream in inhuman pain, the second brought the chorus of that pain and robbed the man of his motor functions. Mevkrean removed his hand and quickly healed the man's body.

[*Perhaps now thou hast the truth of it,*] Mevkrean projected as he lifted his other hand and formed another claw. [*I can and I will heal thee upon every occurrence. And when I say heal, I mean completely. I shall take from thee e'en the memory of just how much it hurt, leaving only that it exceeded the worst thou hast ever seen or heard of. Which means all thou shall retain is the fear of my touch. And this will continue, until we are found out or I cannot continue.*]

"The King!" the man said, choosing an uncertain death over one all too clearly defined for him. He still had the memory of what had happened in his mind and he imagined what he would think awakening to this place, lying in his own waste and not knowing why, just that he was afraid of Mevkrean. It was obvious to him that there should be more people who should be afraid of him. The King himself would be well served to attempt a bit of fear of his Captain.

"This much I know, fool!" Mevkrean barked. "Twas the King who gave the order to a Guardsman! I need to know why!"

"Zargo!" the man said as he was at last able to see again, though not too clearly. "Thou wilt only employ thy tortuous hand but I cannot give thee what I do not know. Take thyself through my mind for I will bear it open for thee. All I know is that Zargo discovered something about King Elior."

"What?"

"I know not the substance, my lord, I swear! Only that Korach said that Zargo could not be allowed to live with the information. That the throne entire would be undone if it rose to the common mind.

"But there is something else I know, Captain," the man was quick to continue. "Two things that I know not the import of, but thine ears and mind may know more of them and their worth than I."

"First thou wilt tell me how thine came by this tale."

"I was once a servant in the castle, my Captain. Dost thou not recall? I fetched thee a drink of well water at thy first tournament. When thou didst take the Blade Stave Championship. It was a magnificent throw!"

Mevkrean remembered it without invoking too much effort. It was the sort of thing one simply does not forget. A center-strike on a moving target at eighty-seven paces! The Fates had been kind to him that day. But he had always possessed a skill for combat. It was that day when he first came to recognize it.

"Aye, thou wert a member of the castle staff," he said softly while thinking. "Which is what thou must be still to put forward such a trap for me. But the talent gathered was hasty and therefore thy choices were limited. Thus the mercenaries. Even the Royal Guardsman who will not follow me do not wish to stand against me and the King needed tongues for which he could be assured of their silence. Then they are dead men too!"

"So what of these questionable facts within thy head? What of them?"

The man still trembled but he gathered enough strength to speak as he looked up at Mevkrean. "Promise me a swift and painless death, my Captain. For we both know I am undone! Thou hast always been truthful if nothing else. Lead me not to a false hope."

Mevkrean looked down on the man and signaled his men to stand him up. They did so and without being told, they cleaned him off. Their Captain thanked them for their effort and he approached the man, looking him in the eyes.

"I swear to thee, I will send thee swiftly and painlessly to thy fathers. For to give thee hope would indeed be false. Thou didst leave the castle upon thy given errand and thou hast not returned. Thou shalt be considered dead or traitorous until given unto death. If thou hast not the stomach or the heart to endure, then death is thy only refuge.

"Know this," Mevkrean continued, "where I tread, only mad men will follow. The Fates hath blessed me with a fair enough share and they are mighty of mind and stout of heart. Yet these attributes are bested by their skills. So if they be mad, no one will speak of it to their faces! That is my trek, for I stand against the throne for the throne's sake! So impart upon me thy knowledge that I might send thee to pastures more graceful than any you have tread in this miserable life."

Leaning forward, the man did speak of it, for he still could not project it into Mevkrean's mind. But he had no fear of eavesdropping as he spoke. These men were loyal to their Captain and there would be no treachery among these mighty war lords. The steel in their Blades was of a weaker mettle than that which forged them apart from the Regular Army and the Regular Royal Guard. They were the Elite and were called such for a reason!

But none of that supported Mevkrean as he was given an old tale too long kept secret. To be sure, Mevkrean did take the man upon his word and explored his mind. Every partially hidden nook and every illusionary preclusion the man had about life. All of these were now possessions of Mevkrean's mind. He found the memory that had been explained to him and every single detail was true. It was a tale that explained so much but forged new questions, burning questions that could not be cooled and still Mevkrean had to hold them. For the sake of the throne he had to hold them. And though he was overwhelmed with choler, he did not have any of that animosity in his movements as he spun around, drew his Blade and removed the man's head from his body. Quick and painless, and as Mevkrean had already disabled the man's nervous system, he felt nothing, he knew nothing. Just that his vision of the world changed abruptly and he slept.

"We are undone!" Mevkrean cried as he joined his men. "We are doomed!"

"Is it the *Deviants*?" Lorthar asked.

"Damn you, Lorthar!" Mevkrean said, as he pushed the archer away. "This plague will not find only one sect, it will attack us all!"

"Forgive me, my Captain," Salkathia said as she slowly approached. "But what can be so sorrowful as to end all three sects?"

"Quite simply, my Bladesman, the throne," Mevkrean answered, lowering himself down to a knee. His men followed suit. "Despite the differences between the three sects, there hath always been an underlying bond that holds us together and that bond be the throne.

"Think, my children," Mevkrean continued, "what would happen if the commoner knew the throne was a fraud?"

Twenty-Nine

He opened his eyes and after looking at his clock, he became aware that he had not actually spent days. Once again, a great length of time at the phantasm took less than one night. William also noticed that his sleeping patterns were returning to something of a norm, and he knew the reason why it had ever diverted. It removed the weird, empty feeling that waking up used to bring. He went over to his window and smiled when he saw no one sitting in the tree looking back at him.

"This might work out to be a pretty good day after all," he thought as he turned to the bathroom to take a shower. He sent his head forward and tried to flip but landed on his back. Suddenly, his disposition for the morning was challenged.

"William!" Adrianna called as she entered the room. She stopped when she saw her son lying in the middle of the floor. "What happened?"

"I'd say I got a three from the Russian judge," William replied, still looking up at the ceiling. He could hear his mother trying her best to suppress laughter but she was failing horribly. "Oh just let it out for goodness sake. You sound like a pressure cooker!" The quip was all the invitation she needed to laugh out loud as she kneeled at her son's head. A simple touch of her finger to his forehead and William felt his back snap. His face twisted at the sound, though there was no real discomfort.

"What did I do to myself?" he asked, slowly sitting up.

"I'll give you the short version. Years ago, the Light-Children used to train the way you did last night. But they found out that the real world had all sorts of twists and turns-"

"And Man-Lords," William added.

"Especially Man-Lords!" she agreed. "So the mental training gets you used to sensations and gives you a pretty good idea as to what your limitations are."

"But there's just no replacement for good ol' fashioned experience," William said.

"Exactly! Let me guess, you started studying movement."

"Yeah," William answered, stretching his back. "I got to double back flips in the arena. Can't even do a forward flip in the real world."

"Sure you can, you just have to concentrate and make sure your body is working here the way it was working in there," she said pointing at his head.

"Mother of Mercy!" she thought. *"Double back flips?!"*

"Moving is what you do best so I'd say you need to stick with it. Just don't get too cocky."

"I'll try to keep that in mind," William replied as he walked over to his desk and spotted his mother's note. "Phantasm, eh?" he said under his breath.

"And like I said, you might be on to something in not telling Elkazzar about this."

"Give what you get?" he asked.

"Something along those lines, yes," Adrianna answered. "He's here to teach you and run the first line of defense against the Council. But don't go thinking he'll tell you everything he knows."

"No doubt," William agreed.

"And if only you knew the things I was keeping from you, Mom," he thought, knowing she could not feel his thoughts. Indeed he had covered a number of things in his training time, the least of which was intentionally performing less than himself just for her and the others in the house to witness. They might be more prone to try to over-extend themselves to protect him, believing he wasn't as advanced as he was, but he had to take that chance. What he had leaned at the phantasm was too important to risk! It was a shame he would have to wait until he went back to bed before he could go back.

"So, that was the Source, huh?"

"Who called it that?" his mother asked, more concerned than he expected. Then he remembered what the Guardsman had told him about his mother's educational pursuits.

"Cov did," he answered, monitoring his voice to make sure his sound did not reflect his thoughts. "Was he wrong?"

Adrianna looked down and considered her options. There were not many. So many questions surrounding the Source, and her own investigations only turned up more questions.

"Too soon," she thought. *"It's too soon to have this happen all over again!"*

"You still with me?" William said, knowing she was very invested in her own thoughts.

"Ah, yeah. Yes, I am. I was just... just, uh... would you mind if we get back to this later? You're getting ready for school and this is not one of those easy answers... I'd rather get back to you after school."

"That deep, eh?"

"That deep!"

"Hmmm," William pondered, feigning innocence. "Learn something new everyday."

"Speaking of something new," his mother mentioned as she leaned in the doorway, folding her arms. "How is the young lady who sent you the flowers?"

"Oh, she's good," William called from the bathroom as he was beginning to brush his teeth. "She's real good!" Adrianna looked down and smiled, just waiting. William leaned out of the bathroom and looked at her.

[*That did not come out right,*] he projected. [*I meant she's doing well.*] He returned to his morning rituals. [*We talked a little, drove a little, talked a little-*]

"Made out some," Adrianna threw in.

[*Well of course we ma-*] William leaned out of the bathroom again. [*You are so enjoying yourself, aren't you?*]

"Having the time of my life!" she smiled back at him. William quickly went back in the bathroom and she giggled, turning for the stairs. "I'll whip you up something for breakfast."

"Yeah, you do that!" William said loud enough for her to hear. He could hear her laughing as she went down the stairs.

"*This will take some getting used to,*" he thought, his sense of hearing able to filter out all other sound except for his mother. Her breathing, unsteady; her steps, uncoordinated; her heartbeat... fast, too fast! She was afraid and it had something to do with the Source. William wondered if it had anything to do with what he had seen *over* the Source.

But he did not choose to dwell on any one thing at that moment. The purpose of the day was to get to the point where he dwelt on one thing, his training. But that would mean asking for some incredibly rare favors that stood little chance of being granted. And then came the temptation to explore his telepathy to the point to where he could have someone give him whatever he desired. To use the weak-minded like puppets and make them dance to his music. How simple life would be for him then.

"*Who am I kidding,*" he thought, looking at his choice of clothes in the mirror. He was gaining muscle mass and it was beginning to show. He would have to wear baggier clothing which was not a tall order for a jock. He turned and left his room, gearing his mind up for the experience... how he hated school!

"There he is," Gordon announced as William entered the kitchen. His mother was at the stove. It looked as if she had finished making him something to eat. William took a whiff and smiled at her. She handed him a plate and ushered him to the dinette table. Arvius was nursing a cup of coffee and Tara looked as if she was finishing her breakfast. "How did you sleep, son?"

"About the same as always," William answered, taking his seat. "But we have a better understanding as to why, so at least I feel better about it." Tara looked at Gordon and William repeatedly, waiting for one of them to fill in the blanks. "Seems my Dad kinda predicted his own death and left a few training manuals in my head."

William's honesty startled Tara and she did not know how to respond. "Well, that was... nice of him... I guess."

"Yeah, he was a real classy guy," Gordon said in half reflection. "The very best!"

"So how did everyone else sleep?" William asked, feeling the weight of the room shifting too much to the serious. "Mom?"

"Like a baby," she replied, still cooking.

"Dad?"

"Oh I slept long and hard, Bill," Gordon smiled brightly. "I think it's been a while since the whole house felt so restful."

"Take a picture," William thought, drinking his orange juice. *"It'll last longer."*

"How about you two?" William continued, looking to his table companions. "Ms. Mifflen?"

"Oh for God's sake, call me Tara, please! I so cannot hang with Ms. Mifflen."

"No problem," William chuckled. "Tara."

"Well I was doing pretty good until I heard Harry here. He was having trouble sleeping soundly, so I went to check on him." William's eyes shifted to Arvius and Adrianna trembled. She had felt this sensation before and she braced for the normal effect, but it did not happen. She turned around from the stove to see William's gaze but this time it was fixed on Arvius and it was the Light-Child Runner who was shaking. Something instinctive was happening with William again. Just as she could not lie to him when his awareness began to manifest, obviously something was amiss. Adrianna's mind went back to the last thing Tara had said. It was not a statement about the former agent. It was about the former Light-Child Councilman.

Caught completely unaware by the mysterious effect, Arvius dropped his glass of orange juice and William caught it with his telekinesis but his eyes never shifted! He did not even look at the glass.

"Oh no, Harry," William said as he put his glass down and slowly got up from the table. "You don't get off that easy!"

"Son?" Gordon looked up from his paper to see a most unexpected sight. Tara jumped up from her chair as Arvius fell to the floor from his.

"William, you're hurting him!" Adrianna called to her son.

"Talk about a funny spin about how the truth hurts!" William said, keeping his gaze on Arvius. But he no longer saw the man who was beginning to shake violently on the floor. He saw a woman, dressed as a flight attendant and a slender man with a particularly bad hair cut and yellow eyes.

Blood began to trickle from Arvius' nose and Tara had seen enough. After the most recent discoveries about Harold Smith, she was not sure she trusted him fully. But it was obvious William was coming off pretty heavy handed.

"Careful," William said, pointing at her. "Heroism seldom yields heroic events so much as it creates a wake of good intentions." Slowly William turned to look at Tara. "But if you feel froggy…"

Tara screamed as she lunged across the table, covering the distance and reaching her hands out for William's neck.

[*Hello, Palshaya,*] William projected as he did a swim move, swinging his left arm up and across his body, smacking both of Tara's arms wide to the right of their target. William caught Tara's head to keep her from going out of the window. He pulled her back and put his hand on either side of Tara's head. Her eyes closed and she screamed long and hard. [*Here I come, Palshaya!*] he projected as he reached into Tara's mind and saw something of a phantasm, but it was nothing like his own. It was a simple farm. The name on the mailbox said Newcombe and William had a pretty good idea where he was. The grass was not green. It was see-through, like a fine crystal. The house and the barn were the same way, even the fence that surrounded the pseudo-property. The sky was black with only three stars and there was no wind, no scent to the air. William's Source had spoiled him.

"We don't have to do this!" William yelled out. He stepped back and a Blade Stave flew in front of his face. He was supposed to look to his left, the origin of the throw of the weapon. But he had felt the energy signature of telekinesis before he heard the weapon. He started to look to his left and then cut to his right to see Palshaya, coming out of her invisibility and attacking him with a Blade. Her studded leather armor seemed to glisten but it fit her well and she moved well in it. Her first swing was meant for his chest but William jumped back in time to cleanly avoid the weapon.

"Okay, so maybe we do!"

"Thou canst not stop me!" she cried as she readied herself for another attack.

"*Okay, so much for asking her if she knows who those faces belong to,*" William thought as he took a quick inventory of his immediate area. This contest was being watched by other minds… sort of.

"Pal, you really don't want to do this."

"You are gifted, Unlawful Son, but you are not yet trained and I am!"

"True," William admitted. "But you are forgetting one thing."

"And what is that, Kador?"

"We're on neutral ground."

Palshaya said nothing in response as she moved toward William quickly, thrusting for his chest. He stepped to the side and avoided the weapon, ducking as she brought the sword around in a wide circle. Palshaya knew the boy was fast. She had seen him move. But he had changed since then. He was so much faster and he only moved as much as he had to, nothing more. It was like fighting with her mentor rather than a stripling of a man.

"Or should I say, we *were* on neutral ground," William said as he closed his eyes. Palshaya thought about moving in to take advantage of his vulnerability but in the next breath, they were both enveloped by darkness.

"Whoops," William ribbed. "Doesn't look so neutral now, does it?" William asked as his voice now contained an echo. Palshaya swung at what she thought the various points of origin were for the voice, but her Blade claimed no hits.

"Nice dancing," a voice commented and Palshaya turned, ready to defend herself. Her muscles loosened when she saw it was Tara speaking to her, caught in a cone of light.

"Tara!"

"Oh, so you do remember my name," Tara said harshly. "I was thinking that if what the kid is telling is true me my name should be Bessie, or Ginger, or Winifred!"

"Of what did he dare to speak?"

"The truth!" Jon cried out. Again Palshaya turned and she saw a wounded Tyro being assisted by William who was still intrigued as to the other faces he saw. "Of how you silenced me and were using the power of my connection with Tara to build this place. What's it called again?" he asked of William.

"A phantasm," William answered, glaring at Palshaya. "But she wasn't planning on training Tara so much as using her." William looked around at the farm. "Hope you like it, Tara. This was going to be your home!"

"WHAT?!" Tara cried, looking back at Palshaya who was backing away slowly. "Were you just going to take over my body?"

"You remember what happened last night?" William asked. "When you went in to check on Arvius?"

"You lie!" Palshaya screamed as she tore into another charge. She was into her second step when the boom of gunfire made both William and Jon jump. Palshaya fell, grabbing her left leg and dropping her Blade. The weapon quickly flew to William's hand. He ran his fingertip along the flat of the weapon and the sword became a crutch for Jon.

"Here you go," he said, handing the device to Jon who quickly took it.

"Thanks," Jon said, knowing William was going to get closer to the action if not take it over completely.

"He's not lying, is he?" Tara said moving closer, her rather large gun in safe position.

"Nice piece!" William commented.

"How many times do you get to make your own gun and actually have it do damage?"

"But something is very wrong here?" Tara said as she looked more carefully at Palshaya.

"Just one thing, Sweets?" Jonathan asked.

"This isn't Palshaya," Tara concluded. "She doesn't act like her. She doesn't move like her. She definitely doesn't deal with pain in the same fashion. Despite the gun size, it's a leg hit. The real Palshaya would have cut off her leg and hit me with it by now!"

"No," William quickly countered. "It's her, but it's Harry's version of her, not the one you spent time with. This is the one you got hit with last night, I'd wager. You probably did hear something, but Arvius wasn't having trouble sleeping. Of course, that begs the question of what you did hear that made you check on him."

"I'm not sure I want that answer," Tara said, looking at the gun, disappointed she could not bring it back to reality with her.

"I'd go along with that wager," Jonathan added. "But that still leaves one thing."

"What was Arvius up to?" Tara said, quickly lifting her eyes up to William. "And we're not going to get the answers here!" She walked over to Jonathan and placed a very passionate kiss on his mouth. He moaned softly as his wounds were healed and his clothes mended. The black sky around the farm began to fill in with pockets of blue and burnt orange. Just after William could smell the wildflowers, he started to form a smile on his face. Then came other fragrances of nature which wiped the smile clean off his face. Obviously Jon's farm came with livestock. Tara slowly pulled away from his lips and looked around in wonder.

"Did we do that?" she asked.

"No sweetheart, you did," Jonathan corrected.

"Jon," William said as he looked around. He was quickly getting used to the smell. It was a matter of telling his olfactory sense to return to Tyro-normal. "That's not an argument you're going to win. Just agree with the woman and kiss her again."

"I like him," Jon said to Tara, smiling at her.

"Oh yeah, he grows on you." The two kissed again, but no further color was added to the scene. Instead ground became firmer and started to take on the aspects of real earth, able to support the life of the vegetation growing out of it. William smiled but kept his happiness to himself. Knowing they would kiss again, he tried to insert his hand into the exchange of energies. He believed if the ground were strong enough, it would do for Jonathan what the Source did for Cov. When their lips finally parted, he knew he had been somewhat successful, but that he did not need to worry about how long it would be before she revisited her Jonathan Newcombe.

"You ready, Will?"

"If you are," he answered. "We're in your mind and time is not passing the way you think."

"Maybe, but I'd still like to know what that bastard did to me."

"You understand, don't you, honey?" she asked of Jonathan.

"Of course I do," Jonathan responded and William had to look away. She was only going to believe the surface of what she saw because that was what she wanted to see. But William could see well beyond it. Jon was saying what he needed to. Tara was about to be the business for which she left the FBI. Her mind needed to be on her work and not her dead fiancé. Yes, they would be able to meet in the phantasm and they would be able to touch. But it would never be real, it would never be fulfilling. Only shadow and smoke and eventually even Tara would come to see it and feel it. But that discussion would come later.

"You go get 'em, Sweets!" Jonathan urged, looking at William for assistance.

William nodded and turned his attentions to Palshaya. He walked over to her. She still had not healed herself. All she could focus on was the fact that she had been injured and was afraid that she was about to be killed. William stood over her and sent probes into her being, looking for something that would remind him of the time Yudara tried to kill him. After beginning the search, he came to realize this image was much like its antecedent, and while driven to a high ideal, it was not prepared to be the one to make its dreams come true.

"*Must be why she was so willing to use Jon,*" William thought. "*This just doesn't do the woman I barely met any sort of justice.*"

"*Wait a second,*" William thought, extending his thought to three places: the downed Palshaya, Tara's memory and his own phantasm.

[*Cov, please help me,*] William projected. [*Help me bring this one home.*]

[*I will add my own memory of her, sire,*] Cov responded. [*Together we shall bring this illusory image closer to the real!*] Tara was looking at Jon, standing in front of his family farm. There was a flash of light and the war cry of Palshaya. She could feel pain and a fair measure of righteous anger in the tone as the memory passed from her mind, seemingly finding some remnants of the woman as it moved and flowed into William's mind. But Tara knew the young man had not opted to keep the energy. Instead it went into the representation Tara had shot. When the light of the phantasm became sunlight coming through the kitchen windows, Tara could not believe how much time had not passed with everything that had happened, but William was holding her and quickly stood her up, his attention already on Arvius who was making a run for it. For a fairly weak Prodigian, he was a gifted runner and his second stride caused him to move at a blur.

"*Oh that can't be the best you have!*" William thought as he could see he was gaining on Arvius.

"William, no!" Adrianna screamed but her son was already by her and the hand she sent to catch him missed.

Arvius was a stride from the front door of the house when he opened it telekinetically. One step out of the door and Arvius looked back at William, less than a full stride away, and smiled.

"Try this trick, son of Zargo!" he said as he jumped forward, throwing his arms in front of himself.

William wanted to jump after him, but something kept him from it and he tried only to run harder. As Arvius fell forward, William noticed that he was not falling too fast.

"*Son of a bitch!*" he thought as Arvius made it out of the doorway, his body completely horizontal and climbing. "*The bastard is flying!*"

"I could use some cover!" William yelled as he pushed for more speed, sprinting out of the house.

"You got it baby!" Adrianna yelled as she focused her thoughts on creating a false image of an empty front yard. But this forced her to slow down and Tara ran by her. Gordon was just barely edged out by the former agent's speed, but his was still better than Adrianna's.

Arvius looked back at William and smiled. He knew with the young one between himself and the others, he was shielded. The only trouble was that William knew Arvius believed that very fact.

"*You've got the height, Harry,*" William thought as he leaned forward and concentrated on his balance. "*But I've got the legs!*"

"Might need a band-aid after this one," he called out as he jumped from the edge of the front porch. His target was the large poplar tree in the front yard. It was the very same tree Elkazzar used to sit in as he first observed William, so William knew where there were at least three good branches. He chose Chidon's simply because it was the highest tested branch. His feet landed squarely on the branch and although the limb gave some, it did not break and he was already set to bound again. He locked his eyes on his destination and allowed his senses to cover his immediate area. He knew the placement of each blade of grass and its status, especially the ones that were bending due to a foot stepping down upon them.

[*Going left,*] he projected. [*Mother, go for sound coverage! Tara, wound or scare only!*]

"Jesus!" Tara whispered as she drew her gun and took aim. "I *really* have to ask King about any illegitimate kids!" William did indeed jump to his left, landing on the top of a telephone pole. His eyes locked on his target again and both Arvius and Kador knew Arvius had to wait for William to make his move. His current altitude and speed were not enough to elude the boy's leaping ability, so only a quick change of course after William left the pole would provide an effective dodge.

[*Checkmate, Harry!*] William projected, flashing an evil smile. Neither man heard the gun go off. William was doing his best to ignore it; the sound might have thrown off his timing. Arvius did not hear it and that was a common occurrence when one is shot. His left shoulder bled and Arvius screamed out in pain, actually beginning to lose altitude. William leapt, but not toward Arvius. He went straight up, and at the apex of his hurdle he performed a spinning clawing motion. In the middle of the air, there was blood and the scream of a man in unexpected yet dire pain. The form of a large man, wearing a beige full-length rain coat was all of a sudden visible. His blue sweater was torn and his chest slashed. But while William had clawed with one hand, he had grabbed with the other and he pulled, twisted and flipped, riding the body of the man like an airborne surfboard. They landed in the front yard and William rolled toward the house. He got up to his feet and ran with a look of desperation on his face. He closed his eyes and leaped forward.

"Too slow, boy!" a haggard voice scratched out. An old man stood behind three bows his talent had suspended over the ground. Each one was already nocked. William knew he could see them but he could not explain how his mother could not. The man released the arrows and William could hear his mother gasp. Gordon stepped in front of her and Adrianna screamed.

"Oh hell no!" Tara said as William landed on his back, an arrow in either grasp, the third in the roof of the porch just over Gordon's head. She played it over in her head how William had taken to the air, grabbing the first arrow, then the second. Still in mid-air he rolled forward, extending his leg. His foot came down on the tail end of the third arrow, forcing it to spin and climb. She lifted her gun to draw aim on the old man but he was already gone, taking the two wounded men with him. Gordon opened his eyes and looked down at William as Adrianna looked around her husband.

"You saved my life," Gordon said softly, his voice barely above a whisper.

"You saved your wife's," William replied. "It was the least I could do."

"Kid, you've got moves for days!" Tara said, offering him a hand up. William quickly took it and smiled at her.

"Let's hope those days outnumber the ones that are coming," he answered, turning the hand up into a grateful handshake. "Very nice shooting!"

"I don't know what it is," she said, looking at her gun. "I was good enough to be Bureau, of course. But to draw, aim and fire like that? Didn't know it was in me."

"I know the feeling!" William said, his brow lifting as he remembered the arrows.

"And what do you think you were doing?!" Elizabeth snapped, turning her husband to face her. "I'm the one with the powers here, not you! I could have healed, baby!"

"Or you could have healed me," Gordon argued. Tara's head gave a slight nod until Elizabeth turned to look at her.

"Healing be damned!" William said dusting himself off. "Those things were bound for his chest."

"And?!" his mother snapped back her retort.

"*And* my ass! His chest is equal to your head! How do even Prodigians heal up from a broke brain?"

Elizabeth started to respond but realized she did not have a response worthy of voicing. She just turned to look at Gordon and wrapped her arms around him.

"That's what I'm talking about!" William said, turning to walk to his car.

"Oh no you don't" Gordon said, delivering his reach to William's shoulder and he snatched the young man back into the embrace. He did not fight it at all. Both of his parents were alive and well. It had ended on a good note. Tara had just finished holstering her weapon when she was grabbed telekinetically and brought into the fold. At first, she did not know how to take it, but she quickly noticed she had four, not three, pairs of arms holding her.

"*Is this what they call breakfast?*" she thought.

"*You should see dinner!*" Jon answered, forcing her to laugh.

Thirty

"That was unexpected," Antal said as he leaned back away from the monitor, blowing smoke up toward the ceiling.

"Which way do you mean?" Cole asked, rubbing the bridge of his nose. "The flying men or the stunt double for Tobey Maguire?!" Brooks pointed at his partner and both men started chuckling.

"Did that impress you?" Rachel snapped harshly. "For that thing to display just how far from human he is?!"

"Lady," Amos said, finishing off yet another beer. "I have to say I like your style. That thing isn't human. We don't know what he or his people are!"

"We know that they *are* human," Cole replied, standing up. "...and in my book that means they get the same chances at life that we all want.

"So I would warn you both about your attitudes!" Cole continued, pointing at both Rachel and Amos. "Because that is where it starts."

"Where what starts?" Amos barked.

"Right about now you're deciding that you don't like William or his people. We won't even get to you substantiating your dislike, beyond your own personal experience, but-"

"I'm not sure I like the way your tone trivializes my personal experience!" Amos snapped, stepping closer to Cole, but a very familiar sound made the man stop. He turned to see Antal smoking his cloves, his pistol drawn and aimed for Amos' center-mass.

"I kinda like where he's going with this," Brooks said with a soft smile. "Let's let him finish, eh?" Amos looked back at Cole and stepped back to his chair. "Go ahead, partner," Brooks signaled. Cole straightened his jacket and nodded.

"I was about to say you're making a decision not to like an entire race and you carry enough weapons to make your dislike something of a point."

"Yeah, so?"

"So what if someone in the same position decides that they don't like buzz-cut survival types. Or older black women," Cole added, cutting his eyes over at Rachel. "We are Descriers, people! We *watch*... and only when the subject or subjects we are watching demonstrates an inarguable threat to others do we take action!

"Now this particular young man is in something of a pickle, and that's putting it nicely!"

"Amen to that," Brooks said under his breath.

"All his life he's been raised to believe he's one of us, what his people call Tyros. Now I don't know what that means to them, but in our tongue it refers to a neophyte which is a beginner, an amateur."

"Insignificant," Rachel added. "I believe that is more along their connotation of the word."

"And it very well may be, ma'am," Cole replied. "But it changes nothing from my perspective. Because that young man was a Tyro until recently. From what I've read up on him, he's extremely bright, very popular and one helluva football player."

"Well no kiddin'!" Amos interrupted. "He can jump on top of telephone poles. Just how hard would it be for him to play football?!"

"Now I know why you get beat up so much, Redding," Cole shot back, removing his glasses. "Because you're too stupid to learn! We've got it on record that his own people are trying to kill him!"

"What?" Rachel asked, allowing genuine feeling to show.

"You heard me, Dr. Pryor. His own people. And they aren't sending the wannabes, they're sending specialists and he's surviving it. Now, from what we do know of his people he is called the Unlawful Son."

"Come again?" Amos asked.

"The Unlawful Son," Cole repeated, donning his glasses again. "His people are broken up into factions… almost warring factions. A man of one side crossed over and fell in love with a woman on the other side. They had William Ferrous. His real name, by the way, is Kadorgyan."

"It seems I owe you gentlemen an apology," Rachel said softly. "I was beginning to think you didn't know what the hell you were doing."

"To be honest ma'am," Cole said, taking his chair again. "We don't!"

"Well you know more than I do and I've known him for years!"

"You really should not judge him too harshly. He didn't know who or what he was when he met you." Cole looked down at the floor and shook his head. "Can you imagine, being that young again? The world is still beautiful to you! You have all of your options and you pull your hair out trying to figure out what you want to be. He won't even get that. He'll either be a warrior, fighting for one cause or another… or he'll be dead!"

"You think he was coming over here to tell me about himself, don't you?" Rachel asked.

"There is a good chance he was," Cole answered.

"Then why did you want me to stop him?" she asserted. "Think of the things we could have learned from him!"

"What makes you think we stopped that from happening?" Cole said looking up at Rachel. His eyes were penetrating and it was all Rachel could do to look confused. "We just made you the forbidden fruit, Rachel." He finally said. "We will continue to monitor him and when he looks the most distressed-"

"You will have me call him," Rachel answered in a tone of newly gained realization. She could hear engines in her driveway, the squeaking of the brakes of heavy vehicles.

"Exactly!" Cole answered, getting up and opening the front door. "But first, we have to treat the house. Physical prowess isn't the only thing he's gained in the past few days. His senses would easily pick up on our presence, and that could make a mess of things."

"But we've learned from them as we watch them," Cole smiled as men came into Rachel's house, toting boxes of equipment. There was something to his smile that she did not like, but there was little she could do other than carry on.

"And this equipment will nullify his physical prowess and his senses?" she asked.

"Dr. Pryor, those are the results of his ability. You see, his people, the Prodigian, have the most powerful minds I've ever seen. Their thoughts can actually move physical objects!"

"And next I suppose you'll tell me they're from a land far, far away," Rachel remarked, bringing a rather loud laugh out of Amos. "My dear young man, I know what I saw. He jumped up into that tree; he didn't just think himself up there."

"And the one he was jumping up after?" Cole asked, stepping in front of the door to reach Rachel. It stopped the flow of traffic into the house for a moment but it picked up again once he was clear. "Was that wire work, Dr. Pryor? Keep in mind that was a live feed. The only reason they're not picking up on the cameras is because there are no living minds around them. But like I said, we are learning. It has taken some time and some sacrifice but we've found ways to contend with their ability, on a certain level."

"They're using me," Rachel thought. *"That comes as no surprise. But it looks like the elaborate act William and I put on didn't fool them."*

"In the end, whatever face we wear is immaterial," a voice said. Everyone looked toward the rear of the house and saw Arvius walking, with a slight limp, toward them. He had changed, abandoning the look of a Tyro and now wearing the raiment of a citizen of New Sumeria. "It is what forces us to wear the face that we must examine. Lest we be fooled!"

"Fooled by what?" Cole asked, truly confused by what his Prodigian contact was saying.

[*By me!*] I projected, signaling Chidon to begin his assault. The front door had been left open (not that the stuff of the door would have stopped his arrows) and he took full advantage of an unobstructed view.

203

"My pleasure, Head Master," he whispered as he released the arrow. He also liked the spacing of Rachel's house, a place he knew very well, and though he could not see all of the men hauling equipment, he knew where they had to have been standing. I had made it clear that it would be best to contend with the unknown enemies, as they seemed to be girded for the likes of us, though none of us knew how. Best if they were dealt with on the first strike. His arrow ripped through the right shoulder of the last man going into the house and stopped in the left shoulder of the man in front of him. Together they were carrying the largest of all the boxes but it dropped and they fell soon after it, screaming in pain.

[*Now, Vada!*] I commanded, taking to the air myself. [*Leena, assist Chidon and then guard the old woman!*] I landed on the roof and waited.

Inside the house, Arvius jumped at the sight of blood splattering all over him. Oh, Chidon, it was a very good shot indeed! He jumped again as Vada came in through the wall, coming face to face with Amos Redding.

"Damn freak!" he yelled, drawing both of his pistols. He pulled the triggers but the hammers did not move forward. He looked up at Vada-Ri who wore a very cold smile.

"Shall we embrace, warrior?" she said, tossing away her Staffling. Amos drew his knife from his boot and charged forward. One step from initiating his thrust, Vada lifted him up into the ceiling and then slammed him down into the floor. She was surprised to see that the man was still conscious. She took one step forward and she screamed, falling to her knees. Chidon stumbled back and even I was stunned by the sound. It was as if one of the great bells of this land was wedged into my head and struck with a war hammer. My vision was blurred and my stomach turned. I fell forward on my hands and knees and tried to focus, but my efforts only worsened my condition.

"Brooks, get the female!" Cole commanded as he looked at the controls for the sonic pulse emitter. He had another forty seconds of this battery cell. If they held one of the Prodigian captive, perhaps they might have some leverage. Brooks stepped forward to the young woman but stopped when a rather large man entered the house, pushed her aside and ran directly toward Cole.

"Bill, toss it!" Antal yelled, holding out his left hand as he moved to his right. His right hand drew his pistol. He fired once and hit the large man in the chest. He was staggered in his run. A second shot hit the leg and he looked to be headed to the ground. His other foot came forward and he spun, making Brooks miss the shoulder.

Cole was too slow to hear and react. By the time he had processed what Brooks wanted, the bleeding man was on top of him. He made the motion of a throw but the man's hand came down as Cole's came up. The large hand swallowed Cole's and the device and as he was shot in the back, he managed to crush both items.

"Dammit!" Brooks yelled.

"Take them!" Arvius ordered. "They may still be conscious, but they have no powers. You have the advantage!"

"Did I hear that right?" Redding said as he sat up, glaring at a still stunned Vada. "Wanna *embrace*, baby?"

Vada-Ri knew she was in a desperate situation, but she thought her skill was still worth consideration. She lunged forward with a fast left-handed straight punch that was easily deflected and countered with a harsh slap across the face that sent her stumbling out on the porch.

"Uh-unh, sweetness!" Redding said, marching her down. "Try that again!"

Another straight punch, this time with her right hand. The only change to the outcome was Redding landed a backhand slap that nearly turned her around. When she corrected herself, he let the same hand fly forward and smacked my daughter off of the porch and down to the ground.

In all of my days since my master passed away, I had never felt so weak, helpless. I was too dizzy to make my way off of the roof, the place I had chosen, knowing it would have been the first point of refuge Arvius would have chosen. I had imagined our meeting; he would have been agog to see me already there waiting for him. I would have told him he was a fool to think that I would ever take a watchful eye off of him. That my withdrawal from him at the house of Gordon and Elizabeth Ferrous was nothing more than a tactical move; placing myself in a more advantageous position to pounce when the moment was right.

Chidon's warning of Arvius' actions echoed through our encampment and I was caught off guard at the haste the others demonstrated. History is often lost on the young, not these youths! And it was my daughter who had led them, demanding even more speed from their quick steps. We were dressed and prepared for combat and I had started to teleport us all to the house but my own recollection of history called me to hesitate. I told Chidon not to act unless it was to save Kador's life. After his relay of the events, it was clear my future instructions would have to be broadened to protect Adrianna and Tara if such instructions were ever given to Chidon again. But I was not surprised that Kador's instincts would eventually flushed Arvius into the light. I recalled the hell they had played upon Adrianna. So we had watched and waited and gave chase, matching his *jump* with my own. It was something of an inconvenience as carrying an Absularian, even one willing to allow our talents to affect them, was akin to carrying ten Prodigian. But Arvius' ability did not match mine, it never had; perhaps that was another reason for my overconfidence. I had not considered the resourcefulness of the Tyros and I was more than a fool for having had that perspective. William had been raised among them, believed he was one of them, and therefore he thought like them. It was obvious these Descriers possessed someone in their ranks who was just as inventive as the son of my mentor.

I could not even summon a weapon. But then again, I was not a warrior and had not trained my War Locke to respond to touch as well as thought. Chidon readied another arrow; his position had already been compromised by his first volley. For a moment I was confused why he chose not to move as the eight remaining men came pouring out of the house toward him. He pulled back on the bowstring and all of the men stopped just in front of the hedges he had been hiding within. Igrileena burst out of the hedges, her Blade Stave drawn, and her wide arcing swing, cut two men across the stomach. The others jumped back and took stances displaying some talent with weaponless combat. Chidon yelled and released his arrow. A third man fell to the ground, an arrow lodged so deeply in his chest, the arrowhead had come through his back.

"Tasers!" one man yelled, reaching for his side. Both Igrileena and Chidon knew what the word meant and with five left to their opponent's number, their chances for victory were soon to be severely diminished. But they were warriors, and loss was something they embraced in every engagement. But it would be as close of a loss as they could manage. Leena's Blade Stave streaked through the air as she gave her battle cry. The man who had given the order, and thus the first to draw his weapon, was her target. The devices the men sought were all on their left hips and they had to reach across their bodies to retrieve the devices. Igrileena's aim won her a shot where her weapon pierced the forearm of the man and it continued into his stomach.

Chidon's ability with the bow, hampered by the sound weapon, was still quite fast. He moved at the same time as the men but he did not move at the same speed. Before Igrileena's effort reached her target, an arrow found the shoulder of one man. With yet another arrow drawn, Chidon rolled forward and he heard one of the tasers fire its electrical darts. Without using his eyes, Chidon fired at the sound and his arrow struck the forearm of the man who had fired at him. There were only two left unmarred, but Leena's dodge, while fast enough to evade one, was not enough to deliver her from two men firing on her. Still she was a warrior and she screamed in more in rage than in pain and she lunged, grabbing the man who had shot her. Sparks flew from the device he held as Igrileena shared her pain with him. They collapsed together on the front lawn.

Amos did not break stride as he approached Vada-Ri. He lifted his foot into her stomach and she rolled away from him, clutching her ribs.

"Don't tell me that's all you got?" Redding needled, drawing close again. He reached for Vada and pulled her up by her hair.

She closed her eyes and tears ran down her face. They did not stop Amos from slapping her again. The man's hands felt like planks of wood against her face.

"You ain't shit!" he yelled as he spat on her face. "And it looks like I'm gonna get my third kill," he whispered in her ear before slapping her again. "And I didn't even need my guns!" he shouted. The clamor of gunfire brought an eerie calm to scene. Amos looked down, but could find no wound. Still holding Vada-Ri, he looked back.

The gun had grown heavy so Rachel dropped it. She had never been shot, but she had heard accounts from those who had and knew she did not want to join their number. It is often the wants of mortal men and women that are the first casualties of life. Her hand went to the sensation. It was not pain as she had expected, but it was cool and wet. She lifted her hand and looked upon her blood. Then her knees gave. Now there was pain and she grimaced. Her eyes closed as her mouth opened wide, suddenly unable to breathe.

"Good shot, Cole," Amos congratulated.

Vada looked at the woman as she mouthed, "Get off of her!" and the tears that fell from Vada's eyes were no longer in response to her own condition. A Tyro had tried to free her from another Tyro and was paying a price that Vada-Ri could not return.

"I'm sorry William," Rachel whispered as she fell forward on her porch. "I tried to help her." Her eyes closed and body went still.

"*Help her?!*" Cole thought as he laid there, smoking gun still in hand. He had shot because he thought the woman was drawing down on the Prodigian. She was not. She had played them and her performance had been too convincing. Now he knew what Arvius had meant by the faces people wear. The face that Dr. Rachel Pryor wore had protected her friend and eventually took her life.

Vada looked on the dead woman and as her senses slowly made their return, she knew they would not be restored in time to save the woman. But as the woman's eyes closed, she found herself not wanting her powers so much as she wanted Redding's face. A sharp strike to his wrist freed her hair, a lifted forearm blocked his hook and her nails tore into the flesh around his eyes.

Amos screamed as he put his hand to his face and Vada leaned forward, landing a jab to his neck. Now he too could not breathe. As he gasped for air, Vada drove her fists into his ribs and sternum, landing a spinning kick to the face. Redding finally fell to the ground and Vada was quick to take the knife from his thigh scabbard. She lifted the weapon and her body jerked, almost instantly robbing her of the strength to hold the weapon. She looked at her chest and there were two tufts of blue feather-like fabric. She saw nothing soon after and she fell unconscious.

Chidon summoned two Edges as he threw his body through the air again. But the man who had his mark did not fire his second and last volley. He waited for Chidon to attempt his dodge and then he fired. Both electrical leads found Chidon's left arm, but the Edge in his right hand cut the wire. His left hand Edge found the man's thigh and the right hand Edge was set to drink from the neck, but one step into his thrust, Chidon's body jerked and he looked at his chest where he saw three of the blue-feathered darts. He looked toward the house before he succumbed to the toxin.

Antal moved out of the house with a special kind of rifle held close to his body. He looked left, right, up and down. There was no need for any more surprises today and he fired two darts into the woman dropped by the taser. As he expected, the sound she made proved she was indeed recovering. He only had two more shots in this clip and that made him nervous. The boys who developed the weapon and the darts had told him that one dart would be enough. But when he tested the weapon, it failed to fire as accurately as they had told him it would. He did not intend to find out if they were just as wrong about the tranquilizer too. As Chidon fell, he made an immediate check of his perimeter, saw it was clear, and took out his own sonic pulse emitter, saturating the area with another twenty-second pulse. I could hear Arvius scream from inside the house as I gritted my teeth, unable to move, and because of my lack of vision, I was unable to summon Vyzoron. We came as predators, we had become prey!

Thirty-One

Though his heart was still back at home in the middle of a very endearing group hug, his mind was fixed on where he was driving. He eased into the same parking spot he had been using for two years and cut off the engine.

"Now this morning is an interesting development," William thought. *"Just how small does the world get in its effort to dump it all on my front door? I can see this is going to lead to one serious question/answer session with Viz.*

"But alas," he whispered, looking at the building. "I've got bigger fish to fry right now. How exactly do I downshift to homeroom after ripping a man's chest open with my bare hands on my front lawn?"

It was not that William hated school, far from it. For him, the institution was the latest greatest example of true human evolution. Everything else was an advance of technology and nothing more. Instead of slaughtering each other with arrows, maces and swords there were knives, night-sticks and guns. The techniques of killing had changed; however mankind forgot to change the killer. Man had also forgotten much that the school needed in order to keep up with the life and times of the citizens of the community and the countries around and beyond them. Students were more reflections of multimedia than their families. Strike up a conversation about an Aretha Franklin movie and the focus would be more on who would play the role and not whether or not her breathtaking performance of *Nesun Dorma* at the Grammys would be part of the film. Teachers had to be more than teachers; they had to be parents too. Given that they lived in the very same economy that was taking parents out of the home, the teachers did not have time to be parents either. Still they were understaffed, overworked and underpaid. All of this made for a rather poor mixture and the children were the first victims of that system. Though they would be the last to admit it, they were all hungry for instruction, and what they could not get from home or from school, the environment was all too happy to provide. In that stride, William knew he had been blessed. Between Gordon and Elizabeth Ferrous he had been given two steadfast parents who occasionally stood as his friends. Friendship, though, took a secondary role to parenthood and thus William had started school knowing how to act and ready to learn how to think. He was a breath of fresh air to some teachers, an irrepressible pain to others, but equally unforgettable in either extreme. He did his best to get all he could out of school and get out. Yes, it would have been easier for him to attend private school and it was not that his parents could not afford the cost, because for a while they had.

William had spent a full year in private school. His seventh grade year was a very prestigious academy of education. But it was without Dexter and a year where he was surrounded by illusions. It just seemed to him that enough of the people there were spending so much time being something they were not, that they failed to be real.

Public school was not a cure to the problem and William discovered that delusion was something that ran rampant in an adolescent's life. But still there was more of the common element in public school and in eighth grade he had made his return. He and Dexter had tried out for the football team and they both made it. They played only five plays the entire season, but each of them was a scoring play and registered enough to where they moved up the Coach Popularity Scale in time for Junior-Varsity football. It was then that there was a separation of sorts. Gillis always played more than William, but it was clear the quarterback had a favorite receiver. One for whom he would miss practice to attend science fairs where he did not know up from down. But it never kept him from showing his interest and always trying to understand the words coming out of friend's mouth. There were many reasons to like school. It just seemed that he had grown tired of all the reasons why he did not like it. He closed the car door and shouldered his bag. His head leaned forward ever so slightly as his eyes closed, his ears lifted and his nostrils flared. Dexter Douglas Gillis.

"How's it going, Gillis?"

"*What the hell?*" Dexter thought, moving up slowly and quietly in an effort to shake William out of his normal pre-school blues. The drum corps was practicing as they did every morning during the season. One of the boons of Columbia High School was its ethnic diversity. So while you had a white man as the band director demanding musicianship, he was surrounded by students and teachers who demanded a good show. As the band practiced bringing sexy back, many of the students around the parking lot were dancing. William could not have heard him.

Dexter always wore cologne, and more often than not William complained. That was half the fun in wearing it. The other half was being a living example of the advertisements currently on television about the effects of using body sprays. But it was the morning, and the cafeteria ladies were still chucking out the non-moving masses of nutrition that was loosely called breakfast. Despite how it looked or tasted, it always smelled good. That might have been the reason everyone always gave them the benefit of the doubt. So he could not have smelled him either.

William was facing the school, allowing the state of the educational system to weigh him down. Dexter had the hardest time getting around that part of his best friend. How he could place the status of the school on his own shoulders and actually try to carry it was beyond description.

"*So how did he know?*" Dexter thought as he walked up to William who was smiling at him.

"And how did you know it was me?" he asked.

"*Oh wonderful!*" William thought, racing through his mind to find a reasonable explanation that was not the truth. "*That's what you get for showing off!*" His eyes darted left and right and he breathed a slight sigh of relief. He put his talents toward substantiating his response.

"Your ego always arrives before you do," William answered as he started laughing, buying himself some time. Dexter nodded and gave a slight chuckle.

"Oh you are just too funny," he said as he finally broke from laughter. "No seriously, how did you know?"

"Dude, relax!" William said as he pointed to his car. The side mirror had been moved, nearly folded, but it was designed to do that instead of breaking. "I saw you in the mirror!"

Dexter's eyes shot to the mirror and sure enough, it was but of place out in a perfect place to reflect his approach. Dexter knew fact that William took care of the car better than most doctors took care of their patients and with that fact, Dexter nodded and laughed off what he was thinking and feeling. William felt like it would have been divinely appropriate for it to rain solely on him.

"*What a difference an assassination attempt makes,*" he thought as he looked at Dexter. He was sinking fast.

"You still with us, Gillis?"

"Huh, oh, yeah! Still here, man! I was just… oh nothing. I think I might have taken one to the head last game."

"You did!" William confirmed. "They caught your slow white ass and had all kinds of fun with it!" Dexter pushed him away as both young men smiled.

"The hell with you, Handyman. I ain't slow! You got me on white, but one of us has to make us look good!"

"Oh, someone's got jokes this morning," William replied.

"Yeah," Dexter said as his eyes shifted. "And someone's got some explaining to do."

William turned to see a familiar limousine entering the parking lot.

"I got word my best pair of hands had them hands all over that after the game *and* yesterday! I guess I am slow compared to your fast ass!"

"You got word?!" William said as he turned to face Dexter. Their eyes locked but William never saw him as his body shuddered and he grabbed his stomach.

"Yeah," Dexter answered, not knowing what was going on with William. "You forgot that girl from Faraday Academy lives in the same neighborhood as young... Miss... Rasner..."

William looked down at his hand, but it was not his hand he saw. It was older and feminine and it was covered in blood.

"Billy?" Dexter called to him. William's eyes and mouth gaped wide open. Gillis looked down and all he saw was the palm of William's hand.

There were no markings, no rings, but William could feel the importance of the hand. It was too great, too strong for William to assume it belonged to someone he did not know. Surprise and shock soon became fixed anger and confusion as William looked up at Dexter.

"I gotta go," he said and unlocked his car, quickly getting in. The car had not started when Dexter jumped into the passenger seat and put on his safety belt. William paused for a moment, but neither best friend said a word to the other. He pulled out of the parking space and the tires screamed as he sped out of the lot and on to the street. Though the car was loud it was never out of control and Dexter took hold of the *Oh Shit* handle and kept a very tight grip. He had been in the car with William before when driving fast was the goal. Typically the car fish-tailed more, there was always some loud music on and even then William's insane wailing could be heard over it. This time the radio was off and Dexter's best friend was not enjoying himself.

She had seen the exchange as the limo pulled into the parking lot. From the way he moved, Linda knew William had experienced a vision, a violent one to say the least. She watched as he turned away from Dexter and got into his car.

"Thank you, Dexter," she said softly, placing her hand on the window. She watched as the car moved out of sight at what had to be its best speed. She trembled as he moved out of her range of sight and she cursed the name and existence of C'Silla. Linda knew too much for her own good and all it did was fill her with indecision and fear.

The door opened and she jumped away from it, almost screaming. "I'm sorry, Miss," Hughes said quickly. "I did not mean to startle you." She looked at him and her tremble grew to shaking and shaking into crying. Alistair Hughes was quick to move. He had always been. Though it was not his place to display tenderness, seldom had Linda Rasner held to those places. Alistair had known Linda's father, Lawrence Derek Rasner, and had stood by her side when she had to bury him. The times that immediately followed were horrid as Mrs. Rasner raced to fill a void that could best be described as spacious yet growing. There were many suitors, all of whom were anything but suitable. But while none of the house staff appreciated Herbert Favonius or his flavor, for some reason Mrs. Rasner took to him. Five months after she had buried her husband, she walked down the aisle to take another man's ring and name.

Linda had lashed out every chance she could get and each time it was Hughes, Miller and Dance that brought her back. Peyton Miller was a fine lawyer and an even better friend who made it possible for Linda to actually protect her estate and, in certain cases, use some of those assets to at least keep Hughes on the payroll. But he was the last of the original house staff and the only true friend Linda had at the household. As she got older, Linda had wanted nothing to do with the world she had been born to and had employed some rather colorful methods to get herself removed from several private schools. Herbert thought he was punishing her by sending her to a public school but it was exactly what she wanted and she had found a place to call her own. However that place had been repeatedly challenged, the latest coming in the form of the limousine Herbert purchased and then fought to argue that buying a car when she already had one was not an acceptable application of her funds. In order to keep his place, Peyton, the executor of the estate, was forced to agree and a very sizeable wedge was driven between Linda and her friends. While the effects of that wedge were beginning to wear off, William came into the picture. The past few weeks had been so much better for his young employer and Alistair was happy to see her smile so much. Now it appeared there was something amiss with William and it looked to be pulling her in as well.

"I'm a coward, Hughes!" she said. "That's why I'm crying. I'm a damn coward!"

"Now see here-"

"Oh come off it, Hughes!" she snapped. "Look at me! He needs all the help he can get and I'm sitting here on my ass and crying!"

"If I or anyone in his life needed help, he wouldn't hesitate," Linda continued. "Not one second!"

"Miss, we do what we can," Hughes argued. "Nothing less and certainly nothing more." Through all of the tears and all of the pain, Linda heard him. Somehow she heard him and the crying soon came to a halt. "Have I offended you, Miss?"

"Take me home, Hughes," she said, wiping her eyes. "Immediately!"

"As you wish, Miss," Hughes said, touching his hand to the brim of his hat as he got out of the car, a smile on his face. He had seen that glimmer in her eyes before. It had been some time since that wondrous afternoon, but he was glad to see some of the dancer make a comeback. He knew better than to ask her again what she was talking about. She had already refused that request once already. To ask again would have been more than rude. All things moved at their own speed and Alistair had lived long enough to know that there was nothing to be gained from rushing Linda Rasner. He did not know what was coming but he was pretty sure it would be something well worth remembering.

"*Alright, you!*" Linda thought, closing her eyes. "*I know you monitor William and I have a pretty good idea you monitor me so please answer me.*" Linda opened her eyes but nothing had changed. She was still in the back of the car alone and on her way home.

"Fine," she said reaching for her purse. "You wanna play that way, all I have to do is call William and let him know you've been playing God with his memory and-" Linda's body went limp as her mind was taken to the Territories.

Thirty-Two

He hated being rushed. There was a lack of precision to haste. *Sloppiness breeds inefficiency*, he had been drilled to know and came to believe. A strong belief only reconfirmed by his demotion; he had gone too far, he had crossed the line. Bey had tried to warn him, he owed her for that, but his mind was not in a place where he could hear her. The demotion had given him plenty of time to think, to sharpen up, to become air-tight!

"*Still, this is damn sloppy!*" he thought as he took off his gloves and helmet, stuffing the former into the latter and handing it to a waiting technician. "Thanks," he said as the young man took the helmet.

"You're welcome, Lambda Scout," he replied, pushing up his glasses. "They are already in session with the Dugout and they're waiting for you."

"Understood," he replied, walking out of the room, not bothering to remove his suit. He could feel the floor shake under his boots but he paid it little mind. He closed his eyes and put his left hand to the side of the corridor. He did not need eyes to walk and being in a new place always made his eyes hungry. Time for those details later, his mindset had to come first. After his delivery, he would have preferred to have been given some time to get his bearings, but when the Dugout calls, sometimes an MVP does not have much of a choice. He focused his thoughts inside and made the most of his time.

"Good to see you, Lambda," Sabrina said, watching him on one of her monitors. Her eyes moved over him casually at first, something of a *if you've seen one MVP, you've seen them all* appraisal. But there was something to his walk that made her do a double-take. His focused eyes made her smile brightly.

The mission was more than rushed and she hated using brand new, and therefore unverified, intelligence. Two of the three main members were injured and though the doctors had given them all the green light, Sabrina had seen what could happen on missions where the doctors were wrong. She did not have much reason to smile. Alpha Scout was going to be assigned a brand new Multi-Frame, one that had not yet been tested and she could not believe he was one hundred percent. But watching Lambda walk while he meditated was good news and she smiled.

"*Real* good to see you!" she said as she prepared her briefing.

The door opened and Lambda Scout walked in. He immediately looked at Alpha Scout and nodded.

"*He's not all here!*" Lambda thought looking at the team leader. "*Boy's still banged up and rattled.*"

"*Okay, this is not what I expected,*" Alpha thought as he watched Terrell Whitaker walk into the room. The view was night and day from the last time he had seen the MVP. He liked this view better, but at the same time, he could feel the air around him tightening. It was no secret that the Owners loved them some Lambda Scout, and he had given them reason to be loved. His mission logs were so damn dynamic, even Lazlo was a fan!

"Lambda," he said, receiving Terrell's respectful nod, returning his own. "You're late."

Terrell immediately saw Lazlo's smile and chuckled himself. "Yeah, well traffic was a mess! How's it going, Alpha Team?"

"Going good and always getting better," Sylvestra nodded, giving the obligatory response to that question. But Terrell looked at Conway who did not speak, though he did smile and nod.

"Whatsahmatta, Sabrina got your tongue?" Terrell joked and everyone, including Conway, laughed. Conway stood up and slapped forearms with Terrell.

"Dugout, this is Alpha Scout. Lambda has arrived and we are ready to receive."

"Received, Alpha," Sabrina replied, activating the view screen in the War Room. The image she sent was their target.

"That does not look like Quantico," Beta said, leaning back in her chair.

"That's because it isn't," Sabrina replied.

"Knew there was a good reason."

The floor shook again and Lambda looked over at Alpha. "Did you feel that?"

"Sure did," he answered, shrugging his shoulders.

"It can't be helped, Lambda," Sabrina offered. "We're on a major time crunch and you of all people should know why."

"Knowing everything in the world doesn't make it a better place," he returned. "I take it you guys have seen the footage?"

"Twice," Sylvestra said, looking down at the table. "But I have to admit, your boy's reel of you on the move was pretty sweet. You've gotten tighter."

"Let's hope it's tight enough," Terrell replied. "What am I on this one? I haven't logged a scenario hour with these guys in seventeen weeks! Things are bound to get sloppy."

"That is a contingency the Owners have given their clearance for," Sabrina informed them and the MVPs looked around the room at each other. To be given such a wide berth was something they always said they wanted but believed they would never receive. Having received it they now wished they had never said anything. "We're allowed to be mysterious, but nothing that can identify you specifically. I am on standby for any cover-up, but we are green for body count!

"To answer your question, Lambda," Sabrina continued, "...allow me to introduce you all to the new Alpha Team. Alpha Scout, you are team lead."

"Received, Dugout," Alpha said as he rubbed the bridge of his nose. "Go for note."

"Go ahead, Alpha," Sabrina said, activating the permanent record.

"Three works and five works. Four just gets in the way of things."

"Received, Alpha," Sabrina answered. "You will meet your fifth team member when you get to the target, call sign Sigma Scout. You will receive exact notes en route, team. We are coming up on your disembark point."

They all got up from their seats at the same time and headed for the door.

"This should be interesting," Alpha said as he reached the door first. His new team followed him down the corridor without a word. This was a relatively light assignment, but that did not mean it did not receive the same level of concentration. All of them were wearing their field deployment suits so when they stepped into the final preparations room, all they had to do was strap their weapons down.

"Multi-Frames are on the ground!" a technician announced, donning an oxygen mask. "Sigma has their location."

"Talk about a built-in life insurance policy," Beta Scout said checking her favored missile weapons, her throwing daggers.

"Tell me about it," Lambda agreed.

"Bad news for the new guy," Alpha said, securing his second pistol. The other technicians began to move the storage bins out of the room. No one was wasting time today.

"Figured," Terrell said, tightening his gloves. "I'll keep a safe eye on Sigma and stay out of your way."

"Much appreciated," Lazlo replied as he walked to the last staging area. He was relieved to be working with another team leader. It meant he did not have to explain himself as much.

"No need, Alpha!" the technician called out and the floor shook once more. "You'll have plenty of time." The technician quickly moved to the frame of the doorway. "Let's get to Ready One, people!"

"Alpha ready," Lazlo said, standing front of one wall. The rest of Alpha Team took his lead and each took a wall. "Everybody take one deep."

"Gear is gone!" the technician announced as he looked in the room and the floor rattled. He checked his own placement and then around the room. Everything was clear. "Alpha Team is gone!"

The floor gave and they were sucked out of the plane. Each member put their body into their practiced maneuvers as they tumbled through the clouds. They ignored the cold and held their breaths. The suits held, they always held, and none of the weapons came free from their bodies, but it was not due to any lack of the laws of physics.

Lambda Scout made a motion with his right hand. Holding their breaths made it impossible to speak, but each MVP knew ASL and as Lambda called for acknowledgement, each member hit their locator. Knowing all eyes were on him, Lambda signed that he had visual of the gear. Specifically, the equipment they were going to need in order to avoid fatal deceleration trauma. Lambda, Delta, Beta and Alpha, in that order formed, a line and followed Lambda's lead.

"Whoa, he's gotten tight!" Alpha thought as he was still clearing the cobwebs of the initial smack of their airspeed. But he could at least see the other members of his team, even if he could not see the Concession Stand. Lambda guided his body directly to it and took his position, as if he had been with the team since its inception. He took the most precarious position, which was usually Alpha's job, and he was glad to be rid of it. First one to the CS was no longer an MVP, they were a Vendor, and it was their job to make sure everyone got to their gear, got it on and got clear of the CS before it self-destructed. Lambda had two packs cleared before Delta floated to him. Conway tumbled by Terrell, and Lambda had the man half-hooked up by the time he glided by. He did the same to Beta as the Concession Stand alarm light started flashing. They had ten seconds and Alpha was five seconds out. Taking the last two packs, Lambda left the Stand and moved toward Alpha who he got hooked as the chutes on the Stand opened. Its rate of descent slowed and three seconds later it blew. Lambda then saw to his own equipment as Beta checked everyone. They were set and ready to open with still 11,000 feet left to their drop.

Helmets went active, Sabrina was now with them and Alpha smiled as he could see that she had arranged for six different channels, one for each member to talk to her specifically and one where everyone could listen.

"You going to whisper sweet nothings in my ear, darlin'?" Lazlo said, checking his helmet readings.

"Why should today be any different?" she answered and he could see the smile on her face.

"Well this is one hero who knows when he's been slammed," Lazlo said before switching to his team channel. "Beta, you've got lead on this one. You know the drill, just call the ball. Delta, you're still our heavy hitter and I'll take Beta's normal position."

"Received, Alpha," Sylvestra replied, allowing her body to fall faster, taking the actual lead of the team. "But we will be moving faster with me in the lead, Grandpa!"

"Ouch," Sabrina said. "I don't care who you are, that one's gotta sting! Go for satellite link, Alpha Team." Each member activated the controls on their arms and their goggles received a satellite feed of their target. It was still pretty dark, but by the time they made it to the ground, there was going to be a blue tint to the sky. Given their escape vector, it was clear Sabrina had lost nothing of her planning genius, even with the accelerated timetable.

"Team, we're going HALO," Beta Scout ordered and Lazlo was relieved. High Altitude Low Opening was Sylvestra's least favorite but conditions were ideal for that type of jump. She went for more speed and the team acted accordingly. "Sigma Scout, this is Beta Scout. Are you mean and green?"

"Beta Scout, this is Sigma Scout. I have front row tickets and I have just gone inside the gate. Name your range."

"Received, Sigma," Beta replied, going into her silent count. "Lambda will join you at the west gate. You will watch the parking lot and you will give me a scouting report. Acknowledge."

His breathing had been taxed, but his need for air was beginning to wane. He had a hold of his weapon but it was useless to him. As many lives as it had taken, it had failed to help him keep his own. The shadow of a man that hit like anything but had taken him, slit his throat and laid him on the ground with his partner only five feet away and completely unaware of what was happening. Finally, the Hispanic man released him and he could move again, but lacked the ability to do what he wanted. Crouched low the man caught up with Mack and thrust his knife into his partner's back. He moved the knife to the right and then twisted the blade before removing it and he laid Mack down, paralyzed.

"Received, Beta," the man said as he looked around. "I am already at the west gate and I've cleared the crowd. FYI, the parking lot is on the south side for this trip."

"Received, Sigma," Beta answered. "Since you have a clearance, we will meet you at the west gate."

"I'll get the popcorn ready, muchachos."

At 1,000 feet, Beta Scout gave the signal for the jumpers to separate and give themselves some room for their packs to open. At seven hundred feet, she gave the signal to open and their bodies tumbled as the specially designed parachutes opened, slowed their descent and, in the case of Beta, Delta and Alpha Scouts, they were released. Lambda kept his parachute and dropped toward the west gate. He separated from his chute and took the last sixty feet on his own. He hit and rolled, coming up with his submachine gun ready to fire.

"Shirley?" Lambda said softly.

"Louise," he received and turned to see Sigma Scout. He was dressed in all black gear. He had to have been new. The way he came out of his cover area with his sniper's rifle at the ready... he moved well, but did not check his corners to Terrell's satisfaction. But he ran toward Lambda Scout and held up his rifle. "One hundred eleven."

"One hundred twenty-two," Terrell replied, giving the new guy his range score for the sniper's rifle.

"SMG," he whispered, tossing his rifle to Terrell. Lambda kept his weapon trained on the approaching new man as he caught the rifle and checked to see if it was really loaded. Verifying that, he placed his submachine gun on safe and tossed it to Sigma.

"What, no trust?" he asked with a smile.

"Trust comes with time, Sigma. We get through this and I'll check you off for a little more trust."

"Fair enough, I'll take lead to the Multi-Frames then."

"First things first," Terrell said, taking a knee and removing his backpack. Sylvestra sent a message via Sabrina and Terrell thought it was a novel notion. "Cover me," he said as he began to assemble the necessary tools.

"Parachutes clear and away," she ordered and each of the three hit the controls to release their parachutes. They placed their arms down their sides and their legs together.

"Go for glide!" Beta commanded, her arms coming away from the body though now there was a thin section of fabric going from the inside of the arms to the ribs and another section between the legs. Delta and Alpha did the same and took her left and right wing positions.

"Silent running, people," Sylvestra said as she banked to her right and brought the house to her center vision. She went infrared and took a sweep over the house. She signed she saw fifteen people counting their target. It was nearly 5:15 AM, local time, and only two people were in bed. Another set of commands told Alpha it was his job to get the two bodies upstairs in case they needed to be used as leverage. At their current speed, Lazlo had just enough speed to afford a slight climb up to the second story balcony. He landed with barely a sound and was soon picking the lock. Six seconds. He had done better, but the time was acceptable and he entered the room with his pistol ready to fire, the built in suppressor active.

"Is that you, baby," a female voice asked.

"Great, I have a light sleeper," Lazlo whispered in his helmet.

"You are cleared for the kill, Alpha," Sabrina replied, hoping he would opt to just knock the poor woman unconscious. But they had a job to do and her job was to be their support and keep her personal feelings out of the picture.

"Received, Dugout," Alpha replied, making his way around the bed and running his hand up the leg of the woman. She moaned in approval and she moved under his touch.

"Hmmmm, someone must be on their medication," she said before Alpha's hand jabbed her in the side of the head.

"Figured," he said. "I know I'm in the master bedroom and this girl is way too young to be our target's wife."

"No," Sabrina said. "She sleeps down the hall."

"Absolute power." Alpha grabbed the woman and carried her over his shoulder, making his way down the hall. Two lovers were better than one. Especially when it was difficult to guess which one the target really cared about. "Freakin' California!"

Sylvestra smiled as Alpha landed on the balcony, he had the easy job. With the time they had left, they were going to get a little loud and sloppy. Even though Sabrina had given them clearance to be exactly that, it did not make it any easier for them. Normally they were been given more room to operate and more time to prep but they were MVPs and they would change their approach to the job because of it.

"Lambda, we are ten seconds out."

"Received, Beta," Lambda replied, still on one knee but aiming his newly assembled grenade launcher. "I've got a one-two of pow-smoke for you."

"Six seconds," she answered.

"Firing!" New to the team or not, Terrell was one of the first MVPs and had seen a few come and die. He was still in the game and still one of the best. Perhaps the punishment given to him was severe, but there was no arguing the result. The grenade arched in front of the Beta and Delta Scouts and would go off precisely two seconds before their arrival which meant they could glide right into the house. Sweet!

He poured another round of brandy. From the looks of the bottle, it would be the last round. But still he was smiling. Though he did not particularly like the occasion, he was always pleased to receive her. She always brought the best gifts for him to smoke or for the two of them to drink. They had been talking for nearly eight hours, him trying to get her to see reason. Once again it appeared he was going to fail, which only served to complicate things. Not that they were not complicated already.

"Thidalia, is there anything I can say or do to get you to change your mind?" He smiled as he handed her the glass.

"You are so delightful, George," she smiled back, taking the glass. She crossed her legs and let the dress she was wearing work its way into his mind. Men were ever so drawn to things they have been told they cannot have. "But you already know the position I am in. I can no more say yes to you than I can say no to him."

"Then perhaps you will be so good as to arrange a meeting," George Austin Howard answered as he took his seat. "We could talk man to man, get some things cleared up."

Rook started to advance but Thidalia raised her hand and tilted her head to the side. She was no longer smiling and she knew that George did not care. She had been afraid of this. His eyes had seen Webster and his treachery. A treachery she had yet to resolve and while Peter Webster was still alive, her credibility was slighted. But perhaps George needed to remember the old adage that warns people to be careful for what they wish. She lifted her glass toward her lips to take a drink but she was cut and blinded by the wave of shattered glass that burst into the room.

"Mistress!" Rook called to her and she waved him off again, keeping her concentration on the view of George's office. Two assailants came into the room, along with a wave of blinding and choking smoke. They restrained George and killed the likenesses of Rook and herself before she had time to get a good view of them. With her likeness killed, her connection to the office was compromised.

"What is this?!" she yelled, getting up too fast for her still-wounded body. She shuddered from the pain and Rook eased her back into her chair. She closed her eyes and returned her efforts to healing her battered body.

"You have looked better, Thidalia," a voice said, announcing himself, and Thidalia jumped at the sound of it, causing herself more pain.

"Oh my, that did not look too good," he continued, leaning back against the window of her bed chambers. He did so love making unannounced visits, especially to Thidalia. She was gracious before the eyes of man or woman, flawless and thought to be so passionate with but the curl of her lips into a smile. Any opportunity to control one so controlling amused him.

"What do you want, Dahvahn?" she barked, trying her best to keep some hold of her body and remove the pain of her sudden movements. "Before I have my Rook show you the other side of that window."

"Rook?" Dahvahn mocked her, brushing back his straight blonde hair, his green eyes flashing with the message that he was not afraid of her servant or her for that matter. "Oh come now, *Thidie*, old girl! Don't you find that name just a bit drab? Well, not just a bit."

"You twig of a man, speak or begone!" Thidalia yelled.

"Oh my!" Dahvahn said, his slender, pale frame hopping down from the windowsill and feigning fear. He wore dark, long, baggy clothing that barely subscribed to their current surroundings and with the extra fabric of his sleeve he fashioned a mask.

"Rook!" Thidalia called and her servant lunged toward Dahvahn.

"Yes, Rook, burn!" Dahvahn said and the massive frame exploded in flames, falling quickly to the ground and rolling, but with every ember he smothered on one side, ten more sprang from the opposite. Dahvahn jumped for joy as though he had just received his favorite toy. "Now all we need are marshmallows!"

"And gauze," Pawn said as she came into the room, firing her gun. The first shot found Dahvahn's hip, the second his left arm, and the third tore through the left shoulder. "Plenty of gauze!" She looked over to Rook who was finally able to smother all of the flames. He stood up. He was weak, almost too weak to continue but he would not show that weakness to Thidalia. Perhaps that was why she preferred him to the others. Pawn grabbed Dahvahn by his arm wound and lifted him up to his feet.

"I left you one arm," she said coldly, placing the gun to the side of his head. "Now heal my Mistress and Rook or die!" Dahvahn looked at Thidalia who hoped he would refuse the request and therefore end his life. But he lifted his one good arm and allowed the reformation of flesh for Thidalia, her precious Rook and himself. After which he tore himself from Pawn's grasp.

"Get your hands off of me!" he demanded before pointing at Thidalia.

"Oh come now, Dahvahn," Thidalia cooed. "She was merely following my directives regarding *any* unannounced visitors. I am sure you know all about the Rule of Etiquette?" Dahvahn trembled at his expenditure but he had enough strength to be away from this place and see to his truest errand.

"Our lord has his eyes upon you, Thidalia," he warned. "And his eyes, like mine, are not so taken with you! These matters begin to spin out of your control and he will make amends if he has to. But we both know what that means for you!"

She knew all too well, having been in Dahvahn's position, what the message meant. Her lord was not one to give warnings of a sort. He would rather send an obvious rival to motivate the one being scrutinized. It was a most ingenious application of personnel. "I know what it means, Dahvahn," she answered nodding her head to have the large windows open. "Go and tell our lord you have indeed delivered the message and I will deliver a message of my own!" Dahvahn flashed a very evil smile before he took flight, the windows closed soon after he departed. Thidalia thanked Pawn for her resourcefulness and Rook for his unwavering loyalty. She then went about the business of trying to see what had happened, as she was not the only one to receive uninvited guests. As the image was created, she could see her likeness was still in one piece though degrading rapidly. But through it she could see that the visitors had made off with George Howard of the Federal Bureau of Investigation.

"But the way they moved, they were not Prodigian," she said as she began to pace.

"Undoubtedly not," Pawn confirmed. "They moved like Tyros. Trained and augmented, but Tyros nonetheless."

"Agreed, but that does not help me much. I will go and make my own report. That should buy me some time to restore my control of the situation."

"If anyone can succeed, it is my Mistress," Pawn replied.

"Twice you have saved me, Pawn," Thidalia said as she placed her hands on the sides of the woman's face. "I will not forget this. While I am gone, find for me what you can about these visitors. Consult with Caprice if you must, but get me answers!"

"By your order, Mistress!" Pawn said as she bowed forward and received a kiss to the forehead. She stood up, turned and left the room.

"As for you and I," Thidalia said to Rook. "We must assume better attire. Between my sleeping robes and your singed clothing, we are not going to make the impression we must in order to continue and succeed. Come!" Rook only bowed his reply and followed his mistress out of the room. The clothes she spoke of were not kept in these closets. They were too valuable and would have caused too much trouble had they been discovered by prying eyes. But she was not looking forward to the reason for wearing them. Whatever aspirations she had held in her heart for her return home, reality had dismissed them. But she had not yet run into a dead end in the maze of mysterious adversaries. She still had options, avenues she hoped her skills and favor with her lord could afford her a chance to explore. And if such an opportunity were given to her, she would return to her assignment with a fury this world had learned to forget!

"And my dear Peter Webster, you shall be the first!"

Thirty-Three

"Nothing about this looks good," Tara said as she drove up to the address she had been given. She knew better than to pull into the driveway, but she got out of the car and quickly used her phone.

"No calls have been placed to 911," Simmons said as he answered the phone. "So it looks like you've got some time.

"And I've also taken the liberty of backdating your PI licensing and gun permit. Sis is working on getting your letter to the Fulton County Police Department."

"Well that's all well and good, Simmons, bu-"

"Having a letter appear in the DeKalb County Sheriff's Office the same day as a committed crime tends to add suspicion, not deter it," Simmons explained.

"Why did I even bother to open my mouth?" Tara replied with a smile. "I should've known you'd have all the bases covered.

"Where's the rest of the team?" she asked, taking out her weapon.

"Why don't you transfer me over to your ear piece and concentrate on where you're at," Simmons replied. Some things, like Death, Taxes and Alfred Simmons would never change. With Lydia out of the picture, he was *ramrod* and if anyone had anything to say about it, all they had to do was present their argument and hope it stood the test of his reasoning.

"*He's right,*" Tara thought. "*Don't know if the area is clear.*"

"*Sweets,*" Jon called to her.

"*This really isn't the time, baby!*" Tara answered before she realized that Jonathan was standing right beside her, in full color and blocking her view of what was on the other side of him. Her hand went to her mouth and she stepped back from Jon as he lowered his head. "It is that time!" she said softly and Jonathan nodded.

"Simmons, we've got a 187 at this address. Jon's going to take me to the scene of the crime."

"Make sure you follow protocols, Mifflen," Simmons said. She could hear him feverishly typing into his computer. Tara made her way down the driveway which went up to the side of the house. As she worked her way around the front, she could see her, an elderly black woman, lying too still on the front porch of the house. Tara quickened her step and as she did, she could see all of the porch and just to the left of the dead woman, the same woman stood over her own body. She looked down in confusion.

"What's wrong with me?" she asked.

"Oh, I am so not geared for this," Tara whispered as she approached.

"You've got no enemies here, Sweets," Jonathan said and Tara quickly holstered her gun.

"Thanks, baby," she replied softly. "What's her name?"

"Rachel, Dr. Rachel Cassandra Pryor." Tara closed her eyes and Jon fed to her conscious mind all he had been able to gather about the woman. She shuddered from the weight of the information; hers was not a life wasted, so much as it would be a life sorely missed. Among those things Rachel would consider her crowning achievements, Tara saw William, and her eyes opened. The sound of tires screeching to a halt made her turn around. At the top of the hill, she could see William getting out of his car. She could not explain how she knew it, but letting William see Rachel's her dead body was not going to serve anything constructive and she ran to meet him halfway.

"William, no!" she cried.

Halfway would have been the far side of the tire tread-ripped rose garden. She was about three meters from it when she threw her arms around William and prayed for the strength to turn this raging bull!

"Rachel!" William cried out, his eyes beginning to fill with tears. His senses had already made their report. There was too little sound, nothing to see, and the smell of gunpowder, ozone and blood. Still, his eyes had to confirm it.

"William, no!" She screamed as her feet slid backward. "William please! You have to listen to me! Stop!" A second pair of hands grabbed William from behind and started to pull.

"C'mon, man," Dexter said as his eyes met Tara's and she silently thanked him for his added efforts. "This is a bad scene, man, and you're only going to make it worse."

"Rachel!" William cried out again, stirring me from my daze. Still he made progress.

"William!" Tara cried, putting her back into her pushing.

"Jesus!" Dex cried, pulling for all he was worth but feeling like he was trying to pull a Mack Truck in gear going down a steep hill. *"He's stronger than Armstrong!"* he thought.

"[*RACHEL!*]" William screamed and even Jon jumped at the power of his projection. Dexter fell to his knees, grabbing his head, and Jon fell, losing color and density. Tara drew her weapon and hammered down across the back of William's head. He was functionally unconscious but still managed three more steps before he collapsed.

"You still there, Simmons?"

"I am, and I finally got a satellite feed," Simmons answered, thinking that it would not be helpful to report he felt something come over the phone. "You've got company on the roof of the house."

Tara flipped her gun and prepared to fire it as she looked up. I was surprised by her speed and the fact she could detect me. I quickly held up my hand to assure the woman I meant her no harm.

"It's me, Tara. It's Elkazzar."

"How the hell did you get up there?"

"It is a long story," I answered. "Per chance you will find some rope or a ladder with which I can climb down?"

"Ladder or rope?" Tara said, shocked at the request. "This is going to be some story." She turned to see Dexter trying to get up.

"What the hell is going on?" he groaned.

"Talk about long stories," Tara replied, getting a handkerchief out of her pocket. "You're the quarterback, right?"

"Yeah," Dexter answered.

Tara nodded as she bent over, picking up one of the stones that acted as a boundary for the garden. She handed Dexter the stone along with the fabric and pointed at the window closest to Elkazzar. She knew from what Jon had given her that the windows on this side of the house were quite normal.

"Think you can nail that window for me? Old man needs a hand."

"I can hear you!" I advised as young Dexter Gillis took the stone, set himself and hurled it with interesting accuracy and power. The window shattered and Tara motioned toward it.

"Nice toss!" Tara commented.

"Thanks," Dexter answered, looking at William. "Man, you really hit him hard."

"Yeah, you keep thinking that, kid. Ever-ready here is going to be up in no time.

"Fresh out of ladders and rope here, Elkee," Tara called up to me as she motioned to her body. "Bruce is still making last minute adjustments to my utility belt. Just make your way down and out, and make sure you don't touch anything."

I came through the house and the low feeling I was already suffering was made worse when I did not see Vastiol's body. They had taken him too. I stood for a moment where he had fallen and looked around the room. They removed any trace of themselves down to the blood of those who were injured or killed. They had had much time!

By the time I joined them, William was conscious and sitting up, rubbing his head. He glared up at Tara but said nothing. Despite his anger, he knew why she acted as she had. Dexter had already walked around the house enough to see Rachel and the sight of her turned his stomach. It was his first time seeing death so close and the distance did not agree with him.

"I need to see her," Williams said.

"That would be colossally bad," Tara answered. "You're liable to take someone's head off when the biscuits get burned. This is too much."

"It is too much," I added, "for an animal!"

"*Man's got a major-sized death wish,*" Tara thought.

"*He's got a monster-sized agenda,*" Jon said to her. "*There's a lot going on here, Sweets.*"

"*Uh, Jon honey,*" Tara thought, her eyes still on William, "*...under 'useless information', I'd have to say that last bit takes the cake!*"

"*Sorry, Sweets,*" he replied. "*Sometimes I get so wrapped up in all of this. All that Harry did trying to control you fed me a lot of information about the Prodigian.*"

"We'll get to that tonight," Tara said. She stood up as William stood up, glaring at Elkazzar.

"I thought we already went through that test," William growled.

"You were tested with mere agitations, boy!" I snapped. "This be life and death! Worse yet, the death of one you held very close!"

"*Hold* close," William corrected me. "And if either of you gets in my way again, you'll see the animal you fear so much!"

"Does that go for me too?" Dexter said as he walked between William and the house.

"Dex, you don't know-"

"And when has that ever meant shit, Bill?" Dexter interrupted. "Man it looks like I haven't been knowing for some time."

"It just seems that way," William answered. "I haven't been knowing all my life, up to about a few weeks ago. That's when everything changed for me."

"Okay," Dexter nodded. "That changes things a bit... you haven't been lying to me all your life, just the past few weeks! Yeah, that takes out some of the sting."

[*Perhaps this changes things a bit,*] William projected and Tara took a step back in disgust. She did not appreciate his means of telling his best friend the truth.

[*Give him room, Tara,*] I projected to her. [*They have seen much of the same sky for many seasons and friends such as these are permitted a harshness those outside of their bond cannot understand.*]

[*No, you aren't freaking out,*] William continued to Dexter, [*...and my lips aren't moving. You're hearing my thoughts. I am projecting my thoughts into your mind. Telepathy is what we call it but believe you me the weirdness doesn't stop there!*] William drew his focus on Dexter's body and the boy's wallet came out of his pocket. It hovered around Dexter's chest and opened. William was showing excellent control.

[*Broke, as usual!*] he projected and the two young men found reason to smile but Dexter did not hold his elation for long, the hovering wallet killed it. [*I can do this because all of my people can do it. That's what changed a few weeks ago. I found out Gordon is not my father, but it turns out my real father is just as black. I guess Mom has particular tastes. I also found out my people are a tribe of humans you and I knew nothing about.*]

"At least, until a few weeks back," Dexter said softly.

"Exactly!" William answered.

"And this woman here?"

"Just another Tyro," William replied. "That is what my people call us... I mean your people."

"So you're like a mutant?!" Dexter asked and I was surprised to her excitement in his voice.

"Dude, the Prodigian have it so over any mutant you've ever heard of. We're not limited to just one power. The mind can be applied to a number of abilities."

"That is an overstatement," I corrected as I approached Dexter. "Your friend, Dexter, is exceptional."

Dexter looked at William and pointed his thumb at me. "He thinks he needed to tell me that," he whispered.

"William," I continued, "...has the ability to apply his power to a number of talents, as do I. But only about one-third of our people have this variance of power. The rest are limited to two or three abilities aside from telepathy. William was simply making an assumption based on those of our kind he has met."

"Met?" William repeated. "You used the word met?

"What he means to say instead of *met* Dex is the assholes who tried to *kill* me. Like the woman at the game!"

"Whoa!" Dexter said loudly, jumping back. "She's one of you guys?! And she tried to kill you?!"

"Did her level best," William admitted. "If it hadn't been for Tara and her friends with the FBI-"

"FBI?!" Dexter yelled, jumping back again.

"Oh, that was smooth," Tara commented.

"Yeah, Dex," William said calmly. "You see, when she was looking for me, he didn't know what I looked like or where I lived. So she killed anyone who might have fit the bill. Killing that many people tends to draw the attention of law enforcement."

"Attention!" William said as he looked down, realizing something that stirred him.

"What is it?" I asked.

"Nothing that can't wait," William said as he turned to walk to the house. Again Tara and Dexter wanted to stop him but I motioned them back.

"If he cannot walk as a man now, he never will!"

"Okay, I'm still missing stuff here," Dexter said to Tara.

"You sure are, kid," Tara said, looking up at me. "Why don't you help him out, Elkee?"

"I will…as soon as I can," I answered following William.

"Well, that wipes out about six or seven of my questions," Tara said. She looked over at Dexter and put her hand on his shoulder. "Hang in there, kid. Shit's gonna get weirder. I can promise you that. Answers are only going to lead to more questions and right about now we are trying to find a fart in a whirlwind. But if you hang in there, it will eventually come around to making sense to you."

"Or you can jump smart and get the hell out of here," Tara offered, holding up the keys to her car.

"Hey, lady, didn't anyone tell you? *He's* the brains around here!" Dexter walked to follow his friend and Tara smiled at what she saw. In a different place, she could see Tara Mifflen following after Lydia King, but they were not as close as friends as these two young men.

"Oh my God!" he whispered as she came into view. His body trembled and his steps became unsure. But he kept walking toward her until walking was not fast enough. He ran up to her dead body and, against Tara's wishes, took it into his arms.

"It means nothing," I said.

"Nothing!" she whispered. "He's tampering with evidence!"

"Of what crime?" I asked, beginning to understand what William was alluding to with that single word. Attention.

How was it that only Yudara's movements provoked an FBI investigation when it was obvious there were other members of the Prodigian tribe living amongst the Tyros? Had none of them ever used their powers to commit crimes? And in that line of questioning, I recalled something I saw in the house. It served little import as I walked by it, as my attention was elsewhere, but now it required further investigation.

"Rachel," he whispered as he kissed her cooling forehead. A gun fell from her grasp on to the porch. Tara was quick to grab it, using a handkerchief to block the passing of her fingerprints.

"What the hell is that?" Dexter said.

"I'd say this is the murder weapon," Tara said as she examined the weapon. "A little big for a little old lady," she commented.

"Especially when you take into account that she was a pacifist and was petrified of guns," William added.

"*So, that's why you didn't shoot,*" Jon said, and Tara turned to see Jonathan talking to Rachel as she gazed upon William. She wanted to touch him, but something around his body prevented her touch. He could not sense her, either, even as he held on to her body.

"Uh, Will?"

"*Easy, Sweets,*" Jonathan warned. "*Once you open that door, it can't be closed, and that kid has enough on his plate!*"

Tara looked down as William looked at her. On one hand she agreed with Jonathan. William already needed another set of shoulders to carry the water he had in front of him. But on the other hand, both of them deserved the chance to say goodbye.

"What is it?" he asked.

"Look through my eyes," Tara requested, preparing herself for another linkage with his mind. "But just look." William quickly took her lead and it was not long before he could see Rachel. She turned to face Tara, knowing William's mind was in the woman's body.

"*There you are!*" she said with a bright smile. "*Now before you even try, I am not long for this world, sweetheart. This is no longer my place.*"

"Rachel," Tara's mouth opened but it was not her voice that came out.

"Whoa!" Dexter said, jumping back into me.

"You were warned," I said. "Tara promised you as much.

"And you may as well know that William's stepfather was his father's best friend. Not just his best among Tyros, truly his best friend! I wonder if you find that as interesting as I do."

"Rachel, I'm sorry!"

"*Son, you didn't shoot me!*" she answered, still smiling. She touched Tara's cheek but William's body shuddered. "*And the man who shot me thought he was protecting Vada-Ri!*"

"Vada!" William exclaimed. Rachel touched Tara again and passed to them the events from her perspective and those other unseen witnesses to the event. They were called *wayfarers*, the faces William saw when he visited the phantasm in Tara's mind, and it was their task to take those from this world to the next. Jon had refused them and had the strength to deny their power. Rachel had only asked for time. She knew her William would come and somehow she knew he would cross over for her. It made her heart glow to know she was right. But her smile was not as bright, for she had added to William's burden.

"No," William argued. "You did not add to anything except my means to survive. You taught me how to deal with being me and without it, I'd be lost! I am just sorry that my world brought you to this."

"*Knowing my fate, I'd do it all again if given the chance. Some things are worth dying for!*" Tears began to roll down William's cheek. "*Your world, as you put it, is a wonderful, beautiful place. But you've got to figure it out, just like you have to figure you out, before you can help it. Find the things worth living for!*"

"And when another of those reasons is taken from me?" William asked.

"*Make their passing mean something,*" she answered quickly and I lowered my head to her wisdom. "*If indeed they are worth living for, let your life reflect what you found in them.*" The *wayfarers* came forward and made their presence known to William and Tara. The glow was a sign for Rachel and a warning to those who were foolish enough to intercede. "*You're so good for saying you give what you get,*" Rachel said as she turned to leave with them. "*My sweet William, what did you get from me?*"

William severed the link. He could withstand no more of the pain; and in that act, he hated himself, for that pain was so thoughtless and selfish... nothing of what he had gotten from Rachel Pryor.

"As much as I am able," he cried, "... I will look after your niece. You have my promise!

"And if I am given the chance, I will find one. One who has the gleam in their eye and is looking down the road. I will teach them how to walk, the way you taught me to walk. Goodbye, Rachel!"

Tara could make no comment. She was too busy crying at the wonder, beauty and agony of it all. The wayfarers were such gentle souls. They could see that Tara was different and one they were meant to collect was hiding within her, uncertain if he held the strength to deny them twice. But they were not there for her, or Jonathan, and the *wayfarers* are ever disciplined. They had seen what happens when one of their kind stumbled in the line of their duties. The world has never been the same.

William looked down on her body and kissed it again. "I've got a grave to dig," he said. Again Dexter said nothing. He took off his jacket and grabbed the obvious tools, allowing William the opportunity to pick Rachel up and walk her to the back of the house where he knew the earth was softer and richer.

The two young men started to dig the grave, working like a machine in two pieces, never getting in each other's way and doing the work of some six men. But Dexter was a Tyro, after all, and could not keep pace for too long. William continued to dig as I offered a hand to Dexter.

"Come, son, let me take a turn." I could have employed my talent to dig but William was not augmenting his body at all and there was a sentiment of respect he was paying with the effort. It was arduous, and much deeper than science or ceremony required, but eventually it was completed.

Dexter and I handed Rachel's body to him and he laid it in the bottom of the grave. He climbed out and we filled the grave. William covered the grave with flowers but he was very particular about the kind and their placement.

"Can someone tell me why the grave is ten feet deep?" Tara whispered.

"Nine and a half feet," William answered, going about his task. "Six feet, which is the norm, and one foot for every year I knew her."

"Good reason," Tara replied as her phone went off. She walked away to answer it.

"That must be Lydia calling to check in," William said as he took a look at his labor. "And you're still here," he said to me. "Which means you don't have a trail to follow."

"They were all either drugged or shot," I replied. "There is no trail to follow."

"Wrong," William said as he walked toward his car. "I'm going to need to rest though. I'm about to drop, and you don't look so good either. We get some rest and we hound 'em down, Viz. You wanna train me? Train me as we hunt that bastard down and get your daughter back."

William took out his keys and tossed them to Dexter who tried to catch them but failed in his attempt. "Yeah, you need to stick to throwing 'em," William smiled as he turned to walk away. "I'll see you around the halls…maybe."

"The hell you will!" Dexter shouted. "I'm going with you!"

"Dexter, just get Sugar and drive her out of here. I won't be needing her where I'm going."

"What the hell is that supposed to mean?" Dexter asked in a confused yet agitated voice. "Where are you going?"

"Dex, believe me, man, you don't want this. Not this! Just please do as I ask."

"Please, my ass!" Dexter yelled; his emotions were beginning to erupt within him. It was his outcry that stirred me and I looked at him. "We've come too far for this late night tear-jerkin' bullshit! You have always been there for me. ALWAYS! You son-of-a-bitch!

"Do you know what it's like to be your friend?" he asked, his feet were moving but he was going nowhere. "Do you know what it's like to always being the one who says *thank you* but never *you're welcome*? Do you know what it is to be the best friend of a man who doesn't need anything?"

"I never made a catch that you didn't throw," William argued. "I've always needed you. But-"

"But what?!" he cried. "This is too much for me? Well that's my choice, not yours. If he can train you then he can train me."

"Dexter," William said.

"Have you ever cheated?" Dexter fired back and the question made William step back.

"What?"

"Have you ever cheated?"

"Never, and what has that got to do with anything?"

"Everything if you never mind-zapped me a play to call or a route to run." I lifted my hand to my chin. The young man had made a very strong argument. The game was barbaric, but it was not merely brute strength which determined the victor, especially when the teams often played were often stronger than the Eagles. "I called those plays. Me! You don't know how to move a team through shit and I've been doing it for years!"

"So you still need me!" Dexter claimed. "You just protect your quarterback and he'll get you to the endzone."

"Cute," William agreed. "But recognize that scrambling in this game may not be an option."

"You just show me the rules. I'll get the rest on my own!"

"Viz?"

"It would be an honor to train the both of you," I said. I was afraid I was seeing history repeat itself, and I was not about to stand in its way.

"I'll run you by your house," William said.

"No need," Dexter replied. "My Mom is home. We're supposed to be in school. I miss class and they just assume I'm doing something with Coach Dranksi."

"And Coach Dranksi?"

"Taking a nap until two o'clock," Dexter answered. "Now you on the other hand, they've probably called the National Guard because William Ferrous didn't show up for atom-splitting 101!" Tara snickered and made her exit toward her car.

William looked at his best friend and smiled. How dare Dexter make him smile on a day like today! But for a moment, he pictured his father and Gordon and he wondered how their friendship had gotten started.

"Let's get that nap," he said, ushering Dexter to the car. Keeping his thoughts secured, he wondered if Dexter was ready for a few hours at the Source.

Thirty-Four

Sword met sword and only the strengths and skills of the wielders decided the brief contest. The student gave ground to the teacher. The eyes of one never left the gaze of the other as the younger withdrew from the elder but kept his stance and skill with the sword, deflecting his teacher's thrust. A quick snap of the wrist and the offending thrust was dismissed, but the elder did not give ground. Such stubbornness did not cause the youth to hesitate as he attacked the exposed and open head. Without sword close enough to afford a block, the teacher ducked his head under the swing.

"*Not this time,*" Matthew thought as he saw his teacher break form. The last time this was done, he had been drawn into an attack and shown the weakness of being too quick to react. As his sword passed over his teacher's head, he prepared his power and jumped back to the wall behind him, his teacher's sword just missing his chest. He landed, hands and feet flat on the thick, black stone that was the wall, and he then sprang from the wall, avoiding a chopping swing from his teacher. He landed but was quickly up again, bounding over a chest-level swing. He flipped forward twice before landing. His back still faced his teacher but his sword managed to block the downward swing of his teacher, whom he had yet to increase distance from. He pushed the sword and swung blindly behind himself and he could hear the tip of his sword claim the fabric of his teacher's tunic. His eyes flared wide at the success and he turned around to look upon his handiwork.

"Pride!" his teacher cried and the core of his sword emitted its silvery white flame, enveloping the young man. Matthew threw back his head, his white hair flew back and he fell to his knees, locked in a pain that did not even allow him to scream. Matthew's teacher quickly lowered his sword and the pain subsided. He fell forward on his hands and was relieved when the ability to breathe returned to him.

"Balance, perception, strength, skill and speed," Joshua said as he looked down on his student. These are yours." He reached down and took a good hold of Matthew's arm, lifting him up to stand. "But I caution you against pride and his six siblings. In the light of the spirit, they bring only torment."

"I give thanks for this lesson as I have all the others," Matthew said as he bowed to his teacher. "And may I have the wisdom to acknowledge the ones you have yet to deliver to me."

"Of that, I have little doubt," Joshua replied. "Your skills increase with every passing, my child." Joshua signaled the young ones who served this room until it was their turn to learn in it. They brought scabbards, refreshment and towels and they were used in that order. "Can you tell me of your studies?"

Matthew had the towel over his face and he had never been more grateful for a veil. But that cover did nothing to aid his tongue and the hesitation had already been noted.

"Did you really expect your examinations went without cognizance, Matthew?" Joshua asked, tossing back his towel. "Your father has asked me to counsel you upon this matter."

"Elder Joshua, I only seek to know why the light of the spirit is set to these ends. Especially against this one," Matthew said as he touched his sheathed sword and extended his free hand toward the center of the room. An image appeared of Kadorgyan, a Prodigian, standing in the middle of the streets at his Source Phantasm as he turned the city folk away from their deadly chases. As William spoke, he experienced a sensation that went beyond the power of his mind and the sensations he experienced, the changes in his spirit were obvious, at least it to Matthew.

"Is it not the law that when one feels of the power of the spirit, he or she is brought to the temple and taught the way of the spirit?"

"It is," Joshua answered as he approached the image. "It has been that way since the first of our kind and it is this way now."

"We are the Knights of Eden and this is our cause and our task."

"And I know what words come from you next, my young student," Joshua smiled. "I will speak to Mother on both your behalf and that of this Kadorgyan of the Prodigian Tribe. It may indeed be time to approach him to see if he can be turned from the path he now follows. Now go. Get yourself to the baths. I will finish here." Smiling and bowing, Matthew was all too happy to comply. He would go and wait for his elder and teacher to return with word of Mother's judgment. The doors closed behind him and already Joshua could feel an additional presence in the room. He excused the young ones but did not acknowledge the one he felt looming in the rafters. He was, after all, one not to be looked upon.

"Go to the bath house and wait for Matthew's bath to be prepared," Joshua commanded as he waved his hand over the image, removing it from existence. If only the subject of the image were as easily remedied. "Make sure his passing is painless!"

Thirty-Five

She lowered her mask and stepped back from the table. The others were certainly able to handle the rest. The worst was over but it only left her feeling more and more out of place. She took off her cap and then her gloves as she walked out of the room. Her apron was removed for her by men in long white lab coats.

"*Right*," she thought, cleaning her glasses. "*I must've gotten some of his blood on me. Gotta get that into a Petri Dish!*" She was careful not to say anything aloud. People who gave Manfred Kaplin a hard time had a tendency to disappear without a trace. More curious, he seemed to be taking orders on this one. That had to be something new for the strange little man. She put her glasses back on and took in a deep breath.

"Well, what is the prognosis, doctor," Kaplin asked as he stood up from a chair. He looked as if he had genuine concern for the man she was operating on, like a family member of a sort. She looked at him for a moment as the man who had told Manfred to get to work stood up; his right hand had to have been kicking the crap out of him the way it had been crushed. He now wore a brace that kept the pins in place.

"Dr. Graham," he said calmly; his voice put a lot of people at ease, she believed. "How is he?"

Fannie Bethany Graham took off her glasses and looked at both men and cleared her throat before she spoke. "He cannot be human!" she said and that was enough for Bill Cole. He turned and walked down the corridor. He had other check-ups ahead of him and the status of a well bound Absularian, while important, was not as significant as the other three *guests* he had in his possession.

Kaplin, on the other hand, was glued. He was a strange fit to any picture, but the Prodigian made him seem so not out of place. He had failed to convince Adrianna to allow young Kador to develop, but circumstances beyond even her control had taken that option out of her hands.

Still, there were many questions he wanted to put to her. Like how she was able to maintain such a powerful veil over her house for such a long period of time without needing to rest. He had attributed her dizzy spells to fatigue but it turned out that meters reading the level of brainwave activity showed her attacks only came when William's mind increased in activity over 150%! But still the veil was maintained. That seemed like a very good trick, even for a Prodigian. Vastiol was no Light-Child but he was another breed of a very special tribe of human and Kaplin would press himself to find out everything he could about them.

"Please continue, doctor."

"There really is very little to report," Fannie said, putting her glasses on again. "As soon as he got some blood and plasma, his body just took over. One of the bullets was actually pushed out before I could get to it. Now would you mind telling me exactly what I was working on?"

"I would be more than happy to tell you," Kaplin answered. "But not out here in such a common area."

"Well, if it's that complicated, it will have to keep," she said, turning to go back into the lab. "I've got tests to run to make sure he is what he appears to be." Kaplin watched her walk back into the lab.

"Smart girl," a voice commented and Kaplin spun on his heels. His hand extended and a knife was hurled, striking the wall inches away from Brooks' head. He was sipping coffee and Kaplin's move did not make him jump in the least.

"Yeah, I know what you mean. The coffee is pretty bad here," Antal said as he looked at the knife. "You want me to hand this back or are you going to come and get it?"

"I might send another," Kaplin answered, "...adjusting my aim slightly."

"Oh yeah, Kappy," Antal said, taking another sip. "I'm all shaking over here."

"Look, we don't need to have a pissing contest. Anyone with eyes can see you're ill-equipped for serious competition. But if you make a move on that woman, please have your affairs in order."

"What is she to you?!" Kaplin said sharply.

"Obviously more than you," Niles interjected as he walked down the corridor. A gust of air blasted Kaplin off his feet and up against the far wall.

"Niles, you old dog!" Brooks smiled as he extended his right hand. "How the hell are you?"

"I am well, my friend," Niles answered with a bright smile, one that faded as he turned to look at Kaplin. "Shall I dispose of this for you?"

"Who, Kappy? No, he's fine. I think he gets the point. You can let him go."

"As you wish," Niles said, blinking once. The wind stopped and Manfred Kaplin dropped to the floor. "I am not here for him anyway."

"For that matter, I am not here for you, old dog!" Niles smiled. "I was actually hoping to receive some information from Bill. We have it from a reliable resource that the Prodigians are sending another assassin after the son of Zargo.

"These people just do not know when to quit," Brooks said as he took out his phone. "And with the most recent events, I don't think we left that kid in the best of positions. Hey, Bill? Niles is here and he's got some info."

"Not to mention something of a gift," Niles added.

"Yeah, we'll be right down," Antal said into his phone before putting it away. "He's waiting for us in the holding chamber. It's only three floors down from here."

"Alas, my time is quite limited," Niles explained, leading Antal over to the window. "But if you would be so kind as to deliver my…gift to Bill, I would very much appreciate it."

Antal took a look out of the small window and on the tarmac he could see two people, a man and a woman, both with long black hair that blew in the winds. Both of them looked as if they were God's gift to the opposite sex.

"Allow me to introduce you to Luciana and Patrizio. Disciples of mine, as it were. They are not as far progressed as our poor departed Milana, however."

"Let me guess," Antal said, looking more at the female than the male. She stood closer to the building and her stance demonstrated a greater level of machismo. "They are better than Milana, right?"

"You are too cruel, my friend. You deprive me of my punch line."

"Niles," Antal chuckled, "…punch lines are in jokes. I've read the file on Milana. There was nothing humorous about that woman! She will be sorely missed."

"You are too gracious," Niles bowed as he stepped back. He looked again at Kaplin who looked completely mystified at Niles. "He is, how do you say it?"

"Not in the loop," Brooks answered. "And no, he isn't. Far as he is concerned, everything begins and ends with the Prodigian."

"Then is there a need to eliminate him?" Niles asked as fire sparked from his hand. Kaplin pressed himself back against the wall as he looked at his hand. He held some sort of scanning device and whatever it told him cause Manfred Kaplin to gasp.

Antal looked at Kaplin as he finally looked back up and Niles and then back at Kaplin. "Nah, no need to serve me some ribs just yet. But can I put that request on a rain check?"

"I tell you what," Niles said as started to float back down the corridor. "If I should return and not find you, I will cash your check and dismiss this one from existence!"

"Even better!" Brooks said, taking another sip of coffee. Niles floated to the end of the corridor and then out of the door. Brooks saw him take to the sky like a missile.

"That guy really knows how to get around," Brooks whispered, envying the man for a moment. He quickly returned his attention to Kaplin who had at least come away from the wall. "That was Niles. He's an

Elemental. They're a tribe of Humans who have been helping us keep tabs on the Prodigian. Didn't know today was coming didya?" Kaplin shook his head no. "So why don't you fix your clothes, cuz you've got that blown look goin' on, and go on out and show our new friends that you can be interpersonal. I'll go tell the good doctor you've been put in your pen. Then I have to go downstairs and report to Cole." Brooks walked by Kaplin with a devilish grin on his face. He handed Kaplin his cup as he walked by. "Freshen that up for me, will ya?"

The doors to the elevator opened and Bill Cole walked out into the large corridor. The lighting was extremely bright down here, but he more than understood the reasons, all three of them. He was not yet in his third stride when the lights dimmed and he could hear screams coming from one of the rooms.

"Chidon," he whispered, looking up at the lights. "*Still he resists. Perhaps I should speak to him last,*" Cole thought as he stopped at the first interrogation room. It was hardly designed for such events but the technicians had done a very good job in their impromptu construction. He entered his code and placed his hand on the reader pad. The door unlocked and he pushed it open.

On the inside there were three guards, two with tranquilizer rifles and one with a stun gun linked to a power pack strapped to the guard's back. Each of them was ready to use their weapons, but Vada-Ri was a very calm young lady. She sat in her chair without moving and she tried to sit comfortably though it was obvious the gear strapped to her head made that highly unlikely.

"Hello there," he said, taking his place opposite the table from the young Prodigian. "I take it the equipment you are wearing has been explained to you?" Vada looked at him but she did not make a sound. "I will take that as a yes," Bill continued. He hated this. He was a director of personnel! He was a strategist and a student of para-psychology. He depended upon Thidalia for such dealings but she was not responding to any of his calls, which forced his hand with his prisoners.

"What we're looking for is information," he stated after clearing his throat, writing notes on his clipboard.

"Three and one makes four," Vada replied. "Now you have information."

"Actually, I was looking more for the location of the Territories." Bill was glad that the eyes she quickly cut over to him were capable of nothing more than signaling a painful shock to be delivered to the young woman's brain. She winced in pain as sparks flew from her body. This of course signaled her restraints strapped to her arms, legs and waist and she was struck with more pain. The domino effect continued until she absorbed the pain without moving or focusing too much thought. Eventually the pain passed and Vada-Ri settled back in her chair.

"*Father, give me strength,*" she thought receiving a warning buzzer for her cogitations.

"As you can see, we have set this particular equipment specifically to contain a Prodigian. Even one as gifted as you is restrained."

"You seem proud," Vada replied. Bill choked a bit and cleared his throat again.

"No, it is not pride, Miss," he argued. "It is that Prodigians tend to do first and ask permission second... even when they are not in New Sumeria. That makes these a necessary precaution."

"And why is it then that you are asking me these questions?" Vada-Ri pondered out loud. "You have Arvius! Hasn't he told you all you wish to know?"

"Actually, he has drawn the line at divulging the location of the Territories," Bill answered plainly.

"And you wish for me to deliver what even a traitor will not?" she asked her captor. "Do you truly have no inkling why we look down upon the Tyros?" The lights grew dim in the room and both Bill and Vada looked up as Chidon screamed again. "He is taking more and more power to restrain," she pointed out.

"I was hoping you could help with that," Bill said, holding up his finger. "You see, each time he does that, a reading is taken of how much of a power feed it takes to stop him. When it reaches a certain point, it will deliver a shock strong enough to literally cook his brain. And that is only if my men do not shoot him first!"

"And what do you want from me?" Vada asked, demonstrating all the expressed rage the machinery would allow.

"He would listen to you," Bill answered. "You are the daughter of a Head Master!"

"My, my, he has been telling you a bit about us, hasn't he?" Vada smiled. "I can't say as I am surprised. He needs as many friends as he can fool into fighting for him."

"If you are referring to the incident that nearly destroyed the Light-Child Council," Cole said, leaning closer to Vada-Ri, "...please bear in mind that I am a man of limited means. I cannot afford to rebuke a resource. Mind you, there are certain alliances I would rather have. Especially if you were to give me your word."

"You would take me at my word?" Vada asked.

"I can't imagine a Prodigian who would have so little honor as to break their word," Cole said.

241

"I can see even less a Prodigian who would give it to you, Tyro!" she replied.

Cole stood up with a sigh. He had far too much to do to continue wasting time on Vada-Ri. He did not even bother to say farewell as he turned to leave.

"Wait!" Vada called to him. "Kiss me."

"What?" Surprise was too weak a word to describe the effect her request had on Cole and he turned back to look at the Prodigian woman. "Vada, you seem t-"

"Your spy may have told you much," Vada interrupted. "But he could not have told you what it is to be a Prodigian woman. Give me your lips, that I might judge your manly honor."

"This is clearly some sort of trick," Cole concluded.

"Shall I give you my word?" Vada asked.

"You'd give me your word about a kiss, but not your assistance."

"I have yet to see one Tyro worth their weight in rotting bones!" Vada criticized. "And your devices prevent my mental talents.

"Satisfy my lips and we will see about your needs," Vada offered. "You have my word that I only wish for your mouth on mine and no harm shall befall you from my hand or mind during our exchange."

"*This can't be happening!*" Cole thought. As he looked around at the guards in the room, it was clear he was not the only man thinking that way.

"A kiss?" he asked and Vada slowly nodded. He approached, leaving his clipboard on the table. He walked up to her and began to think about what he saw. Fortunately, she was no Yudara, plus she was wearing a device designed to prevent mind control. He found it hard to find a means by which this was a trap.

And what sort of trap where she would be allowed to break her word? For that question, he had no answer and he leaned forward, touching his lips to Vada's. He came back slowly and was startled to see the look on her face.

"Call that a kiss?" she asked. "It is a wonder the Tyros reproduce at all! I have s-" Cole pressed his mouth hard against Vada-Ri's and he was shocked to find her receptive, returning his effort as she breathed deep and hard. Their mouths worked against each other at first but eventually found a rhythm that made Vada moan. That was enough for Cole as he pulled back. Vada's eyes were still closed but she opened them slowly, looking at Cole in a different way.

"You have given me much to consider, Tyro. Your people are passionate if they are nothing else. How much time am I given to consider this word of cooperation?" she asked.

"I can give you until I am done with Igrileena," Cole answered. "There is no point in even speaking to Chidon. He borders on the fanatical."

Vada chuckled and closed her eyes. "He's a tracker," she said. "He more than *borders* on the line of the fanatic. But I will take your offer into consideration and when you are done with Igrileena, I should have answer for you."

"I will be back soon then," Cole said as he turned to leave. The moment he got outside of the room, he called Antal and requested he come down to his floor. He had to tell him about this experience. But Antal took too long, so Bill decided to go and talk to Igrileena without him. Brooks could be told about the kiss later.

"Let's wake her up, shall we?" Cole said as he entered the room. He was taking longer strides and he looked at everyone straight on instead of having to lift his head to do so.

The technicians complied and hit Igrileena with enough current to bring her conscious. She was in pain, angry, but awake.

"I will have thine eyes for this!" she screamed, straining against her bonds and being shocked for the effort. It did not take long for her to calm down and become still.

"Well," Cole said, straightening his tie. "Now that we have that out of the way, perhaps we can get down to business." Cole did not bother to take a seat. He put his hands on his hips and approached the woman.

"I have been speaking to Vada-Ri at length," Bill stated matter-of-factly. "And she is prepared to discuss terms of your cooperation with regards to our study of your people, if not becoming a line of information for my organization altogether. I am looking to replace Arvius as soon a humanly possible."

"Seen the error of thy ways, eh?" Igrileena jested and Cole smiled.

"That's one way to put it," Cole said as he began pacing in front of Igrileena. As he passed by, her nostrils flared.

Ah, now that is the daughter of Elkazzar," she thought.

"Whatever Vada-Ri gives her word to," Igrileena stated proudly, her bonds all beginning to flash warnings to her. It did not alter the fervor of her announcement. "I will support with my Blade as well as the blood of those who dare oppose her!" Bill could hardly believe his ears and he stopped, turning to face Igrileena with wonder stretched wide across his face. "But let me taste thy lips!" she added.

"Was is it with your people and kissing?" Cole asked anxiously.

"It is naught I am willing to reveal to any man," Igrileena replied. "But to have my oath, I will require thy lips!"

Cole swallowed hard. It was not that Igrileena was not attractive, she was very shapely and her face, when not twisted in anger or pain, was quite fetching.

"*It's not like this is ever going to happen to me again!*" Cole thought as he approached, grabbed Igrileena by the back of the head and pulled her mouth forward onto his. The strength of his passion surprised the Prodigian woman and she let out a soft moan as she kissed him.

But her tongue quickly invaded his mouth and Cole was taken to places his dreams failed to find, his hand beginning to explore the paradise that was her form. He had just taken hold of her breasts when his world went black.

"You okay in there," a voice called him out of the abyss and Cole opened his eyes. He was on his back and on a cold concrete floor, looking up at Antal Brooks who looked to be struggling not to laugh.

"What happened?" Bill stammered to say.

"I'd say you rocked her world," Antal answered as he motioned over to Igrileena who was unconscious. Smoke rolled off of her skin and he could see burn marks under the restraints. "You both were shocked but she took the brunt of it; from the looks of it, that part was voluntary. The charge should have killed you."

"Is she-"

"She's just sleeping it off, Cole," Antal said in a calming voice. "What happened?"

"I think we just found two new recruits for the Descriers," Bill said with a bright smile.

"Damn, you *did* rock her world!"

Thirty-Six

He stood there for a moment, not knowing what to do. It was obvious to him that she was oblivious to the world and he had issue with bringing that oversight to her attention. It seemed every time she walked out of the door, less of her came back to him. Soon, the door to their home would open and only a ghost of the woman he loved would greet him. She would be, for all intents and purposes, dead to him and at that moment, he felt like being very selfish.

So why could he not just turn and leave her room? Why could he not just let her lay there and sleep? She was asleep, and deeply for her not to have heard the commotion at the front door, not to mention the phone.

He stood there a moment longer, took a deep breath and blew it out slowly. He made his approach in even, steady strides. She was always more sensitive to someone sneaking up on her than someone just walking up to her. He placed his hand on her shoulder very gently.

"Mom," he said softly and her eyes opened, locking on his body, then his face, then his eyes. He knew she had targeted him before she recognized him.

Lydia looked at her son and then she could hear the knocking at the door and the phone ringing. She looked around the room and then at her clock.

"*9:45 AM,*" she thought. "*So much for having the next couple of days off.*" She looked back at her son and smiled. You wanna climb in here and help me turn my back on the world?" she smiled.

"Yes," he said. "But we both know you're not going to do that." Lydia lost much of her smile. She was not happy, but she was proud.

"Right," she replied. "So why didn't you answer the door?"

"I did," he answered, shrugging his shoulders. "But they tried to push their way in and I pushed back."

"Oh my God!" Lydia said quickly getting out of the bed. She was in her slippers and robe before she took three steps. "Percival Morathi King, what did you do?"

"Jab to the neck," he answered in a matter-of-fact tone and Lydia almost fell down running out of her bedroom. She looked back at him in astonishment. "Not hard enough to kill him!" he quickly offered as a sort of explanation.

"Since when do you know how hard that is?" Lydia said running for the front door.

"Well, he ain't dead!"

Lydia opened the door and she saw Annabelle Dawson banging on her front door. They called it a screen door, but Jack Moreland had replaced the screen with bulletproof glass, the lower panel still held the fracture mark of one of her not-so-friendly fellow citizen's testing of that glass. She had put the man's son away for twenty-five to life – that sort of thing tends to agitate a parent and Lydia did not even bother to call it in. He had taken his shot, it missed, and he walked away.

Behind Anna were two agents, one standing over another. The standing one she did not recognize but he was a typical wannabe, looking like a throwback to an era when G-Men used revolvers and wore hats. He was an assistant going somewhere to kiss ass. He was waving her newspaper over Allan Turner who was red in the face and having some difficulty breathing. He was holding his neck and grabbing on to Mr. Clean-Cut like his life depended on it.

"Didn't hit hard enough," Lydia whispered as she slowly opened the screen door. Annabelle was knocking on the frame, but her eyes were on Turner.

"Ms. Dawson," Lydia said and Annabelle jumped turning around so fast that she was thrown off balance. "Good morning."

"King, I think we're going to need paramedics!" Annabelle was coming unglued and that was not going to be pretty or fun. Lydia stepped out on to her porch and Turner saw her approaching. The last thing he wanted was to give Lydia a chance to finish her son's handiwork. He tried to stand three times but failed at all of them.

"We might be in trouble then," Lydia said as she moved the assistant away with her hand. "In this neighborhood, the morgue tends to respond more quickly than an ambulance.

"Easy, Turner," she said, grabbing Turner and forcing him to sit. She tried to move his hand away but Turner struggled with her.

"Son, get Momma her gun so I can make Agent Turner here move his damn hand!"

"Yes Mommy," Percy replied emphatically and disappeared into the house.

"*God, I love that kid!*" Lydia thought as Turner forced himself to comply. Lydia massaged his neck and told him to swallow real hard. As he swallowed, she squeezed and Turner choked and coughed. Lydia stood up with a smile, slapping Turner on his back.

"See there, he should be fine," Lydia said, folding her arms. "Now maybe one of the remaining unmarked can tell me why you tried to Bogart by my son."

"I got your gun, Mommy!" Percy cried out, toting her redesigned Ithaca 37 shotgun and Lydia could not hold back her snicker.

"Joke's over, son," she said, killing his smile. "Put that back in the lockbox."

"Yes, ma'am," he replied, obviously deflated.

"Cute kid, right?" Lydia asked with a mother's pride glowing on her face.

"And he's not in school because…" Dawson asked and she swallowed hard, watching Lydia's friendly face fade into one that broadcasted her taste for *going postal*.

"He's home-schooled, sir!" Lydia replied. "And you're a long way from the reservation, Dawson. I thought you were an East Coast girl!"

"Actually I was called in to aid with your debriefing," Dawson answered. "Agent Turner was just bringing me-"

"To my house on my day off!" Lydia interrupted. "And seeing as how I am off the clock and no one called before they motored on over here, I'm feelin' kind of *civiliany*!"

"Director Howard and his wife have been kidnapped!" Annabelle interrupted, losing more and more control of the moment. Lydia was a dog, an attack dog, and without a specific target to attack, anyone not treating her really nicely risked losing a hand. The pleasantries had been compromised by bringing Turner, and altogether lost when King's son had man-handled a supervising agent. She threw the real bone at King and prayed for the best.

"When?" King asked, her arms dropping to her sides.

"Just before six this morning," Dawson answered. "They took him and his wife."

"*His wife?*" Lydia thought, already aware of George's marital arrangements. "*What the hell was he doing with his wife and where was her lover?*"

"From the looks of it, we believe he was hit by mercenaries."

"Mercenaries?!" Lydia repeated, walking into the house, leaving the door open for anyone to follow. Dawson took the lead but signaled for the other two to remain on the front porch.

"Howard had a visitor," Dawson continued. "We think it was a dignitary of some sort but we have no ID whatsoever."

"Really funky hour to have a guest there, George," Lydia whispered and she walked quickly into her closet. Annabelle stopped at the doorway to the bedroom. "I take it they were taken too?" she said aloud.

"We're really not sure about that," Annabelle replied in a louder voice. She heard a slide locking into place and she spun around, her hand on her pistol but she did not draw. She saw young Percival King preparing his mother's guns and doing a damn fine and quick job at that. "Home-schooled," she whispered. She jumped when Lydia walked by, nearly fully dressed, carrying a jacket to go with the slacks and blouse she was wearing.

"Nice outfit," Annabelle commented.

"Now's not the time," Lydia replied in a tone that told Dawson she was not in the mood for games any longer. "What PN am I?"

PN. Protocol Number! When an agent reaches a certain level of administrative authority or is working on a big enough case, they are asked to generate a Blue File. The first page of the Blue File contained a list of directives for what should be done in the event that an agent went missing or suddenly died in the line of duty. Lydia Diane King was Protocol Number One in Howard's Blue File and Lydia stopped at hearing that information.

"You've got a very special briefing waiting for you," Annabelle advised. "That's why I came out here. Pending the outcome of this investigation, you are hereby reinstated in active duty."

"Didn't know I was otherwise," Lydia replied. "That's why you're in the vicinity?"

"Why I *was* here is moot," Annabelle answered, walking to stand very close to King. She was an agent that would only work with those she respected. Turner's machismo had cost them a fair degree of credibility and she had to show some backbone or Lydia would be handing Dawson her own head on a silver platter. "Why I *am* here is key! Let's not lose focus, Special Agent King."

"*No time like the present,*" Lydia thought. She liked the way things had been laid at her feet, but she did not like the reason. She knew George was into a number of things. How clean or how dirty did not matter. Howard got the job done and had put more than his ass on the line for King, and more than once. There was a high probability that her current course was going to put her toe-to-toe with Howard and she was not looking forward to that day. But all of that aside, Howard was someone only King could take out. Everyone else had to take a number.

"I'll go to the debriefing," Lydia said, putting on her shoulder and leg holsters. "But if you don't have papers detailing my full reinstatement, despite the outcome of this investigation, by the time I get out of said debriefing, you can kiss my black ass goodbye."

"You'd never leave George like that!" Annabelle asserted.

"Wow, Anna," Lydia quickly answered, putting her face in Dawson's. "Are you really calling my bet this early in the game?" The two women stared at each other briefly before Annabelle turned and walked away. Lydia smiled and took a seat in the closest chair.

"*Dammit,*" Annabelle thought as she drew closer to the door. Lydia was supposed to call her back by now, tell her to wait and then change her demands. But Dawson had seen the detailing of Howard's list. King had codes no one else in the Bureau knew. Given what they were last investigating, Dawson knew they needed to act fast if they were going to get Howard back or get the ones who took him.

"It'll take some-"

"Don't even!" Percy said, quickly covering his mouth and looking at his mother who wore a soft smile and nodded at her son, letting him know that they would discuss the matter later.

"Kid's got good lungs," Lydia said. "Needs to work on his manners, but his instincts are pretty sharp, wouldn't you say?"

"I'll have them in writing in an hour," Dawson said.

"Knew that you could," Lydia replied. "And before you even take in the breath, I pick who I work with. Not you, not Turner, and definitely not that butt plug out there waiting for his nose to turn brown!"

"Done" Annabelle quickly said. "Anything else?"

"You'll be the first to know," Lydia said, donning her jacket and walking by Dawson. Annabelle took a moment to look back at Percival. It was hard to put a finger on what she read in his face. Resentment, hate, rage, pride, love and fear were all mixed in there somewhere.

"So who's gonna look after you?"

"Have a good day, Special Agent Dawson," he answered, holding out his hand, ushering her to the door.

Thirty-Seven

QUERY: how does one, being a Man-Lord among other Man-Lords, hurry without looking like one is in a hurry? ANSWER: no bloody idea!

He was late; there had been no way to avoid that. But regardless, he had kept the Master waiting and he had seen his Master destroy others for a lesser offense. So he needed to move quickly. But there were none among the Man-Lords who did not know Daleifner was Jamoreh's man, which meant he always had to conduct himself in such a way as to not bring any undue attention upon himself. He could not be seen moving too quickly; it would be better not to be seen at all. But even the Prodigian know they cannot have everything they want, so Daleifner was not too terribly disappointed when he had to turn down the alley that led to an intersection of several walkways. When he reached the center, he stopped. The crowd in front of him had cleared and he could see an obstruction to both his intent to remain inconspicuous and his intent to remain in Jamoreh's good graces. Shuppim, the Gray Priest! He stood there with one of his Blades and neither pair of eyes was welcoming.

Daleifner's hand moved to his left hip and he breathed easier but only slightly. His favorite Edge was still there and his skill with the weapon was more than simple passing conversation. Fighting alongside Jamoreh meant one had to bear their share of the conflict. Daleifner preferred a scenario where he was not the sole target of multiple opponents, but that was what he saw when he turned around to use the way he came as an escape. The route was now blocked by two more of Shuppim's sycophants. Counting Shuppim, there were twelve in all and Daleifner was trapped.

"Leif?" Shuppim said, feigning innocence. "Doth mine eyes see clearly?"

Daleifner spun around to face the Gray Priest, his face changed, expressing now his level of intention. He knew, they all knew, he was no match for these numbers but his eyes declared he would not die alone and only an offering of Fate would keep the count of the dead low.

Shuppim was not surprised in the least. He was even less impressed. But he could not ignore the opportunity which had been so gracefully given to him. For those who placed their faith in numbers, Bilshan's removal from argumentative perfection was cause to celebrate, but the Gray Priest saw the truest measure of the Crimson Court's last session: Jamoreh had been made to protect something he wanted to destroy! But what was his motivation for such efforts? Surely it was more than the fact that his father had killed Kador's father! Especially since it was common knowledge that Jamoreh was not of Beriah's blood. No, there had to be more and Shuppim felt it had to do with the claim more so than the act. Jamoreh was a junior to him at best. Only his skill and Blood had given him the opportunity to surpass him. But Shuppim had seen skill greater than Jamoreh's, even greater than that of his surrogate father. It was this belief which kept the Gray Priest from openly acknowledging Beriah's claim. He had seen Zargo fight and the man never did so poorly; even when he rated himself as such, his skill and power were surely the stuff of legend! Beriah was no neophyte, but where he could challenge dozens, Zargo could have decimated scores! He had been the only Man-Lord to travel without guide or guard into the Jargahar Mountains and return. So what pressed the Black Priest to risk one of the few things for which he kept and openly displayed true feelings? Why send Yudara after Kadorgyan? And what's more, what would Jamoreh do now that his open campaign had been denied? Such answers Shuppim knew he could never pry that information from the Black Priest. But Daleifner commanded a mere fraction of his Master's mental strength; his mind could be forced open and there were countless treasures awaiting the one who put forth the courage to act on… opportunity!

"Why, mine eyes *do* see clearly!" Shuppim declared as he advanced, slowly, his mind feeling out for a lurking Black Priest, but he was not to be found just here, just now. "It is something of a wonder to me, my friend, as to what Fate hath wrought for us on this day. I wonder what brings thee here at this time and place."

"My reasons are my own, Gray Priest!" Daleifner yelled back, stepping away from Shuppim and keeping his senses sharp on the placement of the others. They were all moving toward the intersection he was nearly in the center of, but Shuppim and his man were clearly the closest pair. "I attend to matters of the Crimson Court!" he cried, looking to see if the evocation of the title caused any of Shuppim's men to hesitate. He knew better, but his list of options had grown fearfully short.

"And I am an officer of that Court," Shuppim answered with a cold smile. "I will have these reasons lest thou canst give reason to deny thy superior Court's man."

"Nay," Jamoreh called out from the night, coming up through the alley floor slowly and menacingly, like a shadow that had just taken whim to become a full form. "Thou art a higher ranking Court's man than my Leif, but hardly his superior! And I can give thee all good reason why his news will not be given unto thine ears," Jamoreh said as he drew both Blade and Edge. "If thou wilt but come closer, Shuppim, I shall embrace thee with this reason though thy mother shall not again claim a living son once this truth comes from…" Jamoreh clanged Edge into Blade twice, "…my lips!"

A moment, dangled in front of him like so much bait, had carried Shuppim from blessed to burdened. But still he had the advantage. Even with Jamoreh present, and after thinking to look below the alley, they were still only two to his twelve. Too many contests had shown Shuppim he could not definitively take Jamoreh, but he could contend with the youth's skill while his men made quick work of Daleifner. There was still an advantage to consider.

"Ah," Jamoreh said, flashing a very cold and cruel grin, "I see thy thoughts without use of any talent. 'Tis true, the side of power belongs to thee... thou hast only to initiate the act, Shuppim. Thou needst only push aside the fear that grips at thy core! The fear of anguish and the solitude of death!" Jamoreh took a moment to look around, turning his back to Shuppim to do so. "Though such solitude may not be unaccompanied this night.

"Thou hast merely to act," he continued, coming to face the Gray Priest again. "That is, before age takes us both!"

Shuppim's hand found his Blade and his teeth ground tight. He had endured the last of the Black Priest's taunts. As he reached, his men drew and summoned their weapons. The sight made Daleifner's eyes flare with fear and Jamoreh's flash with anticipation.

"Yes!" he cried, taking his stance as Daleifner turned his back to his master's.

"I say to thee all, nay!" a voice argued and Shuppim's men looked up and around. The Gray Priest, the Black Priest and Daleifner kept their eyes on their most immediate targets.

"Hold," Jamoreh said softly, knowing his Edger was about to take full advantage of the distraction which was an action he normally would have sanctioned. But recently he had been corralled by the Court, and the High Priest of Air had reminded his colleagues why he was still a power to be reckoned with. Jamoreh did not need a second lesson of the old one's wisdom. There had been no official challenge of any sort and until Shuppim actually drew his weapons, his men legally could not and therefore would not attack.

"Who dares?!" Shuppim shouted, his eyes still locked on Jamoreh.

"Who dares indeed?" the voice answered, but sounding as if it had moved. Heads turned and bodies shifted, but still the source of the sound was not found. "I suppose that is the question of questions!" A soft smile curled Jamoreh's lips as he could see one possible way the scenario might play. Either way, he was both entertained and impressed. "Still, my Priest, to answer thy question would be to weaken my station. And it is too well known the Priests of the Crimson Court traffic only in power."

"*Aye,*" Jamoreh thought. "*But power comes in many forms, my friend.*"

"Then use thy power to wound Jamoreh!" Shuppim cried out and there was no reply. Taking his eyes off of Jamoreh, the Gray Priest looked up and around. "Well?!"

"Strike in my name and great will be thy reward," Jamoreh said calmly, letting his weapons point to the alley floor. "Thou hast my word!"

"Nay, I hath thine enemy!" the voice replied and an arrow was released. One of Shuppim's men fell to the alley floor, clutching his shoulder. Two of Shuppim's men looked up, searching for the sniper and one of them, hoping to face down the still unknown enemy, was shot in the back of the calf and even Jamoreh winced in the placement of the arrow. The rest of Shuppim's men formed a circle around the Gray Priest, their backs facing him, their weapons at the ready to deflect an arrow's flight.

"Enough," Jamoreh said softly, sheathing his Blade and Edge. He turned to walk down the alley, the shortest alley to the street. "The choice is thine. Remain here with my... *enemy*... or thou mayest accompany me and my man to speak of a continued working arrangement." Jamoreh was into this third stride when Daleifner turned to walk with him.

"No, my friend," he said to his Edger. "They will not attack... they cannot afford to do so. Come."

"My lord," Daleifner started to say, but Jamoreh's raised hand cut his speech short.

"A moment, Daleinfer," the Black Priest said calmly as he walked for a while before turning down another alley. "We must see to our... *ally* before we discuss anything." They had not reached the back of the alley when he at last allowed his footsteps to be heard, and again Jamoreh smiled for he too thought it was a wise move, although any maneuver at this point was precarious. "Thou hast earned an audience, young one. This night thy efforts hath carved a smile upon this face and for that thou art rewarded another good night's sleep."

"Thou art gracious, my Master," the voice replied, though now it was attached to a form. The thin frame Jamoreh expected, given its ability to move without making sound. But the height, or rather the lack thereof, surprised him.

"Thy Master, I am not," Jamoreh corrected and he stood more than ready to take back what his words implied he was willing to guarantee. "Speak and do so quickly!"

"I seek it, my Master," the young man said, insisting on Jamoreh's relative rank and at once, the Black Priest could see it, locked inside his deep brown green eyes. A hope that was perhaps of a finer sort even than the lad's archery. "I seek that horizon! The one I know thou hast seen and seek as well."

"Pray tell me more of what thou yearns."

"Take me with thee when next thou dost venture to Old Sumeria!" he said as he stepped even closer and shuddered as Daleifner drew his Edge quickly and readied himself to throw it. His light brown hair was straight, thin and short, dropping no further than his jaw. It made him that much more simple to spot.

"He bears the mark, my Master," Daleifner said coldly and Jamoreh took in a breath to speak. His mouth opened but froze as his eyes looked upon the young man and registered his reaction to the Edger's words. He did indeed bear the mark of a lesser among the Prodigian, the Mark of Kalur! But the mark did not account for the searing glare in the young man's eyes.

"*Indeed!*" Jamoreh thought as he looked the young man over once again, his eye searching for more detail. "*Aye,*" his thought continued as his eyes explored the young man. "*Marked at the neck...*

"*But what of his clothes?*" he asked himself as his scan was aided by his steps toward and then around the young man. "*Whatever his life's stride, it does not afford him much of a wage. The boots are tied to fit his feet but also tied so the soles make as little sound as possible... and the tops of the boots are also tied down around the bottom of the pant leg. Not even the fabric is allowed to flap in the breeze.*

"*The clothes! They are not even of this color; he has darkened them with pitch! Resourceful,*" he thought as he finally stopped in front of the boy and recalled the alley stand against Shuppim.

"Show me thy bow," Jamoreh demanded and the boy was quick to snap his body in response. Jamoreh snorted before walking back to Daleifner. "Ah, a tenant of the Reaches, I see."

So far! So damn far the young man had come in all of his endeavors. Though he would have settled for with a member of the Court Chorus, he thought it was Fate's gift to him, among the many others, that he had been delivered to Jamoreh. Now he was questioned as to the address of his home. How could the man have known? Was his touch all that they had told him? So quick and cold that it sometimes went without being felt! For he had sensed nothing mounted against the defenses of his mind, nothing at all. But he was not so engaged in thought that he did not measure the passing of time, and he had not yet answered the Black Priest.

"Aye. Aye, my Master. How dost thou know of this?"

Daleifner moved forward to discipline the boy. How did he dare to question Jamoreh? Apparently the Mark of Kalur was not enough and he required the mark of Edge as well. His arm was locked within Jamoreh's in his lunging stride and he found his master smiling at him.

"Thou hast more than once proven thy love for me," he said to Daleifner and nodded, assuring his master he not injure the boy. "Which is why we must be quick to dismiss this youth. For the reasons for why thou hast not achieved my requests must be astounding!"

"I am honored by thy trust, sire," Daleifner said with a deep bow. "And fear not for there be more truth to thy words than my Master may dare to ponder." Jamoreh's brow lifted. He had intended for his words to convey the pain he was about to subject Daleifner to for his failure which, given the time he had taken, was as mysterious as the blind faith he had demonstrated. But with his man's answer, he was distractedly intrigued and desired to have his questions answered soon.

"Yes," Jamoreh said, turning to face the boy. As impressive as he had been, he was now a delay. Still, there was something to his eyes and Jamoreh wondered if he would ever get tired of looking upon it. *"The Reaches,"* he reminded himself and resumed his pacing, now in a circular pattern around the young lad again. "Thou art a Man-Lord, so much is not in doubt! But the presentation of your bow showed precision and pride in the weapon. The condition of the bow speaks to the same. Light-Children must have clean weapons; Man-Lords are concerned with skill!" The boy's head began to lower and Jamoreh felt like stabbing himself. He had not extinguished the dual green fire of the boy's eyes, but he had taken it to a place where it questioned itself and found itself less substantiated. That was not the truth of the matter. He had after all, held the Gray Priest at bay and even made him fear for his life. Jamoreh lifted the boy's chin and stretched his eyes open. "I too possess clean weapons," he remarked as he drew his Edge and let it roll and flip about his hand. When it finally came to a crisp stop in his grip, he looked at the boy again. "We may not be drawn to the snake but that does not lessen the power of his bite or erase the power of his poison. Even the Light-Children have a power to be respected if it is ever to be mastered! Remember this as thou dost take leave of me."

"Take me with thee or leave what is left of my life bleeding in this alley floor!" the boy demanded.

"Another Light-Child trait," Jamoreh answered. "Poetry."

"The rhythm of mine words change not their meaning, Master," the young man answered as he stepped away and drew an arrow from his quiver. "If I am refused in this, thou shalt either take my life or my skill with the bow will take thine if I am refused!"

"Thou art Kalur," Jamoreh explained.

"And thou art a Priest of the Court, capable of granting me exception!"

"One, two or th-"

"I am given two talents beyond speech of the mind," the boy interrupted and Jamoreh chuckled. He now knew why the fire burned so brightly. He was ready to proceed beyond the barriers of law or be killed by one of law's stewards.

"What are they?" Jamoreh asked, stunning Daleifner. Without showing much concentration, the boy began to fade from sight. Jamoreh quickly reached for the boy's neck. But his hand passed through the boy as his own solid matter could not grapple with that which was out of phase. "Ah, invisibility," Jamoreh said with a brighter smile. "And dost thou remove thyself from phase by controlling thy density or dost thou simply make thyself intangible?"

"The latter, my Master," the boy answered as he returned to true form and was now quite visible. "My skills with the Bow, the Edge and stealth are mine own!"

"And I wouldst dare to think they too be as equally impressive," Jamoreh said as he motioned Daleifner to follow him. The two started to leave the alley. "I will assume Fate has given thee a name?"

"Fen," the boy replied and again the Black Priest chuckled as he nodded.

"Thou shalt require a writ from the Court for me to sign, Fen. Once thou hast achieved this, thou shalt await me at the House of Beriah."

"Master?" Daleifner asked, still wrapped in the awe of the moment, but Jamoreh would hear nothing of reason now. He himself was a living, breathing example of how standards may indeed be guidelines, but they could not account for the fire within! Fen had passion, one which reminded Jamoreh of himself and for that, he would take the boy into Old Sumeria and see what the Forge of Fate would yield unto the lad.

"Let *that* be, Daleifner," he said, lifting his finger to signify his words should be considered to be more than a suggestion. The boy's screams of triumph made Jamoreh smile genuinely and brightly. "Thy mind shouldst be more fixed to making that which is clouded between us more clear."

"I went to a Medium," Daleifner said, and he knew to stop walking for that is exactly what Jamoreh did. "I always consult her when thy wishes are met with enough difficulty that a second attempt is called for. As thou might mark, my need to consult her is not great."

"Consult... her," Jamoreh repeated, lowering his eyes to the street.

"Thou art a force unlike any other of our time, my Master," Daleifner declared as he lowered himself to his knees and grabbed at Jamoreh's leg. "Even in the alley when our numbers were pressed, I only feared that I would not live long enough to behold thy victory. Thou art living legend, my Black Priest, and I hath seen Fate's Will in the wake of thy strides. Thou art even greater than the House thou dost declare to be thy Blood, for I hath seen thy power achieve beyond what the oldest of our kind still embrace as impossible. I can not speak as to Beriah killing Zargogyan, such is not my place. But I know thou dost exceed Zargo's son and e'en though thy sister did fail, I see not the chance for failure within thee."

Jamoreh waited. He normally went with his first reaction, but that option puzzled him. Why should he embrace Daleifner for doing something other than what he had been told to do? *"Because his eyes see things mine are too taxed to see clearly!"* he concluded. *"When my anger takes my reason, his is unwavering.*

"Can not speak of Beriah killing Zargogyan," he thought, knowing that was his servant's way of saying he did not hold to the commonly accepted belief, and in that stride, Daleifner did not walk alone. Jamoreh could not say one way or the other if it was true. But it was an honor and a power conveyed to the Blood and he would not fail it! He lowered his head and started walking again. Only this time he turned toward his own house and he could hear Daleifner breathe a sigh of relief.

"What did the Medium say, my brother?"

"She could not see the boy clearly, Master," Daleifner answered and both men were slowed by that statement. They regained their pace, but the fact that a Medium could not view someone in Old Sumeria did not weigh well. "But it was not what she said in his regard which kept me at her table and away from thy bidding."

"Wonderful, there be more," Jamoreh said as he felt a surge of power. It was very far away but of such a magnitude that it caught his attention.

"The Light-Children art busy this night and one hath summoned a storm to handle their opponent... opponents. What sort of fool walks into that sort of trap? Light-Child! Foolishness... Continue," he commanded.

"She spoke of another Medium, Master. One that travels with the boy." Again the pace changed, only now there was no pace and Jamoreh slowly turned his head to look at Daleifner.

"The Unlawful Son has a Medium of his own?"

"A powerful one, Master," Daleifner answered, lowering his head. Mediums were near the top of a very short list of things that actually frightened the man. At the very top was the fall of Jamoreh, but that was also at the top of the list of things Daleifner thought he would not be alive to see. "One who has an *Eidolon* bonded to her!"

"Fates be damned!" Jamoreh exclaimed, throwing his arms up and out. What more would be heaped upon him and this sorry task? He placed his hands on his hip and waited for the rest of the report. "And?"

"And the Medium would not see the woman beyond the discovery of the *Eidolon*," Daleifner continued. "She said only that the one bonded to her hath power in both worlds and can deny e'en the Wayfarer's Touch!"

Jamoreh stood there for a moment and then teleported both men to the house where he threw down his cloak and walked over to the fireplace, causing the logs to burst into a hearty flame. The force of the ignition shook the room and Daleifner shuddered as he collected the discarded clothing. He watched as the Black Priest gazed into the fire. He watched as the Black

Priest paced a stride or three and stopped, only to pace again. He watched as the Black Priest looked once more into the fire and lifted his hands, shrugging his shoulders and letting his hands slap against his legs. He shook his head and started to laugh.

"And for only this thou didst not get the others?" he asked in an ironic tone. "Damn thee, Daleifner!" He walked over and took a seat normally reserved for the master of the household, but Jamoreh's mind was not on the old one at the moment.

"Please forgive me, Master," Daleifner begged and Jamoreh quickly waved off the request.

"Nothing to forgive, my brother at Edges," he replied, still gazing into the fire, reminding himself of Fen, pondering what the young one would do at such a development. The answer came much more quickly than the Black Priest had anticipated. "No, absolutely nothing to forgive!" he said as he moved to the edge of the seat, his brown eyes looking up into Daleifner's face. "When the time is right, thou shalt be given an army to command, Daleifner."

"With what purpose, my Master?"

"Whatever the purpose," Jamoreh said, rising from the chair and walking to his friend, placing his hands on the smaller man's able shoulders, "...it will be a point of contention over which I will never again ponder whilst it is thine.

"Now get thee gone again and gather the others, as we will put it to ourselves to be worthy of thy wisdom. Wait, thou art a Man-Lord and for us wisdom is called guile!" Daleifner bowed and took his leave once more. Jamoreh could see the difference in his strides, there was so much less concern for the outcome of their endeavors. Once more he was the ever-faithful fanatic for which Jamoreh often questioned Fate as to why he had been given one such as the Edger. But even in his fanaticism, he had concerns for his Master that afforded him reason within his worship of the Black Priest. Something of a code of preservation of his deity and that code brought a warm feeling to Jamoreh as he once again drew his Edge. He looked at the metal of the blade and smiled.

"Too quick to the strike, were we not, Kadorgyan? This is a hunt, after all, and thou art a cagy prey with both fang and fury enough to turn the tide of the hunt back upon the hunter. Yudara hast born the brunt of that misstep. But this hunter shall watch thee, son of Zargo. I shall watch thee with more eyes than even thy Medium may account for, and from all of the viewings, an approach to the kill shall be divined! A perfect approach to the perfect kill! Then, as so many others who dared and died, thou shalt be just another mark of my Blood Wake!"

The Edge was flourished again, this time with an intensity that made even the air whisper in fear of his weapon's edge. Side to side, up and down, both attack and guard were executed to perfection as the seam separating weapon and flesh blurred. Then he incorporated spins, reaching into the flames, touching logs with his bare hand with such speed that the heat of the fire was avoided. The Edge also sank into the wood and the thrust was coupled with a sharp twist of the Edge and three logs shattered, his bare hand touching the largest pieces, keeping them in the fireplace. The others were maintained by his telekinesis and followed the dance like a finely crafted train to a gown of combat and glory. Jumps came next, but the height was secondary to the continuance of movement and talent. But the Fire Dance was done and with a final spin upon landing from his fourth bounding leap, the embers and the burning debris were returned to the fireplace and the flourishing of the Edge ended with him in a ready stance, the weapon returned, without hesitation or miscalculation, to its scabbard.

Thirty-Eight

Anxiety had become a constant presence but Satashi was prepared for that. She had taken out all of her braids and let her thick, straight black hair fall around her shoulders. It would help with the blending process. She would be considered more mainstream Asian without the braids.

"And they're called glasses, not *opticals*," she said, pushing them up further on her nose, her brown eyes blinking behind them. She had not believed she would get a response from the Comptroller, let alone an approval from Management. It was still surreal to her, but she knew an all too grim reality was waiting for her to show her face. She blinked hard several times, preparing her eyes for the impressions that were coming. She leaned forward over the View and activated the machine. Once again she reviewed the information that had been collected. So many faces and reports were sent to her mind, filed away with so much other data. Heights, weights, hair and eye colors, skin complexions, tribal hierarchies and extra-tribal affiliations (if any), geographical locations and assorted lists of probable objectives. She closed her eyes after the last image and let her eyes adjust. There was not much she could not have recalled with just a bit of thought even without the machine, but she knew she had to be thorough and follow the guidelines of all field researchers. A full View no more than one hour prior to departure was mandatory.

"It is time," he said and she nodded, keeping her eyes closed. She did not know much about the Bondsman, except that his last name was Cho and his first name started with an 'H'. She gathered her jacket and her shoulder bag, putting them both on before walking to the door and stopping in front of him.

He watched as she navigated the room, collected her things and completed dressing herself without the use of her eyes. It was standard training in an operative with field research capability but he had never witnessed it being demonstrated. He wondered if she thought she was being impressive. Those in her position often felt the need to behave in such a manner, thinking that this demonstration might alter his opinion of her and somehow that opinion would affect her ability in the field. Wasted energy! He concluded it was best not to acknowledge her feat and thereby lessen the risk she would make another attempt while they were in the field. For that level of impropriety he might have to liquidate an operative.

"I feel it best if I hold on to the D.S.C.," he said as he straightened his jacket. Already he could hear the generators working hard to generate more energy, the floor vibrated in response, the lights dimmed as mainline capacitors started siphoning larger and large fractions of power, diverting it to the Shutter Chamber.

"No argument there," Satashi said as she walked by him and down the corridor. It was only then he noticed that he had just been standing there, doing nothing. Why? "You're the Bondsman," she announced. "It only makes sense that you hold on to it." Cho put away the argument he had made ready to substantiate his suggestion as he put away the DSC, and turned to follow the young woman.

The Chamber was now the center of attention and activity. Last minute checks were being made before the transmission could commence. He directed Satashi to sit on one of the benches along the wall and he stood next to her.

"Why did you request this assignment?" he asked, keeping an eye on the technician checking the superconductors. He recognized his face and remembered the young man was given to flights of fancy, often losing focus and making mistakes, the sort Cho knew neither he nor Satashi would be able to walk away from.

"Knew this was coming," she thought as she adjusted her glasses. *"I really hate Bondsmen! They have the disposition of arrogant know-it-alls with the courtesy of an elevator with faulty door sensors; if the doors want to close, putting your hand up won't stop a thing!"*

"I feel our observation has to be taken to this level," she replied.

"But there are many operatives who are trained for field-"

"And I happen to be one of them," she quickly added. "That, along with the time I have logged watching them makes me a better candidate for success."

"Success?" he repeated, still watching the technician who looked as if he was getting a hazy look in his eye. "Your tone and word choice suggest you perceive this as a challenge. We are being dispatched to observe."

"Negative, Bondsman!" she argued. "We are being dispatched to resolve the existence of a technology that we did not create and should be beyond those who are using it. Observation is a requirement, but this is an investigation."

"Technician!" Cho barked and Satashi jumped at the volume and harshness of his voice. The young man he was watching also jumped and nearly fell off the scaffolding. "You are relieved! Report to the Comptroller. Your focus is not on your work and we are both aware of your condition. Advise your supervisor that you have been relieved for your work shift and leave the Chamber immediately!"

Satashi looked at Cho and the young man he was dressing down. She then looked to where he was working. She could see nothing wrong from where she was standing and as she stood up, Cho's hand was placed lightly on her shoulder and she was ushered to remain seated.

"His work looks good from here," Satashi said.

"He was working in an area of the apparatus that is vital for the transmission," Cho answered. "I found his attention to detail insufficient."

"He's got a blue patch," she pointed out. "That means he's a Team Leader. It could be that he's worked on that wiring so many times that he can quickly see whether anything is amiss."

"Familiarity with an apparatus is no excuse for a lack of focus while working on it!" Cho declared and Satashi quickly looked away from him, but not so fast that he did not notice her smile.

"So, is this your first transmission?"

"It is," he answered and Satashi's head turned even further away as her body trembled. She was chuckling. "You find something amusing about the number of transmissions I have experienced?"

"There is nothing amusing about the number," Satashi struggled to speak in a clear voice, making a mental note to enter into her personal log that she had been paired with a Bondsman who was afraid of Displacement Transmissions!

Once everything was made ready, the Comptroller sent messages to both of them, letting them know they had clearance for transmission. Satashi smiled when she read that she had been named Team Lead for the mission.

"*Hidelreaux*?!" she thought as she read Cho's first name in the transmission release orders. "*I did not know we were so tasked for names!*" But before another smile could register on her face, Satashi noticed Cho was still reading his message from the Comptroller. As he lifted his eyes, Cho saw Satashi examining the monitors just over his shoulder and he returned to receiving his text.

"*My View Speed might be exceptional, but he's a Bondsman*! *He should be done by now... providing his release orders were the same as mine... and it's obvious they are not.*" Satashi's mind started to fill with numbers. It was her coping mechanism, to work through mathematical formulas and take into account the various approaches to an answer and try to force her view to take a step back from the personal disposition. She was into her second approach when Cho lowered his hand and waved her to follow him onto the platform. She thought it best not to make a point that if anything, she should have been waving him to follow her.

"They have left the declaration of our landing coordinates to you," Cho announced as he took his place and Satashi's face lit up. She was indeed the Lead of the mission, one which the Comptroller did not have a definite overview as to how it should be resolved. "If I may make a suggestion," Cho continued, "everything seems to revolve around this Peter Webster. Perhaps we should transmit to his location."

"I suppose it is a good thing that I am Lead on this," Satashi said coolly as she consulted her hand computer. "Peter Webster and his team have been thrown in on the deep end."

"Excuse me?" Cho said, obviously thrown by what she had said.

"Thought so," she remarked as she entered information into her computer. "Leave the talking to me until you've had some *observation* time.

"What we can't do is to introduce ourselves in such a manner that there is doubt or suspicion. There will probably be some anyway, but I think we will have to maintain on-hand surveillance until I can work through an insertion strategy."

"Very well," Cho replied as he closed his eyes. "Then where we will be landing?"

"I have been monitoring Mr. Webster and the Prodigians they have had some dealings with, one of which they managed to place a transmitter upon and they are tracking it. Unlike their quarry, they cannot land just anywhere, but there is an 89.633% chance they will opt to use a private airport in the Northern Metropolitan area of the city of Atlanta, Georgia." Satashi allowed herself another smile as the room began to tremble.

"Something *else* amuses you?" Cho asked.

"I am easily amused, Hidelreaux," she answered. "And in this case, we are landing at an airport that bears the same name as a popular figure in American history, a cartoon character by the name of Charlie Brown. It is not named for him, but the similarity of names struck a chord."

"And the point of amusement?"

"Having seen many of the animated features with this character, I am just hoping you and I come off more like Lucy Van Pelt and not Charlie Brown in regards to kicking a football.

"And, Cho, if you get the feeling there is no floor," Satashi said as she stowed her computer away and removed her opticals. "…there probably isn't, but looking only makes it worse." Cho's eyes opened as the transmission began. Soon the Chamber was just a memory and an image that soon faded, replaced by a blackness his vision could not penetrate.

"Welcome to the Abyss," was the last thing he heard Satashi say before he felt the floor remove itself from beneath his feet. He looked down. His eyes had been trained, very well trained, and his mind held a great deal of information – enough to know he was moving through Sol. The Fourth Level Surveillance Data Recorder was correct. He would have been better off not looking and realizing that somehow their bodies had passed through Mars without feeling it.

Thirty-Nine

There was a lot to be said for ceremony. Thidalia had monitored many tribes and had come to the conclusion that most members of most tribes would not have agreed with her. Many of their opinions, however, were easily dismissed inasmuch as most of their opinions of ceremony came without too much exploration of the concept. True, there were times when all that went with tradition seemed to be the efforts of the old to add definition and value to their station, but the aims and reasons of the ceremonies predated even them. But it was the young minded who lacked discipline and vision who were the first to make such assumptions regarding ceremony. So focused were they on expressing themselves, they did not pay homage to that which had afforded them the ability of expression. The young were going to be the undoing of the very universe if the elders did not maintain their grips.

Coming to that belief, she considered where she stood on the line that separated the elders and the youths of her kind. Before she began her offering to the Overlord (called the Path of Life – a ceremony that renewed her promise to the Overlord and therefore her people), she looked to the right and acknowledged the elders, a movement of introduction and a respectful request to enter the chambers which stood in front of her. There would be no response to speak of unless admittance was denied. None of the elders moved to do so but a pair of gentle and welcoming female eyes nodded and smiled a greeting to her. Parents and teachers indeed! Then she looked to her left, where the young were still getting to their seats, already showing their disrespect in their tardiness. How could one of her kind be late to anything?! But she could see their faces, at least most of them; she did not know there were so many ways to display distaste. Most looked at the exercises as a means of torture dispensed by cold and cruel masters incapable of feeling. But their attendance of her arrival back to her kind was not mandatory, so she was slightly perplexed as to how she had drawn out so many.

Thidalia looked at her performance as a means to stay connected to the world from which she had been created. Every stride toward to the large drape symbolized growth, which was why there were many steps backward and to the sides. Every life had its fair share of conflict, even if the source of the conflict was self. At the beginning of the path, her hands were close to her sides and her arms did not move. Youth! The ceremony reminded her of herself when she was a child, unable to fend for herself; when her life had been the responsibility of others, her parents and her teachers. As she moved forward, first without music, without direction, for that was a representation of the insistence of instinct, her fingers were allowed some freedom and light sprang forth from her hands, trailing behind spirited bolts that her talent controlled. They sparkled like Tyro fireworks and cascaded shavings of themselves around her body, changing colors as the sparkles slowly drifted to the ground.

Then the music was added, announced by a hail of thunderous drums, a symbol of the dawn of enlightenment, and she was immersed into more of her own history as she recalled being given to her mother to be her instructor and Thidalia could not have been more pleased. Ansharon was then and now one of the most gifted Mavga's of her tribe, credited with the creation of two incredibly powerful incantations. Thidalia's arms came away from her sides and for three steps forward, they flailed about. Then she stepped back and to the left and her arms were pinned again, with movement allowed only from the elbow down. How children often rushed into knowing what they thought they knew and how easily life always taught them that they had overstepped their boundaries. That was why she chose to step to her left, toward the children, posting what Tyros would call a proverbial billboard, warning them that this step toward fulfillment was more voluntary than most believed. She spun again and more light burst from her hands. She now had six bolts, each following its own course around her body. Out of the corner of her eye, she could see one particular head tilt and Thidalia smiled; she had allowed herself a show of pride as only two bolts were required for the progression to the chambers.

Her steps fell were more in time with the music as her life and the instruction she had been given found a common path to tread. As the tempo and the volume rose, her pace became faster, her movements more violent, only to stop. Then she moved at a glide, again in the grace of the notes that were played. As the music approached its climax, she was no longer on the ground, supported by the application of her talent. Now she remembered how she was selected to take point among the Tyros and had been given the awesome responsibility of The Great Façade. It was hers to keep and make stronger if at all possible. To be chosen was the honor of a lifetime. She was of the right blood, a member of one of the three families that had created the Façade. But assumption had so often proven to be the beginnings of crucial downfalls; none of the families could blindly trust that one of their children would be of the skill and strength necessary to assume the objective. Still, she had been chosen, and the order of the three families was changed as hers was moved to the forefront. The former masters of the Façade, the Ambrosius family, having no heirs to present, had bowed out gracefully. Dahvahn's family, the Kourge's, had long since held the third tier and Thidalia's ascension had not changed their position. She was sure there was resentment, but even without an heir to speak of, the Ambrosius bloodline was too powerful to question and their record of service was more legendary than impeccable, though it was that as well.

She brought the bolts together as the music crashed its final note. She was kneeling but still elevated above the ground, and her body slowly lowered to the carpeted stone. As she touched down, she drew applause from the elders but her attention was taken by the youths, and soon the applause of her elders also subsided as they too took heed of what was happening. They were on their feet and cheering her. She could feel the tremors their stomping generated and the shaking rose up and into her heart. Tears welled up in her deep brown eyes as she saw one of them come from his seat. He ran toward her and came to an abrupt stop, dropping to both knees, a motion declaring his voluntary subjugation.

"Lady Thidalia," the young man said in a very clear and strong voice. "The brightest jewel of the crown that is the Pekavali Family, may I have the honor?" His head was lowered, so she could not see his eyes. But his near-gold blonde hair was well combed and kept by a headband normally worn by the more combative sort. He wore traditional robes, but his broad shoulders and the way he ran were both evidence that his body had been well trained. His voice did the same for his level of education.

"You are gracious to ask," she replied. "But I am not worthy-"

"You are the Mistress of the Great Façade!" he said as he stood up. She could see his eyes but not their color, he had already brought power into his body and he was about to cast. "You are the defender of our kind! Who would dare to speak against your worth?

"O, Great Overlord!" he called out, turning to face the chambers. He had changed the air around his mouth and augmented his voice. There were no ears within 100 meters who could not hear him clearly. "May I present to you Mavga Thidalia Anzakasha Pekavali! Rank of Mistress and Chief Facilitator of the Great Façade. She has traversed the Path of Life and in her strides, no Arcanian was left untouched or untaught! Permit her entry into your sight, I beg of you!"

"Let it be known, young Odalius," the Overlord spoke in the same manner as Thidalia's eager Caller but the magic that carried his voice did not need an ear to be received; it was more felt and moved immediately to the mind more than it could have been heard and simply *listened to*. "Mistress Thidalia is embraced in these chambers and that these eyes are pleased to see her Path of Life and her very presence. Enter, Lady Thidalia Pekavali, that your words may be found in equal light as your gesture of tradition and honor." In answer to the Overlord's directions, Thidalia stood and Rook walked over to her rear left. Both sides of the Path began to leave their seats; the time for watching was over. She would wait for the seats to clear as much as they would, but she looked at the young man, Odalius as he bowed very deeply toward the chamber before turning to leave. His every stride was in accordance to their traditions, and she had to admit that his bowing was probably deeper than her own.

"May I have the blessing of knowing your reason, Odalius?" she said softly. He stopped at the sound of her voice but he did not turn around. He did not even turn his head.

"Was I out of place, Mistress?" he asked. His strong and boastful tones were nowhere to be found. His intonation acknowledged her greatness and his respect of who and what she was.

"Far from it, young one. You were inspirational!"

"Nay, Mistress, I was inspired!" he argued. "Surely you can attest to the difference. I am not so much the pebble as I am part of the pond, impacted by your very presence."

"Poetic," she remarked, somewhat glad she did not have this one's eyes. She was not sure she did not look flushed by his words and demeanor. "But hardly an answer."

"But you already have that, Mistress," he replied. "It is there at your feet!" Thidalia looked forward and down and she saw a small hand mirror made of silver and infused crystal instead of glass. The reflection it produced seemed almost three dimensional. "It is a small token of my esteem, Mistress Pekavali, and I hope there is no insult in its offering."

"It is beautiful," she said, almost with no voice coming out of her mouth. Rook stepped forward to pick it up and present it to her.

"It is a mirror, my lady," Odalius answered as his talents were once again applied and he was now teleporting himself. "What it reflects, at least in this case, is beauty!" He was gone before the mirror was placed in her hand.

"The seats have been cleared save for one, Mistress," Rook offered, knowing it would be bad for her to keep the Overlord waiting.

"That seat will be filled when I am done here, my precious Rook," Thidalia answered, still looking at the mirror. There were two gems on the outside of the design and when her fingers touched them both, the mirror folded itself on a hinge that had not existed a moment before. It was now small enough to fit into her small purse and that was where she placed it as she approached the now parting drapes. Rook reassumed his position and walked in with her, his head held high.

The chamber had changed since her last attendance. Then again, when she was last here, she was being given a reward, an honor, a challenge. Now that challenge had proven to be difficult, if not moreso, than the elders had promised. She had lost ground. There was no need to even waste thought toward that argument, but the progress she had made before the events surrounding Peter Webster might still hold as impressive enough to afford her an opportunity to fix what had gone awry. She looked as the colors that had been dark before were now bright and brilliant to the eyes. Yellows and golds had replaced the purples and blacks as long stretches of satins and silk were strewn about the chamber, wrapped around poles that protruded from the walls. Thidalia nearly gasped at the sight of him as she came through the drapery. He was not seated. He was standing and the magnitude of his frame made her shudder with weakness.

"Arch Mavgaran Ambrosius?!" she whispered as she remembered then to bow. It was late, but the surprise of not seeing the Overlord was easily understood.

"Mavga Thidalia," he answered, his clear blue eyes locked on her form. She was still ever so wondrous to look upon, a gift of her mother's blood. Her talent was the gift of both her blood lines, but it had been so precisely crafted by Ansharon. "The Overlord has asked me to receive your report in his stead. There are matters he must tend to that, while they are not more important, have been put off long enough, and at my insistence, I have been given the honor of receiving your Path of Life."

"You what?!" she screamed as she took a step back, energy surrounding both hands. Rook's hand found her shoulder before she could step forward and release her gathered power. Her eyes were sharp as she glared at her servant.

"You will not, Mistress!" he said softly to Thidalia. His strength did not waver. His touch was light, but he stood ready to receive her fury and perhaps even perish from it. That would not get in the way of his service to her position. "You can not," he added as he let his hand slide off and Thidalia quickly dismissed the energies she had so quickly assembled.

"You have your father's temper," Verlson Ambrosius remarked, stroking his long red locks. "A gift you could not have requested, but it has been delivered by your blood nonetheless."

"Arch L- Excuse me! *Overmaster* Ambrosius, I have acted-"

"As one might when taken completely by surprise, Mavga Thidalia, and there is no need for either of us to speak of it any further. Besides, we have more pressing issues, do we not?" Thidalia nodded, but could not find any words to offer but for Verlson, her nodding was enough. "Good," he said as he walked to stand in front of her. "Perhaps that temper will be unleashed on the Tyros who seem to have become something of a problem for you."

Anger was a point that struck a chord in both of them and it was a commonality she appreciated. "Yes," she answered quickly, before realizing she had just been given a pass. Her brow strained and she lifted her eyes up to his. They were of the same tribe and wielded much of the same power, but the depth of his glare made Thidalia feel as if she would drown in his essence. "Overmaster, does this mean-"

"The Pekavali Family will maintain its position in the Great Façade, Thidalia. My ascension is not a measure by which you should feel threatened. Do you not think your mother would have warned you if it were otherwise?"

"Admittedly, sire, I am not proud of the flexibility of my mind at the moment."

"It is a balance that comes and goes, my dear! My time among the Tyros taught me that much."

"But it is the matter of this one that concerns me most," Ambrosius said as he formed an image of William Ferrous.

"Yes, the Unlawful Son," Thidalia said, looking at the picture of a youth that, like Odalius, was surprising and uncommon among his kind. "Or at least that is what the Prodigian call him."

"They may come to call him more than that if he is allowed to live to see the Territories," he replied as the image faded. "And this is not to say that you are tasked with killing him. What you do as a Descrier is what you should continue to do, after you have cleaned up a few matters."

"Peter Webster!" she said coldly.

"Barely the tip of your particular iceberg, Thidalia," he replied. "I have not confirmed it, for to do so would be a trespass between our families, but I would wager that he is but a tool being expertly wielded by Lydia King and, by fateful design, an extension of William Ferrous. For what we must accomplish, we do not need the extension as much as we need Kadorgyan." He walked over to Thidalia and threw his arm around her shoulders, leading her over to a window that was the Overlord's scrying device. It responded to Mavgaran Ambrosius' commands... he was definitely within the embrace of the Overlord and his claim to ascension was true.

"If Verlson is an Overmaster, what has happened to Fandros?" she thought, before wiping away the preclusion that it was Fandros who had been replaced though he was the oldest of the three Overmasters.

But Verlson was not boastful, nor did he in any way remind her of his authority. His attention was fixed on the Tyros and the condition of them. He inquired about her impressions and took full consideration of her suggested resolutions before asking to offer alternatives. When he was done, she thanked him for his time and his observation. She refused his suggestions and gave reasons why she could not act along those lines... none of her dismissals met with argument and he genuinely took in her points of contention. He then offered assistance in a form she could later name and he dismissed her, advising Thidalia that he would report to the Overlord that the situation of the Descriers was in suitable hands... she had indeed been given a pass. Before she left his presence, Verlson reminded her of the folly of arrogance and that the Thidalia who was first assigned to the Great Façade should be the one who returned to the Tyros, not the one who had come to know the Tyros and had judged them weak and scattered. For although such views were not wrong, they were also not wholly right.

"Tyros have no given power of their own," he said as she turned to leave the chamber. "Therefore they often stumble upon one or two from time to time. Mark well the Prodigian and the Elementals, though the former seem to be occupying themselves for the moment."

"I thank you for you kindness and your grace, Overmaster," she said as she bowed. "You do not have to make these efforts and yet, long after you have completed your time as Master of the Great Façade, you endeavor to aid me."

"I aid the Arcanians, Thidalia," he answered. "As do you!" She smiled again and nodded. Then Thidalia walked out of the chamber into the waiting arms of her mother. Rook was allowed to go amongst his people, the SomeVinco, but his time there would be short. His place was ever at her side and she was just beginning to realize what a boon it was to her. Even more, it gave birth to another thought as she wrapped her arms around Ansharon Pekavali. There would be few words exchanged between mother and daughter, Ansharon knew that, witnessing the difference between the Thidalia who entered the chamber versus the one who emerged from it. She quickly flashed a smile and nodded, giving her daughter a mother's and a mentor's blessing to proceed.

"Assemble the others, Rook," she commanded. "It is time the Tyros took full measure of my court!"

Forty

He was not holding back, not anymore. The punch nearly took her chin off and she spun into the wall. But she screamed as she came away from it, her haymaker hook. Her hand missed his jaw but his foot found her stretched abdomen. Lydia's roar of rage became one of pain and her body was seized with pain. But he opponent did not stop and his forearm hammered down on her back. She fell to the floor almost out of breath.

"You sure you wanna keep at this?" Joey asked as he backed away, giving her an opportunity to get up... again.

"You're not gassing out on me, are you?" Lydia asked as she slowly got up. Joey shook his head as he approached knowing her current speed was a feint, his step in drew her out of her façade and he ducked, sinking his ridge hand into her stomach. Lydia folded, and this time it was no ploy. She fell to the floor, keeping her fetal position.

"I think that should do it for today," Joey said, turning to leave. He could hear Lydia giving an effort to resume the session, but he knew her body would fail her ambition. She did not even get up from her knees. "Wanna tell me why you're here?"

"Training," she answered, wracked with pain.

Joey nodded as he took off his t-shirt. He had won, but he had underestimated her zeal and had been made to pay for it. But these bruises would heal. Whatever was hurting Lydia King was not showing signs of subsiding. "That's cool!" he said sarcastically. "No need for us to maintain any sort of professional courtesy. Just tell me to fuck off like you've been telling everyone else around here."

"Fuck off!" she whispered.

"You're not my type," he said, picking up a hand towel and a bottle of water. He walked both of them over toward her, dropping them just out of her reach.

"Son of a bitch!" she moaned.

"Leave my mother out of this!" he replied. "No one saw you walk in, no one has to see you leave."

Lydia strained her muscles to move and she eventually crawled over to the wall and used it to get up to her feet.

"What's happened to you?" he asked, drinking water and rubbing his jaw. Her back kick had found his sternum and nearly knocked the wind out of him. He had taught her that kick, but he would have liked to have known who had taught her the hammering fist. It was unorthodox but potent. He had been dazed long enough for King to land three sharp blows to his back. It was then that he had felt like he was in a fight for his life and he had reacted accordingly. That was the first time Lydia went down. She had taken another three trips, depositing Joey Bui on the mats once more as well. The last trip she took was not especially hard but she had over-extended herself, leaving herself vulnerable. A child could have hit the right spot and downed her. Joey was no child, but he had held back from his real power. "You got nasty," he concluded.

"And you picked up a lot more speed than you ever used on me before," Lydia said, taking out her mouth guard and checking her teeth.

"Never needed to go all out on you before. Someone's taught you how to be vicious!"

"No," Lydia said, walking over to her bag a lot faster than Joey thought she should have been able to. "She taught me to make every shot count!"

"She? Wow! *That* I was not expecting."

"Then this is really going to blow you away!" Lydia said, handing Joey his orders. He had seen these folders before but he had never opened one, nor had he ever thought he would see his name on one.

"What are you up to?" he asked.

"Nothing I'm willing to discuss here," Lydia said as she twisted her back and Joey could here her spine pop.

"Dammit!" he said, walking away from her. "I forgot you did that shit!"

"Of all people, I have to get this from *you*?!"

"I'm a guy. We're supposed to make sounds like that, comes just before the cave painting and after the grunting. You're a girl! You're just supposed to walk around and look sexy."

"Not for you, I'm not," Lydia responded quickly.

"Oh, so Jack finally put his thing down!" Joey was quick to conclude, and Lydia closed her eyes. She was tired, mentally fatigued and physically battered and she had forgotten why she wanted Joey as her partner. He was good! Fast, smart and loose-minded enough to make the transition from the norm to the new norm. But none of that made her feel comfortable that he was now in her personal backyard.

"Take note that these are optional," Lydia said, getting back to business as she rubbed her abdomen. That last shot was going to hurt for a while, she was going to welcome wearing a protective vest. "With what I'm getting into, trust me, it's voluntary."

"That one-way, eh?" Joey answered.

"That's just it, Joey," she replied. "I don't have all the details." She was not facing him, but she could feel his face twist and he turned to face her. "It's for George. He's gone missing."

"Then it's not voluntary," Joey Bui replied. He was bound for the showers but his mind was already going down his 'pre-flight' check list. "I'll see you in the parking lot!"

"Thanks, JB," she said softly, turning to rinse off herself. Still having his trust was bittersweet but she did not have her team any longer and a number of comfortable options went away with them. Joey she could at least trust to give her one hundred and thirty percent, and that would be just at the onset. It was bound to get better the deeper into things they got. She stopped at the door and watched him disappear around the corner; and her mind reflected on Kim and Marshall.

"Go get cleaned up, King," Joey yelled. "We both know how you suck when you over-think things."

"I was just thinking about Kim and Marshall. He's eleven now, right?"

"Going on thirty," he replied. "And I would not be much of a husband, father or a man if I let you go after George alone. We both know how close to the shady stuff he used to run. It's a fool's run to go at that solo."

"George did it," Lydia replied with a smile.

"Thank you for proving my point," Joey exchanged as he went again around the corner. "See you in the parking lot."

"See you there," Lydia whispered, welcoming the warm waters of the shower to come.

From the gymnasium to the estate, it was a quiet ride, and she let Joey drive. It was her second trip and the crime scene technicians were still pretty busy.

"What happened here?" Joey asked and Lydia smiled at the similarity of their reactions. Joey parked the car and got out, looking at where several bodies had been found. Joey took off his sunglasses and squatted, looking in all directions.

"Well the good news is that none of these men died here," Joey said, still looking. "The bad news is that there is no trace of how they got stacked up like this. And that officially opens up the Weird Journal."

"You're going to be better off not asking any questions until you've done a good walk through," Lydia said, getting out car. She did not hesitate and walked for the house. "Meet me on the inside when you're done."

"That I can do," he replied and left to make his sweep over the property. Lydia knew Jack had trained Joey in a few of their outings into the wilderness, and likewise Joey had given Jack an understanding of how to make the most of his size, speed and strength in hand-to-hand combat. As good as Joey was against anyone, he was an even better instructor. Lydia walked into the house and let her smile of convenience fall.

"*Good,*" the woman thought, keeping to her perch. Watching the Tyros had always been something of a boring pastime, but these latest additions had proven worthy of at least keeping her interest. The black woman was making her second appearance, and as it had happened when she first witnessed her arrival, it was clear she was in charge of the scattered and scared Tyros. The Abyss frightened them so and that was indeed good. All one needed to do was surround them with enough darkness and they were easily controlled.

"*And this one,*" Pawn thought as her eyes followed the young man who obviously had some Asian influence to his blood. Still, his swagger was American and his eyes were equally clouded as he walked the grounds. But she watched them, still in the midst of her own investigation of the parties who had attacked the property and made off with George Howard, though she did not know why her Mistress sought to expend her talents in this direction. "*He looks but he sees little!*"

Joey stopped and looked down at the ground, taking a moment to squat low and extended his hand into the grass. "Interesting depressions here," he whispered. "Like someone jumped out of a car..." he stood up and looked around. "...maybe even a truck. So where are the tire tracks?"

"*Since the question has to be asked,*" Pawn thought as she looked back at the house. She could tell they made their way from this direction. The impressions the fool spoke of and the blast marking in the side of the house both were on this side of the-- a well-thrown stone was blindly caught in her hand.

"Or maybe they fell from the sky," Joey said, looking directly at Pawn. She had misjudged him, but she had not removed all her attentions from him. She looked down on him. She jumped down from the thick of the tree and looked at him again, the ground and then back at his face.

"Thirty six and one-third meters," she said as she dropped the stone to the ground. "Forty two point six three degree angle incline. Nice throw!"

"Oh shit!" Joey said, already convinced she was right about every detail of his throw, but that paled to the way she had taken a near three-story drop to the ground and just bent at the knees when she landed. He reached for his gun but came up with nothing as the rock he had thrown was kicked back at him and took his gun out of his grip. From the sparks that flew, he doubted whether the thing would be capable of firing without thorough examination.

"Call for help and you will only succeed in having company in death," Pawn said as she slowly lowered her foot back to the ground.

"Wow!" Joey exclaimed as he turned his left shoulder toward the black woman that made Lydia's normal intimidation factor seem nonexistent. "Got it all figured out, do you? Just like you knew I didn't spot you."

"You should have taken that grace and lived longer," Pawn answered, walking toward her prey. "But with Tyros I have seen that grace and wisdom do not walk in the same stride."

"And here I always give my opponent an opportunity to surprise me and take the fight."

"Just as you consider the chair a worthy opponent when you sit in it?" Pawn asked. "No, you do not give it a second thought. You are not worthy of my first!" She was still fifteen meters away when she jumped and Joey gasped, knowing she was not going to land until she had exceeded that distance. He stepped to the side and she flew by him, a soft ripping sound reaching his ears and he looked down only to see that his ankle holster was missing. He looked at the woman as she made a kicking motion and his spare pistol landed in her hand before it was crushed.

"Lower your guard and I shall make it painless," she said in a tone that actually had some regard for the disadvantage she had over Joey Bui.

"Hey, you've already painted a good picture of me being pretty stupid," Joey replied, taking another stance, one that allowed him maximum movement. Getting his head out of the way was obviously not enough. "This hardly seems like the time to go changin' things up."

"So be it," she said as she nodded and lunged at Joey, leaving a blur of herself as she moved. Joey kept his ground but twisted, moving his torso. It was a guess, expecting her to go for a kill move and therefore limiting the number of targets she could strike and achieve her aims. Her double hand thrust to his neck and chest missed, and his quick jab barely made her blink. He ducked under her sweeping chop and he put his shoulder to the ground, kicking up with both feet. It was like kicking the front bumper of a pickup truck, but he was fortunate she did not weigh as much. She was lifted from the ground but he could tell as she landed that it was hardly a telling blow. By the time he took another stance she was already up and charging. He stepped out of the way of her hook for his head. He smacked her hand thrust wide of his body and spun down her arm as he barely avoided a fierce cross. She brought her arm back and tried to get a headlock on Joey, but came up with only his jacket and his foot across her face. She grabbed for his chest and Joey was topless as he put both feet in her chest and kicked off. She moved back, but only two steps, whereas he was on his back. She lunged in again and Joey lifted one foot while his hands pressed against the ground. His foot met her chest and he slid over the grass from the force of her charge. She stopped and grabbed for his ankle but Joey kicked the hand before she could grab down. He rolled up to his feet and jumped back, her fist inches from his chest. She stepped forward and lost sight of him and his hand peppered her face with slaps. She grabbed for one of his arms and received a solid hook that barely turned her chin. Her diving head bunt was leap-frogged and she passed under him. She landed on her chest and he was on his feet. She got up slowly, cooling her rage. The Tyro was well trained and he was gifted in impromptu applications of his technique. Only her strength, speed and body armor kept her as the superior in this contest, though it was clear he was winning. She turned around and was slightly bewildered to see he had put his jacket back on.

"What?" he said, looking at his jacket and brushing his hair back behind his ear. It did not stay there long. "It's chilly this morning. Don't want to catch my death of cold before you get a chance to kill me!"

Pawn screamed as she charged him. Yes, she had given up her position and others would be coming, but she would have dispatched this one by the time she was clearly in range of their eyes. She jumped toward him, throwing her arms out wide to tackle him to the ground. Joey jumped up and met her in the air, his foot stamping out in the middle of her chest; their bodies were sent away from each other but she was thrown back harder and landed on her back while Joey struggled to keep his stance after he landed, his leg nearly numb from the contact. He staggered back, clearly in pain and off balance, and Pawn smiled at her opportunity. She quickly got up and moved toward her opponent, surprised that he was moving toward her and he closed their distance before she was ready, her grab for his arm missed poorly, a soft rip reaching her ears as she moved past the man. She turned to face the man watched as he brandished a weapon. It was a small, single-edged blade without a hilt and had apparently been kept in the back of the jacket. Pawn looked down to see her stomach had been cut deeply and upon seeing the wound, the pain registered.

"I'll admit, you're a big tree," Joey said, taking a new stance, a lower stance that revealed there was nothing wrong with his leg. "But you're fuckin' with the wrong beaver on this one, lady! Might take me a minute, but I'm about to carve your pretty ass and serve it up for Thanksgiving!"

"I doubt it, little man!" Pawn said, touching her thumb to the wound and it instantly healed. "But let us put that issuance of endurance to the test, shall we?" Three shots! Two to the chest and one to the neck and Pawn was knocked back into a tree that she immediately slid around. Joey quickly ran the other side, taking out his other knife. He thought he was ready for anything but when he saw the woman launch herself nearly seventy meters away, he stopped and lowered his hands to his side. She landed on her side and slid to a stop, coughing and spitting blood. She screamed in rage and pain and spat again, blood and a bullet coming out of her mouth.

"What the hell!" he exclaimed as he saw the other two rounds come out of her chest. The woman looked at him and he was glad she did not have eyes that could actually kill, because he could feel his throat tighten under her glare. He was tackled just as the woman made a throwing motion. The tree behind Joey caught the three bullet spread.

Lydia rolled off of Joey and blindly reached for her second pistol in the small of her back, tossing it to Joey. "Stay mobile!" she shouted as she took aim at the young black woman. She did not have time to even get the first shot off as the woman bound up in the tree and then jumped again as if she had jet assist.

"Well, that's different," she said softly as she checked her weapon. "You okay, JB?"

"Different?" Joey repeated. "That's all you have to say?!"

"Yep," Lydia said matter-of-factly. "That's my first time seeing them move like that though. Normally they use telekinesis or teleport."

"Did you just hear yourself?"

"JB, we can argue what I said..." Lydia said as she walked over and picked up his crushed revolver. "...or we can argue what you saw. Either way, it won't change a thing!

"That was pretty smart, getting that transmission to me," Lydia added.

"It was just one of the perks of getting my jacket back," Joey answered, picking up his primary weapon. He was right, it would not have fired for him. "I also needed my blades."

"You're going to find that you can never pack enough out here," Lydia said, walking up to Joey and touching his shoulder. "Not until you take care of what you're packing here," she said touching his chest, just over his heart. "And like I said, this is strictly voluntary."

"And like I told you, I'm in, but I'm going to need more information!"

"Agreed," Lydia replied, finally putting up her pistol.

"And where is the freakin' cavalry?" Joey asked looking around.

"I sent them to the other side of the property," Lydia answered, making her way back to the house. She picked up his shirt and held it up for him to take. "No sense in filling body bags today.

"You find anything worth talking about?" she asked.

"You first," Joey replied, taking the shirt knowing it was a lost cause. "You name the café and let me get by my place and get a shirt."

"A shirt?" Lydia asked.

"*And* a shirt," he answered.

"Not a problem," Lydia replied, walking back to the car. "Only we do not separate until we can get some reliable backup."

"What would Jack say?" Joey ribbed.

"Just hope he's saying it," Lydia fired back and Joey swallowed hard. Jack had been hard to put down before their mutual training. After they had traded knowledge with each other, each man was only considered more disgustingly capable in the eyes of their colleagues.

"Good point."

"Welcome to the team, Joey," Lydia smiled. "Hope you like your first day."

"*So long as I can get to the point of saying* first," he thought, having ducked death at least a half dozen times back in the woods. Even if he were a cat he was over halfway used up in his first fight since taking on the case. Just what the hell was George into to have something like that hanging around his house? "*And damn if she was not fine!*" Joey thought as he started the car.

Forty-One

    His steps were quick and sure. His pace was dictated by the time parameters he had given himself. He had told Elkazzar that he only needed an hour, but that time had been nearly all taken with the work William had done with Tara. Her time with King's team had been life-changing, especially with the extra talents she had picked up along the way. Thank God for Simmons and his need for an extra pair of steady hands. She was far from being an Electrical Engineer, but she could lay wire and solder a circuit. She was even able to offer some advice as to how to package the particular tool William was trying to jury rig. But that had been the stuff of the waking world and he was now back at the Source, outside the city, and looking for its latest citizen. The scaffolding for the tower proved to be high enough for him to scan the surrounding the area without bringing too much attention to himself.
    She sat at the side of a fire but there was nothing else, no cave, no weapons, no food. She looked as if she was waiting for oblivion to come and take her.
    "If I have anything to say about it," William said as he climbed the rocks. "…it's going to be a pretty long wait."
    "Bless the Fates for my patience," Palshaya replied without looking up.
    "Whoa!" William whispered as he took in the sight of her. His first meeting with the Tracker and Warrior had been through Tara Mifflen and therefore he had not ever seen her true appearance. What he saw sitting on the ground far exceeded the image that Arvius had been able to generate. This said much about the man William now hunted. "You are something else!"
    "I am nothing," she replied. "I am dead and without thy efforts, I would be in the care of the Wayfarers."
    "That's true, and for that I am sorry. My need is great, Pal-"
    "And that is reason enough, eh?" she asked sharply. "Is that all a man needs?"
    "If all you have in you is the bitterness I see and feel, I will see you to the destiny you so desperately seek. Forgive me, but the woman I saw in Tara is truly dead, for this waste of thought that sits on the ground in front of me kills the image of the woman I fought beside." William walked over to her fire and peered over the hill. Nothingness! It was where the Source stopped and ambient, unformed thought was beyond it, the Abyss through which he had fallen to reach this place. It was exactly what he expected.
    "Why do you just sit there?" he asked as he walked to the edge, receiving Palshaya's confused eyes in the act. "You're right here! Why not

just lay back and roll over?" She lifted her hand and moved it in the direction of the edge. There was at first a soft crackle but then her hand stopped at an energy wall. She looked up at William but said nothing. "Oh," he said blankly, robbed of his passion. "That's why. Got it."

"Well, let's try another approach," he said, offering his hand to Palshaya. "Come on, get up off your ass and let's see if this works. I got stuff to do and you're really pissing me off!"

Palshaya at first did not know what to do. She looked up at William who thrust his hand at her again, urging her to move quickly. She got to her feet and slowly approached him. What she had not advised William of was that touching the wall brought pain with it. However, there was no presence of the wall with him there poised on the edge.

"What do you want of me?" she asked.

"What does it matter? I'm just another asshole man squeezing you for what you're worth. I know what it feels like to have a lot of idiots lined up, all of them just waiting for their turn to get a good crack at you. In fact, there's a cloaked asshole back in town who's added himself to their company. Now let's put this in motion. I've got too much ground to cover to give you every little detail. Enough people have used you and I'm sorry I was almost added to them. Let me be a toll you can use this time around."

Palshaya took his hand and there was no crackle, no defensive reaction of the wall whatsoever. But she could feel the Abyss beyond the hill and she could feel herself beginning to get lost in the stream. A true death awaited her. She had only to take one more step.

"You have something to say?" William asked, opening the moment to greater consideration. "I hate to seem rude but I've got to get back and see if my trainer can give me some tracking pointers…since I cannot get them from you."

"I understand," Palshaya said, pulling William into an embrace. "Thank you! You are indeed worth the reason for this meeting in both time and circumstance."

William closed his eyes and wrapped his arms around the woman. "Let's hope I grow to be worthy of that estimation."

"If you grow any further, the estimation will have to be changed," Palshaya assured him, a tear rolling down her cheek. William kissed the tear and the warrior woman was touched in his observation of their culture. It was their belief that a dying warrior does not cry, but that their tears are merely reflections of heaven opening up for their entry. Kissing the tear was to touch the divine and the most gracious salute of the efforts of the warrior who had created the tear. "Tell me, who is this corpse you seek?"

William's face twisted, confused that she did not know, but her inquiry made a number of things quite clear to him. He was no longer in a rush, nor did he have any anger toward Palshaya.

"Harold," he said softly, allowing the memory of her husband to drift from his mind to hers. "Arvius, Palshaya. I seek Arvius and this is why." What started as a soft and slow feed of information quickly turned into a feeding frenzy, and at the memory of Arvius' face when he had looked back at William, hovering over the front yard, Palshaya pushed back from William. He could not keep his eyes on her for long. Where her feet stepped she left burn marks on the ground. They were quickly changing to normal, but the reaction was another surprise of the moment.

"Bastard!" she screamed. "Thou didst promise me, Arvius. Thou swore an oath of thy Blood!" she threw her arms out from her body and William started looking for shelter. A storm had suddenly gathered and Palshaya was the eye of it. "I gave thee my trust! I gave thee my body and passion! [*I gave thee my love!*]" William rolled to his right and avoided a bolt of energy that he assumed was raw thought.

"No!" Palshaya said coldly as she looked at William. "It is not simply thought! It is empathic energy!"

"*Wonderful, I'm about to killed by a tantrum,*" William thought as he looked at Palshaya. Against everything she wanted to do or say, a smile broke across her face and she laughed. The wind and the crackling energy quickly vanished and the sky was once again a clear blue. There was a strong breeze but nothing else aside from Palshaya's growing laughter. Palshaya fell to her back and rolled over on her shoulder as she clutched her sides and the laughter turned painful.

William stood there for a few moments and watched and waited as the tides of laughter rose and fell. After he had seen her go through five different stages of crying and laughing, William projected an image of Yudara into Palshaya's mind and her laughing came to a very sudden stop.

"Well whaddaya know! That worked a helluva lot better than I thought it might," William admitted and he offered his hand to Palshaya.

"Have a care, Unlawful one!" Palshaya warned, taking his hand and getting to her feet. "It is not too late for me to make good on thy head!"

"In your dreams," William smiled, already sensing the insincerity of her glare. It immediately softened and Palshaya began to shake her head.

"I was such a fool!"

"You were my hero," William quickly replied, looking down and her eyes focused on his face. "You had the courage to love, Palshaya. With everything going on around you and the doubt you must have had, still you dared to love him!

"Okay, he wasn't worthy of it, but that's not what we're talking about, is it?" William asked as he turned to face the Abyss. Strangely, he found the blackness calming as he remembered his first encounter with it. "What people do with our love... well, that's on them. But it's on us if we can't give them that love to begin with."

"I am dead so thou must take measure of my words," Palshaya offered, forcing William to laugh. "But I shall tell thee this, Kadorgyan. If thou hast the worry in thy mind, then that which is needed in thy heart is already there. She must be a remarkable woman!" Palshaya concluded.

"Even if I were not Prodigian, she could make me fly!" William answered.

"But this is not why thou hast sought me out, nor is it why I shall give unto thee all I can to find Arvius and those he has taken."

"While we are at it-"

"Have trust, Kador," she quickly added, smiling. "I be not an *asshole* man!" William closed his eyes and opened his mind to Palshaya. The last conscious thought he experienced was the surprise the woman felt for his blind trust of what she would do. They were at the Source and well within the shields of his mind. There was much she could have done, but he trusted her to do what she said and nothing else. When he opened his eyes, he was lying on the bench in the arena and Dexter was sparring with the cloaked man and proving that he was doing rather well with the Edge.

He sat up and found that he was not groggy, nor was he weak. He stretched his neck and it popped fairly loudly and the sound continued into his back.

[*Hark, master of the Source!*] Palshaya projected to his mind, but there was something odd to the sound and feeling of it. It had been recorded and placed in his mind, set to play once he was of the mind to hear it. [*Seek me not, my brother, for I hath given unto thee the best of my own form, mind and spirit. Look to the eastern point and thou shall find that thy Source hath been increased.*] William closed his eyes and let his mind drift to the east. He gasped as he saw and felt it. The rocks yielded to a rolling land of deep green. Wild grass bent and swayed in the wind. The grass continued until it kissed the edge of a deep and rich forest filled with all sorts of trees that might as well have been evergreens, for knew that only when he wished it would the weather change to facilitate lessons to be learned learned in the ice and snow. He could see the rivers and the caves; he could see, hear and smell the flora and fauna and somehow the Source had taken the addition and had conditioned the minds of the city folk to believe the woods had always been there. Some of them even knew the pass through the mountains that were always covered in snow.

[*I am become that which was always the best of my spirit. I am become the wood where I first took to the instruction of my talents. Methinks this place, in thy mind, is far greater than either of us may ever know, and I am glad to add my essence to it. In thy mind thou shall find not only my talents but the very lessons which that were given me in my time. Without request or regret I have given thee every talent given unto me and perhaps in thy mind, more of what they were meant to do and be will remain. Farewell to thee, Kador, Blood of Xargagyan, Unlawful Son and my hero. For in thy mind, I have cheated death!*]

"Indeed you have," William said as he quickly picked up the bow, nocked an arrow and fired without aiming. The shaft hit the target just to the left of the bull's-eye. The target was sixty meters away! "Indeed you have! Okay Harry, I'm coming for you!"

"Is this helping at all?" she asked, and I was nearly too far into euphoria to answer, but I opened my eyes and looked up.

"More than you know," I answered, and Adrianna continued to apply her hands and considerable healing talents to my shoulders, neck and temples. There had been something to the sound attack which caused every muscle in my body to lock up and the aftermath was nearly as painful in body as it was in mind. "Are you sure he is okay?"

"He is fine," she answered, continuing to rub my shoulders and I heard the soft pop of bone in my back. A wave of ease washed over me and I sighed. "For the sixth time, he was working on something with Tara for a few minutes and then he told her to get some rest. Next thing I knew, he and Dexter were asleep in William's room. It's not even noon yet, Elkazzar." She started to say more but she caught herself and just kept to her rubbing. "But minutes have to be lifetimes for you right now."

I place my hand on top of hers. There was no need to say anything else. We were both parents, but I was just beginning to feel what my former protégé had been dealing with for over seventeen years as a passive fear and as a very active fear for months.

Another point of interest for me was the way his room had been packaged. It was as if there were telepathic shields over the walls, floor and ceiling. They were not impenetrable, but that was not their design. They were meant to be a first warning and alert those inside of the presence of projected thought. Curious!

"If he's not up in another ten minutes, I'll go and get him," she offered.

"I can go and get him now, Elizabeth," Gordon offered.

"Oh baby, would you?" she asked, smiling up at her husband.

"No problem," Gordon said as he turned toward the stairs. "Kinda feeling like a knot on a log around here. I need to do something!"

[*His problems are just beginning*?] I projected and Adrianna pinched me, giving a soft chuckle at the same time.

"Okay, sleeping beauty," William said as he nudged Dexter. "Time to walk it off."

Dexter's eyes opened slowly but not as if he was groggy or tired. It just took time for his consciousness to get reconnected; they had both had been warned that for Tyros, that was often the reaction of a prolonged stay. As soon as he had overcome the transfer, his face lit up and he screamed.

"Feeling better?" William asked.

"Keanu can so kiss my ass!" Dexter shouted as he dropped down into a low weaponless battle stance.

"Not bad," William smiled, looking at Dexter's rather impressive form. "But don't think if you move toward me that I'll be all Morpheus-like and just teach you without bitch-slapping you across the room!" The door to the room opened and Gordon stepped in. Dexter attacked quickly without recognizing who it was. Gordon blocked the punch meant for his face and went to put Dexter into an arm-lock but his effort was denied and Dexter backed him out of the room with a flurry of attacks.

"Gillis!" William shouted and Dexter realized who he was fighting and stopped. Gordon threw a punch and Dexter spun out of the way, slapping and guiding Gordon's power away from his body and down the stairs.

"Dexter!" William shouted as he locked his eyes on Gordon. Both fists were clenched and he strained with his telekinesis to catch Gordon just above the bottom of the stairs. He did not have the power to correct his body; he just gently laid him down and fell to his knees.

"Oh shit, I'm so sorry!" Dexter cried, not knowing whether to go downstairs to Gordon or stay with William. He wound up taking twenty steps but never really got beyond the halfway point between his two points of concern.

"It's okay!" Gordon said sharply as he got up from the floor. "It's okay!"

"What happened?" Adrianna asked as she came down the corridor. Gordon had nothing to say and he walked out of the front door. Adrianna called after him but he kept walking. She turned and looked upstairs. Dexter was still walking and still he was not getting anywhere.

"Transporter Gillis here damn near killed Dad," William managed to say, rubbing his head. "Man! I can't wait to get to improving these mental skills! I'm getting the physical stuff down, but I was barely able to stop Dad from going splat on the floor there."

"I am so very sorry!" Dexter apologized again.

"It's okay, Dexter," Adrianna said softly. "I hope you boys got all the rest you need, you've kept the rest of us waiting."

"Not all of us," Tara proclaimed, coming out of the guest room yawning and stretching. "Got to like how you people wake up around here though. Just the right kind of mayhem to bring someone out of a nice deep sleep. I suppose I have you to thank for the mini-coma?" Adrianna could not hold her eyes and Tara nodded. "Thought so. Nothing like a pushy, telepathic, overly-maternal nurse!" Adrianna looked up at Tara and even William's face changed slightly. "Well, what good does it do me to lie around here?" she asked, going back into her room to get dressed.

"Girl's got a point," William added as I walked up in time to hear Tara's exchange and take delight in her candor.

"Just get ready," his mother said, "we're running late."

"No, *we're* not!" William replied. "You're not going. Neither you or Dad for that matter."

"Wow, you must've had one of those really funky dreams, son. That almost sounded like an order."

"Want me to come downstairs and say it louder?" William replied and I dropped my head. "Should I start off by telling you that in my little feed I came across the rules and laws of the Prodigian? Not all of them, mind you, I was feeding, not trying to put myself to sleep.

"I am not yet eighteen, but I am well over thirteen," he said in a calm voice. "And I think we both know I am about my father's business…just like I think we both knew this day was coming." Kador looked at Adrianna and shook his head. "I have no words to comfort you, Mom. And I'm sorry about that. But we've never been that kind of touch-feely anyway. This is going to get worse before it gets better, you know."

"I know," Adrianna admitted. "But you are my son!"

"No one's even beginning to argue that!" William snapped back. His tone was stronger, more authoritative. I wondered if it was genuine or simply what he thought she needed to hear before she would agree to his plans. "Besides, we're not going after wannabes here," he said as he came down the stairs with his shoulder bag. "We might need a cavalry to call on, and you and Dad sure fit my bill!" Adrianna wanted to speak and had she been given the time, she would have said something, but William was the perfect image of a form he did not know he was copying. "Dexter will have his cell phone and he will call you if anything goes wrong."

"Dexter is going and I'm not?!" she said with her hands on her hips.

"Two Prodigians and two Tyros," William said. "Sounds like a balanced team to me."

"Then take Joshua!"

"You take him," William countered. "You might need the extra moves."

"Elkee, you ready?"

"I am indeed, but I am not sure it was wise to wait-"

"Let's get this straight," William interrupted. "Why you're going with me is your own reason. But make no mistake, I am going after the people who killed my Rachel."

"And that is your priority?" I barked.

"Rachel never judged me," he said softly. "She loved me for who and what I am, even when those definitions changed. I can't say the same for the ones those bastards took prisoner."

"You are not in charge of shit other than my training, and even that position is not in stone! Now, decide!"

Tara came back to the corridor and it was clear by the look on her face that she had heard every word. She did not look at me or Adrianna as she walked out the front door. Dexter followed quickly behind her.

"Say it," William said.

"Say what?" I asked.

"Say it!"

I took in a deep breath and kept my mind focused on my daughter. She needed me and I needed the others, as the Great Bridge was still not an option. "I am going with you. I have my own reasons, but this is your hunt."

"Good enough," William said, walking over to his mother. He kissed her on the cheek and turned to leave. She grabbed him and brought him into a tight hug, kissing him on the forehead. He smiled as their eyes met and Adrianna nodded again as she had done so many times before. I walked out the front door, having witnessed this scene at another place, in a different time.

"Tomorrow isn't promised," William said softly and it was all Adrianna could do to keep from crying.

"So give them hell today!" she said and William turned, picked up his shoulder bag and closed the door behind him.

"Are we walking after them?" I asked as William walked out into the front yard. He walked over to the telephone pole and saw some of the blood splatter from the man who had flown to Arvius' aid. He put his hand to the blood. "That is not Arvius' blood!" I exclaimed.

"No, it isn't," William agreed as he closed his eyes. "Don't suppose you want to tell me why you hate the man so much?" He waited only a moment. "I didn't think so.

"Okay, I got a blood mark," he announced before he closed his eyes and lowered his head. I could feel his senses stretching out, but they had changed drastically since last I experienced them. They were more precise and motivated and they did not waste time with the immediate area. He opened his eyes moments later and turned to face me, projecting a place in my mind.

"Can you get us all there?" he asked. I nodded and in the next moment I teleported the group to Charlie Brown Airport.

Forty-Two

Silence! She had been in places where there was an absence of sound, but this place was different. It was as if sound was disallowed and could not exist where she was. No matter what direction she looked in, the walls were close to her. Close enough to see clearly but just out of reach. She stretched out her hand and took a step but she did not move any closer to the wall.

"What?" Linda whispered as she turned around and tried to walk toward a different wall, but her effort yielded the same result. She tried with all four walls but by the time she got to the last wall she was running and still she was no closer. "Dear God, where am I?!"

"Thou art in a place where the God thou doth seek is but one god removed!" she said, and though the arrival of her voice surprised Linda, it did not heighten her sense of fear.

"C'Silla?" Linda called out and the darkness was dispelled. She stood in a large room, a library... a very familiar library. "How did I get to my grandfather's house?"

"Thou hast yet to leave thy carriage," C'Silla said, walking into the room, her hands held one inside the other but behind her back. "This setting pleases thee... eases thy mind and makes for a more suitable location in which to discuss thy threat of extortion."

"You gave me no choice," Linda replied.

"I have given thee much, child!" C'Silla yelled, demanding a deeper sense of respect.

"None of which I asked for and if you didn't know what was going to happen because of what you did, then you're a sorry ass excuse of a guardian!" Linda yelled back, matching her tone and telling the Man-Lord that any respect won of this Tyro was going to be well earned.

"Something's happened an-"

"A woman has been shot and killed," C'Silla said matter-of-factly as she began to look around the room at the display of accumulated books. "A woman by the name of Rachel Pryor."

Tyro knowledge! It seemed to be a contradiction of terms but as C'Silla touched upon each book, she found Linda's memory of reading it and instantly she was made aware of the book and its contents. She was surprised at a few of the selections but C'Silla quickly passed it off as impressions from Linda's mind more so than actually literary worth. After *A Tale of Two Cities*, she decided to leave the books alone altogether.

"William has mentioned her before," Linda said, thinking... trying to remember the occasion. "I think it had something to do with one of his projects." C'Silla looked at the young girl and assisted her capability to recollect. "Right!" Linda said with a gasp, covering her mouth as her discovery also brought to mind the importance the woman held in William's life. "Oh my God!"

"I didst not know thou wert such a devout," C'Silla said as she walked over to Linda. "But this does not address thy demands of me."

"You have to train me," Linda said quickly.

"Train thee?!" C'Silla said, looking the young woman up and down. "Train thee to do what?"

"To stand with him," Linda said softly, keeping in enough air to brace herself against the cry of her reasonable mind that begged her to fall in love with someone else.

"This is m-" a quick jab to the face cut short C'Silla's attempt to define the moment as well as Linda's request.

"Train me!"

"Watch thyself ch-" another jab from Linda was blocked, as were the next two, as C'Silla gave ground and set to return the attack. Her hand thrust was caught by Linda and her arm twisted. But the Tyro was not happy enough with the advantage. She kicked C'Silla in the face and actually hurt the older woman, and Linda did not release the hold. She slammed C'Silla's head into the closest bookshelf and followed in up with a quick knee lift to the ribs.

Linda surrendered her hold to drive her fists down on the back of C'Silla's neck. The Man-Lord woman broke to her knees and her head was kicked forward into the books again and she fell to the floor. Linda reached to grab the woman and pick her up but she jumped as she took hold of the back door of the car instead. Linda looked around and she could see she was back in the limousine and Hughes was looking on her with great concern written across his face.

"Miss Rasner?" Hughes said, opening the door on the other side of the car. "We are home." Linda quickly jumped out of the car and started for the house.

"Hughes, there are going to be a few things going on around which will not make any sense. The less you know the less you are a target for trouble."

"As you wish, Miss," Alistair Hughes answered, trying to keep up with his charge. "Should I then not speak a word of this to your stepfather who has not yet left for work this morning?"

"Oh shit!" Linda gasped as she could see the front door of the house opening.

"Let me aid thee," C'Silla said as she tackled Linda, forcing her to fall into the shrubs. She did not bother trying to cover Linda's mouth. It was simpler to not allow any sound to leave their immediate area, and let Linda scream as the bushes that held thorns made their case as to why no one hides inside of them. As Linda screamed, C'Silla held on to her and did not allow her to move. She waited for the man and Hughes to exchange pleasantries. When he turned to climb into his conveyance, C'Silla pressed Linda further into the brushes and she screamed even more. Linda struggled to free herself from the Man-Lord's grip but it would have been easier to lift a 747 airplane. Eventually, the man drove off and Hughes jumped toward the shrubs to get Linda out. As he touched her, C'Silla dropped her sound-proof envelope and Hughes jumped back causing Linda to fall… fresh wounds! C'Silla slid out of the bushes with two or three thorns stuck in her leg. She removed them and waited for Linda to show herself.

"Bitch!" Linda screamed, she was bleeding and without her shirt. She was swinging that garment and brushed it across C'Silla's face, leaving several thorns along the older woman's cheek, neck and chest. C'Silla reached for her own face, locked in pain and Linda kicked her in the crotch, reducing the woman to a trembling mass of flesh. Linda staggered back and fell into Hughes arm. He gritted his teeth and winced in pain, but Linda Noel Rasner's body did not touch ground again.

It was nearly an hour before he had removed all of the thorns and had seen to her every wound. Being a gentleman, he could not leave the other lady in the middle of the drive. His expressed attitude toward her was never in conflict. Linda had indeed engaged in combat with the woman, but when the woman could not fight any longer, she withdrew from the engagement. She also had not called on Hughes for assistance, so he did not call the police, but he did spend considerable effort and time restraining the woman to the bed in one of the guest rooms.

The welts were at least subsiding and Alistair was thankful for the time he had served as an Emergency Service Technician in England. The bandages he had fixed to her body and the medicines he had applied kept her from falling into a fever, but she was still in a great deal of pain. He did what he could, but he knew she needed to weather this particular storm under her own power.

"Thy concern is touching," the woman said, walking into the room. For reasons he could not name aloud, Alistair was not surprised to see her. The event in the bushes had filled him with questions and all of them had something to do with sound and why it had not traveled the way it should have. "Sound shield," she said as she sat on the side of the bed. She moved her black hair off the side of her face and closed her eyes as she placed a hand on Alistair's leg and the other on Linda's waist.

"Oh my word!" Alistair said as the sensation of elation and invigoration forced him to close his eyes. Suddenly he was thirty, perhaps younger, and the pain in his joints that had become his constant friend was suddenly absent. His clothes once again fit his frame exactly, as they had done years ago.

Linda's eyes opened and her hand went immediately to C'Silla's wrist. The wounds were gone, the pain was gone, the rage was gone and all she had in her heart was sorrow.

"Don't!" she screamed, begging C'Silla to stop. "Don't do this!"

[*No time,*] she projected. [*I have been watching Kador since his birth when his father and my mentor first held him up to the stars and poured his love into the child.*] An easiness moved over Linda and her lids grew heavy.

"Hughes," she whispered. "Don't separate us... until... I... awak-" she fell back to her pillow as the woman collapsed over Linda's legs. She started to roll off the side of the bed but Alistair caught her. His brow strained at the sensation of holding a full grown woman with such ease. In his prime he had not been this strong. What sort of chaos had his young lady fallen into? Would he be strong enough to escort her through it? Alistair lifted the woman up, making sure that at least her hand stayed in contact with Linda's body and he set her down on the bed next to his mistress.

"No one will disturb you, Miss, Hughes will see to that!" He turned and left the room. The particulars of what was happening were the business of Miss Rasner, and only became his business should she decide to take him into that confidence.

"Great!" Linda snapped as she looked around the large room. "We're back in the library?!"

"I was pressed for time," C'Silla said, coming out from the Reference Section. She wore a long black cloak and hood but that was pulled back off the head and her skin was clean, it even glistened in the soft light. "I would ask that you forgive me." Linda's eyebrows shot up from over her eyes. "Yes, I can speak in your dialect if I so choose."

"I was reacting to you asking for forgiveness," Linda advised and C'Silla chuckled. "This is not a laughing matter. Why are you giving up your life?"

"Let's get one thing straight," she said and the soft visage became stern and cool. "I am C'Silla, Blood of Nann and Man-Lord Supreme. I am the sole Man-Lord student of Zargo, Blood of Xargagyan and the key to his claim to legend. I do not *give up* anything!" Her hand made a gesture and Linda could hear the clunking of wood behind her. She turned to see her favorite chair set behind her. It was a chair that was on the third story of the library and bolted to the floor. "You will need to sit down, child. This will not be pleasant or simple."

"Love never is," Linda answered, receiving the back of C'Silla's hand for her effort. She fell back into the chair, the side of her face already throbbing. She wanted to get up and take the fight to the woman but as their eyes met, Linda knew she was fresh out of surprises and C'Silla was not about to be put down again.

"You might as well dispense with your romantic notions of what love is, child!" C'Silla said as she removed her cloak, revealing her armor and weapons. "Because such loftiness will not stop cold steel and THAT is what comes for your William, my Kador. Love is not somber afternoons or sweet songs, foolish Tyro. It is anguish and it is sacrifice."

"Someone needs a hug," Linda replied.

"I am dying because of my love for that boy!" C'Silla screamed. "I am the empress of shadow and stealth and it has been my talent that kept his location from the eyes of the Prodigian King as well as Man-Lord and Light-Child alike."

"You showed me it was William's mother who-"

"Has never been gifted in subterfuge," C'Silla interrupted. "I put the idea in her head and I corrected her initial attempts which failed, slowly teaching her how to hide her essence of thought and power. I added to the veil with my own power and it was my mind that kept the workings of my Master hidden, even from his wife." C'Silla made another gesture and brought another chair in which she sat, looking at the floor, thinking of what her next words needed to be.

"Jesus!" Linda whispered as it dawned on her just how much effort all of these measures must have taken and why she was dying. She had not given up anything, she had instead sacrificed her life to see to her Kador, a child she had loved and would never know. She wanted to console the woman, give her some measure of comfort as these were her last moments among the living but deep down Linda knew she would not accept them. But C'Silla giggled and looked up at Linda.

"You are right, but the thought brings me great comfort, Linda Rasner.

"I failed him," she said as she took their minds back to a New Sumeria when C'Silla had held fast to lofty notions of love. When she was the eager student of Zargogyan, Black Priest and savior of the Prodigian – at least that was her opinion. He had trained Elkazzar and, being the man he was, he had to keep a balance, at least within his own mind, and therefore he had also trained a Man-Lord. He had chosen C'Silla and she had proven to be a very eager student, at least for most of his lessons. She took to weapons and combat quickly enough, but she had dragged her feet when it came to matters of strategy and opening her mind to believing that perhaps there was a bond between the Prodigian. She had fought him every step of the way and it was Man-Lord fashion to simply abandon such a hard-hearted student. But that was another way Zargo sailed over the rest of the Prodigian. In order for him to follow an aspect of culture, it had to be thoroughly explained to him.

C'Silla had chosen not to make her instruction a public matter and that had impressed Zargo. Usually Man-Lords were the kind to boast when they had improved themselves. Perhaps that was why he continued to train her; he had caught a glimpse of C'Silla opening her mind and was invested to see it either open fully or see his flame expire from the realm.

She had taken to stealth, watching Zargo move around and avoiding those he could have easily bested.

"Why not feed that wretch his own entrails?!" she once had barked at him.

"Because I would rather feed him enlightenment!" he had shot back. "Dost thou think once thou hast bested a man that whatever brought thee to the point of conflict hath been truly resolved? The reason is still there, thou hast only moved to a place where the point can no longer be argued! If I disagree with thee today, does my death change my point of view? What's more, in my death thou art deprived of the reason I agreed not with thee. Mayhap my vision caught something thou hast missed."

"Or vice versa," she had quickly added.

"All more to the point, C'Silla!" he had answered, and C'Silla was wondering if she had won the argument. "But thou hast failed to enlighten thy opponent and now thou art deprived what could have been an ally… what could have been a brother… what could have been a love! All to prove thou art a warrior who seeks war more than peace."

"A warrior seeks peace?" she had asked.

"And if their worth is of any consequence, they seek nothing else. They serve war, C'Silla, aye. But still they seek peace!

"Who is born into the world to be an enemy of anyone or anything?" he had asked, and his student did not have an answer. The discussion was over and he had left her in a place where she would need to make a decision.

The first part of that decision had been to use her talents and seek out her counterpart, her Master's student among the Fairies. It was her first exercise of stealth and though she was not very gifted in talent, Fate saw to the compliment of affording her the opportunity to see Elkazzar become Vyzoron. C'Silla was thrown back, and she felt betrayed by her mentor. He had given more to the Light-Child than he ever gave her. She looked to her Edge and thought she might resolve the insult with his blood.

"And how was thy voyage into the lands of the Light-Children?" he had asked as she approached him for the next day's lesson. "I find their buildings beautiful, but those that dwell within them are often quite ugly." C'Silla made no reply. She drew her Edge and stabbed for the back of his head. He moved like the wind. For a man of incredible thought, his body seemed to surpass his genius and his hand caught her wrist, deprived her of the Edge and threw her over the work table where he had laid out today's lesson. C'Silla rolled up to her feet and reached for her Blade. Her Edge was returned to her between the fingers holding the scabbard of her Blade. She shook at his accuracy and speed and then looked up at him, her rage transformed now by her frustration into tears and screams.

"Thou hast failed me!" she had claimed.

"Think that I have fallen short, C'Silla?" he had asked. "Thou hast a strong point. I have never lied to Elkazzar but I have engaged in an ugly duplicity with thee."

"Thou speakest as if there be only one!" she had pressed. "My mind can instantly recall three."

"Dost thou?" Zargo had asked in contemplation. "I was about to come to the truth that when I told thee I was training a Light-Child, I was lying. I had not chosen one to teach at that time. Your interest in learning from me was not a factor until I told you of him.

"In my travels, especially to Old Sumeria, I have learned what many of their kind put as a statement of wisdom: diplomacy begins best at home! So I first put my skills and perspectives to that which was closest to me, my own Man-Lord following. To you, C'Silla!" Zargo had approached, no longer pondering anything. He had come to his conclusion… that was when he was the most dangerous, for that was when thought became action.

"And I sayest to thee this much as an oath 'pon my Blood! It is not I who fell short. Despite his shortcomings, Elkazzar has given me more and it is Vision he hath attained. Something, by my hand, thou shall never behold within thy mind!" He did not strike her. He did not dismiss her. Again he broke with the actions of the Man-Lords that preceded him.

To his credit, he did not teach her of Vision. But he did teach her how to move around it, to foil it and she became the necessary antidote should Elkazzar ever prove to be a poison to the Prodigian. In her estimation, both she Elkazzar had also fallen from the height Zargo had left them, but she had never seen the Head Master sink to a place where she thought the Territories would be better without him.

"I accused him of failing me," C'Silla said as they both drew focus on the library again. "When all along it was I who had failed him!"

"C'Silla," Linda said, placing her hands on the woman's shoulders. "Zargo believed in you! That much is certain. And look what you have done to protect his son! You have failed no one!"

[*HOW INTERESTING THAT THIS CHILD KNOWS WHAT THE MISTRESS DOES NOT!*] a voice projected and both women stood up. C'Silla drew her Blade while Linda took her defensive stance. They faced the double doors of the library which led to the rest of the house. They opened and a bright light blinded them both, but C'Silla recovered almost instantly while Linda turned away, the light burning her eyes.

"Master?" C'Silla whispered.

"No, my Sister, I am no longer that to thee. I have ceased to teach thee anything for quite some time."

"Your lessons live on in me!"

"They did, Sister," he replied softly, as she felt his hand on her arm. It was such a welcome touch and she felt her burdens fall from her body. She was light again. Her strides were no longer labored. "And you have passed them on to this one, who also looks after my son. This could not have been better planned, at least not by my mind, but thou hast seen to the aims of my heart."

"What will happen now... Brother Zargo?" C'Silla said, accepting her fate and the reward of her service.

"They must prepare themselves for the tide of the storm that cometh," he answered as he led her back through the doors. "As must we!" C'Silla's eyes widened with anticipation; a chance to stand beside her master, her mentor, her teacher, her brother and friend. But she looked back at Linda who could not see through the light into which she now strode. Nor could she hear the gentle tones of Zargo. No mortal could. But C'Silla she was not yet fully removed from the realm. The teachings of her master had to be maintained, and she gave a last effort to reach Linda's mind.

[*Hear me, woman,*] she projected and suddenly Linda was still, her eyes closed so the light was not a factor. She directed her full attention to the voice that called to her. [*To thee I pass this burden, and for that I beg thy forgiveness. Fate has given me a daughter, and I could not have wished or prayed for better. But you must know this, the hesitation Elkazzar had in killing Kador was not his own, it was mine! Without my mind, his Prodigian habits will return and in greater strength. You are the antidote to the Vision now, Daughter. Take all that I have, take the Blood of Nann and do with it what thou wilt!*]

As the light passed from the room and the doors closed, Linda could not keep the tears from her eyes and she fell to her knees, only to come back to her bedroom, still garbed in her effects but now covered with a cloak that served as a blanket. She could feel the Blade under her right arm, the Edge under her left and she knew she had the knowledge of how to use them. But Linda took only the cloak as she left her bed, finding her way to the corner of the room, the one most removed from the light. In the darkness she found great comfort. Now, if she could only find direction... if she could only find her William.

"*Linda,*" she thought, "*Blood of Nann, antidote of Vision. Think I prefer Mistress of Shade!*" she smiled, knowing there were few preferences coming her way.

Forty-Three

Matthew smiled as he soaked in the water. The depth of the tub and the warmth of the waters were therapeutic after the thorough workout. He draped his white hair over the side, deciding to wash it later. A soft song escaped his lips as he drew the large ladle from the side and rinsed his shoulders with the waters.

"Would you care for some warmer water, youngling?" a servant inquired and Matthew held up his hand to refuse.

"No, thank you," Matthew said. "The water is perfect!" He took in a deep breath and sank beneath the surface. He looked up to see the servant smiling at him as the man reached into his vest and produced something that resembled a charcoal briquette. Then time seemed to stop. The eyes were a non-distinct brown, but Matthew was struck by the sense of them as the briquette was dropped in the water. His head came up out of the water as he kept his eyes on the servant.

"What are you doing?!" he said sharply.

"Cleaning, youngling," the servant answered and just as there had been little delight in his eyes, the smile had now faded. "I am always cleaning." The next instant the water became stone and Matthew's body was trapped within it. "You would have been better off keeping your head under the surface," the man said as he waved his hand over his face and the image of the servant was replaced with a diminutive man who wore all black clothing and an Elder's sword on his back. "At least it would have been quick and painless."

Matthew had but one tool, his voice, but in order to use it he needed time and a deeper breath. He was given neither, and the man replaced the sword as quickly as he had drawn it. It snapped back into place even before Matthew's head hit the floor and rolled under the tub.

"I suppose it was quick anyway!" the man said as he took his leave of the room. Blood flowed from Matthew's neck, down the shoulders, and over the edge of the tub where some of it came to rest on the gray stone and some of it reached the floor.

"This is going to be a mess to clean up," Rebecca said as she stepped into the room. By the time she reached the tub, the stone had reverted back to water and there was no sign of the briquette. "And to think they used magic too!"

"Is that all you have to say?" Matthew snapped as he walked into the room, looking at what was supposed to be his body.

"You died well?" she replied, brushing back her blonde hair. She tapped the closest shoulder and the false body returned to its more earthen material. It flowed out of the tub as mud and she directed it to rejoin the ground outside the bath house. She did not look again at Matthew, for she knew the glare that waited for her in his face. "Okay, so it was a good idea for me to make you a false body," she admitted as she now used the water in the tub to clean the area of the false blood. "Now you need to tell me what tipped you off about Elder Joshua."

"Like any of the Elders need to be told about someone touching the spirit," Matthew snapped. He was enraged. They tried to kill him. He had just been proclaimed a Eden-Knight and he monitors one person only to be marked for death. Suddenly he needed another sparring session with Elder Joshua.

"You can't beat him," Rebecca said loud enough to shake Matthew from his train of thought. "All he needs to do right now is level that sword at you and say 'Wrath' and you're finished!" Matthew closed his eyes and lowered his head. She was right and the Convert Elemental had proven to be more than helpful… she had saved his life. "And you still haven't answered my question."

"I just didn't think any of the Elders needed to be told when someone touches the spirit," he replied. "I had been led to believe that they could feel it when a kindred spirit was born."

"They can," Rebecca said.

"Then why has no one ever mentioned the Prodigian?" he asked. "And why are there no Convert Prodigians?" he continued as he walked over to the window to check the streets. "Not a single one! We have Converts from all the tribes of Humans. I am a Convert Tyro."

"You are an Eden-Knight," Rebecca corrected. "People like me are only allowed to become Converts, but you are clean and whole."

"How can you say that and still help me?" Matthew said as he turned to face Rebecca and time stopped again. Her brown eyes were empty her hands were not. She had drawn her sword and he was without weapon.

"You must be cleansed," Rebecca said as she drew the weapon back for a thrust.

He looked around the room but he could not see the means of control, which helped him ascertain the way to reign in his friend. "You weakling Elemental! You've been turned into a puppet by an Arcanian Spell!" As Rebecca moved forward, her arm came slightly forward and then upward. Her sword went up through the ceiling and both could hear the soft, wet sound of steel and flesh having a brief yet fatal disagreement. A young, slender form came through the ceiling and crashed into the tub. With no water in it, skin and bone met with porcelain, and both gave. The bath was no longer water tight and the body no longer held life.

"Oh, good one!" Rebecca said as she directed the steel to return to her hand. "You knew that would get to me!"

"No, I didn't, but hope was all I had left," Matthew said collecting his clothes and weapons. "That death was felt," he pointed out and Rebecca stepped toward the back of the room, creating a burst of flame which blasted a large hole into the wall. A small spark of light flashed in the distance.

"Timothy's ready at the docks," she said as she stepped out and looked in all directions. There were many younglings that were armed and looking for an enemy. Too many of them looked hungry when they looked at her. "And we're ready to die if you don't get a move on."

"Right behind you," Matthew said as he jumped out of the hole. Winds rose up to protect them from arrows and Rebecca offered her hand. Matthew took it and the ground under them began to slide forward over the path that led down to the docks. He was reminded of the times spent on his skateboard and he smiled, knowing why she had chosen that particular mode of transport; it cost less, yielded a higher speed and she did not have to worry too much about him losing balance.

"Knowing they felt him touch the spirit doesn't explain your plan, Matt," she yelled as they glided down the hill with younglings engaging their power to give chase. They had used their power to augment their speed and most were at least keeping the distance, while a few were slowly closing.

"One thing I have learned from watching William is to always approach a possible conflict as if your opponent can smack the piss out of ya!" Matthew yelled as he looked back. He could see Elder Joshua at the top of the hill. The chase was robbed of the small degree of fun it had held. "Joshua!" he told Rebecca but she did not look back. This too was part of the plan, though it had been more along the lines of "if the very, very worst happens, this is the plan" and it was not a very good plan. But she knew if they had any chance of escape at all she had to follow Matthew's stratagem and she sent up the fireball. It was answered at the docks by another fireball burst.

"What can you possibly be thinking," Joshua thought as he looked down on this pathetic display of desperation. They had shown their cards too soon and now Joshua knew where they were going. Had Matthew but used his power, they might have been afforded enough time to escape. But Joshua closed his eyes and teleported to the docks which were being prepared by another cohort of Matthew's, an Arcanian Convert that had been named Timothy. Matthew had chosen his allies well, but against the power of the spirit they were doomed.

"Do you think your magic can stand against me?" Joshua bellowed as he drew his sword and leveled it at Timothy. A thin jet of black flame sprang from the tip and tore through Timothy instantaneously. He did not even have time to scream. With that done, Joshua turned and waited. He could hear the makeshift slide approaching. He walked away from the docks with sword ready. Perhaps Matthew would choose to meet his end fighting. He had grown in skill and with the Elemental at his side it was not going to be an easy victory. But the boy was his responsibility and a mark against his position if he did not correct the matter quickly.

"Come, Matthew, one final lesson!"

The Earth Slide came to a stop and both passengers looked at Joshua before looking at each other. They started laughing.

"No!" Joshua muttered as he stepped toward them. The younglings had finally caught up and they fired their arrows. They were so eager to bring down Matthew and Rebecca they did not take note of the result of their arrows should they miss the duo. After the first arrow struck his leg, Joshua screamed in rage and a burst of energy cascaded over the incoming field of arrows, burning them instantly! He then looked back at the laughing pair and sheathed his sword.

"*Damn Elementals!*" he thought as he heard footfalls. He turned his head to see Elder Peter approaching with his mace at the ready.

"What is going on here?" the large man asked, nearly out of breath from his trek. Many years and excessive meals had taken a heavy toll upon the man but he was still an Elder and therefore nothing was said of his massive girth. "Ah, Brother Joshua, there you are."

"You were looking for me?" Joshua asked.

"By your direction I was bade to!" the voluminous man answered. "You said after I tended to your Lord's barge I was to-"

"My Lord's barge?" Joshua asked, but he was not waiting for an answer. He turned back to the docks, a mechanism he had not deactivated after he destroyed Timothy, which meant the door to this place was left open. As he looked up, he could see the Skyward Stream and surely enough, on board his personal barge stood Matthew, Rebecca and Timothy. He was reminded that Elementals were not the only tribe that could create false bodies. But he had felt the soulless puppets of Rebecca's creation. Unlike hers, the Convert Arcanian must have placed something living within his false form. Matthew had taken the barge out on more than one occasion and the crew of the barge would not have asked him any questions about any orders he would have given. The tail end of the barge slipped beyond the docks and to the place the docks were set to send them. Returning to the Control Deck, Joshua sought to get the landing coordinates and pursue. His house had many barges and he would be taking Knights with him; the matter would be concluded quickly.

"Damn Arcanians!" he whispered as he reached the Control Deck. A disembodied hand was moving and had been changing the coordinates. Upon Joshua's arrival, it flipped over on its back and extended its middle finger into the air before bursting into flames. Joshua's head sank as he waited for a sound he knew was not long in the coming. Matthew had been sorely underestimated. Surely once he reached the other side he would send back the barge, most likely taking a landing craft for himself and his friends. Joshua had failed his Lord's House and his only possible lead was the one Matthew had been monitoring. He was the only point Joshua might be able to argue as grounds for his Lord to give him another chance to resolve the matter. He had, after all, been loyal and forthright in his service. Still, he had seen many of greater station die for less.

He turned back toward his hillside estate and as he feared, he heard the bells ringing. The Knights were being called to convene at Mother's request. Soon his Lord would call for him to attend. He gave one last glance to the docks before turning them off. He took three strides before teleporting back to his estate. He had to be made presentable for his probable execution.

Forty-Four

His heart would have been filled with pride, had there been any room. Depression and discontent had claimed most of his capacities. His mind should have been on the task at hand, but even he was now failing the most rudimentary of rules. A hand took hold of his shoulder and gave him a shake. He looked back into Lorthar's eyes and nodded. His Master Archer peaked between his unkempt red locks and smiled.

"It serves thee not, my Captain," he whispered, "...that thou be absent from thyself at the moment of thy death!"

"Aye," Mevrkrean returned. "The executioner wouldst never forgive me!"

"Tragic!" Insra added as she made it to the first turn. Despite the humor in her voice, she was as focused as ever. She kept her head low and her senses sharp. Normally Lorthar took the position of lead but in times when combat was expected, he was second, firing his shot at Insra's direction. Mevkrean moved from second to third position, depending on where in the tunnel way they were. But it was clear to the men that their Captain bore a heavy burden, one that distracted him and made him more of a liability than a member of the team. The trouble was living through telling him that! Insra stepped into the intersection and checked all corners. When she neither saw nor felt anyone or anything, she moved further toward their destination. "Eyes clear but feeling minds ahead," she said softly. "Strong minds!" She looked back at Mevkrean long enough to get the signal to discontinue any communication other than hand signals and she resumed her march. Mevkrean then caught the eyes of Olliento and gave him the signal to engage his talents. He nodded and extended his telepathic veil over the small group of six. It was an easy enough exercise, taking only seconds to complete, but his eyes shot open before he could complete his task.

"Siege left!" he shouted and everyone darted to the right side of the tunnel. Normally the command was a warning of an impending missile attack, but in a tunnel such as the one they traversed, it was difficult to conceive of inbound arrows, sling stones or the like.. Still, the option of questioning Olliento was reserved until after the correct response had been given. There were no arrows or the like to avoid, but everyone in the group was temporarily blinded when a pair of tentacles, four hands thick and nearly thirty strides long, splashed down into the water and just missing Lorthar, the last of the group to move.

"Our effort of shadow and silence is undone!" declared Mevkrean as he unfastened his cloak. "Restrain the beast but do not harm it. Insra, thou art with me!"

"Aye, my Captain!" she called out, also removing her cloak. In unison they jumped up out of the water and ran along the side of the tunnel just above the water line. Insra jumped over to the left side once she felt they were clear of the giant squid.

"Thou hast provided a service beyond measure," Insra quoted as they ran. "...bestowing upon the Princes the benefit of thy experience!" They both smiled as they quickly approached the chamber at the end of the tunnel. They did not know what to expect but Insra followed her Captain's lead as he increased his speed and jumped, almost at a blur, into the area.

"Villain!" Prince Abiron cried as he took to the air himself. He missed Mevkrean but managed to tackle Insra. They landed on the ground and rolled. Insra twisted within his grip and rolled free of him. They stood at the same time with Abiron drawing and swinging his Blade in the same motion. Insra's back bend kept her head upon her shoulders.

"Foul villain!" he screamed as he lunged forward, but the thrust with it was a feint and Insra's move to catch his wrist left her open to his charging shoulder. She was forced back and decided to fall as Abiron swung again. While she was on her back, the Prince pressed his advantage, swinging down for her chest. Her bracers crossed over her face, blocking the sword, and her foot struck Abiron's hand, depriving him of his grip. She pushed the sword to her left while kicking to her right. Hitting just below the knee, she did not do much damage, but it was enough to make him stumble as he drew a second Blade.

"Have a care, your majesty," Insra warned. "I be not one of thy dancers assigned to bolster thy confidence while thy skill wanes!" Abiron snorted as he moved in again, only this time his thrust was genuine and meant for her chest. Insra was up and over the attack before it came forward and her bracer claimed the Prince's nose as she passed by him. Her feet touched ground at the same time as his back.

Mevkrean landed and rolled immediately, a volley of thorns passing over him. He came up without weapon drawn and turned to face Ezra.

"My Prince," he said, half bowing. "I see thou hast taken my advice on where to house thy friends. It is a good hiding place! One that offers both protection from prying minds and comfort for those thou dost deem close and worthy."

Ezra stood, ready to attack. Both men knew the Prince held the advantage. Not because of the two Edges he had drawn, but because of the three score of vines that loomed behind him, and their cousins that they both stood upon. Still, he could not give the order to engage with the Captain.

"Thou hast chosen they words wisely, my Captain," Ezra said, returning his Edges to their housings.

"If I still be thy Captain," Mevkrean answered, relaxing his stance, "...it is not wisdom that affords me such, but thy grace, your majesty." He bowed once more but with no precaution for his safety. "Insra, we yield!"

"Aye!" Insra replied, removing the tip of the older Prince's Blades from his neck. She withdrew, kneeled and offered him his own weapon. "I hear and obey, my Captain." Abiron quickly got up and took the weapon from the woman, tempted to strike her down. But as he looked upon Ezra, taking note of his current demeanor, he could not find the means to attack and he motioned for the soldier to stand.

The vines also relaxed as Ezra approached Mevkrean, still curious as to who this man was. He had grown up beside him, had pestered him for riding lessons, even pitched bad eggs at his parading troops...but until the moment of complete surrender, he had not seen Mevkrean. "Thy nobility exceeds my own," he admitted. "Regardless of station or blood. And I am drawn to ponder this one thing which befuddles me, my Captain: what hath we wrought when one such as thee stands against the throne? How hath we failed thee?"

Mevkrean was quick to take Ezra's hand and put it to his chest. "I am thine!" he said in a loud and defiant tone. "Mark this well and true, my Prince, for I am not one to take many oaths. But I am thine!"

"My lords and future Kings, I must beseech thee for thy indulgence. I seek a boon that I cannot explain a-"

"Thou wouldst dare this?!" Abiron shouted as he approached. "After all which hath passed? Thou wouldst dare more and keep the truth from thy lords?"

"We are not his lords," Ezra corrected. "We be merely his Princes, those he hath *chosen* to call his lords. We command him no more than we command the stars, brother."

"I be not so great as a star," Mevkrean added.

"When thou dost fail to blind me in the brilliance of thy faith, Captain," Ezra quickly argued, "...perhaps then we shall discuss the relativity. Until then, ask thy boon."

"Ezra!" Abiron gasped.

"Name the time, my brother, when he hath failed the Mind Star Clan. Name the instance where doubt stood over him. Name the stride where hath stumbled."

"He hath attacked the throne!" Abiron stated.

"Nay, he hath stood against it at a time when its stance hath ne'er been more in question.

"I shall grant the boon, Abiron, but I am not your master. I canst not force the same of thee," Ezra said as he walked over to his brother.

"Give me one reason to side with thee," Abiron requested.

"We both have sat in the shadow of a throne which acts without explanation. That is not our way, Abiron! Our kind are set to commit deeds of great secrecy in Old Sumeria and we know not why. In the name of that mystery, I will permit the Captain his."

"Damn my soul for its foolishness," Abiron said in a huff. "How long hath I been bested in debate with thee?"

"Long enough to know better," Insra answered. Her eyes flashed wide with surprise, realizing her thoughts had found voice. She placed her hand over her mouth and looked to her Captain.

"Thou doth close the water gate well after the well hath run dry!" Mevkrean commented. "Still, the waters hath not passed without thy notice. Mind thy place, Lieutenant." Insra nodded as Ezra broke into a rich laughter.

"What dost thou ask of us, Captain?" Abiron inquired.

"Thy hand," Mevkrean answered, extending his own. "And even more tolerance." Both Abiron and Ezra extended their hands and Mevkrean quickly drew his Edge, cutting them both on the arm. Abiron withdrew but Ezra merely winced and then glared at Mevkrean.

"*Damn his eyes!*" Mevkrean thought. "*They hath always been quicker than his brother's.*" Mevkrean carefully returned his Edge to its scabbard and gave signal to Insra; it was time to go.

"Is there anything thou canst tell us, Captain Mevkrean?" Abiron pleaded and Mevkrean's feet became stone. How could he deny the very one who was heir to the Throne? Insra also stopped and looked at her Captain. What he had told her and his men, in the strictest of confidence, was a matter too grave for any one of them to fathom, and yet explained one of the more common mysteries of the Light-Child culture: what had forced Xarga, Blood of Gamshygar to leave the way of the Light-Child and become Xargagyan of the Deviants? A man who had been revered in the Council and was earmarked to become its next Arch Lord, wielding a measure of power which rivaled the King's. With all the of the fantasies that children had entertained over the years, they were of greater comfort than the potential truth... a truth that Captain Mevkrean, Blood of Thalls now investigated.

"I canst tell thee this much," Mevkrean said without facing either of them. He had been over and over the scenario in his mind, contemplating the various avenues to resolution. In the final analysis, there was only one true avenue. The others danced around the bitter truth and Mevkrean was no dancer. "I am bound for the castle. If I should go there and face my *King*, mayhap all that has transpired can be explained and put behind us. But if I go there and find the *Throne*, all I can promise thee is that I will spend my last breath insuring it is a throne worthy of thee, for thou shalt sit upon it soon!" He said nothing else and Abiron was ready to press for more. Ezra's hand stalled him and all he could do was watch the Captain and his

Lieutenant walk back into the tunnel where four of the Captain's men waited. They were wet but otherwise untouched.

"My orders were kept?" he asked, walking right by them.

"Aye, Captain," Olliento answered. "Both little beasties are bound and resting."

"Both, eh?" Mevkrean smiled, truly impressed with the man Ezra was becoming. He was not next in line, but one does not get to chose their King, merely whether or not they will serve, and in that choice, it was the hope that both the service rendered and the one serviced will stand as worthy. In Abiron he could place some hope and he was comforted as he looked upon his still undrawn Blade. Soon it might need to be plunged into the chest of Elior.

"Well free them on our way out, they have done nothing wrong save serve the future of the Prodigian Throne! For that, they should be rewarded."

"And our reward?" Insra asked softly enough for only her Captain to hear.

"Look behind thee and find thy reward, Lieutenant," he answered. "As soon as we find the one who scrutinize this blood collected upon my Edge, we shall measure how much more must be spilled to keep the Territories whole!"

Lorthar laughed aloud as he took his position at the rear of the group. Olliento looked back at the archer and shook his head. "Something *else* amuses thee, Lorthar?"

"Aye, it does, my friend. We approach the gambit of history, my friends. Look now and mark well this moment in thy memories."

"I suppose it is too much to ask that some clarity be given to thy speech?" Insra asked and Mevkrean chuckled. She had walked into Lorthar's trap. But given the circumstances and the morale of the men, perhaps she meant to.

"I would be all too happy to comply, Lieutenant," Lorthar bellowed. "Look upon these ragged dogs that muck about under the cities of the Light-Child. Should we win in this endeavor, it will be written that heroes carefully used their knowledge of the city to navigate safely to their target and liberate the Throne."

"And should we lose?" Olliento asked, already smiling.

"The vermin that dared called themselves men met their sticky end in a place befitting their kind!"

"I do not see what bring thee amusement then, Lorthar," Olliento pressed.

"In my case, both accounts are right," Lorthar answered and Mevkrean was glad that the tunnels could contain the sound as his men erupted in laughter. Insra covered her mouth but it was clear her heart joined the men.

[*Aye, Lorthar,*] Mevkrean projected, [*that is most amusing. As the truth often is!*]

Mevkrean kept his smile but his demeanor was changing. Only Olliento had eyes sharp enough to see it, though he knew Insra would soon spy it as well. It was the change their Captain went through before a major confrontation. Though his enemy had always been either beast or Man-Lord in the past, on this evening it would be Light-Child, those he was sworn to protect. In his service to the Throne, Mevkrean openly acknowledged something greater than himself. Now it was his task to impart that perspective upon the Throne itself. Even if it meant the destruction of it, of him, or the removal of both parties... so long as the Territories were maintained, the cost, Mevkrean believed, was insignificant.

Forty-Five

The alarm horns still blasted their crashing sound; the bells still rang out into the depth of the night. Feet shuffled against stone and sand, propelling bodies here and there, all of them pressed to get into position. The traitor had been spotted and he was nearing the castle walls. The guard, which had already been tripled, was increased to the point where passage was possible only in the large corridors. From the outside looking in, there may have been a place where one might have found something humorous. From the inside looking in, there was apprehension, fear and for some, sheer terror!

"Be there any word?" Korach barked upon entering the chamber. He burst through the doors with such force that many Blade Staffs were turned in his direction. But he did not hesitate in his approach, smacking one of the weapons aside. "Well, is there?!"

"No word," one of the sergeants answered. "However the King was recently moved to his chambers. I shall send a man out to retrieve statuses."

"Then let thy actions reflect thy words, sergeant," Korach replied as he approached without bowing and erected a thin telekinetic shield around himself and the king to prevent sound from traveling.

"The trap was not successful," Korach said to the King who looked up at him with contempt.

"Truly, Korach?" he said ironically. "Dost thou mean to imply that perhaps I hath been relocated here because the *flawless* trap thou didst design to catch Mevkrean somehow failed?!

"I abandoned reason advocating it!" Elior said as he started to pace.

"'Twas a risk-"

"Thou knows nothing of risk!" Elior screamed and though Korach knew his king's words were not coherent outside the shield, the fact of his scream was not prevented.

"This hostility yields us nothing!" Korach countered. "Or should I consider myself dismissed to go about my own way?" Elior said nothing. He merely looked away. "I thought not," Korach said as he began to pace. "But I know the reason for thy mood, my King. Thou hast little to worry about. Only Royal Blood uses or even knows of the passages in this section of the castle, and they art even more heavily guarded against phasing. Not even the miraculous Mevkrean can find his way here, save through the corridors, and not even his fifty best couldst wade through these numbers!"

"I am glad the congestion in this castle pleases thee," Elior said softly, returning to his chair. "Perhaps then thou canst tell me why thou didst choose that particular piece of bait for thy failed trap!"

"Mevkrean is no complete fool!" Korach barked. "We had to use someone who had the ring of truth in his words. He wouldst not have shown himself otherwise!"

"But now the man cannot be found!" Elior screamed. "And if Mevkrean has him-"

"Then we have Mevkrean!" Korach eased his face and his stance as he approached Elior. "Hast thou not yet gleaned what the man is? He is a patriot! If thou wert a religious figure, he wouldst be a fanatic!

"To be honest, I am disappointed. I had come to expect so much more from him in the way of guile. This particular brand of warfare is simplistic, pedestrian! Mayhap his accolades are merely the reflection of yet another Light-Child who is refined, yet fights like a Deviant and thusly overpowers his opponents."

"I care not for thy tone of speech," Elior said in a nearly muted tone. "How many true and noble souls can I say would die at my command?"

"If such were true thou wouldst have commanded his death long ago," Korach added. Elior started to speak, but held himself quiet. He wanted to argue but saw nothing of use coming out of it. "I know, my King. The distaste of our arrangement chokes at thee. I-" Korach looked at his own shield which was turning darker by the moment. "Why dost thou draw a veil?"

"I did not," Elior said as he too looked up in confusion. Korach put his back to the wall behind the chamber throne and drew his Blade. "Lower thy shield, man!" Elior commanded as he stood up.

"I can not!" Korach replied as his normal persona of clarity and control was gone, replaced by shock and fear. "It is mine no longer!" Elior put his hand to his Blade but trusted his senses to ascertain if a weapon was necessary. He could not find an adversary anywhere within his range and that extended beyond the castle walls. He approached the shield as it went completely black. It had grown in thickness, capable of stopping so much more than sound, and King Elior put his hand to it, letting his senses slip into the construction of the dome. He could feel the working of three minds weaving as one and even his power would have difficulty in breaking through.

"Stand aside, Korach, we are not so trapped as thou might-" Elior froze as he turned around, looking at Korach who bore the look of dire conflict and anguish on his face. His mouth was open but he did not speak and his muscles appeared to be locked, yet he did not move.

"Art thou still disappointed?" a voice called out. Elior gasped as the point of a Blade slowly came out of Korach's chest. It was in half-phase, an act that often overwhelmed the nervous system of the target, prohibiting the engagement of any talent. But to do it properly, without being felt, was the work of a Master's Master. The drape behind Korach moved, revealing Mevkrean as he continued forward with his sword. "I wouldst hate to disappoint thee, my dear lord Korach!

He placed his hand on the back of the pain-locked man's head. "The upfront attack was indeed mine," he whispered. "I had to be sure where the King would be ushered. I had to know where I might find thee, blackguard! Thou shalt move this Throne no longer, Korach. Thy influence is at an end!" Mevkrean brought the blade back into full phase and Korach's back and chest were ripped. His death was slow and painful. Short of healing him, Mevkrean took every precaution that the man felt as much pain as possible before he removed the Blade and then Korach's head in the very next measure. The body fell but the head remained Mevkrean's possession. Elior took in a breath to release his rage but his mighty voice was silent as the Captain of the Elite Royal Guard cut his eyes to his King.

"Thy rage is unwarranted... my King," Mevkrean said as the dome walls became less dark. The leverage he threatened thee with, he did not possess. He never possessed proof, my Lord, only the claim of it.

"I consulted a Medium and according to her most favored *Wayfarer*, the proof he possessed was equal to your fear: potent but maintained solely by thee!" Mevkrean sheathed his Blade as the dome was once again transparent.

Before the sergeant could call out his name, Elior projected and ordered them all from the room. All save Mevkrean who awaited judgment from his liege. The two men stood face to face, the King looking over his best warrior while Mevkrean's eyes did not move from Elior's.

"So thou hast replaced one serpent with another?" Elior asked and Mevkrean looked down.

"I do not need the Throne to serve me, sire," Mevkrean said as he turned back to the wall from which he came. "I simply need a decent throne to serve." He started down to the doors that led into the corridor where he was sure there were no less than fifty men waiting to arrest him.

"Riddle me one thing, Captain," Elior said walking over to Korach's body. "How did you navigate the passageway meant only for Royal Blood?"

"When next a nurse comes for thy cousin, sire," Mevkrean said with a smile. "...it wouldst serve thee well to make sure your nurse is not my Lieutenant." He reached the doors and opened them. As the weapons came forward, all could hear Elior's voice. It was strong and crisp, as it had been when he first took to the Throne.

"Captain, ready thy men!"

Mevkrean stopped and looked back at his King. "Your majesty?"

"We have released a madman into Old Sumeria. We hath need of thee to go and fetch him for us."

"By thy command, your majesty," the Captain said, bowing low.

"The order is given," Elior replied. "We shall empower the Great Bridge with our reserves and send thee there. How long will it take you to prepare your men?"

"My men are always prepared, your majesty. I shall gather them now."

He could hear their bitter mutterings as he joined Lorthar and the others. He tried not to smile at their resentment.

"It is a fine disservice you do to them," Lorthar said heartily, making no effort to mask his humor at their disposition.

"They are the Princes of the Realm and they shouldst have a personal guard," Mevkrean said softly as he walked toward the platform.

"No argument there, my Captain. But thy Lieutenant and thy best-minded man? I am not sure I love my mother that much!" Mevkrean snorted when he did not wish to and he slapped Lorthar upside the back of his head for his troubles. Olliento was touched and chuckled as he stood behind Ezra. He did not dare to look in Insra's direction. She had been assigned to Abiron which was not that bad of an assignment, but she was not accustomed to being away from Mevkrean's side for too long a time, let alone for an entire mission. Even Lorthar's antics failed to raise a smile on her face. The four of them, Lorthar, Salkathi, Murietta and Mevkrean saluted the King before he gave the signal to activate the Great Bridge. In a flash of light, they were gone. Everyone began to turn away and return to their normal chores.

"Recall them! Recall them now!" a voice cried out and heads turned back to the Great Bridge. Insra was the first one to arrive and ran right by the attendants of the Great Bridge, stopping only when she came to the viewing crystal. All she could see was lava flowing and she screamed at the sight of it.

"Captain!" she shouted, extending her senses into the crystal and feeling nothing but pain and passing life as she did. She lost her bearings and she was being drawn in. Minds grabbed at her thoughts as hands took hold of her collapsing body.

"No, my lady," a healer called out to her. "Thou cannot follow death. It takes its own company and even thee if thou choose to gamble with it! It is a gambit one never wins!" Insra looked at the healer and there was genuine concern in his eyes. It was a quality missing in the eyes of her King. His eyes were cold and without reflection, though his actions were those of a man in shock. Insra started toward him but was caught before she could take a second step.

"Come with me," Abiron said. "I hath need of thy counsel."

"Counsel?"

[*Get **hold** of thyself, woman!*] Abiron projected hard into her mind. [*Be this the product of Mevkrean's teachings?*]

Nothing further needed to be said. Not then... not ever. She took her place behind her Prince and she marched with only her tears left to signify she had been touched by anything. She marched behind Abiron away from the Great Bridge and eventually away from the castle.

"Thou needst not leave thy home on my account, sire," she finally said.

"Then be at ease, for I am not," Abiron answered. "I am a Prince of the Realm, woman, and there are duties I must tend to! Though this be among the sorriest!" Abiron held up Mevkrean's cloak. It had been folded and pinned! Seeing the cloak, Insra knew their destination: the House Thalls.

"Sorry is hardly the word, your highness. But if it means anything to thee... at this moment, the Captain would be most proud!"

"It," Abiron whispered, wiping away a tear. "His pride, I mean, is the least of Captain Mevkrean, Blood of Thalls I wish to have now. The very least!"

Forty-Six

Her steps were smooth and nearly exact in length in each stride. She did not scuff her heel or scrape the floor. Each footfall was distinct, like the drops of water from a faucet not quite closed. Her turns were immediate and did not alter the pace of her walking.

Her thoughts were another matter entirely. They were scattered, but none of them were of the sort that garnered or boosted hope; had they been she would have been suspicious of them and discarded them immediately. She did not want to be painted as paranoid or pessimistic, she was just a mother in a really bad place: she had lost her husband to uncertain circumstances. The man had simply had too many enemies to assign blame to any one of them. Now it was her son's turn, and though he was both quite brilliant and the picture of Prodigian health, he was still her child and no amount of skill could discount maternal concern.

"*Too soon,*" she thought, making another turn. "*It's too damn soon. Zargo was thirty before he started getting into serious trouble.*" The recollection made her smile since he had also been that age when he had met a very young Adrianna.

[BUT THAT IS HARDLY FAIR, MINE HEART,] his voice called out to her and she nearly collapsed in relaxation. [THE AGING FOR US WAS DIFFERENT. HIS TIME IS COMING SOON!]

[*If he lives to see such time, Zargo!*] she projected. She had given up on trying to figure out how her dead husband's thoughts were reaching her mind. He was here, she trusted him to be smarter, so she would use whatever angle she could to help her son. [*He's so young!*]

[IT WOULD BE MORE ACCURATE TO SAY NEITHER OF US ARE READY FOR THIS TIME,] he answered and Adrianna nodded, admitting that once again she was witness to a power which exceeded her own by many measures. But her admission afforded a new consideration and she decided to put it to this energy that claimed to be her mate.

[*But wait, in what way or ways am I not ready?*]

[AH, NOW THAT IS MY LADY!] he answered and she smiled, it was indeed Zargo or something that knew him as well as she did. [FOR THOU ART INDEED A CARING MOTHER, AND THIS IS A TIME NO ONE DARES TO INSTRUCT THEE HOW TO ACT AND REACT. BUT THERE IS ANOTHER WAY THOU ART UNPREPARED FOR THE EVENTS OF OUR CHILD TO COME INTO HIS OWN MIND AND PLACE. JUST AS I MANAGED TO PLACE THE PHANTASM IN HIS MIND WITHOUT THY KNOWLEDGE-]

"You dared to put something in my head?!" she said aloud, turning angry and wishing there was more of a voice present in the room with her.

[*WHAT THOU DOST HOLD, MINE HEART, IS A KEY!*] the voice insisted, and the strength of the projection shook Adrianna out of her anger. [*ONE THAT HOLDS A GREAT DEAL FOR OUR SON! KEEP THY ANGER. I CAN ARGUE NOT AGAINST THEE AND SUCH BLAME IS MINE TO BEAR. BUT DO NOT LET THY BLURRED VISION HAMPER OUR CHILD!*]

She lowered her head and took hold of her emotions. What good would it have done to argue the point anyway? Zargo was dead, or at the very least removed from the Living Realm. Her son had to be her focus and she closed her eyes as she projected the sentiment that she agreed with what had been said.

"I won't fail him," she said. "You have my promise on that!"

[*I WAS FAR FROM A FITTING HUSBAND OR A FITTING FATHER,*] the voice projected into her mind. [*IT IS THE LOVE OF MY WIDOWED WIFE AND NEARLY ORPHANED SON WHICH SUSTAINS THE IMAGE THAT WAS ANYTHING OF A MAN.*]

"Yeah," Adrianna smiled. "Either that or any of the three thousand miraculous feats you performed. You'll be happy to know your son has your humility."

[*SAVE FOR ONE STRIDE, MY SON DOTH EXCEED HIS FATHER IN EVERY FACET OF LIFE. HE HATH YET TO BE CHOSEN BY THE IDEAL MATE!*]

"Give him time, he's been-" Adrianna stopped as she felt the voice leave the room and the house, very abruptly.

"Elizabeth, there you are!" Gordon called out to her as he walked into the room. "I've been looking all over for you."

"Well, it's always the last place you look," she said as she smiled at her husband, still perplexed at Zargo's sudden departure. "What did you need, baby?"

Wrapping his arms around her waist, Gordon smiled as he drew his wife closer. "Nothing of any official importance. It's just that, it's daytime, and we do have the entire house to ourselves."

"Why Gordon Ferrous!" Elizabeth feigned shock. "What would the neighbors say?"

"Where do those two get their prescriptions?" Gordon guessed and Elizabeth laughed aloud, slapping her husband's shoulder.

Gordon feigned pain until she rubbed the spot and then he grinned like a child who has just gotten his way. The playful side of Gordon lessened and he pulled his wife in for a tender kiss. She was happy to oblige him and the eyes that looked into hers after their lips parted let her know she was about to be kissed again, but with more passion. A soft moan told him she was more than happy to return whatever affections he was about to offer.

Their lips did not break again, they simply adjusted to allow for a more passionate exchange, and as Elizabeth felt her husbands arms wrap around the small of her back, her senses once again scanned the room and then the house. There was nothing to observe... which was the problem. Even without people in the house, there should have been people outside the house, animals out back and the like. She was being blocked! As Gordon kissed her harder on the mouth, she could see movement. A shift of body weight and a slight twist and the couple fell to the floor, landing on their sides.

"Oww!" Gordon cried out just before the crash of breaking glass made him get up quickly, assuming a combative stance.

"Watch it!" Adrianna warned as she pushed Gordon toward the wall. He took her lead and rolled again, coming to his feet. He turned in time to see his wife streak into the corridor. She was moving fast and extremely quiet.

[*Stay low and stay quick, baby,*] she projected. [*Follow me.*] Gordon knew not to say anything and he broke into a run to catch up with his wife.

Adrianna was in the kitchen and about to make the turn into the family room when she heard a crash in the room behind her. She knew Gordon was still in it; that was not good. Her ability to feel the grounds of her household was her only means of detecting her attacker, there was no mind she could detect and that was worse.

"You're not scared are you?" a male voice asked as the floor in front of her burst into flames. The debris blinded her and she stepped back away from the heat. Her first step was clear. Her second stride met with a hard object that did not give and she fell backward. Adrianna gasped, closed her eyes and fell through the floor at half phase. She could hear something hard hit the floor. Whoever it was, they were quick to press.

"On her way to you!" the voice called out and Adrianna maintained her phase state and fell through the floor and into the foundation of the house.

"Think you're safe, Runner?" a female voice baited her; it seemed to be coming from the very earth itself. "You're at what, half phase? Gets you through most walls, floors and dirt. How about really dense stone?!" As the voice spoke, Adrianna could tell her descent was slowing, which should not have been the case.

"*Still no minds to trace,*" she thought as she focused and teleported. It was more of a strain than it should have been, as much of the hardening rock was in fact touching her. She was in the middle of her bedroom, encased in solid stone and she knew she would not be able to breathe. A body shield of pure energy burned its way around her body, giving her room so she could come out of phase.

"You're good, Runner!" the female had already found her. How was she able to find her so quickly, let alone move as fast as she had? "But you're out of road and your tires aren't built for this terrain. Let's take this outside!" Adrianna was jostled as her boulder prison was moved, and from the feel of things, it had been hurled through the ceiling at an incredible speed. There was going to be a large need for mind wiping and house repair.

"This bitch is really getting on my nerves!" she thought as she looked at the stone. She did not recognize the formation, but she could see where it could be fractured with just a small application of energy. As soon as she located it and made calculations for the amount of force, the lines shifted.

"The rock is moving?! Oh, the hell with this!" Adrianna teleported out of the stone, moving only ten meters away and immediately started to free fall. Her back faced the ground and she could see the large boulder that had been her holding chamber. A female figure was flying beside it, barely touching the rock. Her eyes were closed, but they soon opened and she quickly put her other hand to the rock.

"This is just too good to pass up!" Adrianna whispered as she took hold of her body with telekinesis and propelled herself through the air. She increased her speed and allowed her talent to augment her physical form. "You lose something, sweetheart?" she called out, and she flew up to the woman and drove her body into the stone. Adrianna's smile was quickly wiped away when the stone fragmented and fell apart from the collision, and the dark-haired woman turned around with a cold smile on her face. Her speed was too much for Adrianna as she took hold of the Light-Child's neck.

"Looks like I found it again," she answered as Adrianna slapped down on the forearm, hoping to separate herself from the choking grasp. The strange woman was much stronger than she was, rivaling the worst she had seen amongst the Absularian feats of strength. She was clearly not Prodigian, but she had been trained how to protect her mind and her defenses were strong.

"Leaves one option," Adrianna thought as she fought off the tendency to panic once the brain is denied oxygen, a training she received from her Zargo. Electricity sprang from every pore of her skin and coursed its way into the woman whose cry of pain echoed through the sky. She quickly released Adrianna but the former Councilwoman maintained her grip and felt the woman's strength quickly wane as well. She continued the flow of energy for a moment longer and then grabbed the woman and held her close. She turned both of their bodies and put her speed toward achieving the ground again.

"You better be glad I need to get back to my man," Adrianna whispered. When she was close enough, she slowed her rate of travel and then teleported back to the bedroom. Another electrical charge coursed through the woman's body and Adrianna let if fall to the floor.

"You have my sister, woman!" the male voice called out. "And I have your husband!" Adrianna closed her eyes and gave herself a quiet bout of persecution. "I propose a trade. What say you?"

"*I say you've made a big mistake coming to my house,*" Adrianna thought as she focused her talent in two different disciplines. She faded into a teleport as her mind generated sound to remain in the room.

"You so much as blemish his skin and I shall kill thee!" her voice from upstairs warned as she landed next to her husband. It appeared he had been thrown through the wall of the dining room and kitchen. He was bleeding and unconscious. The man, who resembled (at least from her perspective) the woman, also stood over Gordon, but his back was to him.

"Let us not engage in empty threats, woman," the man answered her sound source. A closed off mind is proof against the weaker forms of telepathy, but it also had the tendency of making one vulnerable to stealth.

"Yeah, you're right," Adrianna agreed as she generated power. She hoped the cure for the woman would work against the man. "It just wastes time!"

The speed at which the man moved seemed too great for Adrianna's mind to describe. But he turned and jumped at her and before she had time to gasp, he had hold of her left and right shoulder and they were both flying toward the far wall. She could tell by his grip that he was just as strong as the woman, if not stronger – a result of his fear and anger. Adrianna threw her head back and pulled against the man and they tumbled to the point where his back met with the wall instead of hers. They were inverted and she had been shielded from the impact. He was not injured, but he was surprised at her agility and precision of movement. That moment provided Adrianna all the time she needed as she closed her eyes and gave the man a greater amount of energy than she had for the woman, and again there was a scream. They both fell to the floor, but Adrianna was still conscious. She rolled the man off of her and stood up. She was beginning to feel it now, not winded, but she knew she had exerted herself.

"What are you people?" she whispered as she turned to tend to her husband.

Her mind was sent to a place where balance was not something that could be attained and she stumbled back to the wall. She had not even felt the blow, nor did she hear the woman answer, "Resourceful!" before she landed her tremendous punch on Adrianna's jaw. She fell to her knees, struggling to hold on to her consciousness.

Luciana knew she had caught the woman unaware and she pressed to keep her advantage. The woman knew how to wield power and that made her dangerous, too dangerous to be taken lightly again. She lifted her hand

and maintained her near stone-fist as she threw it down for Adrianna's face. A wrist smacked at the inside of Luciana's forearm and the punch went wide.

"Impossible!" she whispered as Adrianna took hold of her forearm and managed a brief but potent electrical charge. Luciana shuddered from the burst and her strength was removed a second time.

"*Don't need balance to fry you, bitch!*" Adrianna thought as she held out her hand. "*And I know my house with my eyes closed!*" The cable from the stove flew to Adrianna's grasp and the lights of the house grew dim as Luciana screamed until she was unconscious. Adrianna maintained the flow of power even after releasing her mysterious attacker, but now she applied the energy to healing herself. The dark haired woman had managed to break her jaw with that punch. Adrianna could not recall a time when she had been hit that hard. She set her jaw and mended the damage before the power from the cable stopped.

"*Probably tripped the breaker,*" she thought as she stood up slowly. She was still dizzy and nearly half of her reserves had been spent. The two siblings were indeed unconscious but her attention was on Gordon who moaned in pain.

"On my way baby," she whispered and slowly walked toward him. She looked back at the pair and gave them another charge of electricity. "Bastards!" she whispered.

"And thou didst dispatched them as such," a voice called to her and Adrianna extended her senses. A large man walked into the room, but her vision was still not focused enough to see him clearly. "As I must now dispatch thee!"

She leaned to the side as a fast moving solid object just missed her head. She was not sure, but she thought it might have been her television. She ducked under what had to be her dining room table.

"*Dear God,*" she prayed, "*another assassin!*" Feeling the slightest tremble, she jumped to her right just before the floor erupted in an explosion of an energy Adrianna did not recognize. It was bright and extremely potent; the eight foot hole in the floor was evidence of that.

Adrianna spun as she landed and she could feel the man move by her, his attack just missing her face. But the way he landed, the softness of his step told her she was facing a master, one that perhaps rivaled her husband in combative technique. She had to extend the engagement, get to her husband and escape. She jumped back from his spinning kick. Normally a duck would have been her response but she would have fallen prey to the open palm thrust that followed the foot. Even with the jump, she was just barely out of range. Her hands went up in an windmill fashion as she blocked a series of rapid punches and she gave more ground, using the hole to temporarily slow his onslaught.

"*Pain!*" she thought as she invested her focus into her telepathic talent. Strong mind or not, it was time to test it and he grunted in pain, stumbling for a moment before he jumped over the hole in the floor, performing a flipping side kick that caught Adrianna in the sternum. One kick and he knocked the wind out of her. The wall stopped her flight and she started to slide to the floor. A burst of energy struck her chest before she could reach it.

"Gordon," she whispered before succumbing to unconsciousness.

"Considerable," he said, looking down on the woman before turning his attentions to the downed Elementals. A wave of his hand and two more bursts of the white energy struck their bodies, waking them from their pain-induced slumber.

"Get up and repair the house," he commanded. Patrizio quickly brought his mind into focus and went immediately to work. Appliances like the television could be made to look undamaged, but his lack of knowledge of electronics made it impossible or him to make it work.

"Forgive us, Master," Luciana said as she kneeled. "We were sent to replace Milana and we have faired far worse."

"No," he said softly, standing over Adrianna. "You faced a far superior opponent in Adrianna. Cov was a machine! A killing machine who spent most of his time standing in his own way. He used surprise and tremendous amounts of power to achieve his victories. His victory over Milana was slight and aided by sheer luck.

"No, this woman has been trained to aspire to heights of thought, wisdom, emotion and pure combative capability." He smiled as he considered the confrontation. "She also has an affinity for the one energy to which we have no immunity.

"Do as you have been told!" he barked as he walked toward the window facing the front of the house. "Everything must be made ready for our guest."

Forty-Seven

George Austin Howard knew the moment he opened his eyes that is was not going to be a good day. He expected to be bound, he was not. He expected to be in a cold concrete room, dimly lit and damp; the queen sized bed he was in was more comfortable than his own and the comforter that had been draped over him was imported, one could not easily get Japanese silk in the States. He was wearing loose clothing that kept him warm, they felt somewhat like pajamas. The room was very large and well furnished with everything save a computer or a phone. He could see a door that probably led to a bathroom as well as double doors that did not have hinges. His eyes focused on the slide track the doors were mounted on. They were solid state and looked to be made of stainless steel. The wall mounted large flat screen plasma television was already on, turned to an all-news network. He had awakened just in time to get the weather report. He chuckled at the fact that the local forecast was blurred on the screen as was the time of day.

"No, this can't be good," he said as the doors to the room opened and a young woman walked in wearing something out of a very bad episode of Stargate SG-1. She wore a uniform along the lines of coveralls but it was very form-fitting, and what a form to fit! She was as tall as he was and was definitely in better shape. Her straight black hair and facial features made him think she was European, probably Greek. George was beginning to think his declaration was proving to be all too accurate.

"What makes you say that?" Beta Scout inquired. She smiled as George refused to answer. She was carrying a tray of food and beverages and walked over to the nightstand. "I was asked to bring you this," she said, placing the tray down.

"Don't!" she warned as George moved toward the small table in the room. He took hold of the chair and came around swinging. He missed on the first swing and she rolled over the bed to avoid the second. George fell on to the bed in his haste to give chase. Sylvestra caught the chair and helped George balance it as he got back to the floor. "Should I have said, 'Don't please'?" she asked just before ducking. The wall gave instead of the chair and George knew he had a serious weapon, so he gathered himself, checked his footing and looked at his opponent.

"*Man's got some scrap to him,*" Beta Scout surmised as she took one step back. "*But he is about to press my buttons and I promised Sabrina I'd leave this old scab alive and kicking. So...*"

Sylvestra stepped forward and punched through the chair, stopping centimeters from George's chest. Her index finger came away from her fist and shook toward George as if to call him a naughty boy. George looked at the chair, her hand and then nodded as he stood up straight. He had tested his cage and found it to be sturdy... so far.

"Thank you," she smiled as he put the chair down. "I was about to say that we don't have to take the classical approach to this because we don't need to. If you don't answer our questions, we hook you up to a machine that makes you answer. It hurts like hell, but it works like a charm."

"No such machine exists," George rebuked.

"Right, and a flying woman didn't just explode her way into your house and take you out from under the noses of at least a dozen Mercs dressed up like Federal Agents! I can see where that line of thinking pays off for you.

"I'll be sure to tell them to warm up the machine," she said as she turned to leave.

"Wait!" George cried out. "You didn't even ask me any questions yet."

"Then I'll tell them to get the conference room ready," Sylvestra replied. She nodded and left the room. The doors closed behind her and George could hear the magnetic lock kick in.

"Yep," he sighed, "they do know how to pad a cell around these parts."

"What do you think?" Hubris asked. He had never been so jumpy. True, it was the first time the MVPs had ever been asked to bring a live body back to the Dugout for questioning. Usually a facility was fabricated in the field, Sabrina preferred that method. It allowed more freedom and was of substantially lower risk to the organization.

"I think we've got an old tiger by the tail," Sabrina replied as she moved away from the monitor. "We might have bit off more than we can chew here, sir."

"Noted, Sabrina," Michael said as he read over Beta Scout's report. "What is the update on the identity of the woman he was talking to?"

"Facial recognition programs have located several pictures taken by surveillance units," Sabrina said, entering in commands to bring up the file. "All of the photos, however, are secondary. She was spotted in the background when we were investigating several targets associating with our bogey."

"And?"

"And there is a good chance she is involved with the organization of people who deal with the bogeys," Sabrina replied, receiving Michael's eyes in response.

"Hubris, could you give us the room, please?"

"Yes sir!" he said quickly as he jumped up from his chair and made his way quickly to the stairs leading out. Only when the doors closed behind him did Michael take his eyes away from Sabrina. "Talk to me."

"Sir, I've had a file on these people for three months now an-"

"Consider us crucified for not giving you an open ear, Bey," he interrupted and Sabrina gained something from that. The Owners were feeling heat. She was not sure how or why, but things were not going well among them. Those reasons she would uncover later.

"Her appearance in the stills," Sabrina started to explain, putting the mysterious woman's image on all the monitors. "The way she moves in the video records... she's not eye candy, sir... even though she's incredibly attractive.

"We're dealing with a player. From my observations, I'd say she was the one behind all of these guys we're investigating."

"Really?" Michael said and she knew he did not believe her.

"The greatest trick the devil ever played was fooling the world into thinking he didn't exist," Sabrina countered. "You take that Neanderthal chauvinistic train of thought forward into this and you miss the fact *I* am the brains behind the MVPs, that Beta is one helluva Mission Lead and that this woman is telling our dorky boys when to jump. Of all the people we've photographed, she is the only one we don't have an ID on!" The Owners prided themselves on a number of things: anonymity and the ability to access information were prime among them. Kidnapping George Howard threatened the first, but his guest at his house, the one who should have been dead or at the least gravely injured, all but destroyed the latter! Sabrina knew the last fact of her report would hit hardest and stood the best chance of getting the results she felt were needed.

Michael paced as he thought. He had to make sure the next action was well thought out. The entire organization could be lost if the response to this problem was not handled correctly. The Bogeys were one thing, they were not altogether human. But those that associated with them, they seemed to be people of capability and some level of influence. They came from various walks of life and some of them, like Kaplin, were difficult to track down. But not this woman... this voraciously beautiful woman. How could a surveillance agent not get a picture of her? The more Michael looked at her, the more he wanted to look at her. Images of her body, draped in Egyptian Lace, flashed in his mind.

"Sir," Sabrina said, looking at Michael but he did not respond.

The woman danced for him, only for him. But he could not truly see the moves she made. He could only see her eyes... her incredible eyes! He was lost within them.

"*Are you a man of authority?*" she asked him as she smiled and danced for him.

"I am. I am a man of great authority."

"Sir?" Sabrina asked, taking a step away from Michael. She knew he was not talking to her and she could derive no scenario where such a reaction was a good thing! Sabrina put her right hand on top of her left arm and activated her wrist top computer.

"Give me a full scan of the Dugout and run it until I give the stop command."

"I am a man if immense authority!" Michael sang aloud. "I am an Owner!"

"Oh shit!" Sabrina whispered as she moved her hand slightly up her arm and activated her radio. She did not bother to open up any one particular channel, she opened them all!

"This is Dugout," she said calmly. "I've got a level nine situation here. Stat!"

"*Are you opposed to me or any you have seen me consorting with?*" the dancing woman inquired.

"I don't know you and only a little about your little friends," Michael answered. "But your element-wielding friends are toast!"

"*Michael, I cannot have that,*" she answered and she stopped dancing.

"No, no, no, no! Don't stop dancing!" Michael begged.

"*But it displeases me to hear this!*" she stated and Michael stroked the face of the picture with his hand.

"What can I do to make it better?"

"*Destroy all of this organization that you can before you are forced to take your own life!*" she answered as she smiled. "*And then I will do much more than simply dance for you!*" A dim light shot from the picture to Michael's face and his head shot back as if he had been punched by a professional fighter.

"I hear and I obey!" Michael said as he turned to look at Sabrina. "I need for you to initiate the self destruct sequence, Omega Level."

"Absolutely sir," Sabrina said as she moved to a terminal. She began entering in commands and Michael put his hands on his hips.

"Sabrina?"

"Yes sir?"

"That is not the terminal where the sequence is housed," he pointed out.

"No sir," Sabrina answered quickly, still working at the station she chose. "I have since hacked the codes, sir, and I moved them over here."

"Shame on you, Bey," Michael said as he took out his gun.

"Level One Lockout instituted," the computer voice announced. "All exits are now fixed."

"What are you doing?" Michael said, getting a little angry.

"I figured you wanted everybody to go up with the blast, right?"

Giving it a moment of thought, Michael nodded and walked over to his chair. "Well done. Commence the countdown!" The door to the Dugout opened and Hubris came in with his pistol already drawn.

"Freeze... sir!"

"Computer, protect the Owner from all threats!"

"Threat detected, Dugout," the voice declared.

Sabrina shouted, "Hubris, drop your gun!" but it was too late. Three of the five guns had a clear shot of him before the announcement was done. The chain guns fired until Hubris' body could no longer stand. All five then trained on Sabrina but they did not fire. She had not presented herself to be a threat so they just kept Sabrina Bey in their sights. Two of them turned when the door to the Dugout opened and Alpha Scout walked in.

"*Lazlo, no!*" she thought as he flashed his normal smile at her.

"Say Mike," Lazlo said, making deliberate eye contact with Sabrina. "Anything you want me to do? You know, seeing as how I am Alpha Scout. You know, ALPHA Scout!" Sabrina could have put her head in a hydraulic press as she blinked and finally understood what Lazlo was doing.

"Owner compromised by unknown agent!" she barked at the computer.

"Alpha confirms, belay all directives given by Owner!" The gun retreated back into their housings.

"Unable to comply, Dugout operative is down. Kill order has already been initiated and confirmed."

"Acknowledged," Alpha said as he looked at what was left of Hubris. "Some things you just can't undo."

"NO!" Michael yelled as he came down the stairs toward Alpha receiving a lightning-fast punch to the face. Lazlo barely broke the form of his stance and Michael was unconscious before he hit the ground.

"Lucy, you got some 'splainin' to do!" Lazlo joked as he started to look around the room. Sabrina was very quick to turn off all the monitors, only to see Lazlo blink several times as if he had just awakened.

"What happened?" he asked.

"Oh my God!"

Sabrina declared a state of emergency and told the liaison in the Owner's Front Office that the Dugout was about to go on a field run. They would be on communications lock until further notice. She then had Michael's synthesized voice give his authorization to confirm the report.

Poor George could not have known his prediction would come to pass so clearly. Sabrina did not bother with the first stage of questioning. She had Lazlo take Howard from the conference room to the interrogation room and hook him up to the machine. Howard had never seen an operative so young which meant the determined look in her eyes was not about to be discouraged.

"Before you turn the machine on," he started.

"No options, old man!" Sabrina barked before she replayed the footage of Michael's meltdown. She knew he was a man of great intelligence and she trusted that to apply to the two most popular definitions of the word. She had to appeal to both definitions to have any hopes of getting anything quickly out of him.

"Last I checked, hypnotism had nothing to do with elemental control!" Sabrina yelled.

"And you would be quite right in your assumptions, my dear," Thidalia said as she materialized in the room with Rook at her side.

"We have a Level Ten Breach," the computer announced. Seven unknown entities have been detected!"

"My, that was fast!" Thidalia said as she looked at Sabrina. Already she could see the potential of the young life that stood before her. But the Great Façade was ever so demanding and she would not fail Arcanian Blood! She extended her hand and let fly a bolt of energy. The young girl was more than just intelligent, she was trained. She was not the fastest Thidalia had ever seen, but she was quick and clever enough to evade the first passing of the bolt. She was also mart enough to keep enough of an eye on it to see it was still live and coming around for another attack.

Rook stepped in front of Thidalia, his hand catching a knife meant for Thidalia's neck. He quickly bent the blade and let the steel drop to the ground. He looked to his shoulder and Thidalia nodded in a fashion indicative of his insignificance to her. But it was enough for Rook who marched toward his opponent.

"Ho-Boy," Lazlo whispered looking at his knife, a weapon which had been designed for the MVPs not to bend when they exerted themselves. "I always get the interesting ones.

"One, Seven, Eight, Eight!" he screamed and he could hear the members of his team acknowledge his orders. "Oh that does it, big boy. You better kill me quick, cupcake. I've got friends on the way and when they get here, you are going to be so ugly!"

"Should your friends survive mine," Rook said softly, "I will accept my death at their hands!"

"Room go green!" Lazlo yelled and he lunged at Rook. A half instant before he reached Rook, the lights went out.

Thidalia hurled another bolt of energy that whizzed by Sabrina's head and she spun toward the far wall and ran. She knew the room backwards and forward, so she knew why Alpha had the room go dark. She found the wall and the panel that controlled the trap door and she slid into the passage. It closed just as light began illuminating the room. *"Get clear, Lazlo!"* she thought as she ran down the passageway.

Rook grabbed nothing but air as two fists slammed into his either side of his Adam's Apple, cracking the bone. Rook choked for one breath and Lazlo heard the neck snap a second time. He side-stepped a back kick that felt more like a massive piston being shot up out of an engine the size of a Multi-Frame.

"Whoa," he thought. *"Big, strong, fast and immune to throat crushing hits. Why is this not the place for me?"* Lazlo jumped up and over his opponent, flipping forward and just out of reach of the large man. He landed in a hand stand and caught his opponent with a righteous mule kick that lifted him up and away. A spark of orange light flashed brightly before the large man's body collided with the source of the spark.

"Two ball, corner pocket!" Alpha said as he ran for the door. "Room go green!" he commanded as he stepped out and the lights came on again.

Rook quickly got up off of Thidalia and applied his healing touch to her. She jumped awake and moved Rook aside, looking for either of their opponents. Facing and losing to Tyros in such a fashion was getting tiresome and she was beginning to lose her patience. She wanted to scream but she unexpectedly saw an old friend, bound to a rather interesting looking device.

"George!' she said with a bright smile.

"What the hell are you?!" he growled through clinched teeth. She could tell from the coldness in his eyes that George had somehow realized what she was and now questioned how many times he had done what she wanted him to do only to forget anything had ever happened.

"Well, to your kind I would be a wizardress," she answered, motioning to Rook to gather the others. "Sometimes my people were called Sorcerers, Illusionists-"

"Witches?" George added and Thidalia dropped her veil and looked on George with the face she was born with.

"Witches, Witch-Doctors, the Pharaoh's advisors, Nostradamus, Aristotle, Rasputin… the list is endless."

"I wonder if you'd put Hitler on that list?"

"Goodbye George!" Thidalia said, casting a small orb of water suspended around his head. She did not look back as she left the room, but she could hear George yell inside the water. "That only quickens the process, George," she whispered.

Rook came to her, his clothes slightly ripped, and the blood on his hands and arms obviously not his own.

"How many?" she asked.

"By my accounts, at least fifty, Mistress. But there are a few exceptions. Ones with bodies unlike any Tyro I have ever seen. That would include the man we found in the room. They are augmented, but there be no magic about them."

"No, Rook, of course not!" she said as she walked down the corridor. "They prefer the magic of silicone instead."

"Then they have insured no one else can use their magic," Rook added quickly. "And though they are the sort to stand their ground and fight, their means of flight is respectable and we are not able to maintain an engagement with them while we fight on their ground."

"Mysterious and thorough," Thidalia said as shook her head and stopped. "Thorough!" she whispered.

Watching the Dugout burst into so many explosions of light and fire cut deeply into her heart. However, she took heart in the fact she was holding the brain of the master computer and that she was aboard the last Multi-Frame stored at the facility. Aside from a few suits of form-fitting body armor and some radios that would put James Bond to shame, the only true losses were support personnel and a geographical location.

"How are you doing back there?" Sylvestra added, wiping her mouth yet again.

"I'm alive," Sabrina answered. "Which is more than I can say for most of them. What did we make off with?"

"All five of the Alpha Team made it out," Beta Scout answered. "But Sigma and myself got a little dented by God knows what. All I can say is there is one mean movin' black woman down there who likes punching steel doors off the hinges!"

"Jesus!" Sabrina whispered.

"Yeah, from the sounds of it, he was done there too and man was he pissed. We have five Multi-Frames piloted, the other three on auto pilot and carrying technicians. Thor told me to say hello."

"Thor?"

"Yeah, he had the Multis prepped and cookin' before we got to the hangar."

Then there was another series of explosions. Those had to be the generators and as they went, she could see a golden sphere of light arc up and head eastward.

"Beta," she called out.

"Yeah, I see it, Sabe," she replied, her voice thick with disgust. "Since when did this become Oz?"

"Who knows, Beta? Maybe on that third click Dorothy didn't go home. Maybe she brought Oz to us!"

"Does that make us Flying Monkeys?"

"I'm not sure, Beta." Sabrina said, still looking at the sphere. It had to be doing about three-quarter Mach and getting faster. "But I get the feeling we just met one seriously wicked witch.

"Let's do a two-three-two split along the Alpha, Beta and Lambda lines," Sabrina commanded as she consulted her small computer. "You're the 3 Lead. Take us to Platform Three."

"What about Alpha and Lambda?"

"I'm sending them their orders now." A signatory beep was her acknowledgement. "That's it, let move out!"

Beta spread the word to the rest of the pilots. One good thing about the Multi-Frames was that it was not going to be too long of a flight. Each Multi-Frame activated its Stealth Shield and went supersonic.

Forty-Eight

"Okay people," Jack's voice called out over the intercom, one of the few things still working on the plane. "We've just about gotten all we're going to get out of this one. Simmons has made arrangements for us to pick up a new ride near Boston. He's been able to maintain tracking on our target and it finally came to a stop about fifteen minutes ago at an airport near the city of Bankhead, Georgia."

"Bankhead?" Caleb repeated. "Where the hell is that?"

"Too damn close to Decatur!" Peter answered.

"And the truth shall set you free," Caleb sighed, sitting back in his chair. He would get around to apologizing to Marianne later. Right now she was doing what he should have been doing, getting his head right, trying to prepare for the tsunami of impossibility that seemed to be waiting for them.

By the time they landed in Boston, everyone was silent. Only Jack spoke as the disembarked from one plane and boarded another. It too was a private jet but it was hardly commercial.

"*Wonderful*!" Peter thought as he took his seat and strapped himself in. "Looks like Simmons found us some kind of college thesis to ride in! Damn thing probably has a Warp Speed setting."

"Warp Speed might be what we need," Jack said as he was putting his radio away. "I have a status update for us and it isn't good.

"Tara's made contact with Simmons and King and they have the info I'm about to give you. We don't have all of the answers yet, but Harry's been playing both ends against the middle. According to Mifflen, the Head Master can't stand him and when last seen he was mixing it up with our friend William."

"You have to be shitting me!" Peter whispered.

"Also," Jack continued, giving Peter a look that conveyed he had not gotten to the good part yet. "We should expect company of the human sort. It looks like the group Webster was trying to penetrate has operatives here in the States and they've taken the Head Master's daughter. This was after they managed to kill one of William's contacts. Our boy is in the field and smelling blood, according to Tara."

"So we've got watchers-"

"Descriers," Webster corrected.

"Sorry," Marianne replied. "Descriers and Prodigian working together?"

"It looks like Harry's had his own agenda all along, Cooper," Jack replied. "Simmons believes they have had a Prodigian contact for some time and our Harry may just be their man.

"But there's more. Simmons did some cyber digging and cross-referenced the info that Peter got to us before he got made and had to get away from Whattawoman. He has found Bill Cole and even managed to get his current location." Peter started laughing out loud and slapping his leg.

"Did I miss something?" Marianne asked.

"Peter's just guessing," Jack said softly. "He's right, but he's only guessing. Cole's current location is less than 100 meters from our tagged girl, and given that they are at an airport, we can presume they are working together."

"Charlie Brown's getting crowded," Cooper said.

"Hah! Jack's just reading from the invited list, Babe," Peter commented. "I get the feeling that place is going to be thick with freaks!"

"That's not a nice word," Marianne said quickly.

"Anyone willingly going to where Head Folk, especially rebel Head Folk, are cannot be considered altogether glued. Now we've added Descriers to the mix so we can look for some serious toys and capable personnel.

"But wait! I forgot to mention our teenage assassin-killer is coming for them and according to Mifflen, he's pissed! Now Tara's a little emotive herself. So for her to say someone is pissed means they are enraged and ready to bite the heads off people. And to think that used to be a figurative statement.

"Does that wrap up the news?" he looked at Jack.

"Howard's gone missing and King's received his red file!" Jack added, lacking the strength to look any of them in the eye. The plane was silent. "She's recruited JB and when they went to Howard's home, they went up against someone who King thought was a Prodigian. But we've never seen them spit out a bullet they took in the neck or heal completely in under five seconds. Caleb?" The doctor closed his eyes and shook his head no. "Okay," Jack replied. "That means I get back on this thing before we take off and let Simmons know that whatever they came across was not Prodigian, but no less weird or capable.

"Last but not least," Jack said taking a knee in the aisle. "King was able to download footage from Howard's house. She sent it to Simmons and when he ran it, he saw a familiar face. One your phone sent us, Webster. Thidalia's alive!"

"Never thought otherwise," Peter replied. "And if she's not Prodigian then what the hell is she? That is the question we all want to ask." Peter looked around the cabin of the plane, taking in each pair of eyes. "Hell with it, everybody's got to die some time. Kick this pig and get 'er flyin', will ya Moreland?"

"That I can do." Three minutes into the air, everyone could feel the plane accelerate. The wings folded backward toward the fuselage and there was a soft boom. Jack piloted while Peter and Marianne found a quiet corner. Caleb meditated, going over everything Arvius had taught him, wondering if the information had been slighted in any way to give the Prodigian any measure of an advantage.

"*Dear God,*" he thought. "*The last time I felt this way we at least had King and Tara with us. Now Lydia's in California and Tara's in another world. Feels like we're short-handed, but the game's gone up a level.*"

Forty-Nine

"Be this normal, sir?" one of the Blades asked his commander.

"Inquire not unto me," D'Hano answered. "I know not of such things!"

"Thou doth speak as though thine assignment vexes thee," Wolf Lord remarked. His eyes were still closed and he was still walking in a large circle. All but one of them stood there with the hunter; D'Hano had dispatched one of his men to use his talents on the minds of passersby's; keeping the knowledge of what they saw from their eyes. Oddly enough, the brute did not need the protection. During the transit from New Sumeria, his clothes had changed and were now fashioned from leather; his unkempt hair was now combed back and kept in a ponytail. Wrapped around his waist and torso were a number of chains. D'Hano could see he kept his War Locke there. "Perhaps we should have brought with thee a bathing maiden, or at least thy scented oils."

"Stay thy mind to thy task, Deviant!" D'Hano barked.

"My mind hath never left the task," Wolf Lord answered. "But I am curious as to how we came to this place in all of Old Sumeria."

"Cov last reported from this location," D'Hano answered. "We must know his whereabouts, and we seek the Unlawful Son."

"Well, if this be the Unlawful Son, he be far weaker than his father," Wolf Lord commented. "An effect of this place, no doubt.

"But much hath happened here," Wolf Lord continued. "Conflict of many minds and souls. Engaged deeply and full of purpose. There was also death and birth."

"Birth?" D'Hano was confused.

"Aye," Wolf Lord replied as he squatted low, removed one of his leather gloves and touched the ground. "There are many births to a life, Captain. On this field, in this battle, the one you seek to kill was born into death. He took a life." Wolf Lord opened his eyes and looked around. "Or at least he tried. It was not for lack of effort he did fail."

"*A Man-Lord Bridge Door,*" he thought. "*Much transpires here that not even mine eye canst discern.*"

"Then where is he? What trail do we follow?"

"Ah, that be the bane of this place," Wolf Lord said as he smiled and stood up. "So many minds, all excited, some empowered, they serve as cover to his trail. I cannot sense his thoughts.

"But his feelings are another matter," Wolf Lord said with a cold smile forming on his face.

"His feelings?" one of the Blades whispered and D'Hano raised his hand to silence him.

[*The beast of a man is a master of empathy,*] D'Hano projected. [*He can truly track thee by the sentiment thou demonstrates.*]

"Thou hast found an emotion that strong and that sustained?" D'Hano asked, knowing it was rare.

"Aye," Wolf Lord said as he walked toward the road. He took sight of the field once again and marked in his memory the burn marks along the ground, the skid marks of a heavy conveyance that had been used as a weapon and the place where the Unlawful Son stood when he abandoned the laws of the land and consciously decided to take a life. He had lied to D'Hano, believing that duplicity deserved little honesty in return. The boy was naïve and innocent to the ways of the Prodigian, but he was not weak. A warrior untried does not move so quickly to kill. With all of the emotions Wolf Lord detected, there was no guilt!

"Love," Wolf Lord said as he reached the road. "He loves his conveyance, how convenient!"

"Art thou fit for a run, Captain?" Wolf Lord asked before running down the road. D'Hano and his men were quick to take up running behind him, but Wolf Lord was not about to change his pace to accommodate them. First he called for greater speed from his body and when it answered his summons, he engaged in *jumping* and skipped in and out of sight, his strides taking greater and greater distances.

He stopped at the corner, several houses away from his destination and his wards finally caught up, two of them sounding winded. Wolf Lord did not bother to show them his disgust; he kept his eye on the target.

"There," he said pointing at the parked car. "That be his conveyance."

"Then that must be where he dwells," D'Hano said, drawing his Blade, his men following his lead.

"And what of thy agent?" Wolf Lord asked.

"I canst see the remains of a great amount of psionic energies," D'Hano stated as he peered through a crystal. "Much of it belongs to Cov."

"Of that I have no doubt," Wolf Lord said, spinning to face D'Hano. "It is a shame that crystal sees little else!"

D'Hano moved the crystal aside so that he could see the Blade Staff that had been thrust through him and into the chest of the man behind him. The weapon was left in him as Wolf Lord spun away from him, hurling two Edges. D'Hano's second man was struck in the neck, the third in the eye. The last of his men looked too long upon his fallen comrades to avoid Wolf Lord's initial lunging slash to his neck and was too stunned to respond to the second which tore out the back of his skull.

"Forgive my Deviant ways," Wolf Lord said, turning back to D'Hano and sending energy to his Blade Staff which coursed into both men.

D'Hano's man was nearly unconscious and D'Hano's attempt to heal himself was dissuaded. "But I knew my time was drawing near and I wouldst prefer not to fall before thee." Wolf Lord broke the neck of the man who had his Edge lodged in his throat. Prodigian simply could not be counted as dead while their minds were still active. Wolf Lord knew that lesson well. He collected his weapons, directing several energy bursts to the pole of his favored weapon. By the time he was done seeing to D'Hano's other three men, the fourth was dead on his spear and D'Hano was not far behind him.

"Thy crystal sees not the power of the mind, foolish whelp, it sees the power of thought. What it doth not see is the tremendous wave of rage and frustration that Cov experienced before his death. Thy man is dead, Captain, and thou art about to follow his lead. Yet before I allow thee passage, I will rake thy mind for the answer to one inquiry: what Man-Lord hath given thee the accounts of Yudara? There be no report from Cov. That much my Master knoweth for fact. Such wouldst mean thou hast retained a means of communication into the Crimson Court; and my Master will not have that. So, the choice remains before thee, wilt thy passing be gracious or grievous?"

D'Hano begged for his life and Wolf Lord gave him a sample of what a grievous passing would entail and then he healed his wound, knowing his mind was in no condition to put up any resistance. D'Hano closed his eyes, forcing a lone tear from his eye and gave the name of Wushedann, a member of the Congregation who aspired to little else, the perfect spy! Wolf Lord then tore into D'Hano's mind and found the name he had been given was indeed true, but the Captain was not a man to be trusted and it was most grievously he passed away but not before Wolf Lord could feed on his reserves which were increased at the moment of death, when the *Wayfarer's Touch* added great levels of power to a mind and soul. Wolf Lord filled his reserves, placed the overage in his War Locke and lowered himself to one knee.

[*I seek thy counsel, Master,*] he projected.

[*I shouldst think so,*] Beriah answered, linking with his apprentice. [*Hast thou found him?*]

[*I hath found his home, sire but he is not here. I sense his mother is about.*]

[*Then take her and bring her to me,*] Beriah commanded. [*Alive, Sulrynn, alive!*]

[*By thy command and to thy glory, Master!*] The link was severed and Sulrynn could feel his Master's failing health and a sense of desperation, but perhaps it was an urgency he felt himself and was misinterpreting. But there were other matters that called for Wolf Lord's attentions

"Thy sister should have come with thee," he said before he jumped straight up. Patrizio shuddered at the realization that his soft approach had not been soft enough. He hesitated and Wolf Lord teleported at the height of his jump. In the space of that movement, the hunter became the hunted.

Patrizio thought it best to be mobile and he let the winds take him straight up. He was just above the trees when an arrow shattered against his back.

"Now I have your mark!" he said as he turned and increased the speed of his flight. He saw nothing but a clear field of low grass and Wolf Lord landed on his back, grabbing his shoulders and releasing electricity into Patrizio's body.

"In truth, I have thy mark!" Wolf Lord declared as he increased the power and Patrizio wailed in sound that was an orchestration of delight to Wolf Lord. "Indeed, I see the pain thou hast felt and I know its reason. Thou art strong of mind but this pain weakens thee." He pulled on the man's shoulders and like the reins of a horse, Wolf Lord had control of the flight as Patrizio's body turned upward.

[*I have thy mind!*] he declared as Patrizio stopped screaming, for there was no more pain, at least not from being electrocuted. But his consciousness had been trapped within his mind. He could still see and hear, but he was no longer in control of his body, his thoughts or his powers. [*Aaahhh, I see thy fear now! Whatever thou art, thou hast known of my kind for some time and this is a thing thou doth fear t-*] A gigantic fireball struck them both and Wolf Lord screamed in pain and fear. He fell from Patrizio's body and struggled against the flames.

"How interesting that the animal does not like fire," Luciana said as she followed the body of the burning Man-Lord down. Patrizio roared in anger and flew past his sister, becoming a thing of stone as he did. He snuffed out the flames surrounding Wolf Lord moments before he collided with the Prodigian.

Luciana summoned stone from the red clay of the ground and as it flew toward her, she blinked and it shattered, each fragment flying free and shaped by air and fire into razor sharp clay darts. They fell back to the ground and curved in many directions. Luciana did not know what a mailman was and she did not care. But there would be no living witnesses of this confrontation. The same went for those who were drawn out of their houses or to their windows, all trying to gain a glimpse of what was happening. It was the last that many saw. Others actually saw Luciana look at them before fire burst around them.

Wolf Lord met with the ground and did not move. Patrizio landed near him and the ground shook under his tremendous weight. Each stride he took was heavy and the ground shook.

"What do you have to say now?" he said as he reached down and lifted Wolf Lord from the ground. Wolf Lord moaned and opened his eyes for a moment before spitting blood and smiling.

"I know thy fear!" he whispered before life was driven from his body by Patrizio's fists. He pounded his body long after he knew he was dead.

"What are you doing?!" his sister shot at him as she landed, looking in all directions.

"I know," Patrizio said, breathing heavy and returning to his normal density. "Overkill, but this bastard had it coming!"

"What are you talking about? You're punching the ground!"

Patrizio's brow strained as he looked upon the dead form whose head now turned to look at him.

"I told thee, I have thy mind!"

Patrizio screamed and was brought out of his delusion. He had not been saved, but he had hoped he would be and Wolf Lord had fed the illusion with his talent, delving even further into Patrizio's mind. His grip was now beyond the Elemental's ability to expel and Wolf Lord was curious as to how the young warrior had been taught how to resist telepathy so well.

"Patrizio!" she called out to him as the front door opened.

"I am fine, sister," Patrizio answered as he staggered into the house, carrying Wolf Lord's body over his shoulder. He walked into the living room and put the body down on the sofa. "This one put up some fight but like most Prodigian, he places too much faith in his telepathy.

"I can barely see," he continued, "but I will be fine."

"Your vision's been impaired alright," Luciana answered coming from the other side of the room, the false body reverting to dirt. "But you'll excuse me if I make sure you are my brother and of your own mind. What is my real name?"

"*This one be clever!*" Wolf Lord contemplated. Though he did have control of the boy's body and power, his most sacred thoughts were still kept from him and though he could have pulled it from him, he did not have the time.

"Corpse!" Patrizio answered, lifting his hand, but nothing happened. Something was blocking the boy's control of fire and he could not set the woman ablaze. Luciana shook her head and grabbed Wolf Lord by the neck. He was stunned to discover she was stronger than the boy as she began to choke the life out of him. Wolf Lord released the boy and he fell to the ground. He turned his talent to his best power and roared, sending his claws into the arm and shoulder of the woman. She was surprised to see her arm bleeding and she stepped back from the man. Wolf Lord jumped to press but winds caught him in mid-flight and threw him through the living room window. He landed in the front yard where the ground quickly started to swallow him.

["*Nay!*"] Wolf Lord screamed as he lifted his hands. They were charged with energy as he sent them into the ground, displacing all of the earth that had grabbed at his body. Luciana shuddered in pain and Wolf Lord had discovered yet another weakness of the Elementals. He lunged forward and recovered every inch the woman had thrown him, but she ducked under his slashing attack.

"Fine," she said, reaching toward the discarded pile of earth that had been her false form. The earth became a pair of short Blades. "We settle this by hand-to-hand combat!"

"Agreed!" Wolf Lord said, summoning his axes.

They circled but only briefly as she knew the Deviant was not one to waste time in combat. He came forward, swinging both axes down for her head. She deflected both with one sword and spun around, landing both a foot and her other blade to Wolf Lord's back. He fell forward into the fake television and grunted in pain. Luciana pressed the issue, thrusting for his back. Wolf Lord felt her approach and jumped up, back-flipping over her. Her weapons sank into the wall as his axes drank from her back. There were initially sparks from his blades, but halfway down, Wolf Lord could see blood. His action did not stop as he made full circles with his weapons and lodged his axes in the woman's shoulders. She released her swords but she did not scream.

Wolf Lord quickly released his weapons and drove his clawed hands into the woman's back.

"It is hard to contend with steel which be not of full phase, eh, stone skin?" he hissed at her, twisting his claws inside her body. Still she did not scream. "Thou art perhaps the finest warrior I hath ever faced, yet the only fair fight is the one thou hast won!" Wolf Lord released electricity into the woman as he tore out her kidneys. He removed his hands and she fell slowly to the floor.

"I have seen many Prodigian fight," he said walking into the room, tending to the wounds of Lavisdion's champions. They had fought well, and in truth, Luciana's skill did surpass Wolf Lord's but he had much more than skill on his side. His instincts made him far more than a simple combatant, they made him gifted. "But you stand far and apart from them all." Wolf Lord turned to face his new opponent but the look in the man's eye and the form of his face caused him to hesitate.

"I know thee!"

"It is good to be remembered," he answered as he moved the bodies of the resting Elementals into another room. "Perhaps that is enough reason for you to hold your wrath long enough to converse with me."

"I have not the time!" Wolf Lord said as his axes flew into his hands. He lunged forward slashing for the bridge of the man's nose; he struck air. The other axe came down for a shoulder. The man struck the flat of the blade and pushed it wide of his body. Wolf Lord blinked as he saw two blurred images pass in front of his face. He could not tell if they were hands or feet and he lowered his weapons. The man used an easily recognizable combative style, the one Wolf Lord had been taught, but it was obvious his knowledge of the form was not as great as the mysterious Elemental.

"How about now?" the man asked.

"I fear thee not," Wolf Lord.

"Let's not waste words, my friend," the man said as he relaxed his stance. "It is the folly of fools that seek to make any Man-Lord fear anything, especially one with your abilities.

"What I seek is a pact with you, a secret pact."

"I keep no secrets from my Master!" Wolf Lord said as his knees bent, ready to begin the next pass of combat.

"Even though he kept secrets from you?" the man asked with an all too knowing smile. "Take the truth of the thought now passing in my mind." Wolf Lord took a step back and formed a shield around his body before seeking the mind of the man in front of him. His precaution drew a smile from the man, but he did not defend his mind from the memory he had invited Wolf Lord to view.

What the hunter saw made him drop his axes! He relived the memory over and over again, a dozen times before he turned away from the man. Sulrynn lifted his hands to hammer the wall, but they were both caught by the winds.

"This house has seen enough damage," the man said calmly. "It is bad enough that the damages of the neighborhood will be impossible to cover completely."

"Thou shalt mend the homes and I shalt deal with the bodies," Wolf Lord said as he returned his axes to his Locke. "Mystery, I hath found, confounds Tyros and they art very quick to dismiss it!"

"And you are helping me because?"

"Because I accept thy pact," Wolf Lord answered. "Thy memory was not all of what I saw"

"It wasn't the only thing I left open for you to see," the man replied. "And you will continue to serve your Master?"

Images flashed in front of his mind's eye. Memories of his youth and all the things he had witnessed in Utopia, New Sumeria, and his many trips to Old Sumeria, a number he had intentionally misquoted to D'Hano. He had believed in all the things he had been told even though all he had seen spoke against many of his lessons. But he had remained true, only to find he had been duped. Like all of the Man-Lords, he had been misled. The man, the very mysterious man, had in mind a plan that would not only afford him a sweet revenge but a position of power beyond his dreams. Once more, there was little to doubt about the man. Here he was seeing to his plans. With all of his power he was still on the battlefield, where the truest of generals belong... at the front of their armies. This was one field marshal Wolf Lord could and would follow.

"I am serving my Master," Wolf Lord replied as he turned and knelt. "If he will but have me."

"Why wouldst I refuse?" the man answered, his language had shifted and he spoke as a Prodigian. "Thou art without question or doubt within my mind, Wolf Lord, now called Sirian. In thy hands I commit a grand degree of my plans and therefore my fate. Carry thyself into the face of those who would practice their deceits and let them feast on their own duplicity. Their time cometh more quickly than they can fathom!"

"But the boy cannot be harmed!" the man insisted and Wolf Lord was quick to nod in agreement.

"The one who was my master hath set me to another quest. I am to return with the boy's mother."

"Then take her," the man replied. "She lies beside her husband in their chambers upstairs."

"The boy is sacred to thee?" Wolf Lord asked.

"That boy is sacred to us all!" the man asserted. "I go now to ensure his latest action doth not yield him death. I shall remedy the houses as I depart."

"And I shall tend to the fallen forms," Wolf Lord said as he took to the stairway. As promised he did find Adrianna, battle-scarred and unconscious. He could feel the presence of his new Master about her form and she had fallen before him. Zargo was legendary, but it was often the subject of conversations that Adrianna, Blood of Abinadab, had managed to outlive him while defying the *Fairie* Council, The Crimson Court and the Throne. He closed his eyes and did as he told his Master he would. Empty homes and cars would draw interest and many questions but there would be no evidence of anything having happened. For a time, they would investigate, but that would pass like the seasons and they too would be forgotten.

"This choice doth serve me well!" Wolf Lord said as he took the limp body of Adrianna. His arm was grabbed by her husband who was still face down in the bed.

"No!" he struggled to speak but still his grip was worth noting. It held for a moment even after Wolf Lord's fist pounded the back of his head.

"Yes, Tyro," Wolf Lord replied as he took Adrianna over his shoulder. "And thou art a fool to mix thy weak blood into matters of those greater than thee!" Wolf Lord teleported to the field where he and the Light-Child Blades had landed. He buried his feelings deep within his mind and made contact with Beriah, the Great Liar. Suddenly the former Black Priest's insistence was clearly understood. He feared the boy as he feared the boy's father. As the link was restored, Beriah sent a doorway back to the Territories. Liar or not, the old fat fool had his abilities. Wolf Lord would make those resources his own before he would drink in Beriah's blood!

Fifty

"What was that?" Timothy asked as they all looked up.

"Three Elementals," Rebecca answered softly. She did not recognize any of them but the power signatures of the one who flew in the center made her glad that they had missed them. "One of them is more powerful than the masters who taught me how to use my powers!"

"What?!" Timothy snapped.

"Don't worry," Rebecca quickly replied. "He didn't feel me."

"But he might have heard you!" Matthew snapped as he stepped toward the middle of the longboat.

They hand landed in the back yard of the house, one of the most veiled parts of the house, from what Matthew had witnessed and he checked the Eden Star, another stolen relic of his most recent past. It inhibited viewing from Eden and also kept the longboat under his control. He had already sent back the barge of the House Adamson and it had taken them nearly two hours to get to Atlanta from New York, thanks to Timothy's spell increasing the speed of the craft. Matthew, as far as he knew, had been the only one to monitor the young Prodigian in the House, and in his research he found only one other House had ever looked in on William Ferrous. Timothy had been good enough to bring those records with him when he left the House of Tavor, which left the Eden-Knights with only the history of William's father Zargogyan and the plight of his mother Adrianna having been banished from New Sumeria.

Matthew hopped over the side of the boat and fell to the ground as his feet touched earth. There was so much pain and death. He had not prepared himself for the reception of so much emotion.

"Matthew!" Rebecca screamed as she extended her hands toward Matthew's quivering form. Timothy's hand slapped her arm hard and broke her concentration.

"Did you or did you not say the man who just took off was more powerful than the Elemental version of the Boogeyman?" Timothy asked as he made a gesture and levitated Matthew's body.

Rebecca put her hand over her mouth and looked up and around. She did not see or feel any of the three Elementals, but what Timothy had said was true, for what she felt coming from the man, his perceptions were most definitely stronger than hers. Summoning the winds to lift Matthew's body would have been a very bad thing!

"Sorry," she said softly. "I-"

"I know," Timothy said in an easy tone as he motioned Matthew's body back into the boat. "You're in love with the guy!"

"Well, yes," Rebecca said plainly before she gasped, recognizing that she had actually voiced something she had kept silent for nearly a year. Again her hand was over her mouth.

"You may want to keep that there," Timothy said with a smile. He received a slap on his shoulder as he squatted to check Matthew. He was always quick to recover and once separated from the ground, he was doing so once again. "When are you going to get around to telling him?"

"Matthew has always had his eyes on other things," she said as she turned away.

"Matthew is a perpetual student!" Timothy argued. "Why don't you teach him a lesson he's obviously been missing?"

"And what if he doesn't want to study the lesson?"

"The risk we take drawing our first breath, Rebecca," Timothy answered. "And now that you've turned your back on Eden, what do you really have to lose?" Rebecca looked at her friend and fellow Convert. They each had been in Eden nearly the same length of time; Rebecca had been brought to the realm less than a week before his arrival, and in that time a true friendship had developed; one that had survived even when they were assigned to rival Houses.

"I would be kind of stupid to argue your wisdom, wouldn't I?"

"Hang on, you said 'kind of'," Timothy said standing up. "Like there is room to argue not telling someone that you love them."

"Not much room, I guess," she replied and Timothy pointed down. Rebecca looked down to see a fully conscious Matthew looking up at her.

"I suppose you have even less room now," Timothy said as he began to levitate. "I'll go take a look about. You two need to talk!"

Ascending toward the house, the Convert Arcanian hoped his particular take on what to do to help two very good friends would turn out for the best. He just could not help feeling he had overstepped his boundaries. After searching the house and the neighborhood, he returned to the longboat, hoping to find good news; he had received enough of the bad sort. As he slowly descended to the boat, his heart found reason to smile, seeing Rebecca resting in Matthew's arms. They were still were not speaking, but it appeared that everything necessary was being said.

"Did you find him?" Matthew asked with a half dazed smile spread wide across his face, his eyes gazing upon Rebecca.

"He's not here," Timothy answered. "And from what I could find, it's a good thing." His response caught the attention of both and they came away from their embrace. Timothy told them what he found and the marks of death that plagued the area.

"Can you track them, Rebecca?" Matthew asked. "The three Elementals?"

"I'm not sure that's a good idea, Ma-" the boat rocked suddenly and was aloft in the next instant. "What are you doing?" Rebecca asked.

"I'm not doing anything!" Matthew claimed and it made it clear who was making the boat move. Only the House Lord could recall the longboat with the crystal active and as they all looked at each other, Timothy lifted his hands, only to be shocked by the mast. He shuddered and fell unconscious.

"Timothy!" Rebecca screamed and she started to move toward him, but Matthew prevented her and held just shy of the next blast.

"Don't move!" Matthew instructed as he summoned his Spiritual Sword and took stance in time to deflect the next blast. Three more deflections and Matthew found himself giving ground. Rebecca knew that she had to move to give him room but her action caused the Eden Star to fire two bursts.

"By the will of the Father!" she gasped as Matthew deflected one blast into the second causing it to flare out inches from her face. She had a slight flash burn but she was made of stern stuff and she focused, directing a blast of flame toward the housing of the Eden Star. Forced to defend itself, the Star formed a small orb shield.

"*Big mistake!*" Matthew thought as he took his blade with both hands and swung into the base of the mast, separating the mast from the boat itself. The mast ascended as the longboat fell.

"Beka!" Matthew yelled as he could feel the boat fall out from beneath his feet. He had forgotten the amenities provided by the power of the Eden Star, but having an Elemental around once again proved beneficial. Commanding the winds, she glided the boat back down to the back yard of the Ferrous household. Matthew sighed as he turned to face Rebecca. She could see burn marks about his face and arms and she ran to him.

"Oh, I'm okay," he said quickly as they embraced. "A couple of those blasts got a little too close for comfort, that's all.

"We need to check on the Timster over there."

Blue eyes slowly opened to look up at slightly charred friends and Timothy managed a smile.

"Now isn't this pleasant," he whispered with a slight cough. "The couple that flambés together, stays together."

"Let's get him out of the boat," Matthew said, taking hold of Timothy's shoulders. Rebecca looked at Matthew as if to convey some confusion as winds took all three of them to the roof of the house. In mid transport, Matthew smiled in embarrassment and released his grip.

"While you're showing off, make sure you burn that boat to a crisp. That mast gets back before you're done and they'll know exactly where we are."

"Talk about motivation!" Rebecca said as she pointed at the boat. It burst into flames and her finger-pointing slowly turned to her hand gesturing as if it was taking hold of the boat, and the flames burned brighter and hotter. As she made a fist, the flames changed color, eventually turning blue.

"I love a woman who can cook!" Matthew said as he saw to Timothy who was rapidly gaining strength.

"Oh, that was classically foul!" Timothy replied.

"I have to take that from the flambé jokester?" Matthew ribbed.

"Good point."

"That's it," Rebecca reported as the flames died, having nothing else to burn. A gust of wind then scattered the ashes. "Now what do we do?"

"Being away from Eden and down a wizard kind of limits our search options," Matthew said. "Maybe we should just get inside and wait for him to show up."

"And here I was about to say that anything beats staying exposed on this roof like this."

"It is a partially good plan," Timothy said as he gestured toward a window. It opened and he started crawling toward it. "I am of no use to anyone right now. Let me stay behind and guard the fort as it were. You two march on and see if you can find this William. The Knights may not know how to find him via record, but you said he had touched the spirit. That is something of a beacon, don't you think?"

Matthew's face went blank, as if he had just found out he had lost his best friend. He looked up and started to move off when Rebecca grabbed him.

"Oh no you don't! We don't have any room for macho heroics!"

"Rebecca, you heard what Tim said."

"Right, which means you'll be needing all the help you can get if the Knights show up around him!" He looked into her eyes; short of death she was going with him, and he was not about to raise a hand against her.

"Then we'll need some altitude so I can search for him," Matthew said in a half apologetic tone.

"That's more like it," Rebecca replied and she lifted her hands. A slight breeze spun around both bodies before it died. She looked up and around and then looked at her hands. Matthew did not need to look around. He just closed his eyes and slowly turned around to see who it was that the Knights of Eden had sent. He stood there in his armor which shined like silver but was of much sterner stuff. His shoulders were broad and his legs were sturdy, but the rest of his frame told the tale of a man who loved food. His helm was tucked under his arm, allowing his bearded face to show. Unlike the hair on the top of his head, it remained black and he kept it shaved close. The gray-touched black locks that blew around his shoulder were another matter.

"Lord Praldicut?!" Matthew said, surprised at the choice that the Mothers had made.

"Nay, Brother," Praldicut answered as he gestured to what was behind Matthew. I am not here for you… I am here for that which belongs to my house. I am here for my Convert."

"Just as I am here for mine," cried Lord Tavor. He was on the opposite side of the house and his thick red hair was timeless. It would probably start to gray only after his death. But his slender form was without beard and too much muscle. "If you would be so kind as to direct me to where I can find him."

Rebecca and Matthew stood back to back and both drew their swords. Rebecca faced Lord Tavor while Matthew faced Lord Praldicut who shook his head in disgust as he donned his helmet.

"The youths of our kind disgust me," he huffed. "Boy, you are my chance to have just a bit of the revenge due me!"

"Try not to tire yourself walking over here," Matthew snipped. "For I have something for your disgust!"

"Oh do you now?" Lord Tavor said as he drew his sword and pointed it at Matthew. "Before you expire, perhaps you would be so kind as to show us what you have in mind."

"Get inside as fast as you can and close the window." Matthew whispered to Rebecca. "This isn't macho heroics, trust me!"

Sighing heavily, Rebecca launched herself toward the window which closed after she entered. Matthew could see Timothy close it just after she flew in.

Matthew went into a fanfare with his sword and by the second move it was glowing. But that glow was something that Knights of Eden were quite used to and they continued their approach, unaffected by the demonstration of skill.

"One fat old man and one skinny old man," Matthew smiled. "This is almost too comical for words!"

"Do not kill him too quickly, Tavor. Leave some for me!"

"No promises, Praldicut!" Both Knights made a speedy approach to the latest initiate into their order who completed his fanfare and thrust his sword into the roof, lowering himself to one knee.

"Wrath!" he yelled and his blade sent energy into the roof that shot out toward Praldicut and Tavor. They both screamed at the energy pouring into their bodies. Praldicut was closer and received a slash from Matthew's sword that opened his chest and heart. Matthew turned and hurled his sword into Tavor's chest. Matthew stepped back from being directly between both men and pointed at their swords.

"Swords of the Spirit!" he called and his voice echoed. "If I be but righteous in my actions, take heed of my command!" Matthew moved his hands, passing one over the other and his intention was quite clear. Tavor's sword flew out of his hand and into Praldicut. The large knight's blade was ripped from his grip and killed Tavor.

"Judgment has been rendered!" Matthew declared and the Spiritual Swords exploded in white flames. Matthew reached for his sword which flew to his hand and he lifted the blade over his head. "Judgment is mine!" he cried as the two sources of white fire fed into his sword. When the light finally died down, Matthew was on his knees, looking at his sword. The blade of it flashed white and Matthew was gone. Rebecca screamed after him but Timothy would not let her out of his grasp. He knew where Matthew had gone and the only assistance they could give him was prayer.

Fifty-One

Bankhead, Georgia! The grassy hill was a favorable choice of arrival point pads. It was just east of the airport and had some upthrow to it. Tara and Dexter made as good a landings as they could, being the true definition of Tyro to the process of teleportation. Kador was at last beginning to act as if he had Prodigian blood in his veins as he materialized. His stance was sturdy and his eyes promptly drew focus on the airport. I returned my talent to keeping our presence concealed from those with any awareness above the expected Tyro capability.

"I can detect nothing," I said as I looked around.

"Which is exactly how they want it," Kador said as he started down the hill toward the large fence. He reached his hand back and made a gesture toward Dexter and Tara. They were quick to follow his lead and I ran to stay in their number. Kador reached into their minds and added power to their legs. The four of us jumped the fence in the same stride. Upon landing, he directed us to place where we would not be easily seen.

"This foolish running about is not necessary," I said. "I can render-"

"Invisibility is something I would rather you not spend energy on right now, Elkee" Kador said as he removed his shoulder bag.

"I cannot tell you how I dislike your bastardization of my name."

"At least you got to keep yours," William snapped back. "Now, if there is nothing else, I would rather discuss how we're going to get your daughter back!" I had neither the time nor severe enough weapon with which to impale myself. What had happened to my mind? I was willing to argue my name while my focus should have been on Vada and the others!

"My apologies," I replied. William nodded and started to speak, but stopped as he looked at the lights on the runway grow dim for a moment. His eyes moved from light to light until he came to one particular hangar. The doors on the large building began to open and William's eyes strained. The man wore a suit of not so fine quality and was obviously in very good shape.

"I think I found our target," William said as he pointed at the building. Neither Tara nor Dexter could see what he was talking about and I myself could barely make it out. But there was no stopping William as he took off running. We were about to lose the advantage of stealth, but William had already lost his concern for maintaining it.

"Okay, I guess we're making our move," Dexter said as he began to run.

"Don't kid yourself, kid," Tara replied. "Strategy is so out the window here! Let's just do our best to keep up!"

The hangar in question was on the other side of the runway from where we were but William would not have us cross just yet. Still, his speed was hard to match and I chose to lift the Tyros and glide in behind him.

"You're pretty handy to have around there, Elkee," Dexter said with a smile. I did not respond but I did look over at Tara who was no longer looking at me. She was looking at the hangar we were hoping to attain. But she did not see a building, she could only see a man housed somewhere within it and the sight of him set fire to her soul. Mayhap the anger would add the necessary edge these Tyros needed to survive what awaited us all in that building.

"It won't be much longer," Jack announced as he turned the plane toward the airport. "We will probably be arrested by the Feds for all the laws we're breaking, but it won't be much longer."

"That's good to hear," Marianne said, taking the co-pilot's chair. She was dressed in body armor and the weapons harness that Al had designed for them. She checked the instrumentation and breaking the law was right. They were nearly at Mach Two and the plane was flying nice and steady.

"Peter was right, this is some thesis!"

"He has no idea," Jack said with a smile and a turn of the wheel. "I take it he needs his time back there?"

"Yeah," she answered, forcing a smile. "He's got his rifle again and he just put it together."

"You mean he put *her* together," Jack mentioned.

"Don't tell me you believe in that crap too?" Marianne pleaded.

"When a man shoots the way Peter Webster does, whatever he says about the gun that is his premium weapon of choice is my mantra!"

"I suppose you have a point," Marianne chuckled as the plane shook violently and she lost her smile. "What the hell was that?"

"You got me," Jack said as he quickly checked the engines, but they were doing just fine. Whatever they had felt was inside the plane and they had been through too much to dismiss the seemingly impossible. "I think we just got boarded!"

Marianne Cooper started to remove her seatbelt and get out of her chair, but she looked up to see an unfamiliar man's face looking at her through the portal of the door separating the cockpit and the cabin.

"Jack!" she screamed.

Peter had just placed his baby in her sleeve and zipped her up when he looked out of the window. He was looking westward and it looked like there were two suns.

"We are still a Class-M Planet, aren't we?" he said as he got up out of his chair. Caleb looked up from his own weapons preparation and did a double take before walking to the window closest to the sight.

"Last time I checked," Caleb answered. "You think this thing moves so fast we wound up on another Earth?"

"Man we've been on another Earth since we took this case," Peter answered. The second sun suddenly flared brightly, turned and approached the plane. As Peter jumped back from the window, there was a bright flash that blinded Caleb. He fell down when the plane shook violently.

Peter looked up to see Thidalia looking down on him. She was not alone. She had brought her chauffeur and five other muscle-bound minions, though they did not have the same air about them as the large driver. They seemed more assertive, more capable and certainly better dressed. The largest man was twirling a very fine cane.

Both of them moved quickly, Arcanian and Tyro sniper, and it was clear that Webster was faster than her. But a finger gesture of a spell took less total movement than drawing a pistol and Peter felt a powerful push to his chest. He was pinned to the floor, unable to move.

"My, this is most fortuitous!" Thidalia said, genuinely glad to see Webster again. Her eyes glowed as Webster could hear Marianne scream Jack's name. The smallest of the men had quickly made his way to the cockpit door and was reaching for it.

"Student body Port!" Jack yelled and although Peter knew what was coming, there was little he could do other than grab the frame of a chair.

The plane quickly did a barrel roll counter-clockwise and everyone in the cabin was thrown to the left side. Thidalia stepped on Webster as she tried to catch herself. As she slammed into the left side of the cabin, Peter could feel the force pinning him to the floor break off and his body came up from the floor, but his grip on the chair held fast.

"Let's try this again," Peter thought as he reached for his pistol and swung his feet around to support his weight as the plane came back to its upright position.

Peter fired, but not before Rook put himself between the gun and Thidalia. He scored a shoulder and the man's facial expression did not change. Quickly adjusting his aim, Peter fired again and as the first bullet was coming out of the large man's shoulder, the second hit just over his right eye and Rook was dead. His large body slowly slid out of the way and Peter shifted his aim.

"Go right, Jack!" Caleb yelled and the plane rolled once again counter-clockwise once again. Peter screamed as the dagger meant for his heart hit his left shoulder instead. It was just a grazing cut, but the force of the throw spun him around and he lost his grip on his weapon, but not before it went off, shooting out a window. The plane no longer flew steadily and alarms sounded as oxygen masks dropped from the ceiling.

Pawn made it to Rook and prayed she had not taken too long to be of use to her comrade. She put her hand to his forehead and dedicated nearly all of her reserves to his body. She removed her hand and the bullet flew out, the wound slowly mending.

"You are a hard Tyro to kill, Peter Webster!" Thidalia announced as she made another gesture. She and all of her party were suddenly gone.

"Bitch!" Peter screamed as he made his way to his chair. He passed Caleb along the way and helped him into his own.

"We're clear back here, Moreland!" Peter announced. "I shot a hole in this thing but it looks like some silly putty grew over the hole!"

"Roger that!" Jack yelled back. "I'm going for an emergency landing."

"GOODBYE, PETER WEBSTER!" Thidalia's voice echoed through the plane as it was rocked again. The nose of the plane dipped and did not come back up.

"We're hit and I mean hard," Jack reported. "Both engines are up and gone and the wings won't open, so I can't glide her in."

"Jesus, Webster!" Caleb shouted. "When you piss off a woman, you really piss off a woman!"

"I got no control over this thing," Jack said as he came out of the cockpit. "And we got about thirty seconds before we suffer from an extreme case of Sudden Stop!" He opened a door to the storage bin and pulled out two parachutes. "You have got to be kidding!"

"Hell, man," Peter laughed. "That's two more than I was expecting. Weight-wise it should be you and Mari, me and Chalk. Mari and I are wearing!"

Jack put one arm into the harness and reached for Marianne before opening the door. He expected to be sucked out, but he was glad the engines were gone. That would be one less piece of the plane they could make contact with as they jumped. As expected, he was sucked out but to his surprise Marianne was pulled out of his grasp. Still he managed to keep his grip on the parachute.

Peter knew he did not have Jack's strength, but he did possess about three times his speed and ten times the experience. Even with the shoulder wound he was in the harness and ready to go in no time, but there was no Dr. Caleb Chalk to be found.

"Doc, now is not the time!" Peter yelled and Caleb came from the back of the plane toting his medical kit and Peter's rifle. Both men jumped and Caleb kept his grip on Peter's body and the two articles he nearly died for. The chute opened and Peter hoped it would be a landing they could both walk away from.

Jack looked around but he could not see her. There was plenty of daylight, but that did not help matters at all. He went about the business of getting into the chute but he kept looking, hearing only the hard hitting wind and the sound of jet engines.

"Dear God, not her. Please, not her! Not on my watch!"

Fifty-Two

The alarms sounded and his time with her was cut short. He had often heard the big, strong, swarthy types always complaining about such events and thought Bill Cole would admit to fantasizing of such anguish, he had long ago confirmed it would be an episode he would die without experiencing. But as he pulled his lips from Vada-Ri's he wished he had remained among the blissfully ignorant.

"I have to go," he said, looking down.

"I know, Bill!" Vada-Ri replied, touching her lips to his forehead. "Go quickly so that you may return quickly." Bill stood up and looked at her as she rose from the bench they were seated upon. He was trying to speak but could not find the words. Vada smiled and touched her finger to his lips.

"Have the guards return me to my binds, Bill! You may need your full faculties for this and-" Bill was getting better and better at expressing his passions. Again her retort was cut off and again his arms wrapped around her body, pulling her close to him. Again she moaned and touched the side of his face as she slowly pulled away. "Guards!" she commanded and they placed the restraints back on her arms and head. Bill turned away so he could not see it happening and quickly left the room. Antal was waiting in the corridor, finishing a second cigarette.

"You two set a date yet?" he asked.

"Well, it is clear she wants to make some sort of arrangement," Bill said, adjusting his glasses. "A pact if you will. Just can't seem to come to terms."

"Yeah, I can imagine terms are pretty damn hard to come by when your mouth is full," Brooks smiled as he looked to his cell phone. "The alarm was for an inbound plane from the North. Supersonic and seemed to be headed right for us but it turned west and at last report was losing altitude fast."

"It could be just getting under radar," Bill suggested. Antal nodded in agreement. "Let's get ready to scramble interceptors."

"I already gave the order. They're airborne and our particular ride out of here is just about ready to go. The big guy and the crazy-go-nuts archer will be the first to be secured. Flight Engineer says the way the crazy man is drawing power we may have to put him down before we can go up."

"I can go along with that. He is really a pain!"

"I thought low lights kind of set the mood," Brooks remarked.

"You're not jealous, are you, Brooks?"

"Why would he be?" Amos barked as he came away from the makeshift cafeteria.

"Oh well, there went the fun," Antal sighed.

"You done swapping spit with the freaks?" Amos asked as he lifted his hand to point into Bill's chest. Cole's drawn pistol pointed at Redding's head kept him very still.

"Let me see if I can explain this clearly," Bill said in a very calm voice. "Keep your hands off of me for the rest of your life. However short that may be! Was that clear?" Redding nodded and Bill grabbed his shoulder and turned the man around. "Now go back to the hole you just crawled out of and pray I don't need to lighten the load on my transport plane!"

"I must be under some sort of enchantment," Thidalia said as she walked down the middle of the corridor, Pawn and Rook walking behind her. "Bill, is that you?!"

"Thidalia!" Bill said excited. "I have been trying to reach you."

"I know," she said, surprised again as Bill took her into a friendly embrace.

"Dude, easy on the confidence!" Antal thought.

"I have had to deal with a few matters of import." Thidalia looked up and motioned to the flashing lights. "Have I arrived just in time to be attacked?"

"Oh, no!" Bill said quickly, motioning to Antal. "We just have security pretty tight around here and there was an inbound unregistered plane. They have since turned off. We're staying at alert status because we are ready to transport our prisoners."

"Prisoners?" Thidalia asked, her smile quickly fading.

"We ran into a situation," Bill said, ushering Thidalia to walk with him. "Several, actually. First of all Arvius took it upon himself to deal with the Peter Webster issue."

"Did he now?"

"Yes, and he did so without any authorization from me. I have not been in touch with Sebastian to see if the order came from him."

"I seriously doubt that it did," Thidalia said as she picked up the pace. It did not go without notice from Bill but he expected her to be aggravated by the actions that were definitely out of the status quo. "And?"

"Well, he got Kendra involved in an assassination attempt," Bill answered.

"A failed attempt," Thidalia said.

"Yes, it failed." Bill swallowed hard, thankful he was not at fault.

"And?"

"I sent Leone into the field," Bill said softly and Thidalia came to an abrupt halt. "But he was successful in rescuing Kendra and getting her away from Webster and company."

"What?!" Thidalia asked, her mind going through the number of possibilities of the past few minutes. It was not coincidence that she had come across Webster. He was not headed here to see a colleague; he was en route to come to this very place!

"Webster actually managed to capture Kendra using, of all things, a sonic pulse generator."

"How in God's name did they get their hands on that?"

"From what our intelligence has been able to put together, this was a homemade generator and only good for one usage."

"*Ho-kay,*" Brooks thought as he scratched the back of his neck. "*What is going on?*" He looked up and around but there was nothing to see.

"Something amiss, Mr. Brooks?" Thidalia asked.

"Much as I would like to say that there's nothing wrong," Antal said as his hand began to itch for his weapon. He looked at his hand and his uncertainty receded instantly. "We're being zeroed!" he whispered.

"This is Cole," Bill said into his cell phone. "I need a corner to corner security sweep immediately and until further notice, I need to see weapons drawn."

"Bill?!" Thidalia said shocked at the new man she saw standing in front of her.

"Antal doesn't itch unless there is something to scratch, ma'am. Forgive me, but I think we need to get you to safety."

"I appreciate the concern, Mr. Cole, but I will see to myself. Please advise your men that I have four other people with me at this time! They are waiting for me on the surface.

"I am afraid I will have to insist," Bill said as he motioned for one of the guards to approach.

"Yes, sir!"

"Please see this lady to the transport plane and send the word that there are four additional associates of our Director on the premises. They are to be treated with the utmost respect.

"Director," Bill lifted his arm up to give Thidalia the direction she was to walk in. She nodded and followed the guard assigned to her. Bill watched her walk and seeing her leave safely gave him reason to smile.

"How sure are you of this feeling?" Bill asked. Gunfire answered Bill's questions. "Forget I asked. You see to perimeter defense and I'll get the prisoners on to the transport!" Bill ran off before Antal could give him a response.

"*Too bad he's jumping to the other extreme,*" Antal thought as he ran for his area. He needed his rifle if he was going to deal with this itch. "*I was really getting to like him.*" Antal took a few steps before his hand reminded him of an advantage he held. He held up the knife Niles had given him and looked around. One bad thing about being underground was there was very little open ground. He would have to get outside to make the knife work. It was a good thing his weapon was on the way to the door leading up and out.

"I don't get it," Dexter said as he looked around. "No one said 'halt' or 'hey' or nothing! All of a sudden, an alarm goes off!"

"This isn't a video game, Dex," William said as he looked around but saw no activity coming in their direction. "But I am a little puzzled myself."

"And who are they shooting at?" Dexter asked, straining to maintain cover and see as much as possible at the same time. "Not that I should presume it's a *who*."

"Well said, Tyro," I replied, extending my senses to sweep the grounds. There were three entities the guards sought to engage, and each had been fired upon with no result to speak of save the irritation of the intended targets. I tried to reach into their minds but my efforts were reflected back upon me. "*Prodigians?*" I thought. "*But how? Why?*"

"I must take my leave of you for the moment!" I said.

"Oh, this is so not the time!" Tara said, reaching into her cargo pants pocket. It was her phone; she had just received a text message and in my reaction to what she said, William had time to reach my arm.

"No solo heroics, Elkazzar!" he ordered and my jaw drew tight. "Prodigian or not, if it's not who we came for, they're secondary."

"I thought you were here to settle a score for Rachel?" I asked, reminding him of his own claim.

"Sometimes, just sometimes, Viz, you say what you have to say and you do what you have to do! Rachel did not give her life for me to go off like a madman, and I'm not about to have you lose the people you brought here to train me. This is not what they signed up for."

"I cannot argue any point you have made, Kador," I answered, and I began to question my anger, my resentment. I knew they were in me, but I could not understand their reason for being. "It is too bad we are one short of a fist, but you have your small army – we shall follow your lead!"

Tara smiled as she read the text: *Guess who… brought some friends. P is on your 6, bum rush on your 9… Luv J.* Tara did not know whether to laugh or cry. "I don't fucking believe it!" she whispered. "We got backup!" she said as she smiled brightly at William.

"Not the guys again?" he said, becoming half excited himself, and Tara nodded yes emphatically. His eyes cut up at me and I had to smile. Perhaps the whole of them might be the missing fifth we needed. "Alright, let's see if we can go for two-and-oh. We just got bumped up to a more direct approach, especially with all hell breaking loose on the other side of the airport. Let's just take it to 'em!"

Thidalia and her entourage of the well-dressed hard bodies were escorted to the transport plane, but the smallest of her male companions walked in front of her to stop her.

"Prodigians are about, at least two!" Knight warned. Thidalia nodded and directed everyone to board the plane anyway.

"We will let them draw themselves out, my friends!" she answered. "Then we shall make our move." She took her seat and was surrounded by her people, none of whom liked being in a confined space in the case of a powerful flank attack.

I kept the four of us invisible as we made our approach. I was foolishly under the misconception that we were simply going to charge in and rescue my daughter and kinsmen. But our attacking quartet veered off to engage a group of armed men who seemed to be in the process of establishing a perimeter guard. William tackled two of the five men; Dexter took on one, leaving one for myself and Tara. Tara did not have to struggle and neither did I. William had dispensed the second by the time Dexter had suitably restrained his man. He was sloppy and he shook like a frightened child.

"Can you tell me why we did that?" I asked.

"Dude, get with your boy!" Dexter said as he tossed the pistol Tara had given him back to Tara. "No offense."

"None taken," she replied as she too also started collecting weapons. William took only a pistol, a magazine of ammunition, a knife, a section of rope, a radio and a very small tool kit.

"Rope?" I asked.

"Some other time, Elkee," William answered as he looked around. "If we're lucky, we got a few seconds. Let's move this inside!"

"Too late!" Dexter said as he pointed. The large plane was moving out of the hangar, though the back of it was still open.

"Okay," William said as he reached into his shoulder bag and pulled out a piecemeal box bound together with tape and fishing line. He handed the contraption to Tara. "You go with Elkazzar from the left. Me and Dex will head in from the right."

"Dex and I," Dexter corrected as he set his weapons for the attack.

"Oh my God we're in trouble," William concluded as he moved toward his attack point.

"This was not what I was expecting," Satashi said sadly as she looked down on the hangar. The transference platform was good for only fifteen minutes and she had already used eight of those, searching around the ground.

"I take it we are Charlie Brown then?" Cho asked.

"Actually we are Charlie Brown's Christmas tree," she answered as she finally found a suitable landing point.

"From what I am able to detect, we have more than two Tribes in the same area," Cho concluded. "This is no longer a mission of surveillance!" Cho turned and looked at Satashi and she knew her fate. She wanted to argue but there was little chance she would be able to get him consider her argument, let alone suspend his necessary action. She just nodded and fought back the tears.

"Just give me a moment," she asked and Cho nodded. "Do you have a sharp edged device?" she asked and Cho reached inside his shirt, at the small of his back. Satashi turned and jumped off the platform, the high pitched whipping sound behind her head told her that his first cut had just missed her.

"Somebody help me!" she screamed on the way down to the ground, the equivalent of a forty-story fall. Her scream found the ears of William Ferrous and he looked up to see a speck of a body falling to the ground far off in the distance.

[*Elkazzar, can you catch her?*] he projected as I continued my progress inside toward the hangar. William could see the woman's body stop just shy of the ground and then she fell the last ten feet.

"William!" Dexter cried as he tackled his friend. A hail of machine gun fire poured out over their location. About half of the clip was gone when the man was shot in the chest and fell to the ground. Both young men looked up and then at each other.

"Nice tackle," William said.

"Told you I should've played defense!" Dexter replied.

"Nowhere near as much play, man. Just ask Tom Brady! Thanks for the save!"

"Thanks for the advice!" Dexter said, pulling William up to his feet.

"Sure helps to have a sniper on your side," William whispered as he moved toward the rear of the plane. He and Dexter moved up the ramp to see two technicians who were not armed with guns come at them with tools instead. William leaned back to avoid the first man's wild swing and he came forward with chop to the side of the face. The man fell unconscious and was joined by a man holding on to his crotch for dear life. Dexter lifted his weapon toward the seven people in the far corner.

"Freeze!" he yelled as William looked over the plane. "You people look way too nice to get your clothes all wrinkled and bloody."

"My, how cordial!" Thidalia said, leaning forward so that her face could be seen.

"Just keep your seats and everything will be fine," Dexter said calmly and Thidalia was shaken; neither young man had the normal reaction to seeing her. She nodded to Knight who stood up and started toward Dexter. "Hey, easy partner! These things tend to go off and... KILL people!"

"Then shoot!" Knight said callously.

"You got it!" Dexter fired a three round burst into Knight's chest and he fell to the floor. The sound of the gunfire made William return to the room. He entered quickly and appeared ready for battle but Thidalia quickly realized he had not drawn a weapon.

"Everything okay in here?" William asked of his best friend.

"He said shoot!" Dexter said with that ever popular Columbia High School look on his face.

William shrugged his shoulders and started to continue his search. But he stopped and looked at Knight. His mind! William felt his still very active mind.

"What in the world?!" William said as the man sat up and glared at Dexter. Dexter was also flabbergasted as Knight stood up, straightened his jacket and made a throwing motion. William could see the bullets but he knew that Dexter could not.

"No!" William said as he focused his telekinesis. With very little effort assembled, Dexter flew out of the back of the plane and carried for about forty meters before he hit the ground and rolled to a stop. William's eyes flared wide with shock. He had moved Dexter out of the way but he could not believe his push was that strong. He blinked and the shutter of his eyes closing brought him back into focus and he stepped back, avoiding a flying kick from a shapely black woman. Her foot struck the wall of the plane and the wall gave! William knew he would have to address his faux pas with Dexter later. The woman landed from the kick and reached for him; William split her uprights with an uppercut that backed her up but did not knock her down. William looked at the finest dressed woman of the grouping.

"Do we talk or do we die?" he asked.

"Hold!" Thidalia commanded. She was struck by his candor. For one so young he was a very old soul. His eyes did not shake in fear and his movements showed a master of conservation, which he would need to fight just one of the SomeVinco. Fighting six of the Body Masters was suicidal. "We can talk," she finally answered him. "Given what is said, you may not have to die."

"And your name?"

"Thidalia," she smiled.

"Pekavali?" William asked. His head tilted as his mind tried to engage.

"*Why did I ask her that?*" he thought. Before he could get too distracted, he had taken note of her reaction to the inquiry.

"There are other paths to war!" she said as she turned her face away from William. "Kill the Prodigian!"

Bishop was the first to act after a kill command. She was always first. She charged William with a hand thrust that could have penetrated a brick wall, but William caught her wrist and twisted her arm. He used it to block Knight's axe-kick. The arm broke, but the woman did not even grunt in pain, and William pushed them both off. Bishop stepped away and grabbed her arm. She threw her brown hair out of her face and set the break herself.

"*Damn these boys heal fast!*" William thought as the largest man, standing about seven feet in height, ushered his slightly smaller colleague toward him. He swung for William's head but missed. William had his hand on the man's chest and was going to push, him but the force of the charge was too strong and William slid toward the back of the plane. "*And they're stronger than me!*" Rook grabbed William's arm and pulled sharply, trying to get William into a position where the large man could grab and throw the young man's body. William kept his weight moving and flipped over Rook, landing in the midst of the six warriors. Thidalia crossed her legs as she raised her brow and smiled. Her 'what now' look made William smile as he knelt, ducking a swing for his head. He put his hand on the floor of the plane and brought the all the electricity he could find into this section of the plane. All seven enemies screamed and William was glad that Dexter was not on the plane after all.

"Enough!" King said as his cane slipped from its guise, becoming a Battle Staff. King drew his share of the electricity into his weapon and lunged for William in a series of grabs that were either blocked or avoided. William spun around the man and sidestepped a powerful front kick from Bishop. King was struck instead and was flying toward Thidalia, but his weapon stopped him. William landed an open handed thrust and Bishop took two steps back. William jumped up and split-kicked Rook and Knight, while blocking Queen's chop for his groin.

He knew he was not hurting them and he could only continue to avoid them for so long. Fighting as a unit, he could see them adapting to his technique. He took stance and focused on everything he had learned at the Source.

"Like how to duck!" he yelled as he jumped forward. Something burst through the side of the plane and collided with King. The two forms continued to the other side of the plane and stopped only after King's body was wedged into the framework of the plane. Cho got up from a stunned King and turned to look at both Thidalia and William. The SomeVinco were the property of the Arcanians and Thidalia was a ranking member of the Great Façade. She had to be dealt with first. Cho stepped toward her and Knight landed a downward hook that barely turned Cho's face. Knight displayed his first sign of pain as he staggered back from Cho.

"Impossible," Thidalia whispered as she looked to the ring on her right hand index finger. The ruby was not glowing. "You're not an Elemental!"

"Indeed!" Cho said as he lunged for Thidalia. She leaned back in her chair and his hand closed tight, brushing her cheek but touching nothing else. Cho had been caught, lifted and thrown by Queen and Bishop. He flew out of the very same hole he had made. He landed on his back and bounced off the ground. He flipped over and came down on his feet. He glared up at the plane and extended his hand toward it.

"*Definitely my cue to leave!*" William thought as he jumped out of the back in the direction where Dexter was getting up.

An energy bolt left Cho's palm and Thidalia's manna bolt intercepted it just before it could hit the side of the plane. King came out through the hole next. His suit was gone. He was topless except for criss-crossing bands of studded leather across his chest, along with black leather pants and boots. Queen, a lovely looking Amazon that stood nearly six feet tall, joined him dressed in chain mail and playing with her exceptionally long ponytail. Both of them had jumped out of the hole in the plane and covered twenty meters before touching the ground.

"Like I said," Peter repeated himself as he kept his scope on the action. "You don't want to be down there!"

"I think our new friends just might agree with you, Webster," Jack said over the radio. "Or do I assume too much?" Jack asked, lowering his mike.

"I'm still trying to get a handle on the little Japanese man," Lambda Scout answered. "That is like an armored C-130 transport plane. He just ripped through it like it was rice paper."

"Yeah, but he got thrown out just the same," Marianne said offering her savior a drink of water. "I did thank you, right?"

"More than once," Terrell answered with a smile. "With the heads up you guys have given us, I think we still owe you one!"

"I'll second that," Delta Scout added. "How long does this go on?"

"It is usually winding up when we start bleeding," Jack answered, and neither Marianne nor Caleb could argue the point.

Fifty-Three

King and Queen charged together and Cho thought it best to give ground. He was stronger and faster than the two combined, but they were still capable of doing a great deal of damage to his body. Queen shot her head forward and her ponytail came up and over her head, wrapping around both of Cho's leg. A jerk of her neck and Cho was flying toward King who had his Battle Staff charged and waiting. He swung and there was a bright flash of light that blinded everyone watching the fight. As the light faded down, Queen was pulled off her feet and toward the light. She arrived just as it died. King lay at Cho's feet, his chest gaping open and smoldering, the Battle Staff shattered in bits around Cho who caught Queen by her face and squeezed. She did not have time to scream. Her body fell to the ground as life abandoned King. His chest wound had partially healed but he had taken too much punishment. Cho looked back at the plane and a manna bolt exploded against his chest. He was thrown back but he was quick to get up as Thidalia came out of the plane.

"I don't know who or what you are," Thidalia said through clenched teeth. "But I will destroy you!"

"Have a care, Arcanian," Cho said, taking a combative stance. "It sounds as if you are trying to convince yourself more than you are trying to convince me!"

Thidalia spoke in a low tone, chanting words that could not easily be translated and winds kicked up as she spoke. Her dress faded into a gown of chain mail and silk and she held a scepter that seemed to glow from within.

"The rest of you," Thidalia commanded as she and Cho started to close the distance between each other. "See to the Prodigian! He must die as well!"

"Okay, that's our signal," Jack said as he picked up his weapon and started toward the airport. "We'll understand if you two can't tag along."

"Us, stand still?" Terrell said as he checked his guns. "That's not likely to happen." He turned his head to look at his larger friend. "You want to take this one in a Multi-Frame?"

"I hate to make you go solo, but we might need the firepower," Conway answered.

"I'm thinking more than 'might need'," Terrell answered.

"Then I'm on it!" Conway said before turning to run to where the Multi-Frames were parked.

"You might want to let me take point," Lambda Scout suggested. "There's a bit more to us than a cool ride and serious weapons."

"I wouldn't be a bit surprised," Jack answered as he waved Marianne back.

I walked down the large corridor with Tara at my side though she was a few steps back. She had her gun ready to shoot and I walked with my Staffling in hand. We had left Dexter and William at the transport plane and from the sounds of it, the device was no longer functional. It would only be moments before they would join us but I could not wait for the child. His distractions kept me from my daughter, my people. I did not know what intentions the boy was entertaining, but he did not need me to be part of his audience.

"You might want to slow down that walk," Tara warned. "We are in someone else's back yard!"

"We are in a Tyro backyard!" I corrected her.

"Isn't that the same attitude you had when these same Tyros took your daughter and left you babbling like an idiot?" Tara asked and I started to put my eyes on her, but I sensed another mind ready to enact a very severe action against me. I stepped quickly to avoid the attack. Tara had no such warning. The device is called a shotgun and it fired a very powerful burst and threw Tara to the ground. The man, calling himself Amos Redding, lifted the weapon in order to load another round into the device. The slide moved toward him at the same time I committed to my approach. He leveled the weapon at me as I readied my weapon. The slide moved away from him as I swung my weapon. My Staffling struck the barrel of the device just before it fired. His shot missed flesh but struck lights in the ceiling instead. I continued my motion and swept the Tyro off his feet. Before his back met with the ground, my Staffling met with his chest. I felt his sternum give more air than it could normally afford and the Tyro was stunned. Another swing deprived him of the weapon and I continued my path down the corridor.

William and Dexter came down the corridor and saw Tara laid out near the wall. Dexter had just gotten the use of his legs back and William left his side to tend to Mifflen.

"Tara!" he cried and he kneeled by her side. She was wearing the vest she had taken off the agent they encountered outside, but she was still bleeding.

"Oh, man this shit hurts!" she cried. She was in pain and she was scared. "Jon!" she yelled.

"You leave him out of this!" William barked at her, grabbing at her wound. Tara locked in pain and looked at William with surprise. "You leave him the hell out of this!" he commanded as he reached into her mind, finding her pain centers. She could do without them for the moment and he rendered them inactive.

"What did you do?" Tara asked.

"I made you easier to deal with," William answered, removing the vest. "Where's Elkazzar?"

"I guess he figured he'd trade his Tyro partner for one of his own kind!" Tara said as she watched William work. "You spend time at Med School recently?" she asked.

"You could say that," William answered, continuing to clean the wound, administer some of his talent toward repair and then binding it in gauze. "That should last you for the time being. I have to bring the pain back though."

"Typical man," Tara smiled. You never last long e-" her speech became a scream as her mind allowed her to process pain again.

"Dex, you have to stay with her," William said as he started to stand. Tara grabbed him and glared at him.

"That is not part of the plan!" she hissed. "Now you get your little tail moving and finish this job. I'll be fine!" She held up her cell phone and mouthed 'backup'. William nodded and looked up at Dexter.

"You still got my back?"

"Man, you are wasting time!" Dexter said. Another gunshot sounded off in the distance. "Sounds like your boy has found some more friends to play with."

William's nostrils flared wide, followed in action by his eyes. "Aye, he has found quite a few playthings." He started off the corridor and Dexter ran behind him.

"Some genius," Tara thought as she tried to get up. *"Like this damn thing works down here. 'Course, from what I just heard, he's not going solo even if Dexter wasn't with him."*

"Stay down, sweets!" Jon called to her.

"Oh there you are," she replied, turning to look at him. But Jon was not alone. There were figures standing around him, blurred figures who looked hungry; ravenous and waiting for a bell or starting pistol shot before they would release themselves.

"Jon, who are they?"

"Not who, baby. They are a what. These are Wayfarers*!"*

"I thought they were a friendly sort," she said softly.

"They were... for me!" Jon looked down. *"If you stay down..."*

"I'll cease to be me!" Tara answered and used the wall to climb up to a weak stance. "Kid does great work for a rookie. Trouble is I've lost a lot of blood! I feel cold, my body is going to shock and these party favors you brought with you are getting closer."

"Stay out of this one, sweets!"

"Not even for you, baby," she cried her reply. "Too much Lydia in me I guess." Tara drew her pistol and took a deep breath before limping after William.

"*I can't go with you this time!*" Jon pleaded. "*If you go...*"

"I know, baby. It's all good!"

"Give him a maximum dose!" Bill commanded.

"We can't, sir," one of the technicians replied. "We won't have enough for anyone else if we do!"

"Then split it between him and the Absularian," Cole decided as he looked at his watch.

"Sir!" an armed agent cried as he came running down the path. "The plane is compromised, sir! Way too much structural damage!"

"We go with Plan B then," Bill commanded. "Use the underground access way to get them all to Hangar 12. There is a smaller transport there. Alert Brooks and his team of the change." Bill turned to face Vada-Ri who looked worried. He approached her and put his hand to her face.

"Don't worry, I'll be fine."

"Daughter!" I cried, tossing the latest obstacle away from my person. He did not quite reach the wall but he was unconscious nonetheless. I could see my daughter and the Tyro who held her prisoner. The only guide I had was my rage and I reached my hand forward, grabbing the body of the Tyro with my talent. I squeezed. His left arm and one of his ribs had given when a whip slashed across my arm and I dropped my Staffling. I lost my grip and the Tyro fell to the ground. Another whip slash deprived me of my War Locke and I stepped back.

"You!" I gargled in anger, watching Arvius, Blood of Salpanor, called Harry Smith, lift my target to his feet and mend his broken bones. The man did not say much more than a hushed thank you before he turned and ran with his technicians, my daughter and my people. Arvius remained and smiled back at me.

"Yes, Head Master, it is I," Arvius answered, but I could hear the soft and nearly silent footfalls of the owner of the whip circling around me quickly. I had already repaired the first wound and my Staffling was still close, though I could not detect my War Locke. The Staffling was a trap!

"Or should I just call you *Master*?" Arvius smiled, reminding me of perhaps my single greatest failure in life. He had followed Adrianna as my student and thank the Fates others followed him. But he alone stood as an example of how far failure could take a person.

"You may use whatever name you wish, Arvius. This is the day that shall see the end of your life, take this as my oath.

"And think me not a fool," I said as I slowly approached him, leaving my Staffling behind. "For you to stand so calmly in front of me means only that you have found someone *else* to do your fighting for you. Someone *else* you have managed to convince that you deserve to walk on two legs!" Arvius lost his smile and found his anger. My counter-trap was working but not knowing all of what he had in store still had me at a major disadvantage.

"Then why don't we all get acquainted!" Arvius yelled. "Leone!"

A tall, slender man with yellow eyes and black hair ending in silver tips came out of an invisibility veil to Arvius' right. He was not wielding a whip but he appeared to be a very capable Prodigian.

"But perhaps you know him better as the Man-Lord Treldeshyar, Blood of Krannis. Kendra!"

A thin woman appeared to Arvius' left. With brown hair and hazel eyes, I could feel her prowess of mind. She was even better trained than the Man-Lord.

"Quillioni, a Light-Child of no true Blood," Arvius continued. "Then there are those who have yet to receive their Old Sumeria names; Turgle, Keskia, and Yalquim!" Three more came into my eyesight. The large Light-Child who had received Kador's clawing attack, a Man-Lord female who looked all too eager to engage me and the elderly Prodigian who had drawn several bows on Adrianna, again to assist Arvius in his escape from the Ferrous household. A quick inspection told me none of these were my whipping assailant. The footwear of choice was too hard to sound as soft as it had. So there was at least one more. Typical of Arvius to speak in such tones and not come fully to the truth of the matter. So, I was to face some six Prodigians on my own. I have to admit, a smile escaped my lips as I glared on Arvius.

"Is this all you have to keep your life in your own skin?" I asked, taking another step. "Have they been among Tyros long enough to buy into their foolish belief systems?

"Then send them, Arvius. Send them into their destiny with death!" I shouted and took another step forward. I leaned forward and reached back for my Staffling. But my actions had not fooled everyone and a whip took my staff before my talent could take hold of it, snatching it even further away. Away, the perfect position for the whip wielder, with the exception of one or two things.

Kador's hand took hold of my staff while it was in mid-air as was he. He flipped and unfurled the whip in the same action, landing on his feet and twirling my Staffling. "You lose something?" he asked tossing me my Staffling. As soon as it left his hand, I could hear the whip coming forward. Kadorygyan reacted before I could, already he was matching his father's speed, and his hand caught the invisible whip. I caught my Staffling and took position at Kador's back as he held the whip and kept his stance.

"Might as well come on out and make the acquaintance official," he baited, employing the same disgusting degree of humor in a conflictive situation as his father had. This was neither the time nor the place for such antics.

"Mind on your work!" I whispered sharply.

"You just be glad I'm willing to wait until after we're done before I pick my bone with you, old man," Kador whispered back. "Just know it's a big bone and you and I got some pickin' to do!"

"You presume that we will both be able to pick this bone of yours when we're done," I pointed out.

"Elkee, I'm not done until I get my hands on you!" he replied, promising me a fate out of my control to avoid.

"But all things being equal, Harry," he shouted. "I need to come over there and arrange a few of your organs!"

"My friends might have something to say about that, Kador!" Arvius shouted, his eyes showing that he had been generating extra energy for this fight. "But you may cling to whatever delusions you prefer to hold on to, child! Soon you shall hold to nothing!"

Kador looked to the hand that was still engaged in a tug-of-war with its invisible wielder and he sent an energy wave down the length of the weapon.

"Ow!" a female voice said as she fell down, becoming quite visible and had the others attacked at that moment, Kador and I would have been lost.

She was young, about Kador's age, perhaps older, but there was little innocence across her face. There was nothing in her emerald green eyes but bitterness and resentment. Even still, she was a site to behold, dressed in red Old Sumeria leathers that were form fitting and which set well against the fiery red hair that flowed from the top of her head and crested around her shoulders.

"What was that?" she barked, halfway demanding an answer.

"A lesson in manners," Kador answered, snatching up the end of the whip as if he had true talent with the weapon. A talent of which I was completely unaware.

"Get up, Jassa!" Kendra called to her as she moved to lend a hand to that task. The hand was received and the young girl stood and looked at Kador.

"You're going to pay for that!" she vowed.

"Do you take large bills?" Kadorgyan inquired. The young girl struggled to withhold a smile.

"Sorry about that, Harry," Kador said, turning to face Arvius. "You ready to die now?"

"Thou art delusional!" Arvius growled.

"I'm the Unlawful Son, Harry," Kador admitted, "According to our lore I shouldn't be able to walk in a straight line. Just who's delusional around here?" Kador gave Arvius a wink and a kiss.

My grip on my Staffling grew tighter. I could not understand the gesture and I am not sure Kador could either, logically. But he believed he knew what the reaction would be to his stimulus. Arvius was at first confused, having never received such gestures from another man. But the message Kadorgyan sent touched Arvius in a place where reason does not often reach. Rage swept over him and he threw his fist in the air, giving the order to charge.

The wall buckled and the one after it was not any stronger than the first, but it managed to hold, the lion share of the momentum was taken in the impact with the outer wall. Again Cho got up quickly only to receive another blast to his chest. This time the wall did not prevent him and he flew through it. Thidalia strode into the shambled office and looked at the path her opponent's body must have taken. She was glad to have received the respite as she could feel herself beginning to tire out. A simple gesture and she summoned King's Battle Staff and used its reserves to create a shield around herself. It had just formed when Cho came back through the wall, hammering relentlessly at her. By the fourth strike, she could see her protective spell beginning to crack. The fifth blow sent her back outside where the clouds had at last formed around the airport. It was bad enough that everyone at the airport would need to be killed to maintain the Great Façade, but Thidalia did not want to risk having to kill any more than that in order to resolve this incident. She sat up and fired a beam of pure energy through the Battle Staff which caught Cho on the leg and he missed his leap's destination by ten feet. Another blast caught him in the chest; he was only two feet away after making one step. The blast threw him forty meters and his jacket and shirt were both burned from around him. Again he got up quickly and this time a wide black beam struck him in the chest and had no effect.

"*What?!*" Thidalia thought as the Japanese man started to run toward her. "*How could he have lived through that? Unless... he was not alive to begin with!*" Thidalia screamed as her hands uttered streaks of sparkling lights into Cho's chest. He was running toward her when they hit and walking when she finally released her hold on the spell and fell to her knees. Five feet from her Cho fell forward, his chest, mangled by the spell and his back covered in exposed wire and hydraulic gels.

"Don't you just hate it," Satashi said as she limped up toward the smoldering heap. "They say they're sending you in with a Bondsman and they actually set you up with an android!"

"It was the only way we could ensure a control of the situation, Satashi." Both women knew the voice and were equally surprised to hear it. They turned around and both of them blinked as they watched him approach.

"Augustus?" Satashi whispered.

"Caprice?" Thidalia inquired.

"Dr. Augustus Donovan Caprice to be correct," Augustus replied with a smile. "I cannot say how much of a disappointment you both have been! But, you can't make an omelet without breaking a few eggs!"

"What are you doing here?" Thidalia asked as she reached over for Satashi and moved the young girl to stand behind her; a gesture that surprised Satashi and nearly floored Augustus.

"Well," he replied, looking around. "First of all we need to define here. You see, with all of you coming into the name region, you could not be trusted to keep things... oh how do they say it here, Satashi? *On the down low.* So I had to do some quick thinking."

"This is a simulation?!" Thidalia started to look around. With her hand still behind her, she managed to take off her sapphire ring and offer it to Satashi. The young girl quickly took it.

"Oh very good, Thidalia!" Augustus replied, giving applause. "It is, but you can be sure we're not in a warehouse in Europe."

"Antarctica!" Satashi yelled in realization.

"I can see someone has been studying! Yes, it is the only earthbound facility where we have the power reserves necessary to handle these levels of demands."

"Earthbound?" Thidalia repeated. "You're not human?"

"Idiot Arcanian, we're all human! I am just not a Tyro. Satashi and I are members of a tribe called the Genii, a tribe that knows all about the Arcanians and their aims and while you have been tending to the Great Façade, we've been assisting you to make sure you don't make a mess of things. Dare I go further down the line of obvious conclusions?" he paused, smiled condescendingly and then continued. "Of course, without the Arcanians, we would not have found the Elementals as they were finding the Prodigian. It sort of makes me wonder who might be watching us, hmmmm. Amazing, isn't it, the need each tribe has to try and control the other?"

"And what do the Genii think they can control?"

"Well, with the right application of a switch, quite a bit." Augustus answered, losing his smile. You see, it was one thing to teleport a section of the airport, but to move all of the underground levels would have taken an amount of power we could not have masked sufficiently. As you have witnessed during your brief engagement with the augmented Tyros calling themselves MVPs, Tyros can be inventive, though they do not yet possess the intelligence to advance their mentality along with their technology. Kill ten men with a sword yesterday, kill a hundred with a machine gun today, kill whole races with gas tomorrow; oh, how exciting. The Genii always weigh the impact of their technological advances before introducing them. But I digress!"

"You often did," Thidalia said as her eyes began to glow.

"Oh my!" Augustus gasped before he was blasted with flame that shot from Thidalia's mouth. The breath was long and taxing and Thidalia staggered after she expended nearly the full remains of her power. The ground was nearly all glass where Augustus had been standing, the combination of magical energy and extreme heat had cut through the concrete like a compressed water hose pushing through tissue paper.

"I wish you had told me you were going to do that," Satashi said, looking to Thidalia's left. "I could have told you what you were talking to was just a holographic image."

"That was very impressive!" Augustus said as the view of the airport faded, replaced with the gigantic structure they were standing in side of. Augustus looked over at the place that had received Thidalia's Dragon Breath spell and shook his head as he motioned his fifteen androids into place. "Tremendous power, but as always, applied with Arcanian incompetence!

"As I was saying before you interrupted, I could only move the surface of the airport. I did so just before William's friends reached the grounds, which was fairly close to the time when your SomeVinco goons were about to proceed underground, chasing after William. Though it would have been interesting to see him deal with them, only Knight and Pawn made it down before the transference. It should prove interesting to see how they will act without you.

"But I now need to remove you and then send back the three Elementals I have in stasis."

"You are powerful," Thidalia said, letting her head sink.

"No, you can't kill her!" Satashi said, coming out from behind the suddenly maternal Arcanian.

"Very good, Observations Technician Number Twenty-Five, Satashi Sayuri Soroku!" As he spoke, Satashi's face lost its emotion. "Now, Number Twenty-Five, did that nasty little Arcanian give you anything?" Satashi immediately held up the ring and Thidalia's eyes flared in surprise and anger. "Like I said, we consider the applications of technology. Toss it here, Number Twenty-five."

"I heard what you had to say, Caprice," Thidalia replied, realizing her fate was inescapable. But it was not the failure of her position that loomed regret over her hindsight. She had held to the Façade and held her place well. It was the path she had taken in holding it she wished she could take back. The Tyros had a saying... something about backing the wrong horse.

"I have seen the worst of my kind in looking upon yours," Thidalia said. "The Façade is not our right and in our fear of the Prodigian, we have tried to manipulate them and they are now on the brink of a civil war."

"Indeed!"

"And even if William is able to stop that, he will only be killed by you or some other operative of some other tribe."

"We all play our parts. You are released, Number Twenty-five." Satashi blinked and looked around, realizing she had lost moments. She looked up at Thidalia who gave her an understanding smile.

"I take it now that I am spent, he is not using images," she said softly and Satashi nodded. "You know, it could have been Yudara screaming for help and I think he still would have acted."

"I agree," Satashi replied, fighting back tears. She moved toward Thidalia and threw her arms around her. Thidalia closed her eyes and let the tears fall freely as she wrapped her arms around the young girl she would not have time to know.

Augustus, who had no stomach for such things, put his attention to his arm top controls. He sent back the three Elementals and left them in a stasis that would fade in five minutes time. "Well, that is that. All I have is you two and I can let the rest of this all play out. Given that most of operatives for the Descriers are here, they will die with you and that should give William enough of an advantage to live through this scenario. I will give you two one last moment."

"I have one spell left to me," Thidalia whispered.

"It won't work!" Satashi cried. "He's thought of everything!"

"It will work!" Thidalia assured. "You just have to know how to use it. It is time to stop watching and start doing, my young friend! It is your time. Let the one you have been watching be your guide. But that will only work if you guide him as well."

"Before I am retired," Thidalia said, facing Caprice. "Tell me, was it all an act?"

"If you mean my adoration of you, the answer is no. But you would be surprised what we have been able to create to control that impulse."

"Sounds inhuman," Thidalia said as her body started to glow. "It is a shame that while you were watching, you missed something to see worth seeing. I know only two men who have been able to resist my enchantments and I am glad I had the opportunity to meet them."

"A shame it will not be a prolonged acquaintance," Augustus said harshly. He held up his hand to ready the androids. Satashi and Thidalia could hear generators in their bodies charging up.

"Fly, my little friend," Thidalia said as she made a gesture over Satashi's body. "I am so glad you are true to your passions. Remember, be swift!"

Glowing wings of fire formed on Satashi's back and she was aloft before she knew what was happening.

"That was some last spell, Thidalia," Augustus said as his hand fell forward.

"Return!" Thidalia shouted and thunder boomed throughout the facility. The androids fired their energy bolts into her body and without her shields, she fell prey to their tremendous power. There was no time to scream... perhaps there was no time to feel pain.

The thunder now announced lightning as bolts descended down through the roof and all around Augustus. The androids activated their jets and started to ascend after Satashi.

"Wait!" Augustus commanded as a bolt came so close that part of its energy arched and struck him. It tore though the fabric of his slacks and just as quickly through the flesh of his left leg. He screamed as he fell to the ground, unable to move or speak, his scream was his only sign of life.

"*Be swift!*" Satashi thought as she looked down on his writhing form. She did not see his body so much as she saw his computer, the one that had access to this facility and the androids. "*Time to do!*" Wiping away tears, Satashi went into a steep dive, weaving between the floating androids. They were still but it would not be long before their logic programs would deduce their commander was unable to command them. They would then fire at will and destroy anyone coming to this place. A place that had to be making a heat bloom that showed up on just about every satellite pointed in the direction of the continent.

"*Let's see if we can improvise,*" she thought as she rolled and looked back at the androids, commanding her wings to hurl feathers of living flame at the androids. Six such feathers were hurled and each of them struck an android and tore through their chassis, causing them to explode. Six exploded causing three more to explode in a chain reaction. The three furthest from her flew out of the blast radius in time to preserve themselves, but they had to ascend to do so. Satashi rolled back over and continued her trek for Augustus, only now she had to dodge numerous bolts of lightning that seemed to be attracted to metals. Satashi threw her computer aside, hoping to draw the fire of the storm. Eight bolts tore into the device before it hit the ground and Satashi wove her way through the raining power display, flying by Augustus and grabbing for his computer. It came free of his arm as two bolts hit him. An energy bolt just missed Satashi's head, letting her know that the androids had resumed their chase. To make matters worse, the fire on her wings was beginning to give out! Already close to the ground, she decided not to climb and put her attentions to the computer. Its access was still open and the commands were easily entered. A flash of light was the last thing Satashi saw.

Fifty-Four

"Did you see that?" Marianne asked as they ran toward the hangar.

"You mean the big flash of light that made each and every swinging dick in sight just up and disappear?" Jack asked. "Nope, missed it! Just keep running."

They made their way to the hangar where the plane was still parked in front, a hole in its port side.

"Okay, so this really did happen," Caleb said, looking at the plane.

"Yeah and so did they," Terrell said as he looked into the hangar and saw the path leading down. Coming up it was one of the six that had attacked the Dugout. Lambda had only caught a glimpse of them then but he had seen the footage Sigma and Beta had taken. The one that approached was the smallest male of the group, only six feet tall! He also seemed to be the best at their hand-to-hand techniques. "You guys stay clear of this," Lambda commanded. "Delta, you're with me!"

"You got it!"

"Kind of overbearing, aren't they?" Caleb asked.

"Not if that guy is anything like what JB and Lydia took on," Jack replied and Caleb winced in pain.

"Maybe I should hang back and see to their wounds," he suggested.

"Sounds like a plan, Doc," Peter said as he ran up to the hangar. "I'll hang back with him, Jack. You get down there and take care of our girl!" Jack nodded and he and Marianne moved to the far right side. Jack kept Marianne close and they moved slowly, never taking their eyes off of Knight as he walked forward. He looked over at them but his attention was on the two MVPs.

"We have unfinished business," Knight said before looking at Jack. "I'll be down for you in a minute." Jack gave a left-handed salute and ran for the stairs.

"Hey Doc, I think we should find some cover," Peter said softly.

"Why?"

"Because all three of these guys are packing guns and I'm not sure we want to see how accurate they are."

"Too late, Webster!" Knight said quickly drawing his pistol and firing. Webster fell to the ground. Caleb quickly moved his friend to cover and started to examine him.

Lambda and Delta Scouts drew their guns and started firing. Knight was fast enough to dodge their first shots as he jumped to his left side then went horizontal as he spun on air and fired again, killing Delta Scout. Lambda led his target with his shot and when he fired, he smiled at the gun that flew out of Knight's hand. Knight, however, landed and changed direction causing Lambda's next shots to miss. He jumped back, crossing both arms in front of his face and Lambda Scout emptied his clips into Knight's chest. The man did not land on his feet and slid to a stop.

"Dammit!" Terrell yelled as he ran over to Conway. It was a perfect headshot and Delta Scout was long dead. "It was an honor, baby!" Terrell took Conway's gun and fired under his arm, shooting Knight in the knee. The young man was staggered and Lambda quickly shot him in the other knee.

"How is he, Doc?" Lambda yelled.

"He got caught in the chest, just over the armor!" Caleb yelled.

"Figured," Terrell whispered shooting Knight in the elbows. Knight actually cried out in pain at those two shots.

"I figure you have to eventually give out," he said softly. "But there's one thing you didn't know about my boy Conway, I might pack two guns..." Terrell ripped Conway's uniform open, revealing eight spare clips. "... Conway was a cowboy at heart! And I haven't even moved to his grenades!

"You want to live to see another day, you'll heal the man you shot and then, *maybe* then I'll let you live! And if you can't heal other bodies, well, it's been good fuckin' you up!"

"I can heal him!" Knight yelled. "But not if you keep shooting me!"

"Awww, you're breakin' my heart!" Lambda said as he grabbed Knight by his wounded arm and began dragging him.

["*HOLD*!"] William projected and allowed his power to resonate in all directions and the signaled charge was halted. "I know your names!" he said, trying to recall where he knew them from.

"You lie!" Arvius argued. "He tried to trick us!"

"How interesting you would ever accuse someone else of that, Arvius. In truth, Kador does not know your names. But Palshaya did!"

"That's it!" Kador realized. "You are all runners!" he blinked his eyes as more of the memory came to his conscious mind. "Runners that Palshaya reported as dead?!"

"How does he know this?" Leone snapped. If anyone was going to lose trust of a Light-Child first, it was going to be a Man-Lord. "He was here already on Old Sumeria and without his powers!

[*Hello, my friends,*] Palshaya projected and I stepped away from Kador, shocked to receive that projection. His eyes were closed but it was clear that the sensation was pleasing to him. It was a conscious mind that sent the thoughts to us all and even Arvius could not argue the actuality of its origin. With the feeling of her thoughts came an image that moved with Kador's power to take us all into a special place. We stood in the midst of a valley that felt like Palshaya. My surprise was overwhelmed by the beauty of the serene scene. A fawn approached and nuzzled me. I shuddered, feeling Palshaya's touch. In the gentle animal's eyes, I saw myself, all of myself, and I knew why William wanted to speak with me should we both see the end of this endeavor. I could see how my thoughts were forming and knew that they had always been that way, but something about being in the presence of the son of my mentor had altered my perspective.

[*What we hath found is an ugly impasse and I wotteth not how to instruct thee on where thy strides shouldst take thee. But know this: I am with this boy who emerges with every breath into manhood. I ask not that thou take up arms with him, yet I also bid thee not to stand in his way. I hunted each of thee and through the instruction of the man I thought I loved, I set thee all free. I hath never set before any of thee a boon of any kind... not until now. Thou dost not need to join Kador, Blood of Xargagyan. But serve neither to hinder his passage.*]

The Man-Lord now called Leone was the first to act, putting away his weapons. The others were quick to follow and step away, giving William plenty of room to contend with Arvius. His eyes opened and he looked upon the traitor.

"This is not the ending you had in mind, is it?" William asked. "I know, it's kind of anti-climatic. But the story doesn't end here, you do! I thought I needed to know what you did to draw such anger out of a man who is *normally* pretty cool. But I have seen how you used Tara, Palshaya, all of these people here and God knows who else. I don't need to know, not from you. Your story is no longer that interesting. You're a scar on the face of the world that I love and for some reason I have been called to remove that mark. Up until a few moments ago, I hated that about my life. Right now, I'm just really feeling like Palshaya died defending you and that is something I cannot let you live with!

"So, do you have any last words?"

She walked down the pathway, looking for her target... the one called William Ferrous. Her strides were even but she did not walk with the usual hardness of her steps. The world of the Tyros had proven to be quite challenging and now her Mistress battled something that had managed to dispatch King and Queen with relative ease. It was a mistake of strategy to have all of her SomeVinco to go after the young Prodigian, but it was not her place to argue.

"*Tyros!*" she thought, disgusted with the existence of them. "*Their need for stealth and they do not even understand the concept.*" Pawn moved her body ahead and then changed direction, dashing into the darkness of the corner of the wall.

She did not fire; she did not have a shot. If nothing else, her experience had taught her that much. No sense shooting at wind when the wind was not the trouble, she could recall Peter once telling her at one of his gun ranges. The primary emphasis of Peter's was teaching when to shoot first. Once that was mastered, he saw to how to shoot. Tara cursed all the offers to spend extra time on the range she had turned down, and blessed Lydia for making the classes mandatory. Tara moved out from her place of cover, a few stacked crates. She did not want them being used against her since she still did not know what she was up against. As she cleared the crates, she heard the clamor of wood breaking. She rolled over the crate and looked back, seeing a black woman pull her arm out of the crate that had been her cover a heartbeat ago.

"*Damn she's fast!*" Tara thought as she continued to roll. Her body fell off the side to avoid being struck by the crate thrown by Pawn. "*Jesus she's strong!*"

Pawn came up and over the crate and Tara was still on her back; her wound was still slowing her down. Tara lifted her legs and used them as a brace, keeping the woman's hand from her face. But it was only a temporary resolution as Pawn pressed down and forced Tara's legs to fold. Tara screamed, trying to find the strength to push the woman off, but it was not going to happen.

"Say cheese, bitch!" Tara said, lifting her gun and firing into Pawn's face. The woman jerked back and Tara continued to fire her weapon, hitting center mass with every shot until the slide locked in the back position. Tara was effectively one-handed and hit the switch to eject the clip. She placed her gun between her legs and reached to the sleeve on the body armor for another magazine. Pawn's body began to jerk as bullets started to fall on to the ground.

"*Move, Mifflen, move!*" she thought as she took out the magazine, only to realize that the body armor was not hers and the ammunition did not fit her pistol.

"Problems?" Pawn asked as her head came up, her eyes locked on Tara's. She kicked up to her feet and charged, and Tara lifted her feet again. Pawn stopped just shy of them and grabbed Tara's ankles and spread Tara's legs. "Did you really think this was going to work twice?" Pawn punched into Tara's stomach and even through the body armor it was a telling blow. Pawn lifted Tara up to her face and sneered. "You might consider yourself courageous. You sicken me!"

"You should trade places with me," Tara winced. "They make breath mints where you come from?"

Pawn punched for Tara's face and screamed as she drew her hand back and found a knife lodged up to the hilt between her second and third knuckles. Tara fell to the floor and rolled, sweeping Pawn's feet. She screamed as she rolled over her wounded arm, but the movement was crisp and clean and Pawn's back smacked hard to the ground.

"*No one's going to save me,*" Tara thought, "*Jon made that pretty clear. So I gotta pull my own fat out of the fire!*" Tara rolled once more and though it hurt to put any pressure on the wound, this time she did not scream.

"*Damn, she's up already!*" Tara thought just before she felt a hand on her leg. She looked down to see Pawn, still with knife in her hand, but her other hand held her ankle and she started to squeeze. Tara screamed as pain shot through her body.

"I will kill you slow, Tyro!" Pawn gargled, straining to maintain her strength. She was near her threshold of maximum pain absorption, but she was not about to run from another Tyro. The woman's kick to her face was negligible and Pawn continued to exert more pressure through her grip. Tara screamed Jon's name but she knew he was not going to come. Still, calling his name helped as she could hear his voice, telling her what to do as he had before.

"*Right, the other gun!*" she thought as reached to the small of her back. The moment it cleared where she had it tucked, Pawn's eyes widened and her grip softened. Tara fired and suddenly her arm fell limp.

"Well, well, well, your bug ass has the same nerve endings as us Tyros," Tara shuddered to say. She knew she would soon collapse and the trigger was going to be impossible to pull. But the gun kicked once more and she shot the woman directly between the eyes and she fell dead. Tara looked over to her left and she saw them, the *Wayfarers*.

"Kicking and screaming, you sons of bitches!" Tara whispered as she dropped the gun. The Wayfarers approached and the closer they came, the more they did not appear to be wraiths, but soft, gentle faces who had only hope and love in their eyes.

"Jon was right about this one," one of them declared. Voices were raised in agreement and they nodded and smiled at Tara. She could see four of them turn toward Pawn and as they turned, Tara jumped. Their forms changed and they were suddenly had long claws and fangs and they tore into Pawn's body. Pawn screamed as they removed her ethereal image out of her body. She struggled but she had no power now, she was just a ghost-like form.

"I bet her breath still stinks," Tara said as she let her head rest against the cold concrete. "But I'm full of shit if I think I'm not about to join her."

"You cannot!" a voice argued as a young Latin boy came through the crowd. He kneeled beside Tara and placed his hand on her gunshot wound. Tara jumped as the pain ran through her body.

But the pain did not last long as a cool sensation soon took over after it and Tara looked up at the child. He smiled at her and then looked up at the others. Five others also smiled and kneeled around Tara, laying their hands on her battered body. Suddenly a glow shone about her and Tara cried as life ran through her body. She could feel their touch and she knew what they were doing. They would be *Wayfarers* no longer, but Eidolons, and it was time for them to pass into the light and on to the next journey.

"Oh my God!" she gasped as she reached up and took hold of the boy's arm. "I'll tell her," she whispered, knowing that he had not been able to find her in all of his travels. Nothing had looked like home to him and he simply traveled with the others so he would not be alone. He wanted so desperately to tell his older sister that it was not her fault, but he had failed to find her and he had chosen to give his power to sustain Tara's life. "I'll tell her, little *Hermano*!" Tara collapsed as the light became too much for her conscious mind to fathom.

"I do not fear thee!" Arvius declared.

"It isn't about fear," William responded as he started walking toward the Light-Child that was anything but. "It is about those things we can avoid and the things we cannot evade. You've lived much longer than you should have."

A roaring sound filled the corridor and I felt as though I was back on the roof of Rachel Pryor's house. My mind pounded inside my head as I fell to the ground. The last sight I could draw focus on was Arvius just standing there, unaffected by the sonic pulse.

Eventually the sound died down and Arvius turned to see Bill walking up the corridor with his prisoners and the last of his men. The smile he flashed to the Descrier was nearly as bright as a newborn star. Arvius cackled with delight as he summoned his Blade.

"No, Arvius!" Bill shouted. "I know who you have in mind for that and it will not happen!"

"My Bill, you *have* found your manhood!" Arvius said, his smile declining slightly. "Kaplin?"

Bill's face did not change though his body did shudder. He looked down and he saw a long slender blade sticking out of his chest. A stiletto, Kaplin's kill weapon of choice. Bill looked back at Vada-Ri and he tried to apologize without using words. The sentiment he felt for her was not returned, but she was not going to let him die thinking that as she mouthed 'I love you' before he fell.

Cole's men were floored by a powerful telekinetic push. They burst into flames before they could stop rolling and Arvius began to cackle again as he turned to face his next prey. A stiff punch floored him and William turned his talents to suppressing the flames. None of the men had perished in the flames, but they needed immediate medical attention. William turned to face Kaplin and he looked at his dagger. Kaplin took a combative stance and William's ears lifted. He went into a shoulder roll and could hear a Blade just miss his head. He rolled, he could hear Arvius pressing. His footfalls were close but there was little balance to them. Kaplin's steps showed he was moving away from the fight so William focused primarily on Arvius.

"Going for the thrust," William said as he started to get to his feet but rolled to his right. He saw the Blade and it was closer than he wanted it to be. Placing his hand on the ground, William exerted the power of his body and he went up and over Arvius. The move was completely unexpected and Arvius' reaction was too slow for his Blade to taste flesh. He turned around with a fierce swing but it met with a Blade and with a slight push, Arvius was off balance. William's second swing struck the sword away from Arvius' body. It was a classic maneuver, one that Arvius' late wife had always warned him might claim his life should he ever fight one who knew what they were doing with the Blade.

"No!" Arvius screamed as William remained in motion, spinning and thrusting his Blade into his chest. William looked up at Arvius and he brought up the image of Palshaya's face over his own.

"Told ya!" he said in her voice as he pulled the weapon free and spun around, removing the head of the traitor! He had just finished his dismissal fanfare when he heard it, a very fast and powerful approach. He put up his sword and went into a spinning move. He deflected Vastiol's attack but was still knocked to the floor. William rolled across the floor and tumbled up to a stance. Vastiol walked toward him but his strides were labored and William could see his head was covered with a strange apparatus. He then looked back to see Kaplin wearing a wired helmet and he glared at William. His desperation to see William dead could be seen without applying talent.

"You got him, Dex?" William said, readying himself for another defensive stand.

"I got him!" Dexter answered. Kaplin looked over to see Dexter lying across the large Light-Child who had been laid low by the sonic pulse. He had his submachine gun trained on Kaplin. "You were right about the whole playing possum plan. We need to work that into the playbook!"

"I hear you, brother," William replied, looking at Vastiol who was no longer moving. He merely stood there and William could see the anger in his eyes. He smacked himself in the forehead and extended his hand toward the Absularian, shocking him. His body convulsed as the devices on his head shorted out. William ceased the flow of power and as expected, Vastiol recovered quickly. He nodded at William and then turned to find Kaplin, the man who had dared to turn him into a puppet.

"I think he's being handled," William said as he looked over at Jassa, surprised that she had not been affected by the pulse. But riddles would have to wait. He looked at the bindings of Chidon, Vada-Ri and Igrileena and waved his hand across the three of them. Bindings unlocked and wires were removed.

"Now that is some cool looking shit!" Dexter said as he got up. "How are you feeling?"

"Real bad headache," William admitted as he returned the Blade to my War Locke. Jassa jumped as she felt the Locke jump in her pocket. "You'll find him easier to deal with if he wakes up and that is back on his person," he suggested. William turned to find himself assailed by Igrileena as she took hold of his head and kissed him deeply!

"If thou wilt but forgive-" William put his finger over her lips.

"Let's all start over!" he said softly. "May I have the honor of your training?"

"What little thou needs is thine!" she smiled.

"Father!" Vada-Ri said as she ran over to my body. It was a moment I shall not soon forget to awaken to see her face smiling down on me. I touched her face and smiled.

"I thought-"

"I am alright," she cried as she embraced me. "You came for me!"

"What little good I did," I replied.

"Oh, boo-hockey!" William snapped. "Don't believe a word of it, Vada. Your father put down some moves these Tyros are not soon to forget." William looked at Kaplin, being dragged back to the group by Vastiol.

"Do you have need of this one?" Vastiol asked as he bowed. Absularians did not bow often outside a Royal presence!

"Thanks for asking," William smiled, grabbing Kaplin's face. He tore into the man's mind and then released him, leaving Kaplin shaking in Vastiol's grasp. "Not any more," he said and returned Vastiol's bow. "I know the way out now. We just have to get everyone together and make tracks."

Like obedient little soldiers we followed his commands, collecting everyone, even the dead we fought and those that had been with us when this day began. The man called Conway and the old Light-Child, Yalquim, who did not survive the torment of the sonic pulse, were celebrated as they were ushered into the graces of the *Wayfarers* as the sun finally set on what had been too long a day. Our camp site was nearly overrun in sheer numbers but for a moment, we shared drink and we shared victory. It was a sentiment that was washed away when William tried to contact his mother and found no mind to give him response.

Dexter, Terrell, William, Jack and myself rushed to the residence. The others remained to watch over those that were still weak or unconscious. I brought us to the home cautiously but William would have none of that as he ran to the front door. No one tried to call him back, but Dexter and Jack did their best to keep stride with him as he ran up the stairs. I scanned the house and Terrell thought he was best served guarding me should I be assaulted during my search. Admittedly, I was touched by the sentiment and as I scanned the house, I saw what Lambda Scout was capable of and found the gesture even more moving!

There was only one mind still inside the house though, I could detect the traces of many and most of them had to have been Prodigian, given how little ambient thought remained. Only a well trained mind passes without leaving some trail of ambient thought, at least that is what I told William for that is what I used to believe. If I had known then what I know so well now…

He found Gordon unconscious in his parents' bed chamber, and he could tell that at one time his mother had been laid beside Gordon. She was equally unconscious, equally wounded and bleeding slightly. He pressed his face in the sheets and he picked up a scent… two, no *three* scents of people that did not belong in the house. Then, a fourth scent. One that was not of a person so much as it was of an incidence.

"*What is that?*" he thought. "*Ozone? I'm not sure, but it's on both of them! Both of them… there's just too many damn questions!*"

Applying his talent to Gordon's mind, William brought him out of unconsciousness and threw so many questions at the man that Jack moved up and took hold of William's shoulders. William was stronger than Jack Moreland and both of them knew it. But there was something to be said for the large man's overwhelmingly gentle and yet substantial touch, and William was calmed enough to hear Gordon tell of the attack and how bravely his mother had fought; the bits of rock in the bedroom were evidence of that. William picked up the rock and took in its scent… it was his mother's and he quickly dropped it on the floor. But he did not fall into tears. No, not the son of Zargogyan! He closed his eyes for a moment and focused. His nostrils flared wide and he started to look around the room. He was not three minutes into his search when he found it, a small vial left open on his mother's nightstand. Ripping the pillowcase, William collected the bottle and brought it to his nose.

"Flaryn Oil," he said. "Trackers use this when they don't want to be tracked." I quickly set aside the question of how he had come into so much knowledge of the technique of Prodigian trackers. "This is both a calling card and a stop. We know it was a tracker but we don't know which one. Not yet.

"He covered his tracks on the Prodigian level, but I doubt he wore gloves."

"Uh, not to sound like an ass," Jack offered carefully, "but it's not like the guy has an address around here, does he?"

"We'll need to eliminate that possibility, but I believe you are right. Still, it is a means of identification."

"We all could use some food and rest," William said as he paced and thought. It was like looking into yesterday and I could feel his mind considering so many things at once, just as his father often did. "We will have to wait. There's no way around it! I need to get my training truly going and finish it before I try to go to the Territories or else I'll just be a liability that will slow us up.

"Jack, I need for you to do me a favor, if you would,"

"You just name it," Jack assured.

"Go back to the party and make sure it gets going again. We need to relax." Jack started to say something but William cut him off. "I know I don't have to tell you how people in tight groups get on edge. It starts off as a conversation and then it all seems to spiral out of control."

"Well, not anymore anyway," Moreland replied.

"Thanks," he smiled. "I would join you, but I am dead tired and this headache just won't quit."

"Mind if we bunk up, man?" Dexter asked. "Id rather not explain this one to the folks right now."

"Mi casa es su casa," William replied. "Just make sure you call them before you call it quits. Don't have those people freakin' out trying to find where their soon-to-be college superstar has gone off to. Goodnight everyone!"

And with that he turned and walked for the door out, stopping long enough to give Gordon a hug and whisper into his ear that everything was going to work out. He and Dexter went to his room and closed the door.

Gordon got up from the bed and looked at the latest additions to the house before he took his leave. He was bound for the bar and I was bound to follow him. Interestingly enough, without any of us saying a word, Gordon, Terrell, Jack and I enjoyed several rounds of very stiff alcohol, made more potent by my talent, before we too felt the need to retire. Terrell remained at the house while Jack and I returned to the others. Jack kept his word, conveying William's wishes and his concerns, knowing what affect that would have. The celebration was indeed over and they all needed rest. Most returned to their own places knowing our paths would cross again – which would indeed be welcomed, but it would also be too soon! For those that had no place of their own, I insisted that they remain with us. William was already of the mind he would need to have words with me, allowing the others to stray would have only added to his justified onslaught. So room was made at the encampment and I made every effort to make them feel at home in his name. To my surprise, and utter delight, my daughter was more than slightly helpful in that endeavor and though they were confused and possibly even frightened, they chose to stay. This left only the nearly insurmountable task of persuading the weary Chidon that perhaps I should take the watch this evening. Not surprising, Vastiol was able to assist in both the delivery of argument and the facilitation of being Chidon's replacement as we embraced a gentle night.

"Did you see how he moved, Head Master?" Vastiol asked, believing everyone was asleep. But I could feel two minds hanging on our every word. Jassa and Igrileena; though the former puzzled me, the latter was busy arranging her dedication of loyalty to her benefactor. Gazing up at the stars, I could find little argument in her choice, and I would not withhold her from the act.

"Alas, I did not," I answered. "I was too busy succumbing to that damnable sound. How he withstood it I do not know."

"I could hear it, Head Master," Vastiol advised. "I could hear a second sound and it came from him! The air seemed to vibrate around him as he stood there, defiant. I knew when he fell that it was a ruse."

"No doubt a feeling confirmed when the Tyro- when Dexter also fell," I added.

"Confirmed indeed! It was an excellent plan!

"But it was the way he moved with your Blade that I remember most," Vastiol continued, sounding as if he were a child taken to see the spectacle for the first time. "He dispatched Arvius with such ease! Even when I was made to attack him, only the surprise of my actions and the power of my attack made him give ground. In my controlled state I would not have survived a reprisal from him."

"Then we shall both be glad he did not move against you," I replied. "It is a restraint he will not show the captor of his mother. And for the life of me I must admit to one thing… for the sake of that life, the life of the one responsible, I pray when we find Adrianna that she is unharmed. For between that child's skill and my wrath, even Hell will fail to be a sanctuary!"

"Then she is well," Vastiol concluded. "And from what I have gathered from her… she is also well bound!" His comment was given in such a tone that I could not keep from laughing which led only to the exchange of memories of the woman we were missing.

"It was a good plan," Igrileena whispered as she joined Vada-Ri in her tent. "The speed of our saviors was too great for thee to enact it but I am sure it would have worked and worked well!"

"Then we shall keep it secret," Vada-Ri answered. "These Descriers know much, but they do not know all, and in that we have power at least to protect ourselves." Igrileena smiled and patted my daughter on the shoulder as she was about to take her leave.

"Did..." she started, causing Leena to stop. "...did you enjoy the kiss?"

Leena looked down on Vada-Ri and realized there had not been any previous of such encounters for the young Councilwoman. She would keep her personal judgments to herself which included her belief that William kissed much better.

"The man had passion if he had nothing else," she answered. "You gave him a kindness in his passing. His heart, at least, deserved that much." She left the tent and Vada to her own musings.

Fifty-Five

Wolf Lord had been sorely underestimated. Not only was it apparent that he had survived Elior's plans, but he had achieved a means wherein he could slaughter members of the Royal Elite Guard and actually be paid for it. When the messengers came with word of what had happened at the Council Hall, Elior knew he had judged Wolf Lord too poorly as he had praised D'Hano too highly. Mevkrean had, even in death, proven himself right. He had always purported that he appreciated the passions of the soldier, but did not much like the way he went about fulfilling them. Such short-sightedness would never serve the Throne, or anything else, too well or too long.

When he arrived at the Hall, only to see D'Hano and his four men, displayed like beasts of the hunt, King Elior ordered them cut down. That was when the receipt for services rendered was found. It named D'Hano and his four finest Blades as facilitators of runners, per the Throne's suspicions, and as such runners themselves. Wolf Lord expected to be paid according to the measure of the individual, as was the common pricing. King Elior found himself caught within another forced agreement. He could not afford not to disallow what the note more than implied. He was fortunate that Mevkrean's dislike and distrust of the Guardsman was known fairly well throughout the Council. It made his explanation simpler to deliver and have received without question or suspicion. If anything, the King was praised for his prudence and his vision. They cheered his name and formed a reception line.

"And thus begins the parade of the pressed hand," Ezra said from his perch. "It makes one wonder just who is King, does it not?" Olliento patted his charge on the shoulder. Given what the young Prince had said, Olliento wondered why his beloved Captain had chosen him to protect him. Of the two, Ezra was the more resourceful and the more wise. Olliento felt like so much wasted material as he watched the young Prince turn and face him.

"All my life I have learned of things my father would have rather forgotten or denied of me. Wilt thou teach me of the one man who hath been more a father to me than mine own? Wilt thou teach me of Mevkrean? I know how he died but I wish to know how he lived." Olliento pondered no more!

"The lesson is both long and arduous," he said as he started to walk away from the ledge, leaving Abiron and Insra who still observed the events below. "But there be reward beyond measure to the careful eye and open mind that doth take the lesson in."

"Then I shall endeavor to possess both," Ezra replied, mounting his winged steed. "I trust that is why the Captain left one of his wisest with me."

"Trust the Captain," Olliento said, mounting up behind the Prince. He did not know if he would ever be comfortable within the Prince's menagerie, but he found balance in the Prince's comfort. "If nothing else is learned of him, take that he was as constant as the wind!"

"Nay, my lord," the Prince argued as his mount took flight. "The wind dies! Wilt not our memory keep Mevkrean alive?"

"The wind does not die, your majesty," Olliento smiled. It seemed that his greatest toiling would be in keeping the young Ezra still while matters with his brother unfolded. "It simply moves on to be felt elsewhere. But worry not, it always returns in one form or another."

Hagar whinnied as she climbed higher in the air. Abiron smiled, knowing his younger brother was having fun with Olliento, who did not appreciate heights.

"They are quite a fit for each other," Abiron said.

"Indeed they are, my Prince," Insra agreed.

"Is this still then all according to his plan?"

"My Captain did not take me into his greatest confidence, your majesty," Insra replied. "But I wouldst think so."

"That is an untruth, Lieutenant," Abiron said, his eyes still upon his brother. I can see why my brother prefers the company of his friends."

"A mother would lie just as well to protect her child, my Prince."

"And just where dost thy protection lie?"

"Perhaps I am protecting my Prince!" Insra said, facing the young man. She kept her true face away from the surface for there were few remaining who could understand it. And it would have been challenging to separate her awe of her Captain and all that he predicted would happen and the wonder of being told to watch for the moment that was happening at that very moment, right in front of her.

"Ezra will go peacefully," Mevkrean had counseled them both. "Such is his nature and only the one he trusts shall ever see his thoughts or beliefs. But Abiron, upon my most dire hope, will either fly or fold.. and I pray for the former. Shouldst he fly, he shall struggle with the truth of things and as he questions old truths, so shall he mistrust new ones. Be vigilant unto this cause, my Lieutenant, for though we have a second by Fate, we cannot discard the first. Soon Elior will fail, and even sooner after that, he shall fall, and the heavy weight that will be the Throne must be placed on but a single set of shoulders. Abiron hath the strength but thy guidance he shall need. Giveth him deceit until thou dost see the young flower unfold! Only then wilt thy tongue speak of the truths I entrust to thee!"

"It matters not what we protect, Insra," Abiron's smile faded as his eyes lowered. "Safety is a means measured by fate."

"Thou shalt walk alone in such beliefs, my Prince," Insra replied.

"Dost thou truly believe thou art in my stride?!" he snapped, clenching his fists and holding them up between the two of them. "From this moment on I shall walk alone. I may not be of my brother's temperament, but I am not given unto blindness, woman! I possess eyes and they do see!" Insra erected a sound shield around them and it went without notice from Abiron.

"I see my father before me!" he yelled as he pointed at the Council Hall Floor. "The father who, mere hours before this moment was the greatest star in the skies of my dreams. I dreamt, woman, of being worthy of him, of our people!"

"Then be worthy of thy people!" Insra interrupted. She was not one to tolerate self-pity. Her own history could be correctly called a tragedy and yet still she stood tall. Her eyes dropped to Abiron's hands as they moved to his Blade. Her eyes squinted tight and she looked at Abiron and took a step forward.

"If it is fear of my skill surpassing thine which gives thee pause, then draw thy weapon and let me rid the Territories of a coward and a traitor!" she said implying they would both be dead. "But if it is reason which pushes through the woes to which thou dost now cling, release thy grip and step toward me a man who may not yet be ready for a Throne, but is ready to learn."

Taking a step forward but not releasing his grip, Abiron looked at Insra. "What if I am both?"

Insra smiled immediately and chuckled, remembering a stand at a pass that, in retrospect, had not been one of Mevkrean's better moments. "Then I shouldst say thou doth possess enough cowardice to avoid a bad stand!" Insra offered her hand and Abiron took hold of it at the forearm. He should not have been surprised at the strength of her grip, but he did his best to not show the wonder that did register.

"I am Insra, Blood of Lakar and I am thine, my lord, for I shall call you Prince no longer."

"But I am still only a Prince," Abiron was confused.

"Be a man first, my lord, and let the crown serve as all the symbol that be necessary!"

"And what of my father?" he asked.

"Your father, I suspect, is dead," she answered. It was time to bring the boy into manhood and into the truth he would need to question most in order to find his way. She looked back upon Elior and let her smile slowly fade. "Dost thou recall when Mevkrean trained both thy brother and thine own hand?"

"It remains a joy of my mind and memory," Abiron said as he stepped closer, releasing the scabbard but shifting his left hand to the pommel of his Blade.

"And the day thy father- when King Elior insisted on trying Mevkrean?"

"Thou wert still a sergeant," Abiron answered, drawing Insra's attention. That much detail she had not expected him to recall. "Mevkrean blooded my father. It was an accident, my father had not given Mevkrean enough credit and he was too slow, too off balance. It was a miracle that the cut was not of greater consequence. Mevkrean did what he could to remove his weapon."

"It is a weapon which hath never experienced another service," Insra said softly. "A Blade that he couldst not destroy, as it had Royal Blood upon its edge, and one he wouldst not take into battle for the very same reason.

"But the Blade and the blood remain to this day. Blood, your majesty, which has no heir!" Abiron wanted to speak but words would not form in his mind, let alone his mouth. "Bear in mind the blood Mevkrean took from thee and thy brother does show link to thy mother."

"If such is a ploy to have me seek out my mother, who hath lied to me all this time then it is a refused option, Insra! If the blood hath been viewed in the means of which I am familiar, then two faces were shown. Whose face was shown as my father?"

She took in a deep breath and trusted her instincts and the teachings of her mentor, Captain and friend. "Xarga, Blood of Gamshygar was both your father and Ezra's, my lord. We were able to view also that thy mother held the seed of Xarga for some time before she let it pass into her body. It was after Xarga became a Man-Lord and his name was changed to Xargagyan that she allowed the first of the seeds to fertilize within her womb." Insra let Abiron stand silent for a while as she struggled with herself. There was more and she had already kept it from Mevkrean; she could not do so against her Prince Lord.

"Xarga passed enough for thy mother to seed thrice, my lord." Abiron looked up at her, his face still torn with the burden of the answer to his question. "Thy mother hath given birth to three children but thou art not the first of her births.

"Thy cousin, Kamala is thy older sister and the true heir to the throne!"

Sometime very soon, I am going to wake up," he thought as he was led out of the dressing chambers. The weight of the cape was new to him but he found it to be more uplifting than burdensome, and he walked with more sway to his shoulders. He liked the sound of the boots as they made contact with the floor and echoed each stride throughout the room. They applauded as he approached the mirror, each one of the servants had their assigned duties to primp and press, cut and comb. He had to be made presentable. *"How could I have come to this?"* he questioned as he was sent toward the doors. They led out to the balcony where he would receive his fate. When they opened he was greeted with light and cheers, both of which took him by surprise, but he managed to keep walking forward to the edge of the balcony. To his left and right, on a level lower than his place, were the Eden-Knights in all of their regalia. He now wore the same clothes as they did and he wore his sword much in the same fashion. But the ropes across his chest and the girdle around his waist put him on par with those that were on his level to his left and right. They were the Lords and Ladies of Eden. They were also Knights, but they had houses to command, regions for which they were responsible, and he wore affectations like them, but his gauntlets were slightly different than most. In fact only four total wore such gauntlets, two with two stones as his were, one with three and one set that held four stones. Those belonged to the High Lord, Mark Adamson, Matthew's former House Lord and he applauded with all the others, smiling brightly and waving for the crowd to cheer even louder.

"This is ridiculous!" Sister Tirzah snapped as the procession made its way to the highest of all balconies, the Perch of the Mothers. Each of the Sisters wore their navy blue and silver robes which covered everything but their faces.

"Would you have us turn our backs on our own laws, Tirzah?" Ruth asked. "The boy was challenged by two House Lords and he defeated them by calling on the spirit to judge him against his opponents and react accordingly! Need I remind you that a Knight cannot be harmed by his own sword, nor will it act in a manner the wielder does not wish unless a higher power is visited upon it! Who are we to question the will of the spirit?"

"But to make him a House Lord?!" Tirzah pressed.

"Mother has made a very wise move in my opinion," Sister Eunice added. "Far better for this boy, who has had little time to be swept up in the politics of the Lord and Ladies, to be a ranking House Lord, than to pass the power over to council. Far less blood is spilled this way."

"And Mother gains an ally," Ruth concluded. "For though he is untouched by politics, he is ever the plaything of idealism! A knight he has been made and knightly is how he must act!" The Sisters stepped up to the edge and stopped, parting into two lines for Mother to walk between as she made her way to the balcony. As always, she was punctual; her glistening white and gold robes draped all around her but never touched the ground. As she approached, her green eyes looked at each of the Sisters in turn, looking over every facet of them before she moved on to the next.

"Mother Zebudah," Ruth said as she bowed.

"Sister Ruth," she replied, touching the sleeve of the Sister's robes. "Have you been setting the Sisters straight in regards to my ineptitude?"

"Such claim was never made, my Mother!" she said softly. "It is simply that your wisdom exceeds us."

"Were I to approach a musician, Ruth, I would expect music. Can you tell me how is it that without instrument or choir you cast a song before my ears?"

"I am moved by the spirit!" Ruth answered, bowing again.

"Take note, Sisters, for Ruth has set the tone. When you are ever foolish enough to raise your thinking to judge me, seek the wisdom and solace of the spirit or it will be to the spirit that I commit you!" The Mother took her last steps and was basked in the adoration of her people. Normally she would let such cheering go on for some time, but what Ruth had said was very true and it was proof positive why Ruth was her most trusted advisor. Properly used, the boy was a weapon against the declining values of the Lords, Ladies and all the Knights of Eden which came at a time when they could not afford it. So she called Matthew into place and gave his House the name Samson. He seemed to glow when it was bestowed upon him.

After the Naming Celebration, Mother took the new Lord aside and into a Viewing Chamber, a place with which he had become quite familiar.

"I still cannot believe this is happening!" Matthew said as he followed her into his own Viewing Chamber.

"You trusted the spirit to deliver you, my son. What did you expect to happen?"

"I was under the impression-"

"Lord Adamson does not speak for me nor does he allow my voice to speak for him. And do not speak in response to that, young Matthew. It is knowledge meant to guard you, not guide you."

"If I am to be an Eden-Knight," Matthew said, his shoulders broadening, "I must stand against all of our enemies, Mother, not just the ones that are convenient to fight!"

"You shall be of great service to Eden, Lord Samson," she replied as she approached the viewer. "Now let us speak of the one who caused your... difference of opinion." With a wave of her hand, the image of William Ferrous asleep on his bed appeared. "Yes, I know of this one, even if our records have been slightly... *challenged* by your grace," she smiled.

"Mother, if I may speak," he said, bowing.

"That is why we are here," she replied.

"I do not see the reason for the way we regard the Prodigian. "I-"

"But wait, what transpires here?" she asked, looking at the image. "Our talk is a most timely one it seems. Look, Lord Samson! Look upon this one who has indeed touched the spirit."

Matthew looked at the image of William sleeping in his room. Dexter Gillis was in the room too, on a makeshift palette and fast asleep himself.

"*The phantasm!*" Matthew thought, still awed by the concept.

"Thanks for following my lead," William said to Dexter as they stood in the arena and William held up his hand to the cloaked figure to let him know there would not be that sort of training at the moment.

"Hey, what gives?"

"We're going for a little trip," William said as he started calming himself. "Sorry about that big push back at the plane."

"Hey, from what you told me, it was better than standing there and getting hit with thrown bullets!"

"I don't get it," William continued. "It took so much for me to stop Dad and I nearly threw you into the next county!"

"Well that's not really accurate," Dexter said. "That airport is on the county line. You damn near had me in Alabama!"

"I'm getting a little tired of you and the brain-flexing," William replied. "It's not natural!"

"Oh, speaking of natural!" Dexter was excited. "Maybe your Dad had that moving stuff."

"You mean momentum?"

"Yeah! Plus he is a *solid* dude! Bro-ham works out on the regular! Sorry I didn't know about the momentus stuff."

"Not knowing the name is one thing, Dex. You knew what you were talking about and you actually might have something there. His weight plus gravity… it might have taken more from me to stop him.

"But we've got people to see and things to do!" William said, grabbing his friend and using his telekinesis to lift them both.

"What are we doing up here?"

"Something that always happens when I'm above the phantasm," William answered as he looked down. Look!"

Dexter looked to the ground below and he was impressed with what he saw. Again the phantasm went through a time shift and the Tower was again being built. This time, William engaged his telepathy and brought his awareness closer to the phantasm as he and Dexter hovered. "Wait until the tower is finished!"

Again the arrow was shot into the air and the psionic pulses were sent out all around the area but with William's enhanced view, he saw more than the waves of energy, he saw faces and more importantly he saw reactions! Some were caught unawares and did not know what was going on, others looked angry while others were shocked and horrified.

Zebudah removed both herself and Matthew from the viewing and she looked up at Matthew who was confused. That worked in her favor.

"I don't understand," he finally said. "Somehow, he has come into the truth. His father must have been-"

"One who nearly drove us all to destruction!" she interrupted before taking hold of Matthew's face. "Think on this, my son. We all have our slate towards power but while spirit cannot be measured, how can it be called upon without the mind?

"Now look again into the viewer and tell me what you see in the boy's heart, as I know you will try to defend him without viewing."

Matthew did as he had been told but he did not look long before he turned away.

"No!" he whispered. "There is so much hate! Anxiety, rage, pain and... he has taken a life, willingly and he was... relieved, satisfied! But how?!"

"He is a Prodigian, but he is a Man-Lord, and their ethics are not like our own. Now this one is on course to rejoin his people. The Man-Lords have ceased their aggressions against him and the Light-Children have sent one of their highest ranking Councilmen to be his aide! His *aide*, as if to say this child possesses the qualities of a fair minded leader!

"We have safeguards against those that would threaten what we stand for...

The Arcanians – we have armors that prevent their magic; the Genii they are too bright to ever attempt to undo faith; the Elementals – our spiritual steels do not heed their commands; the SomeVinco – they trust too much in their bodies instead of the force that created them! For all of these we have an answer, Matthew. But what answer do we have for the Prodigian? When they can reach into our minds and make us forget again?

"How is it that they knew how to change our languages but did not bother to change our minds?!" she said with a taste of emotion that touched Matthew. He could feel her pain and more than that, her fear. "Imagine... in the morning you are my son and in the evening you are still my family, but I cannot understand you and you must go to be with those with whom you can communicate. Parent lost child and husband lost wife after the Tower of Babel! It was the power of the spirit that kept a bond between our people, for though we could not understand the sounds from our mouths, we shared the light and the love of the spirit."

"Will that not stand as enough, then?" Matthew asked.

"Only if the Prodigian decided to remain separated from the rest of the tribes!" Mother said, looking sternly in Matthew's eyes. "But the Man-Lords do not seek isolation, they seek domination! Our agents have taken lifetimes weaving a delicate veil that this boy now threatens to destroy."

Matthew looked to his sword and then back to Mother. "Then the boy must be destroyed. It was my hand that sought to bring him into the spirit, it will be my hand that will deliver him into its judgment!"

"Assemble your house," Mother directed. It will take time, yes, and it will be in that time he too prepares. But you will need more than your considerable skills to survive this fate."

"Then upon your order, Mother," Matthew said, lowering his head, but he did not bring it up.

"The order is given!" she said and Matthew stood, spun on his heels and strode out of the room, full of purpose!

Zebudah looked back at the viewer and smiled as she ran her hand along the edges of the pedestal that held the viewing crystal in place.

"How timely indeed!" She gathered herself and made her way out. It was time to deliver Elder Joshua from his death and into the role of the fanatic!

Epilogue

"Oh, don't you just love Canada?" she asked, sipping on a very large mug of hot chocolate. She was listening to music, metal rock from what he could hear of it, as he walked out to meet her. He was toting a metal box on his back and he dropped the box loudly onto the patio.

"Let's not forget that even with everything that was done to me, I'm still a black person, so hell no, I do not love Canada in November!"

Sabrina suppressed her laughter and just nodded. "Point taken, Chocolate Thunder!"

"Cute," he replied as he took in a deep breath and sighed. He was giving his words a final review before actually saying them. To the rest of humanity this was called caution; to an MVP, it was hesitation. "I think we're in over our heads on this one."

"Hmmm, the owners aren't going to like that assessment," Sabrina reviewed as she put down her magazine. She did so without closing it!

"Signal one is received," she heard in her earpiece mixed in with the music.

"Bump a damn owner! Let *them* deal with these people! And because I know the type of woman you are..." Lambda Scout kicked over the box and it fell open. Sabrina screamed as she saw a nearly flattened face looking back at her.

"Jesus Christ, what the hell is that!" she yelled.

"A major pain in the ass that call themselves the SomeVinco."

"Somevin- Body... conquer! Body Master?! Oh my God! He's alive!"

"That he is," Terrell confirmed as he closed the box. "Just barely, but alive. He gets out, you're dead. He gets out and only one of us is around... you're dead!"

"So that is what killed Delta?"

"Leaping, spinning in mid-air and firing from the hip, he nailed a headshot. And I think he was like the smallest one too."

"Yeah, I've seen the footage on what they did at the Dugout," Sabrina said as Lambda turned to walk away. "Hey, where are you going?"

"I figure if I don't tell you, you won't have to lie," Lambda answered, stopping long enough to answer her question. Sabrina stood up and she did so without putting down her mug.

"Signal two has been received," the voice in the earpiece replied. "Weapons at the ready."

"They will find you!"

"Tell 'em to bring friends. Nobody should die alone!"

"Don't do this Sabe," Beta said, breaking in on the line. Sabrina quickly tapped her ear lobe.

"Locking out all other transmissions," the voice reported.

"You really think you can get this out of your blood?" Sabrina asked, yelling at the top of her voice, hoping to strike some sort of chord. It had been well over twenty-four hours, and she had been in the company of the Owners and their answer to the MVPs. They were barely human and, with the candidates they had chosen, they preferred it that way. Her greatest difficulty with these people was that one of them was parked outside the home of Allan and Alicia Bey, jumping at the bit to receive the order to wipe the existence of the Dugout, its personnel and their families from existence. Until she had a better hold of things, she had to play it their way.

"Not even going to try," she heard Terrell respond. "Just not doing it for them anymore!" She could hear the door to the apartment close. He would be outside soon and her head lowered while she waited for...

"This is Lambda Prime," she heard over her earpiece. "I do not have the green and I see Lambda Scout leaving the premises. Do I go for the shot?"

"Alpha Prime, are you in position?" Sabrina asked, lighting a cigarette. This was the part of the job she hated most.

"Affirmative," he answered.

Sabrina blew out the smoke of her long drag and tried to think of an alternative. She was coming up blank and running out of time. Sylvestra was only going to hate her more for this one. It had been nothing but one word answers since Sabrina had gotten off the line with the Owners. It was obvious that the Bogeys and this latest entity were not one in the same. The energy readings alone were off the scale. If anything she needed *more* unity, not solidarity!

"Lambda Prime, take the shot!" she commanded and she shuddered when the gun went off. "Alpha Prime, confirm the kill!"

A few moments went by before she could hear the thick voice of Alpha Prime open his communications line. "Kill confirmed, center mass!"

Sabrina had technicians pick up the body and make their verifications while she made her report to the Owners. They were very much impressed with her ability to implement duplicity and information control. "Even Owners can panic!" one particular reviewer said. Plus, even with the breach, their security had not been compromised. Sabrina Bey was to be commended in their eyes.

Early morning of the very next day Sabrina, along with Alpha and Beta Scouts, stood on the observation deck when the scientists opened the box to look at this SomeVinco individual. They opened the box and out poured a cross between rubber and raw sewage. It was vile and three of the scientists could not keep from vomiting all over themselves.

"Doesn't look these things have too long of a shelf life," Alpha said as he left the room. "You did what you had to do, darlin'," he consoled. If you hadn't given the order, they had a backup who would've, and you would've been added to the hit list."

"Thanks, Laz," she said softly. "I really appreciate that."

"*SomeVinco*," Sylvestra thought as a soft smile formed on her face. "*I wonder if they can look like anyone else too.*"

"So what happens now?" he asked as he walked up to a man wearing a full length coat in the middle of the bus station.

"First of all, you can stop looking like me," Terrell said as he looked over at another version of himself that smiled, shrugged its shoulders and quickly changed shape and form, becoming Knight once more.

"I was beginning to like that form," he ribbed.

"Yeah well, one of me pushes the limits as it is." Terrell offered his hand and Knight shook it. "Well, you kept your word and I think, all in all, that squares things between us. We were both doing our jobs, after all. But I think we're pretty shitty in who we picked to work for!"

"I envy you, Lambda," Knight admitted. "At least you had a choice."

"Funny you should bring that up," Terrell said, handing over the bottle of grain alcohol. He had added some cane syrup for flavor but it was the only thing he knew, short of a certain Prodigian mixture, which gave him the response he was looking for in a drink. "Seems that there is someone looking to buck the system. And maybe he'll get me a heart and you a brain."

"What?" Knight took a very good sip.

"Never mind," Terrell laughed. "I'm headed back to William's. Once they review the Multi-Frame records I couldn't get to and erased, they'll piece it together and that poor kid's going to be covered in MVPs... unless we make it both unsavory and unprofitable for the Owners to do so. But we'll have one helluva case to prove."

"If I were to help the Prodigian, what do you suppose I will gain from it?" Knight inquired.

"I'm not the kid's agent," Terrell replied. "But he comes across as a pretty straight shooter to me. If you ask him, I get the feeling he'll give you the truth."

"You would not be able to stop an army of MVPs," Knight concluded. "Not if any of them are like you."

"Nice compliment," Terrell agreed. "But even with that, a man's gotta die sometime. I think I'm in the mood to die for a reason that actually *helps* me sleep at night. God knows I've killed enough for the almighty dividend!"

"Then I shall ask this Kador, and if his answer suits me, you shall die an old man."

"Promises, promises!"

At last! The night sky begins to grow dark, to where I will not even be able to see the stars. I felt their minds and these were indeed dark and dismal creatures. They were enjoying what they were doing, fully cognizant of their actions and what they brought to their victim.

I was foolish enough to contemplate why no one had ever bothered to chronicle this fact, and the oversight actually brought a moment of gaiety to my mind. Suddenly, I could see the moon again and I was able to blink. I could hear one of the leeches explode from backlash.

"*From jesting?!*" I thought as they quickly maneuvered to regain their lost ground. Being leeches, their 'quickly' was to relative to the passing of a season for me.

"But what if?" I heard a voice scrutinize the possibility and then I was reminded of another one who faced their fate. "Kicking and screaming," Tara had remonstrated, and her fear was transposed. My right eye closed as a dagger-like sensation shot through the pupil, straight into the optic nerve. They were not yet undone, these leeches. But I now possessed a Guard, a means through which I could defend myself.

I started with the memory of Dexter Gillis correcting William's grammar and I soon felt the grip of another of the leeches wane. The gauntlet had been thrown down, and there was more to the tales of Elkazzar that still remained to be told! Though they shall always pale beside those of my friend, William Anthony Ferrous… *Kador, Blood of Xargagyan*!

Made in the USA
Charleston, SC
07 August 2011